Beverley Harper was born in New South Wales. At age 26 she travelled to Africa, intending to stay for a year en route to Europe. Instead, she stayed nearly 20 years. She has had a number of short stories and a novel published. Beverley is married with three sons and now lives in the New England tablelands region of New South Wales.

Also by Beverley Harper

Storms Over Africa

EDGE
OF THE
RAIN

BEVERLEY HARPER

MACMILLAN
Pan Macmillan Australia

First published 1997 in Macmillan by Pan Macmillan Australia Pty Limited
St Martins Tower, 31 Market Street, Sydney

National Library of Australia
cataloguing-in-publication data:

Harper, Beverley.
Edge of the rain.

ISBN 0 7329 0899 X.

I. Title.

A823.3

Typeset in 11.5/13pt Bembo by Post Typesetters
Printed in Australia by Australian Print Group

this book is for Robert, Piers, Miles and Adam

with thanks to my agent and friend Selwa Anthony
special thanks to Jennifer and Peter Gill who found the
time and patience to tell me about diamonds
and to
John Counihan, Peter McIntyre and Wally Vize in Botswana

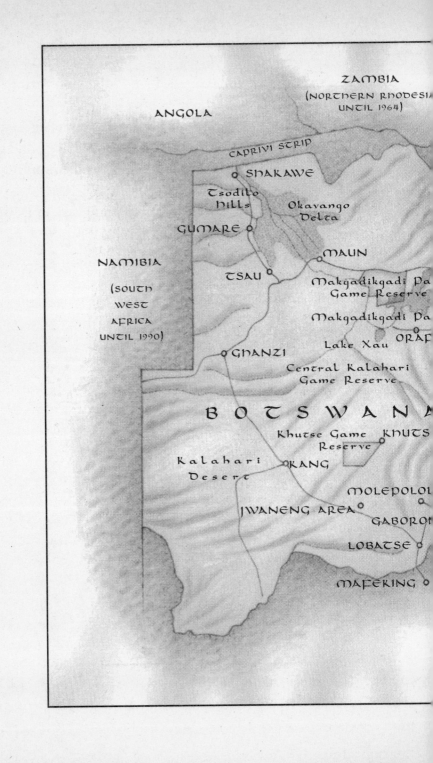

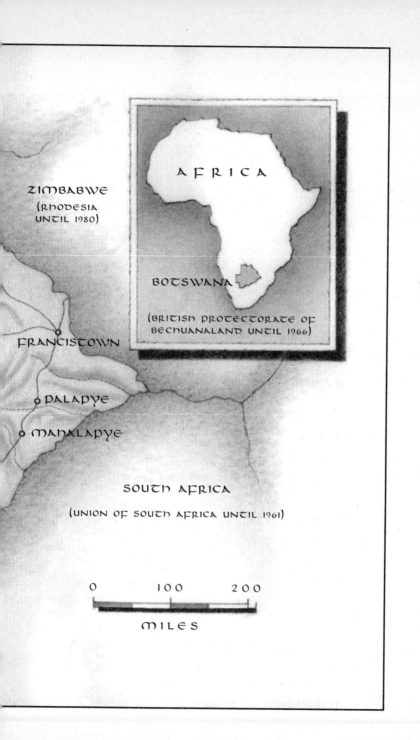

ZIMBABWE
(RHODESIA
UNTIL 1980)

AFRICA

BOTSWANA

(BRITISH PROTECTORATE OF
BECHUANALAND UNTIL 1966)

FRANCISTOWN

o PALAPYE

o MAHALAPYE

SOUTH AFRICA

(UNION OF SOUTH AFRICA UNTIL 1961)

0   100   200

MILES

ONE

The blood scent was fresh. Pungent and rich, the acrid smell of it stung her taste buds, bringing saliva. She stopped, turning her head until she caught it again. In the distance, a clump of trees. Years of fending for herself had her instincts honed to perfection. A light breeze floated the scent to her and she savoured it. It came from the trees. But she was wary. Along with the scent of blood, something else, something alien.

Hunger ached in her belly. Cautious, for she could not identify the other smell, she made her way towards the trees, stopping every few seconds to sniff at the breeze. Her eyes flicked over the surrounding land. Nothing there. The blood scent was stronger. Like a wraith she slipped into the shade, moving with exquisite precision, all her senses alert. When she found the source of the scent she slid forward as close as she dared and settled down to watch. She would remain hidden until she was sure—such was her nature.

Fifteen minutes later the lioness still lay, motionless as carved stone. Tawny eyes showed she was alert and focused. Invisible

1

from all but the sharpest observer, she was cleverly camou-
flaged by the dappled shade of a low scrubby bush and the
sparse dun coloured grass around her. Muscles tensed along
her back and haunches, rippling beige, twenty-three stone of
power and speed. Her concentration was total. She was very,
very hungry.

The little boy thirty seconds away from death was two,
maybe three years old. His fair skin burned crimson from too
much sun. Silky blond curls lay damp on his head in the
intense heat. A cut on his leg was crusted with dried blood.
Face grubby and streaked with recent tears, sobs still surfaced
from deep inside him and shook his sturdy little body. He had
done the unthinkable, the unbelievable. He was lost in the
vast, barren, heat soaked sand that was the Kalahari Desert.

For now, he was absorbed by what he had found on the
ground and had no idea the lioness lay, no more than thirty
feet away, planning to eat him. Even if he had known, there
was nothing he could have done to stop her.

Impending death stilled all sounds. Even the birds were
silent, awed by the savage drama unfolding in a land where
conscience has no meaning. They watched and waited. The
little boy was just another meal but his death would be
viciously spectacular.

The lioness tested the child's scent. Her mouth became a
silent snarl as she drew her lips back, exposing large yellow
teeth, sucking and blowing air over sensitive taste buds. Her
stomach rumbled in its hunger, but she hesitated. The small
creature before her was edible—she could tell by the blood
scent—but it smelled like nothing she had eaten before,
looked like nothing she had seen before and sounded like
nothing she had heard before.

The object of her interest was squatting beside the remains

of a long-dead ostrich. Jackals, vultures and ants had eaten all but a few bones, and the gritty contents of the bird's gizzard. The child was absorbed by a stone which shone with a thousand different lights in the fierce desert sunshine. When he held it up against the sky, and the colours danced and changed as he twisted it in his hand, he chuckled in pure enjoyment, his terror at finding himself alone temporarily forgotten.

The lioness was nearly committed. She knew this was easy prey. One flash of a heavy paw, one slice of razor-sharp claws, one crunch of jaws on that small head, and she could rip out the intestines, then feed to her heart's content. Still she hesitated; caution and stealth had kept her alive till now. As one who lived instinctively, she had a deeply rooted fear of human beings. Her instincts told her to be careful.

On his haunches, the boy hopped sideways around the skeletal remains of the dead bird looking for more shining stones. The movement took him closer to the bush where the lioness lay. She tensed, ready to strike out and bring him down, but he had seen something on the other side of the ostrich, rose and toddled over to it, remaining out of reach. Sobs still shuddered through him but, with the myopic concentration of the very young, he no longer noticed them.

The large and hungry cat inched forward on her belly. Hunger rumbled again. She had not eaten in four days. A front paw throbbed with the poison from a suppurating abscess, caused by a thorn which had broken off and remained embedded. Hundreds of ticks itched as they feasted on her blood but she ignored them. Flies stung as they fed on the sunburned raw edges of her ears. She ignored them as well. Discomfort was as much a part of her life as her instinct to hunt.

Then the little boy began to talk to himself. It was his high-pitched childlike voice which convinced the lioness she was safe. The strange hairless animal was defenceless. Completely committed now, she rose in one fluid motion, disturbing not so much as a leaf. Her tail twitched involuntarily. Tensing front legs she bunched herself, ready to execute her fast, low, deadly rush. The warning growl, something she was powerless to prevent, rose in her throat. It was time to eat.

In that last, intense split second before she acted, her excellent hearing picked up a sound. Self-preservation is strong in those who live by their wits and hunting skills. Hungry as she was, the lioness slid silently from her covering bush and put as much distance between herself and the sound as she possibly could. So great was her ability to move silently, the little boy was unaware she had ever been there.

TWO

The family of warthog, mother, father and three half-grown babies, were busily foraging for roots, bulbs and tubers, using their long curving upper tusks to dig in the soft sandy earth. Trotting briskly from one clump of grass to the other, intent on their task, they were unaware of the two Bushmen hunters who watched and waited.

!Ka reached into his reed matting bag and brought out a flea-beetle pupa which he rolled between his fingers to soften. !Oma chewed on a wad of acacia gum, sticking his tongue into it, then churning it around in his mouth to mix it with saliva. When both the gum and pupa were soft, !Oma spat the sticky mess onto a saucer of bark and !Ka squeezed the orange coloured fluid out of the pupa and mixed it with the gum. They worked in silence, knowing the keen sense of hearing of their quarry would send them scurrying for safety at the merest whisper of sound.

!Oma nodded that the poison was ready. Dipping tiny arrow heads into it they rose quietly and, unseen by the warthog, moved to within firing distance. Without exchanging a glance both hunters sent their poisoned arrows to the same youngster. He was the biggest of the three piglets and some of the mud he rolled in earlier in the day had flaked off his flank, leaving the tough skin vulnerable.

The lightweight reed arrows seemed impossibly fragile as they danced towards their prey and bounced, like twigs, off his side. But not before their tiny sharp heads cut the tough hide sufficiently to poison his bloodstream. The injured youngster screamed at the sudden sharp pain and he and his family took off alarmed. The two Bushmen returned to collect their hunting kits before setting off after the warthog. They were in no hurry. They knew exactly where the animals were going.

The warthog sought cover in some old porcupine holes next to a dried-up waterhole, the boar being the last to disappear in a bottom-first, backwards wriggle. The hunters, who had followed in a deceptively easy lope which they could keep up all day if necessary, slowed and stopped. !Oma unstrapped an ostrich egg from his hip and offered it to his friend. !Ka sipped sparingly at the lukewarm water before passing it back. Then both men squatted down to wait, making no attempt to be quiet. They wanted the warthog to hear them and thus remain hidden.

They knew the poison would work slowly. Ideally, they would have preferred to shoot the animal at dusk and return in the morning to collect it. But with so many lions in the area, this was impractical. Occasionally they had to drive lion away from a kill, something they did readily, with no qualms. But a flying mantis passing briefly by their cooking fires last evening was taken as an omen that something either very good or very bad was in the offing and neither man wanted to put it to the test. The Mantis was a good fellow more often than not but sometimes he used his supernatural powers to play tricks on his subjects. Some six hours elapsed before they considered the poison would have done its work.

When the sun had passed its zenith and was halfway towards its journey into darkness, !Ka and !Oma rose and walked towards where the animals had assumed sanctuary. They stood atop the hole which the big male disappeared down and stamped their feet hard on the baked earth. The boar charged up and out of the hole like a shooting star which sometimes flashed over the night sky, snorting in anger and fright and, without looking back, took off at a fast canter with his tail held high. !Ka relaxed the tight grip on his spear. They had taken a calculated risk the boar would not attack and it had worked.

The sow was less obliging. She had her injured baby in the same hole as herself and, although she wanted to flee, maternal instinct held her back. Her head bobbed in and out of the hole as she changed her mind several times. Acting from instinct more than past experience, and from a deep understanding of wild animals, !Ka and !Oma stopped stamping on the ground and rapidly climbed a stunted acacia tree as the sow finally took a decision, boiled out of the hole, turned with incredible speed and charged. There was nothing there. Confused, she stopped dead. Then, calling her babies to her, she set off quickly in the same direction the boar had taken.

The poison, because it had been freshly made, was working well. The injured warthog, already unsteady on his feet, lagged behind, falling occasionally. The rest of his sounder milled near some distant bushes, waiting for him. The young warthog stopped, sniffing and disoriented, then set off in the wrong direction. Unpredictably, his family simply vanished, deserting him.

!Ka and !Oma jumped out of the tree and followed, spears

held ready. The distress calls of the warthog would be heard by predators who would come quickly to take advantage of an easy meal. However, the young warthog did not manage to get very far. The poison, the heat of the porcupine hole, the weight of his mother sitting on him, had rendered him defenceless. He was lying on the sand breathing quickly and then, just as quickly, he died.

The two hunters took a minute to apologise to the dead animal. The old people had taught them that all animals were once people and, although it was permissible to kill for food, or in self-defence, all the animals belonged to the Great God and their lives could only be taken with due respect. Satisfied they had not angered the Great God, they set off towards camp, happy in the knowledge that their inner compulsion to hunt was blessed with good fortune on this day.

!Oma, being younger, carried the heavy animal first. After half an hour, !Ka took his turn. Chattering to each other, their conversation interspersed with a collection of clicks and loud pops, !Ka asked !Oma if his wife's birth blood had stopped running.

'No,' !Oma replied morosely.

'Can you wait?'

'I must wait.' To touch a woman at this time, or even during her monthly bleeding, made a man thin and took away the power of his hunting tools.

'Do what the buck do. Go and rub your horns against a soft bush.'

'Do not think I haven't thought of it.'

Both men laughed.

!Ka shifted the dead weight of the warthog on his shoulders without breaking the rhythm of his steady half-run, half-walk. It had been a long day. Starting shortly after daybreak they had travelled thirteen miles before coming across the family of warthog.

Their conversation carried far in the hot, motionless air. They made no effort to be quiet; their natural love of spirited debate had them laughing and shouting as they walked. After all, no-one lived out in the desert but the San people and the two hunters had nothing to hide from their own kin.

They had covered more than half the distance back to camp and were near where they had seen the skeletal remains of an ostrich when they heard an astonishing sound.

!Ka stopped dead in his tracks. His small black eyes, brightly bird-like, scanned the way ahead. They heard it again. A baby was talking.

'Over there,' !Oma said, pointing to a clump of trees.

!Ka lowered the warthog to the ground and, very quietly, like stalking leopards, the two Bushmen advanced on the sound. They were intrigued by it. They knew no other clan lived in the vicinity. Besides, the child's voice did not sound like one of their own. Living as they did, as instinctively as the animals they hunted, both men would have known of the presence of strangers in their hunting territory. This young child, they were sure of it, was quite alone. And yet, they knew this would be impossible.

As they entered the shade !Ka caught the dreaded scent of lion. '*Si'isate.*'

!Oma nodded and glanced quickly about.

Then they saw the child, dressed in blue towelling shorts with a nappy trying to escape down one chubby leg. He wore no shirt or hat but, on his feet, a pair of once white takkies without laces. The boy had, as yet, not seen them. He held a stone in his hand which sparkled and shone, flashing like a sunset one minute and a deep blue sky the next. The

Bushmen had seen such stones before in the gizzard of ostrich. They always threw them away; pretty as they were, they had no useful purpose.

The boy hopped sideways, looking for more stones.

'He is like *!ebili* [the water bug],' !Ka whispered.

The little boy heard him and looked up at the two San men, unafraid. !Ka and !Oma advanced slowly, reluctantly. They had seen no signs of others but they were still cautious. The white man was a species about whom they knew very little. The little they knew made them distrusting.

!Ka dropped down in front of the child who looked back at him with blue-green eyes which never wavered and were full of innocent curiosity. His hair was the colour of spun silver, the colour of the moon. 'Da,' he said in a high clear voice, holding out his hand with the sparkling stone.

!Ka had no knowledge of the white man's tongue but thought the child was offering him the stone. 'Da,' he repeated politely, stretching out his own hand to take the diamond.

The boy snatched his hand back, shaking his head.

!Ka looked up at !Oma. 'This little *!ebili* will feed the lions tonight.'

!Oma pointed to the bush. 'Her With The Bad Foot was here.' He walked to the bush and looked at the sand. 'She was ready to kill.'

'That would be a very bad thing.' !Ka knew lions. He knew once they had killed a human they lost their fear of them and quickly included them in their diet. 'She must be very hungry. Her bad foot makes her bold.'

!Oma laughed. 'Not so very much bold. She must still remember your spear for she ran away.'

!Ka nodded, remembering the day he had defended his kill against Her With The Bad Foot and very nearly lost his life.

More by good luck than good defence, because she had taken him by surprise, he had jabbed his spear at the lioness and punctured her sensitive nose. He returned his gaze to the boy who smiled, showing perfectly spaced, even white teeth. 'How did he come here? He is alone. We must take him with us tonight and try to find his people tomorrow.' He rose and held out his hand. The child stood easily and took it trustingly. 'If that is possible,' !Ka added, worried.

!Oma agreed. He too had seen the frantic activity of the ants and beetles. Both men had read the signs: the weather was changing bringing something in, something big, the insects were never wrong. 'I will carry the meat.' !Oma concentrated on practical things for there was no point in worrying about the inevitable.

The little boy tried gamely to walk but stumbled. !Ka could feel the weariness in the small, sturdy body and wondered again where the boy came from. He hefted the child and was about to put him on his shoulders when he caught a whiff from his shorts. 'Pooh! He smells like a dead thing.' The child's diet caused his faeces to be very different from that of San children.

!Ka pulled off the boy's shorts and nappy and, using up their precious store of water from the ostrich egg, wiped the child's soiled bottom with his hand. Then, leaving the clothing on the ground—for he could not imagine anything more uncomfortable, nor could he work out how the nappy was supposed to fit—he picked him up and hoisted him on his shoulders. The child shrieked with pleasure, chuckling constantly, remarkable considering his sunburn and exhaustion. Soon both !Ka and !Oma were laughing with him, particularly when the boy urinated and his warm water ran down !Ka's shoulders and chest.

'The little *!ebili* makes good water.' !Oma cupped his hand and caught up some of the urine to smell.

'His water smells good, not like his food' !Ka agreed.

'He is brave.' !Oma remarked in admiration.

!Ka was certain that this child was why they saw the flying mantis last night. The Great God was testing them somehow. He had sent this young boy for a reason. !Ka hoped he was doing the right thing by rescuing the boy. He did not want the Great God to be displeased and send the Lesser God to punish him.

From his position on !Ka's shoulders, the child was still fascinated by the shining lights in his diamond, holding it up to see better. 'Da,' he said, again and again. In this manner, the warthog and the child were carried back to camp.

The camp was semi-permanent, which meant the clan had lived there for some five months, a long time for a nomadic tribe. Accommodating some twenty-seven individuals, the camp was a simple circle of grass huts with doors facing inwards, set around a flat dancing ground. They were due to move on shortly as they had all but cleaned out the roots and nuts, wild honey, termites, fruits and leopard tortoise which were their staple diet. The clan had stayed longer than usual because there was an underground spring nearby which gave them an abundance of water. But they knew, because they lived as one with their environment, that if this camp was to be enjoyed at some time in the future they had to give nature a chance to recover.

One of !Ka's children saw them coming and ran to tell his mother, Be, that his father was bringing something strange back from the hunting trip. The entire clan gathered in the centre of the camp and the murmur of speculation as to what strange animal !Ka carried on his shoulders quickly turned to excitement and disbelief. The young boy had fallen asleep, rocked by !Ka's steady walk, his silvery head dropped over !Ka's forehead, one hand resting on the Bushman's left shoulder, the other tucked behind his neck, still clutching the diamond.

'Oh, oh, oh, what have you done?' Be cried, agitated beyond belief, for she truly believed her husband had killed the boy. 'Why have you killed one so young?'

'We found this little *!ebili* alone. The lions would have eaten him,' !Ka told her disapprovingly. To take the life of another, particularly a child and especially a strange white child, would have been behaviour so alien to the San that he felt his wife should have given him the benefit of the doubt.

'*Ntsa, ntsa,* poor little beetle. Here, give him to me.'

The movement of transferring him to Be's caring arms woke the child. 'Da,' he said, staring at her face. She must have presented a strange sight to him indeed. Her yellow skin, tufted peppercorn hair, strong cheekbones, bulging forehead, folded eyelids and flat nose all set in a tiny childlike face creased with hundreds of wrinkles and bearing tribal scars representing a zebra's stripes would have had most children his age screaming with fear. Instead, he beamed at her.

Be rounded on one of her older children. 'Bring water,' she ordered. Then she turned back to her husband. 'Did you give him water?'

!Ka hung his head. 'We used the water to clean him.'

Be clucked and shook her head, then taking a gourd from her daughter she offered it to the child who drank so fast he began to cough. Then he chuckled and drank some more.

'He's a brave little beetle,' !Ka said.

Although most of the light of day had gone, it was still very hot. Be carried the baby to the waterhole, followed by the entire clan who were dumbfounded by the strange child.

The boy sat in the lukewarm water and splashed, laughing and happy. Then he fell over backwards and got up slowly, spitting water, thoroughly enjoying himself.

'Oh, oh, oh, what have we done?' Be asked in a low, scared voice.

The clan looked on, horrified. The boy's beautiful silver curls had been washed away, replaced by a darker colour which clung to his head in long straight strands.

'We have washed away the light of the Moon,' someone said.

They removed the child and carried him back to the camp. They sat him in the centre of an admiring throng as they stared and stared at his impossibly fair skin and blue-green eyes. Then a miracle occurred: in the warmth of the evening first one, then another, then another curl whitened and sprang back until his face was, once again, framed by silvery white curls. 'He *is* a child of the Moon,' one of them whispered in awe.

This explanation pleased them all; they distrusted the white man. Once upon a time, in the days when things were different, all the San and all the white men, as well as all the sheep and cattle and goats, lived together. But the white men and the San argued over who should own the livestock. So the white men said, 'Let us have a tug-of-war to settle this matter,' and provided a rope. The rope broke with most of it remaining in the Bushmen's hands. 'You have the rope,' said the white men. 'Use it to trap the steenbok and the duiker while your women gather other food. We will keep the live-stock.' This story, like all their stories, had been handed down through the generations. The little beetle was more palatable as a child of the Moon. For although the San have a great love of children, and often lamented that the Great God gives them so few, he was still a white man in the making.

Suddenly the child yawned and Be sprang up. 'He must eat with us,' she commanded. Her cooking pot was bubbling on the fire. Their meal this night was a mixture of tubers and tortoise meat, thickened with a paste of ground mongongo nut.

Visits by members of the camp to the cooking fires of others was a common enough occurrence. Hospitality was the key word. Children particularly were invited to try the food of others and no good wife would prepare a meal which could not cater for visitors. But the arrival of the white baby had the entire clan at Be's cooking fire so she built it up and the women were sent scurrying away to bring their own meal to join hers. Everyone wanted to gaze at the little *!ebili* and touch his hair in reverence.

If the young child thought the meal and the attention of everyone strange, his appetite was not affected and he tucked into it with the same gusto as the clan members, using his fingers as though he had been born to eating this way. Almost immediately he finished, he burped loudly, piddled where he sat, watching with natural enjoyment as his urine sank into the warm sand. Then, crawling over to Be, he curled up against her and fell fast asleep, seeming to sense she was the comfort figure, despite her strange appearance.

'What are we to do with this little beetle?' Be asked, touching the fair head gently which rested on her thigh.

'We will take him to his people,' !Ka answered. 'I hope we can track his steps tomorrow.'

'How could they have lost him?' she wondered, derision and disbelief clear by her tone. This child, with his silver head, infectious laugh and obvious courage had touched her heart. Maternal instincts had already stirred in her and she admired the boy and wanted to protect him. She wondered again how his people could have been so careless as to lose him.

'We may never know,' !Ka said sternly although, like Be, he wondered how the child came to be wandering in the vast Kalahari on his own. 'But we cannot keep him, there would be much trouble for us if we tried.'

!Ka and his clan spent the next three hours enjoying a spirited debate as to how the boy became lost, and how best to return him to his own people. Wild speculations, laced with superstitious fear of the white race and the Bushmen's own belief in the magic of the moon, spoken in their strange clicking language, were put forward, rejected, enlarged on, argued about and laughed over.

A pale sickle moon sailed lazily on its back above them and the clan fell silent, staring upwards at the shoe which the Mantis had thrown into the sky so he could have light. 'Does he search for his son?' !Ka wondered aloud, watching the silvery sliver.

!Oma expressed the worry of them all. 'If he thinks we have stolen his son he will not send us rain.'

'Do not be foolish,' another said. 'This boy is of the earth. I have seen others with hair like his.'

'Perhaps he was stolen by the Hare,' one of them suggested.

Diverted, the clan asked !Ka to tell them the story of the Moon and the Hare and, although they knew the story by heart, they listened avidly as !Ka, a gifted and favourite storyteller, related the tale of the origin of death.

'A very long time ago, before we were born, before our fathers were born, the Moon and the Hare were having an argument,' !Ka began. He rose, sucking on his pipe and then, holding out his arms to resemble the curve of a new moon he played the part of the new moon, and continued in a high and tremulous voice. 'When a person dies, as I die every night, that person is reborn. Just as I come back the next

16

night, so do men come back. All men die and return, die and return,' he said, flopping and straightening, flopping and straightening to match his words. He inhaled more smoke with quiet contentment.

'Tell us what the Hare said,' a listener implored, although he knew the story as well as !Ka.

!Ka, by wrinkling his nose, baring his teeth and lowering his voice, became the Hare. 'I . . .' !Ka gave a hearty laugh, '... laughed at the Moon. "Dead people rot and smell," I said to him. "They do not return."'

!Ka began circling, his hands turned into claws. 'The Moon and I argued and fought all night and all the next day.' !Ka shot out his hand. Several men jumped in fright. 'I scratched the face of the Moon with my nails. Now he carries my black marks for all to see our fight.'

'Tell us what the Moon did!' the same listener begged, hanging onto every word.

!Ka became the Moon. 'I took a shoe,' he said, bending and picking an imaginary shoe from the ground. He lunged forward. 'And I split the lip of the Hare with the shoe. To this day the Hare's lip is split in two.'

!Ka sat down again and his voice returned to normal. 'These are the signs of their quarrel. The argument was won by neither. Since then, men have died and not returned.' Heads nodded in satisfied agreement. The spirits of the dead lived in the eastern sky with the Great God. Sometimes they turned into bad spirits. It was comforting to know, however, that they would not return as bad men.

'This child . . .' !Ka said, '. . . has been sent to test us. We must return him. It is true he has been touched by the Moon but he is of men and to men he must be returned.'

'How?' !Oma asked. 'We do not know where he is from.'

'The Great God will show us the way.'

The clan then reminisced on past signs sent to them by the Great God and while the conversation ebbed and flowed around him, the child slumbered peacefully against Be, his small pudgy hand still clutching the large diamond, his dreams spinning with shining light images of brilliant reds, shimmering greens and incandescent blues.

!Ka had intended to leave at first light with the child. An excellent tracker, he knew he would have no difficulty in tracing the boy's steps and hoped to return him to his people quickly. But the message of the ants and beetles in the sand, warning of a change in the weather, came true more quickly than expected. During the night, wind whipped up a vicious sandstorm which raged all the next day, leaving the San helplessly pinned down in their lightweight huts. Dust-devils, restless spirits of those who had taken their own lives, spun across their dancing ground ensuring no-one would venture into that raging, stinging maelstrom.

The sandstorm broke around five in the afternoon, only to be followed by a heavy downpour of violent Male Rain which came to the Kalahari only once every few years and had the sands running in gushing rivulets and the men shouting abuse through the open doors of their huts so the Male Rain would see they were not frightened. When the rain finally stopped all hopes of tracking the child's footsteps were lost. Nature had wiped the sandy landscape clean. Be was delighted and began to think the baby had been sent by the Mantis for her to keep.

After the stinging, suffocating sandstorm and the clinging stickiness which followed the rain, the clan went down to their waterhole. Childlike, they all frolicked in the water, the white baby receiving a great deal of attention from everyone, his infectious laughter rising and falling with the delighted shrieks of the San who were always ready to laugh and play games. It was then Be noticed the boy's birthmark—a small, brown half-melon shape on his left buttock. 'The child has the mark of the Moon on his body,' she said, plucking worriedly at the strands of hair on his head, trying to tease back the silver curls which she was convinced had washed away for good this time.

'Do not look for signs that are not there.' !Ka could see his wife was becoming too attached to the child.

'You will not be able to find his people now,' she replied happily.

'I will find them,' he said, 'it will just take longer.'

The baby toddled over to them, still holding the diamond. 'Da.' He showed it to Be. They were used to this by now and instead of trying to take the stone she simply leaned over and admired it. 'Da,' she replied. He beamed at her.

'He is very fond of that stone,' !Oma's wife told Be. 'He will lose it if we don't do something.'

'He has already dropped it many times,' Be agreed.

'I have the very thing,' !Oma's wife said. 'I made it for your husband.'

!Ka heard. 'Then I give it to my wife.'

'Then I in turn give it to the child,' Be said, delighted that their gift-giving tradition had found the answer.

It was a small pouch, made from the skin of a springbok's scrotum, threaded at the opening with sinew which acted as a drawstring. The pouch was designed to carry the flea-beetle pupa with which the San made their hunting poison. It was perfect for the diamond.

'Da,' Be said to the boy, holding out the pouch.

He looked at her, uncomprehending.

She reached out and took the diamond between thumb and forefinger, holding it in such a way so he knew she was not taking it from him. After dropping the stone into the pouch she drew it shut and placed the drawstring over his head. The child shook his head vigorously. Be gently removed the drawstring, opened the pouch and showed him the diamond. The boy smiled and those watching laughed, relieved he approved. Then, with an avid audience, the boy amused himself for a long time, opening and shutting the pouch, pulling the drawstring over his head, taking it off again and reassuring himself constantly that the beautiful shining stone was still here. He fell asleep against Be that night with the drawstring wrapped around his hand.

'Why does he like it so?' Be wondered aloud.

'He is white. They are different from us,' !Ka replied. It was the only explanation he could think of.

That night the men spontaneously initiated a dance. The women clapped and sang songs about the giraffe, the elephant and the mamba snake, strong medicine songs which would empower !Ka and !Oma to find the baby's own people. Despite Be's longing to keep the small white child, despite clear signs the boy had been touched by the Moon, they all knew in their hearts he had come from somewhere and belonged to someone and every effort had to be made to return him to his family.

After the dance, and to be sure that returning the little beetle was what the Great God wanted, !Ka threw his divining tablets, watched avidly by the rest of the clan. He took five discs from his hunting bag and touched each of the thick animal hide tablets in turn, naming them.

'Earth. Water. Fire,' he said slowly, touching the three 'life things'. 'Sun. Brown Hyena,' he added, touching the 'death things'. A superstitious shudder ran through the onlookers. Different people named their divining tablets different things but there was always a Brown Hyena among them and the position in which it fell was the first thing they looked for.

!Ka cupped the discs in his hands and blew on them. Then he lowered his hands and shouted, 'Fire,' before snatching them away, allowing the tablets to land where destiny took them.

A stunned silence followed. Brown Hyena had fallen upside down. !Ka studied the tablets impassively. Finally, 'See that Earth and Water lie far from me,' he said. 'See that Fire lies close.' He looked at the tablets carefully. 'We will find the home of the little beetle but it will be very far from here.'

'Which way do you have to travel?' Be asked fearfully. The face down position of Brown Hyena filled her with dread.

'I do not know,' !Ka answered simply.

'There is trouble ahead,' Be said, hoping her husband would heed the warning and not go.

'Yes,' !Ka agreed. 'But I cannot see who it is for.'

!Oma stepped forward. 'We will face the trouble when it comes. This is what the Great God wants us to do. Not to obey would bring more trouble.'

!Ka picked up the tablets and rose. '!Oma speaks well. We leave after this night.' He walked to his hut and turned at the doorway. 'Come, wife, I will be gone three moons. You cannot send your man away with nothing more than senseless fears.'

Be followed him into their hut. He had made his decision. It was her duty to abide by it. It was what the Great God wanted. The ways of the Great God were sometimes hard to understand but she knew he had sent the little boy to them for a reason. Perhaps she had done something wrong. Perhaps she was being punished. It certainly felt like punishment. The child with blue-green eyes and hair like the Moon had already crept into her heart and she knew, with absolute certainty, he would remain there for as long as she lived.

In the morning Be smeared the boy's small body with some of her precious collection of *tsamma* ointment. This greasy substance, made from a tangy wild melon and rubbed briskly into the skin, over which a fine layer of Kalahari sand is allowed to stick, would protect his fair skin from further burning. She paid particular attention to his birthmark, not wanting any harm to come to, what she considered to be, the mark of the child having been touched by the Mantis or the Moon or both. She gave !Ka more of the ointment so he could use it along the way.

Suitably protected from the sun, which threatened to bring on another very hot day, and hoisted naked on !Ka's shoulders, Be approached the child to say farewell, her tiny black eyes brimming with tears. The baby felt her rough hand on his bare leg and seemed to understand her pain. 'Da,' he said, and traced his finger gently along the tribal scars on her wrinkled and weathered face.

'Da,' she replied, touched beyond belief.

'We go,' !Ka said, turning.

The last view she had of the baby was his plump little bottom bouncing on her husband's shoulders, his bright and miraculously restored silver curls shining in the early morning sun. 'Da, little beetle,' she murmured to herself. 'Go well, my son.'

There were shoe prints and car tracks at the place where the boy had been found. His shorts and nappy were gone.

'A man and a woman were here.' !Ka pointed, reading the signs.

!Oma agreed. 'See how they searched for something.' Two sets of shoe prints were clearly visible, going in all directions.

!Ka squatted. 'The woman knelt here. She found *!ebili's* clothing.' He rose and studied the vehicle tracks. One set led straight to where the shorts and nappy had been left; the other weaved erratically, as though whoever made them had suddenly lost their sight. 'There is great sadness here,' !Ka said finally.

'Will we follow these marks?' !Oma asked, indicating the tyre tracks.

'No,' !Ka said quietly. 'We will find these people our own way. If we follow these marks we will become as lost as they were when they made them.'

!Oma nodded. 'Which way will we go?' he asked. 'From where did *!ebili* come?'

'He did not come from behind,' !Ka said, pointing back the way they had come. 'We would have seen his tracks when we took him back to camp.' He turned and squinted into the sun. 'He did not come from where we killed the warthog,' he added, 'and I do not think he came from where the sun sets because there are many lion there. Therefore,' he decided, 'this little beetle must have come from the direction of the Mantis,' and with that, and with no comment from !Oma who agreed with his observations, the two men turned north.

Thirty miles west lay a small outpost of police who administered the vast Central Kalahari district. Permanently manned, they had a radio which would have made finding the child's parents easy. But, although the two San men knew the police were there they knew nothing of radios and how they worked. Nor would they have approached the outpost if they had known. It was manned by white men and several Bantu. To the north lay the barren wilderness of central Bechuanaland, 250 miles of flat desert country, practically waterless, unpopulated but for wandering clans of Bushmen and the occasional white hunter. !Ka and !Oma were undaunted by this land which they knew intimately. They knew where to dig for water, unearth succulent tubers and even where to find honey. They knew where the spring hare and the ant bear burrowed and where to collect the mongongo nut and the sour plum. With nothing more in their hearts than to find the family of the little beetle and return him to his rightful place, the two Bushmen headed towards some of the most hostile terrain on earth.

They met other clans along the way. Both men had distant relatives in many of them and the opportunity to catch up on each other's news was eagerly taken. !Ka was delighted to be reunited with a younger brother who had left years earlier in search of a wife. !Ka had not seen his brother for twelve seasons. As they sat and talked far into the night he learned of cousins and uncles, nephews and nieces and he carefully memorised the details of each so he could relate them back to his own clan when he returned. Such was the way the San stayed in touch.

Wherever they went, they were invited to spend the night and !Ka always accepted, glad of a chance to hand the boy over to the care and attention of a woman, unless of course she had her monthly bleeding which might have affected the child's health. He worried all the way that the boy would become ill and was always relieved to have the responsibility of his well-being taken out of his hands for a night. To protect the child he constantly wiped his hand across his own armpit, collecting up his perspiration which he spread on the young boy's head. Sweat from the healthy was a powerful medicine and the child endured more than his fair share of it. !Ka and !Oma asked everyone they met if they had heard of a white baby disappearing but news of that nature does not affect the wandering clans and no-one had heard of such an event.

As they walked further north however, one person told them there was rumour of a white child being lost in the desert, but was unable to say from where the child had come. So !Ka and !Oma kept heading north, convinced they were going the right way.

Up around Lake Xau, a mainly dry lake south of the Makgadikgadi Pans, they heard more positive news. A young white child had disappeared down south and all attempts to find him had failed. The grieving parents had reluctantly returned to their home, far to the northwest, convinced their child had either fallen prey to the many lions in the area or had perished in a severe sandstorm. All that had been found of the baby had been some of his clothes.

Encouraged by this, !Ka and !Oma turned more to the west. A few days later they were told the child came from somewhere near 'the bracelets of the morning', those mystical hills the Bantu called the Tsodilo Hills. Neither !Ka or !Oma had ventured this far north before but both men knew the legend of how, long ago, when the world was not the same as it is now, the biggest of the four hills had actually been a man. This man had two wives but he loved only his second wife. There was a terrible quarrel between the man and his first wife and she took a stick and hit him over the head, causing a deep wound which can still be seen to this day. Then she threw down their youngest child and ran away.

The Great God came to the man and asked him where she had gone. When he learned of their fight the Great God thought that since they had no peace between them as humans, it would be best if he turned them all into stone. And they remain as stone, to this day.

The Okavango Delta came as a wonderful surprise to !Ka and !Oma. After a lifetime spent in the hot, dry, sandy southern Kalahari, both simply stopped and stared in wonder. 'This must be the land of the Mantis,' !Oma whispered, awed. Palms, wild figs, islands of living papyrus, reeds, thick woodlands and great open areas of lush grasslands stretched into the distance as far as they could see.

They did not know it but they were seeing the Okavango Delta at its absolute best, before the waters rise, as they do each year, from earlier rains in Angola, 600 miles from where they stood, and flow eastward, spilling out over the flat floodplains of the Okavango Delta into an enormous complex of twisting waterways and islands. But now, in the height of summer, the Okavango River flowed smoothly between well-defined banks, some more than a hundred yards apart. When the waters are high, walking through the Delta is difficult, if not impossible. The waters not having yet arrived, the Bushmen were able to follow ridges and navigate easily, some primitive instinct showing them the way. Naturally shy of contact with other Africans and deeply reluctant to make contact with whites, they avoided speaking with anyone other than those of their own race. Although the northern dialect varied from their own, at least they could be assured of a friendly welcome.

At Sepopa, on the northwestern edge of the Delta, they learned that the child belonged to white farmers only two days' walk further. 'You should give him to the police,' they were advised. 'They will take him home.' But !Ka and !Oma had become deeply attached to the young boy and believed it was their Great God's wish that they deliver him themselves. Once again they set off.

This strange little trio, two diminutive Bushmen and a small white child, had barely raised a flicker of excitement in the animals further south. But up in the Delta hunting had made the animals skittish. !Ka and !Oma, used to reading the signs of the wild in an arid desert, found the long grass and swampy marshes of the Delta most confusing.

A browsing herd of buffalo appeared from nowhere. The Bushmen had never seen such big cattle, for buffalo do not venture into the Kalahari. Not yet alarmed, they carried on walking, chattering to each other, expecting the very large cows would ignore them as the occasional herd of cattle they encountered down south always did. A large bull raised his head and saw them. He snorted at the sudden appearance of the Bushmen. Then !Oma, having a bit of child-like fun, made a rush at him, thinking he would run away as cattle always did at home. The bull snorted again and tossed his massive head.

'Go away and eat your grass,' !Oma told him gleefully, turning back to join !Ka.

The bull charged. Still thinking it was a game !Oma went shrieking and leaping towards the river. He could outrun most people and most animals. He could always climb a tree if necessary. He was having a great game.

But !Ka was having doubts. This bull was not halfheartedly chasing !Oma away with his head lowered and heels kicking.

He had his head raised as he thundered after his friend. He looked as though he meant business. And he was gaining on !Oma very fast.

!Ka looked at the rest of the herd. Suddenly they did not look like the cattle at home. Another bull was trotting forward towards the front of the herd, his giant head swinging from the bull chasing !Oma and then back to stare at !Ka.

Reacting instinctively, !Ka turned and ran in the opposite direction with all the reserves of strength he had in his small wiry body, the child bouncing on his shoulders. He reached a large tree, threw the boy into the lower branches, clambered up past him and hauled the child to safety in higher branches. From there he had a perfect view of the fate of his friend, hunting companion, kinsman and clansman, !Oma. The divining tablets were never wrong. The little Bushman had not stood a chance.

It was several hours before he felt safe to leave the haven of the tree. He mourned for his friend. The bull had left little for him to bury. However, he scraped a shallow grave in the soft soil with his hands, and placed !Oma's remains in it. He could find no stones or rocks to protect his friend from hyaena but he broke branches and stacked them over the grave. The child helped, carrying smaller sticks. He seemed to sense !Ka's sorrow. He was unusually silent.

!Ka had done his best. He had not been able to bury !Oma in a squatting position as is Bushman custom but he arranged his remains so that he faced the Great God to the east and he broke all !Oma's arrows and his bow and scattered them over the grave so that others would know what it was and keep away.

Worried that !Oma's premature death would cause his spirit to try and capture his own to keep him company (because those who die young often resent it and resort to such tactics) but satisfied his friend was as suitably buried as he could manage, !Ka hoisted the boy on his shoulders and set off again.

They reached their destination the next day. A small clan of northern San who were camped close to a well worn vehicle track told !Ka that they had indeed arrived at the place where some white people grieved for the loss of their small son. !Ka took a circuitous route to the farmhouse, avoiding the cattle and the native workers, and set the child gently down at the gate. 'Go,' he said, pointing to the house.

'Da.' The child looked up at him and smiled.

'Go, little beetle, this is your home.'

The boy looked over to the house. A sudden shudder ran through him and he started to run on his plump little legs. 'Mama, mama.'

A woman came tearing out of the house, skirts flying, at the sound of her son. 'Ali,' she screamed. 'Ali, my darling.' She scooped him up in her arms, kissing him, rubbing his head, stroking him, hugging him. 'Alexander, my darling baby, where have you been, where on earth did you come from?' She burst into a storm of weeping and held him to her as though she were afraid he would disappear again.

A man hurried from the house and saw them. 'Jesus Christ, I don't believe it.'

All this was double talk to the little San but he saw the child was safe and he saw the love on the faces of the white couple and he knew he had done the right thing and he knew his friend !Oma had not died in vain. He turned away and left, unhurried and alone. He had over 400 miles to make on the return journey so he might as well get started.

The man lifted his tear-stained face from his son's head

and saw !Ka turn and leave. 'Wait,' he shouted. But the little San did not wait and the man was too distracted by his son's sudden reappearance to go after him.

'Da,' Alexander said, reaching for the pouch to show his father the stone which sparked with hundreds of beautiful lights.

But the pouch was no longer there. It had snagged on a twig when they climbed the tree in their flight from the buffalo. And the little boy who had borne sunburn, separation from his parents, strange food and even stranger people, a gruelling six-week trek from the Kalahari way down south, to Shakawe right up near the Angolan border, not to mention a fatal buffalo charge, burst into heartbroken tears.

THREE

When he was six, Alexander Theron had the worrying thought that his mother was not normal. He remembered the incident quite clearly. She had stood alone, defiantly facing the wind. The approaching storm boiled, slate grey, like a swirling whirlpool, from the ground to the sky and as far as he could see in each direction. Ragged remnants of earlier white cloud were caught up and churned, like cream in a coffee cup, in the violent vortex as nature vented her fury on the landscape. The distant Tsodilo Hills had disappeared, their rugged sandy boulders and craggy faces hidden as the full force of the wind from Angola hurtled over and around and pelted them with rain before boring down onto the flat white country.

'We'll get it this time,' she called to Alex's father. Sand blew against her but she ignored its sting. Dropping to her knees she raised her hands imploringly. 'Please, God,' she prayed out loud. 'Please send us that rain.' But the only moisture around were the tears pouring down her face.

Alex looked up from the game of jacks he was playing with Paulie. His brother was a bit young and the jacks usually fell off the back of his small hand but he gamely tried to copy his older brother. Alex saw his mother's tears and felt afraid. She had been crying a lot lately. It was then he thought that maybe his mother was not normal.

'Come inside, Mum,' he called to her. He looked over to his father. 'Tell her to come in, Pa.'

But his father was watching her with a strange and sad expression on his face and appeared not to have heard him.

Alex saw several drops of rain hit the sandy soil. They were so big and heavy they formed a crater the size of a penny. 'Please let it rain,' he prayed. Not to God, as his mother had done, just to anyone who might be listening. 'Please make Mum happy again.'

'Your turn.' Paulie thrust the jacks at him impatiently.

Alex threw them into the air and caught four on the back of his hand.

'Wow!' Paulie was impressed.

Lightning flashed, jagged and dangerous in the midst of the swirling grey rain which seemed close enough to touch. Alex counted slowly as Pa had taught him. 'One hundred and one . . . one hundred and two . . . one hundred and three . . . one hundred and four . . . one hundred and five . . . one hundred and six.' Thunder rolled. 'Six miles, it's six miles away, Pa.' Panic was rising in him for his mother.

'Come on,' Paulie urged. 'Finish your turn.'

Alex threw the four jacks in the air, whipped his hand down, picked up the fifth and caught the other four.

'Wow!' Paulie breathed. 'I wish I could do that.'

'You will,' Alex said kindly. 'You just have to wait for your hand to grow up.' He threw another despairing look at his father.

'Come back to the verandah, Peta,' his father finally called.

But she stayed where she was, hands raised to her God, begging for rain.

The storm blew away to the north, its rain–laden centre a taunting black curtain in the distance. The few drops which had fallen had not even settled the dust. Peta Theron lowered her arms and rose to her feet. Her shoulders dropped. She went up the steps of the verandah and flung herself into a wicker chair beside her husband. 'It's always the same. We always miss out.' She turned on him angrily. 'Why did we have to buy this stupid farm? No wonder it was cheap. It's right on the edge of the rain.'

'It's the hills.'

'I know it's the hills.'

'We get rain sometimes.' He was placating her, imploring her not to be angry.

'Never enough. It stops just out there.'

Alex collected up the jacks. 'Come on, Paulie, let's play with the cars.' The cars were out back, away from his parents, away from his angry mother and sad father. As they left he heard her say, 'God is punishing us.'

Paulie heard it too. 'Why would God punish us?' he asked when they were out of earshot.

Alex had no idea.

Later that night, tucked up in bed and waiting for sleep, he heard his parents outside on the verandah. Paulie, as usual, had fallen asleep as soon as his head hit the pillow. Alex always took a little longer. He heard his father tap out his pipe against his shoe. 'I meant what I said at dinner, Pets. Paulie will be lonely when Alex goes away. He should have a companion.'

Alex felt the fear in his stomach. He was going away to school, far away from his family and the thought of it scared him.

His mother sighed and was silent.

'Pets?'

'I know.'

'Well?'

'Well what?' She was angry again. 'That's all you think about. It's wrong.'

'That's not fair, Pets.' Pa's voice was quiet but Alex sensed his sadness. 'I've been patient but Paulie's three now. A man has needs.'

'It's wrong,' she repeated.

Pa sighed. 'How can it be wrong? We're married.'

'It just is.' He said nothing so she added, 'It's against the law.'

Alex's ears pricked. He had heard his mother say that before. He knew what the law was. Was this why God was punishing them all?

Pa kept his voice low. Alex had to strain to hear. 'South African law perhaps. But we live in Bechuanaland.'

'All the same . . .'

Scrape. His father's chair moved on the wooden verandah. 'Peta, for Heaven's sake! Just because my family is about to be classified coloured by some idiotic selection process. Christ! Half the South African parliament wouldn't stand up to scrutiny.'

'Don't blaspheme.'

'Peta, this is getting me down. Where did you go? We used to be so happy.'

His mother was crying again. Alex could hear her sniffing. 'We're being punished. God is punishing us.'

'That's bullshit and you know it.'

Wow! Pa rarely swore. Alex listened intently.

'You're ashamed of me aren't you? You're just like the others. It was okay for a while but now you're ashamed because

34

I've got a smidgen of black blood. Jesus, Pets, I'm the same man you sneaked out to be with all those years ago. I'm more white than some of the others we went to school with. And what is more, it doesn't matter a damn in this country.'

'I hate Bechuanaland.' She was really crying now.

'Pets, honey. Would you like to go home for a visit?'

'You know I can't. My parents have disowned me. I can't take the boys.'

Why can't she take us?

'No-one would know. They don't look black. Anyway, Pets, it's not a law yet.'

Black! I'm black! Whoopee! I'm black. Alex, who—apart from his parents and more recently Paulie—had spent most of his time in the company of the farm workers' children was not encumbered with prejudice of any kind. He had always thought of himself as being different from them. Now it seemed, he wasn't. He hopped out of bed and shook Paulie. 'Paulie, wake up, wake up.'

'Wha . . .'

'Sshh. Listen.'

'Well that's what they'd be called in South Africa. Black. Officially, our boys will be black.'

'Officially *I'll* be black,' Pa shouted, frustrated.

Wow! Pa's black too. This is good stuff.

'Paulie, did you hear that—we're black!' Alex whispered.

Confused and frightened, Paulie started to cry.

'Sshh.'

But it was too late. Their parents had heard and came into the room. 'Am I black, Mum?' Alex asked.

Their mother fled crying. Pa sat on Paulie's bed. 'No, son, you're not black. But in South Africa that is what you would be called.'

35

'Why?'

'Because they have different laws there. Because you live in a black country, they'd call you black.'

'What's a black country?'

'It means that one day this country will be ruled by its own people, the black people. South Africa is ruled by white people. They'll call you black because of it.'

Paulie settled down in his bed. 'Will I turn black, Pa?'

'No, son, you'll stay the same colour you've always been.' Pa had a smile in his voice. He got off Paulie's bed and looked over at Alex. 'Okay, son? Do you understand?'

'Yes, Pa.'

'Remember this, you two. It's what's inside your heart that's important.' He left their room, gently closing the door behind him.

Alex did not believe him. He had heard too much.

In the morning he tried to talk to his mother about being black but she was reading her Bible and frowned at the interruption before he could say a word. Bursting to tell someone, he went to their servant. 'Denao, guess what?'

She looked down at him and shrugged. He did not like her very much. Servants didn't stay long in their house, unlike the farm workers, and this one was sulky and silent and made no attempt to be nice to him. She wore those funny long dresses the Herero women always wore and was always talking about going home to South West Africa, or, as she called it, the old country. Pa said she never would because it was run by South Africa. Still, she was all he had.

'I'm black.'

Long skirts and a multitude of petticoats rustled as she moved around the kitchen. 'Tch! Don't be silly. Of course you're not black.' She brushed past him and he had to skip backwards to make way for the voluminous folds of her skirts.

Well, she should know. After all, she was very black. Maybe Pa was right. Perhaps it was because they lived in Bechuanaland. Deflated, for the thought of being black meant that he was just like his friends, he went outside to play with Paulie.

FOUR

The question of his colour remained a mystery to Alex for three years. Whenever he tried to talk to his mother about it she would either get angry, or more often, cry. So he stopped asking her. His father would tell him, 'One day when you're older, son.' By the time he was nine Alex was wondering just how old he had to be. Most of the time he forgot about it because, now he was at school and mixing with whites and Indians, as well as blacks, his own colour was no longer of much interest to him.

He had settled well into school. He was homesick for the first term but, once he had been home for the school holidays and realised he would get to see his family regularly, he started to enjoy himself. By the time Paulie joined him three years later he was a veteran. Both boys liked their aunt Dorie with whom they stayed in Francistown, although Uncle Hugh was someone they avoided if they could; he was a bit too fond of a drink.

Alex was on the under eleven rugby team, not bad going considering he was only just nine. His size got him on the team. That, and his excellent physical coordination. Alex was taller than most boys of ten and Paulie was shaping up the same way. Both boys had quick minds and revelled in the learning process. Compared to Shakawe, Francistown was a big city and they loved it.

Getting from Shakawe to Francistown and back was not normally a problem. The village of Shakawe evolved because the mine labour recruiting organisation, Wenela, had set up a major depot there. Men from the area, and as far afield as Angola and South West Africa, signed up for work in the South African mines. Wenela flew these men in and out of Shakawe in DC3s. The same planes were used to ferry the children of Wenela's management staff backwards and for-wards to Francistown where they then caught connecting flights to either Southern Rhodesia or South Africa to attend boarding school. Alex was able to hitch a lift.

Not this time, though. Somehow, his mother had learned that Shakawe was to get a resident preacher. She was so excited by the news that she offered him the services of her two young sons from Francistown to Shakawe. 'It's such a long journey,' she had written to the Southern African Mission Office. 'The boys can tell him about the area and keep him company.'

Paulie leaned towards the front seat of the Land Rover. 'How much longer?'

Alex sympathised. It was Paulie's first return journey and he had the misfortune to have to make it by road. Two-and-a-half days of boring, bone jarring, hot and dusty driving, with cramped six hours of sleep snatched along the way at night.

The Reverend Frith looked briefly into the rear vision mirror and smiled. 'Another couple of hours.'

Paulie groaned and sat back.

The Reverend went back to his concentration of the road. It was a constant battle. The route was mainly traversed by larger vehicles. The narrow wheelbase of the Land Rover could not quite settle comfortably on their wider tracks— one wheel was always on the sandy, sloping edge. In places, the bush grew right up to the edge of the road, drooping dust-laden leaves, the sharp thorns of acacias ready to cut an unsuspecting arm to the bone. The Reverend's right arm had been lacerated twice yesterday before he realised it would be prudent to keep it off the open window. Alex had never heard a man of the cloth say 'shit' before.

He'd never heard one say 'Holy fucking Jesus!' before either. Three elephants had just crossed in front of them, ears flapping wildly. They appeared from nowhere and disappeared into the trees and were quickly gone from sight. The Reverend was visibly shaken by their size and the swiftness with which they came and went. 'Sorry, boys. I didn't expect that.'

'That's okay.' Alex was trying hard not to laugh.

The Reverend was embarrassed. 'Do you have elephants on your farm?'

'Not elephants. Sometimes we get lions.'

'Don't they eat the cattle?' The Reverend was fresh out from England and anxious to learn as much as possible about the savage land which was his first posting.

'Not often. Sometimes they do.' Well it was true. A mangy old lion, desperate for a meal, had once brought down one of their calves. His teeth had been so rotten he roared with pain every time he tried to take a bite. Pa had watched him with sympathy for a while and then shot him to end his misery.

Paulie leaned forward again. 'Wonder if Michael-John has grown much.'

'Who's Michael-John?'

'He's our brother,' Paulie said from the back seat.

'How old is he?'

'Two,' Alex said.

'I guess he'll be going to school with you chaps in a few years.'

'I dunno. Maybe.' Alex didn't think so. Michael-John had been born sickly and stayed sickly. He was a thin boy who had something wrong with his legs and spine. Paget's disease he thought it was. Well, that's what Pa once said. His mother refused to discuss it although he had heard her say more than once it was another sign of their being punished.

'What's Shakawe like?' The Reverend swerved to avoid a pothole. 'How big is it?'

'Well . . .' Alex had no idea. 'There's Wright's Trading Store and the Wenela depot. There's a really big African village that kind of wanders all over the place. There's a police station too.' He stopped, trying to remember. 'There's the school of course.'

'Why don't you go to school in Shakawe?'

'It's for black kids.'

'Oh.' The Reverend grinned at his bluntness.

Alex tried to be helpful. 'I've seen your house. It's nice.'

'No it isn't, it's a dump.' Nothing if not honest was Paulie.

The Reverend laughed. 'Maybe it's a nice dump.'

Alex laughed too. He liked the new Reverend.

They were getting into familiar country. The road followed the Panhandle, a narrow arm of the Okavango Delta which stretched to the South West African border. Small villages every twenty miles or so sprawled out along the southwestern side of the life-giving waters. They caught their first sight of Shakawe at four in the afternoon. 'Here we are, we're home,' Paulie said, excited.

'This is *it*?' The Reverend looked astonished. A couple of huts appeared beside the deep sandy bush track. In the distance he could see more huts. The track wound randomly in front of them. It was no different from the country they had been driving through for the past six hours, nothing to indicate they had reached a village.

'There's Wenela,' Alex pointed.

The recruiting depot was basic but at least it was European. The Reverend looked relieved.

On their right, the river offered tantalising glimpses through the dense stands of trees which grew on the banks. They were the only substantial vegetation around, the rest was mainly barren sand.

Mum and Pa were waiting outside Wright's Trading Store. Built mainly of corrugated iron, it was the only establishment in Shakawe where provisions could be bought. Even then, being able to buy what you wanted was not a foregone conclusion since most of its stock came in by air, as and when the DC3s had the carrying capacity. Still, the sight of its sagging roof and crooked verandah was the most welcome thing Alex had seen in three days.

As usual it was Pa who hugged the boys and welcomed them home. Mum was too busy thanking and blessing the Reverend and inviting him to lunch. Alex had once heard one of the Wenela pilots telling Aunty Dorie why he did not like giving Alex a lift. 'It's not the kid, he's a nice enough boy. It's his bloody mother. She drives you crazy. Half the time you don't know if she's talking to you or praying.'

Alex, listening to the hippo gargling and grunting in the river, watching Mum fall all over the Reverend, seeing old Ndete, the butcher, under his tree selling meat, felt a great sense of having come home, even though they still had more than two hours over some of the roughest road imaginable to go before they reached the farm.

There was a surprise waiting for them at home. 'Go and see your room,' Pa said.

The house had evolved with no planning. A single room initially with a curtained area at one end for sleeping, it had been haphazardly enlarged over the years, as and when money permitted. First a wide verandah at the front. Then a kitchen and dining room at the other end. Then two bedrooms and a bathroom.

Alex ran to open the bedroom door, Paulie just behind him. They stopped in surprise. Where the door had opened into their room before, now it opened into a hallway with three doors leading from it.

'Yours is the last one, Alex, you're in the middle, Paulie.' Pa had followed them into the hall.

'Wowee!' Paulie rushed into his room.

'Gee, Pa, when did you do this?' Alex wanted to run to his room too but Pa looked so pleased he knew he should ask some questions.

'Just after Christmas. We wanted to surprise you.' Pa guessed at Alex's impatience. 'Go and see.'

Paulie raced back into the hall. 'Wait'll you see, Alex, it's the best thing. Oh boy!'

Alex opened his door and, with Paulie jumping up and down behind him trying to see, took in his new domain. There was a window looking over the back garden, a built-in wardrobe, his bed against one wall, a chest of drawers and a bookcase. A round cotton mat was in the middle of the floor, red and brown and white.

'Like it?' Pa was smiling at Paulie's enthusiasm.

'I love it.' Alex had enjoyed having his own room at Aunty Dorie's but now Paulie shared it with him. As fond as he was of his younger brother, sometimes he wanted privacy.

'Oh boy, I can't wait to go to bed.' Paulie was running from his room to Alex's and back again.

'Hey, man!' Pa caught him by the seat of his pants. 'Slow down, you'll wear yourself out.'

But Paulie, having been cooped up in the Land Rover for three days, could not be contained. He went running outside to play with the dog.

The Reverend Frith had been invited for lunch on Wednesday as a way of thanking him for giving the boys a lift home. He arrived wearing khaki shorts and shirt and long, lace-up snake boots. He shook hands with Pa and clapped him on the arm. 'Nice to see you again, Mr Theron.'

'Danie, please.'

'Fine with me. My name's Harry.'

Pa scratched the cowlick at the front of his head. 'Is that okay? I mean, to call a cleric by his first name?' The clergy made Pa uneasy. He was never sure how to speak to them.

Harry Frith laughed. 'Why not? I've got one, might as well use it.'

Pa's face lost its hunted look. 'Well then, Harry it is. Mind you, the wife won't like it. Come up onto the verandah. Do you drink beer?'

Mum, alerted by Paulie, came out onto the verandah untying her apron. 'My this is nice. Welcome, Father, welcome to our humble home. The Good Lord has seen fit to send us another beautiful day. Mind you, we could do with some rain. Still, one mustn't complain. We're all healthy, praise the Lord.'

Uh oh. She's not being normal.

'Please.' The Reverend Frith smiled at her. 'Call me Harry.'

'Oh Father, I couldn't. After all, a man in your position . . .'

The Reverend kept smiling but Alex thought it looked kind of forced.

Mum excused herself and went to fuss over the new servant in the kitchen. Pa poured the Reverend a beer.

'How long have you lived here, Danie?' The Reverend sipped his beer and raised eyebrows in appreciation. 'Gosh, this is good.'

'Bit different to your beer.' Pa grinned. 'Do you really drink it off the shelf?'

Harry Frith nodded. 'Bear in mind the shelf is a good bit cooler than here.'

'Still . . .' Pa could not imagine anything worse.

'Sorry, I interrupted. You were about to tell me how long you'd been here.'

'We came here in 1940.' Alex heard the tone of his father's voice. He didn't know why but Pa always sounded a bit angry whenever he was questioned about his reasons for settling in Bechuanaland.

Harry Frith whistled. 'Thirteen years. That's a long time to live in such an isolated place. What made you choose Shakawe?'

It was a good question. They were the only farmers in the area and, although he was city born and bred, the Reverend could see that there was very little fodder for the cattle.

'We liked it,' Pa answered brusquely.

Alex, sitting on the steps with his back to them, grinned.

It was so unlike his father's usual courteous friendliness it amused him.

The Reverend blithely carried on. 'Are you South African?'

'Yes we are.' Good manners prevented Danie Theron from telling the Reverend to mind his own business.

'So why live here? Couldn't you farm in South Africa?' Alex heard slurping as the Reverend Frith sipped his beer. 'You don't mind do you? I'm just curious.'

Pa was silent for so long Alex thought he hadn't heard the Reverend. Finally, 'You're new to this continent, Harry. South Africa is . . . well . . . things happen there. We had to leave.'

'Why?'

Good! Alex wanted to know why too.

'Go help your mother, son.'

'But Pa—'

'Do it.'

When Pa spoke like that you did it. Alex went inside, straight out the back door and sat, just around the corner, out of sight. He could hear every word.

'. . . so it's been forty years in the making. General Louis Botha started it back in 1910. Jan Smuts and James Hertzog kept it alive. The whites wanted it so it became a political issue. A big one. Now Dr Malan has made it official. Mixed marriages are illegal.'

'How does that affect you?'

Alex heard puzzlement in the Reverend's voice. He also heard the sadness in his father's.

'My great-grandmother married a man who had a quarter black in him. It wasn't something that happened often, even back then, but it did happen occasionally. Apparently it was impossible to tell—my great-grandfather looked like every other white man. But when everyone was classified into a racial group this fact came to light. Our whole family is officially black, even my father who's as white as you. When Peta fell pregnant we had to leave. Now do you understand?'

'You have an older child?'

This was news to Alex.

'No.' Pa sounded sad. 'Peta miscarried. Even so, we couldn't go back to South Africa if we wanted to stay together.'

'What would have happened if you'd gone back?'

'I would have gone to prison. Peta might have been imprisoned as well but, even if she wasn't, she'd have been a social outcast all her life.'

'That's outrageous.' Harry Frith was shocked. 'I've heard of apartheid but I had no idea . . .'

'They haven't finished yet. You wait, they'll take it all the way, no-one can stop them. They've even requested the administration responsibilities of Bechuanaland so they can shunt half the black population into here.' Pa chuckled suddenly. 'Britain won't go for it, luckily. They can see what's happening.'

'And they call themselves Christians!'

'It's what they hear at church every Sunday. The blacks are inferior.' Pa raised his voice. 'Okay, son, did you get all that?'

Uh oh! He walked around the side of the house. 'Sorry, Pa.'

But his father was smiling. 'It's probably time you knew. Just don't tell your mother. She doesn't think you're ready.'

That cleared up the mystery but Alex was disappointed by the ordinariness of it. He had expected something more dramatic. A distant relative back in the olden days with a bit of black blood hardly qualified Alex to be black. He could not understand why his parents made such a fuss about it. He knew nothing about the process of apartheid and all it stood for.

A few minutes later they were called inside for lunch. His mother had outdone herself. Gleaming glassware, the best china and cutlery and a floral centrepiece which would have been more at home in a church than on the table. She had put out her best china beer mugs. Pa hated them, they made his beer flat, but he said nothing and poured the Reverend and himself another beer.

Mum waited, hovering over the sumptuous meal like an anxious mother hen, until they were all sitting down. 'It would be a great honour—' she said, her eyes shining, '—if you would say grace.'

Alex resigned himself to a long monologue.

Paulie stole a meatball from the dish near him.

Mum clasped her hands reverently.

Pa got that hunted look on his face.

Michael-John was howling in the kitchen because he could not join them.

Paulie chewed surreptitiously.

The Reverend Frith, fresh out from England, cleared his throat.

'Here we go,' Alex thought.

'God bless this bunch as they munch their lunch.'

The half-eaten meatball shot out of Paulie's mouth, hit the table once, bounced in the air and—almost in slow motion, spinning and flicking gravy, and with unerring inevitability as though it had been programmed—landed in the Reverend's beer mug with a small splash, unnoticed by everyone barring Alex and Paulie.

'Well now.' Pa was smiling with relief and reaching for a dish. 'Well now, let's dig in.'

48

Mum was looking at the Reverend in open amazement.

He saw her look. 'I hope you don't mind, Mrs Theron. This meal looks wonderful and I'm starving. I couldn't wait another moment.'

Alex held his breath as the Reverend picked up his china beer mug and took a sip. He didn't dare look at Paulie who appeared to be choking.

The Reverend put down the mug. Pa passed him a dish and he helped himself to potato and onion pie. Pa passed him another dish. Alex stared at the beer mug. It was too far away for him to knock over. He steeled himself and shot a glance at Paulie. Then he wished he hadn't. His brother's eyes were brimming with tears in his effort not to laugh out loud. In desperation Alex concentrated on helping himself to food but his stomach began to shake, then his shoulders. His own eyes filled with tears. Paulie was snorting. Alex thought if he coughed it would take away the overwhelming desire to laugh. He opened his mouth to cough. Instead a shouted bark of laughter shot out. Paulie snorted again and some of his food sprang from his nose. A slimy mess of half-chewed meatball and snot. Paulie clapped his hand to his nose, his eyes pleading with Alex for help.

'What on earth is wrong, Paulie?' his mother asked.

Paulie was helpless. Choking and laughing he put his head on the table and banged his fist up and down.

'The boy's choking,' Pa said, rising quickly. He thumped Paulie on the back.

Alex couldn't stand it. In a gargantuan effort not to laugh, he was making the same noise the cat did just before it was sick. He pushed his chair back and fled, out through the lounge, off the verandah, through the gate, out into the bush where he flung himself against a tree and screamed and screamed with laughter.

No-one came to get him. He knew he was in trouble. He tried five times to return to the house. Each time, just as he reached the verandah, he would get a vision of the meatball in the Reverend's beer or the look on Paulie's face and the laughter would well inside him again and he had to get far away and let it out. In the end he gave up on the idea of lunch.

He was sitting under a tree contemplating the trouble he was in when Paulie found him. 'Mum told me to leave the table.'

'We're in trouble.'

'The Reverend nearly choked on the meatball.'

This set them off again.

'What did Pa say?' Alex wiped his eyes. His stomach muscles ached from laughing.

'I think he's going to get his strap.'

Uh oh.

'I'm hungry,' Paulie complained.

'Well you shouldn't have stolen the meatball.'

'Some of it's stuck up my nose.'

'No kidding! You can get rid of it if you kind of sniff hard backwards then spit.'

Paulie hawked and spat it on the ground. 'How many times you reckon Pa'll hit us?'

'At least ten,' Alex said morosely.

'It doesn't hurt as much as the cane.'

'When did you get caned?'

'Just before the holidays. Old Leadbottom at school caught me pissing against the fence.'

'Why'd you do that?'

'I needed to pee.'

They rolled on the ground laughing.

They sat under the tree for two hours. Finally they saw the Reverend come out of the house, get in his Land Rover and, with Pa and Mum standing on the verandah waving, disappear down the road in a cloud of sandy dust.

'Here comes Pa.' Paulie needn't have bothered. Alex was watching his father like a hawk. 'He doesn't look mad,' Paulie whispered.

Pa joined them under the tree. He sat down in his best trousers, not minding the sand. 'What was all that about?'

'Sorry, Pa,' both boys chorused.

'Alex?'

'Nothing.' Alex didn't want to get Paulie into any more trouble than he already was.

'Paulie?'

Paulie looked at the ground and made swirling patterns in the sand with his finger.

'Paulie?'

'I couldn't help it, Pa. The meatball just sort of came out.'

Alex tried not to but he was laughing again.

'It's not funny,' Pa snapped but his mouth twitched. He ducked his head but his shoulders shook. Pretty soon he was rolling around laughing as hard as his boys. 'That was one helluva shot, son,' he managed finally.

'Bet you couldn't do it if you tried,' Alex said, delighted.

'If you ever pull a stunt like that again, either of you, I'll whip your hides. Your mother is very angry.' But Pa was laughing as he spoke. 'That poor man nearly choked to death.'

'We weren't laughing at the Reverend, Pa—honest.' Alex was worried his father thought they had been cruel.

Pa put his arm around Alex. 'I know, son, I understand.'

With a six-year-old's directness, Paulie put his finger on it. 'It was the grace, Pa.'

Pa gathered Paulie to his side with his other arm. 'You boys believe in God don't you?'

'Yes, Pa,' they chorused.

'So does Reverend Frith,' Pa said. 'He's a good man and he believes in the same things as Mum.'

'But Mum talks about God all the time,' Paulie objected. 'And she's not even a Reverend.'

Pa chuckled.

'We thought the Reverend would say a long Grace like Mum does,' Alex said. 'We were sort of waiting for it.'

'Don't you like saying grace?'

Alex sensed his father was treading carefully. In all respects but religion, Pa was fair and honest with them. Alex could not understand why, whenever the subject of religion came up, his father seemed to develop double standards. However, he knew better than to challenge his father, especially at the moment. 'We say short ones at school. The food doesn't get cold. I don't mind grace, Pa, but I hate eating cold food.'

Pa squeezed his shoulder sympathetically.

'Why is Mum like that?' Alex held his breath. It was the first time he'd dared ask that question. Pa might not tell him the answer.

Silence stretched across the hot afternoon. Pa appeared deep in thought. Finally, 'When Mum was your age her parents took her to the Kirk every Sunday. They said grace before every meal. Mum said her prayers every night. She is a very religious person and talking to God gives her comfort. She loves reading the Bible, it makes her feel closer to God. Everyone is different, son. Reverend Frith might not talk about God as much as Mum . . .' he grinned, '. . . and his grace was certainly a surprise, but he is every bit as religious as she is.'

'But why does she have to talk about it *all* the time?' Alex persisted. 'It makes me feel kind of yucky.'

Pa's eyebrows went up. 'Yucky?' There was an edge to his voice. Alex had gone too far.

'I feel yucky too.' Paulie had not picked up on Pa's sudden anger.

Pa stood suddenly, put his hands on his hips and stared down at his sons. 'You listen to me, you two. Your mother loves you very much. She would do anything for you. Don't ever let me hear you say anything like that again. Do you understand?' He left them without waiting for a response.

Alex watched his father walk away, mixed emotions running through him; he had angered Pa and that upset him. He loved his father deeply. He sensed that Pa sympathised with his and Paulie's feelings. But Alex was too young to understand that, despite Pa's sympathy, he would allow no criticism of his beloved Peta.

There were the things he overheard Pa saying to the Reverend Frith. Alex knew there was more to it. It was all mixed up with being punished and being coloured and not getting rain and Mum crying all the time.

'Well I *do* feel yucky,' Paulie said rebelliously.

'So do I,' Alex agreed, his three extra years giving him wisdom Paulie did not yet possess. 'But I don't think we'd better say it again.'

The boys rose and returned slowly to the house. They would receive a lecture from Mum who would go out of her way to make them both feel guilty. And then, to punish them, she would extend the ritual half-hour Bible reading to a full hour. But Alex did not mind. He would do anything to get back into Pa's good books.

FIVE

There was nothing secret about Annie Carter's predilection for rugby heroes. She liked to fuck them. Simple as that. The only thing was, she got no pleasure from the act.

Pocket money had been wagered. The boy who got Annie to react would collect the pot. Adjudicators hid around the river bend—insurance against any temptation to exaggerate.

A week before leaving school behind him forever, Alex became a rugby hero by saving the final game in its dying minutes.

'I'll wait for you outside the showers,' Annie said. That was her sign.

With some good-natured ribald remarks and some impractical or downright impossible advice ringing in his ears, Alex tried nonchalance as he sauntered from the shower block.

He was sixteen and fully matured. His voice had broken two years earlier and his body was hard and muscular. He'd started shaving seriously six months ago. He was tall, six foot two, and his silvery curls had darkened and hardened to a honey shade which he kept clipped short. He abused the top and sides with a stiff brush, forcing it flat, but at the back where it sat on his neck, his hair curled in tight ringlets. Girls found him attractive and his open good looks and friendly manner made him popular with his peers. His experience with girls, however, was sadly lacking. Until today.

She was waiting for him. 'Hi.'

'Hi.'

She took his arm. 'Great game.'

'Yeah.'

'You were great.'

'Thanks.'

Her long dark red hair tickled his arm. The pressure of her fingers felt hot on his skin. 'Where are we going?' He knew where—she took all of them to the same spot—he was just making conversation.

'The river.'

The Tati River ran through Francistown, splitting it in two. Mainly nothing more than a dry river course, over the years its sandy bed and grassy banks had witnessed the deflowering of half the teenage population of Francistown, all of whom were certain no-one else went there. She led him to her usual place, about a mile from town.

'Here we are. Let's sit down.'

Alex sank gratefully to the ground; his legs were threatening to give way. 'This is a nice place.' He looked around, his heart racing, trying to think what to say next.

'No-one comes here.'

'You sure?' He thought about the others, hiding just around the bend.

She grinned at him. 'Come here.' She seemed so composed compared to him.

He crawled over to her. She ran her fingers over his face, lingering on his lips. He tried to kiss her but she shook her head impatiently and lay back on the grass. 'Now you can kiss me.'

He leaned over her and kissed her, his lips pressed firmly together.

'Not like that, open your mouth.'

He opened his mouth and felt her soft warm tongue licking him. He was as hard as a rock and his breathing was unsteady.

'Do you like me?'

He nodded, not trusting himself to speak.

She ran her fingers down his chest. 'Do you want to do it?'

He nodded again, his heart doing extra big leaps up as far as his throat.

'Well take off your clothes, silly.'

He was out of his clothes within five seconds. Then an agonising wait while she slowly removed hers. He caught his breath when he saw her naked. Small hillocks of breasts, pink tipped. Dark red thatch between her legs. 'Come on.' She lay back, opening her legs.

With no experience to draw on he nonetheless felt a moment's disappointment. Perhaps it was instinct but something told him her manner was too clinical. However, he was too excited to dwell on it. He rose above her, guiding his engorged penis into her. For a brief second he panicked. He was too big. She was too small. He'd never get it in. But he slid into her, past the hairy lips, into the soft inner depths. His breathing was ragged, as though he had run a fast 100 yards. His last thought was to wonder why she didn't feel the same as him. She was lying on her back watching the sky, a small smile on her face.

It didn't take long. With no movement from Annie he

pumped erratically. He felt his climax start, gather momentum, and then the jerking release. It took him by surprise. He had masturbated a few times. This was quicker, more intense. As soon as his breathing returned to normal he wanted to move away from her. She made no attempt to hold him back. 'Did you like that?'

He didn't want to discuss it. 'Yeah.' Suddenly he was embarrassed.

'Have you ever done it before?'

'Course. Plenty of times.'

'Who with?'

Now he was stuck. He had enough of the gentleman in him not to want to name names and get some innocent girl into trouble. But, on the other hand he could not admit he had lied. Inspiration was slow, but it did come to him. 'I promised not to tell.'

She tossed her head. Alex watched her. 'Did you like it?'

She was pulling on her skirt. 'It was okay I guess.'

It was 1960. The explosion of sexual freedom of that decade was on a roll around the world but in Francistown, it was a long way off. Alex's knowledge of girls had come from a well-thumbed, dog-eared book which someone at school had loaned him.

Some of the stuff he had read hadn't made much sense. Other things were almost unbelievable. But he decided to give it a go. Besides, apart from his fledgling male ego wanting to turn her indifference into moaning, writhing ecstasy like the heroine in the book, he had a lot of exploring to do. And there was also the money from the bet. 'Wait.'

She stopped in the act of pulling on her blouse.

'Take it off.'

Shrugging, she took off her blouse.

'The skirt too.' His heart was hammering again.

He parted her legs and then the secret lips encased in dark red hair. There it was, just like in the book. A little bud. The book called it a manikin. He lowered his face between her legs. 'What are you doing?' She sounded scared.

Then his tongue touched the manikin. 'Oh, oh God, oh yes, yes, yes.' It was working. He licked all around. She had a pleasant yeasty smell. He hadn't expected that. 'Yes, oh God, yes.' She was breathing hard.

He went back to the bud. 'Oh Christ, oh Jesus.'

He felt her legs around him stiffen.

'Oh my God, yes.'

Then she was shuddering and jumping and yelling. 'Fuck me, oh my God, fuck me.' This time she was not watching the sky.

She lay for a long time afterwards, eyes closed, languid, not covering herself. Alex moved away slightly but he was grinning. The book had been right: girls liked it just as much as boys, you just had to turn the right key. She rolled her head sideways and looked at him through half-closed eyes. 'I've never felt like that before.'

'Did you like it this time?'

'God, yes.'

'Want to do it again some time?'

'I want to do it again now.'

Now! He wasn't sure he could. His penis hung limply, ravaged and sore.

'We don't have to do it all. You could just . . . you know . . . do that to me again.'

He moved over to her. The book said something about nipples too.

Walking back into town an hour later Annie asked him to go steady.

'I'm leaving Francistown next week,' he reminded her.

'Where are you planning to live?' She was not about to let him go.

'Home I guess. For a while anyway.' He had no idea what he wanted to do other than have fun and make money. Without Annie.

They reached her gate. 'We will do it again before you leave won't we?'

'You bet, Annie.'

She grinned at him. 'See ya.' She turned and ran down the path.

'See ya, Annie.' He waved guiltily at her mother at the front door. 'Hello, Mrs Carter.'

'Hello, young Alex. I heard you scored!'

The others were waiting for him just around the corner. 'Jesus, man, what did you do to her?'

Suddenly he felt ashamed. Annie had no idea the others had been hiding. She might be easy but she was a nice girl at heart. 'Uh, nothing much.'

'C'mon, man, we heard her.'

'Yeah, man, cough up.'

'Uh, look fellas I don't want to say.'

They watched him in disbelief.

He dived into his school bag and tossed the well-thumbed book to one of them. 'Read that.' Then he was off and running with the others whooping after him. They chased him to the Bakers' front gate.

'I've read this.' Colin Tigg, the captain of the rugby team, waved the book high. 'You didn't really do that stuff did you?'

He was a new man. The wisdom in that little book gave

him more knowledge than he had learned in ten years of school. 'What do you think?' he drawled, before turning to saunter, in a manner he hoped was superior, into the house.

Paulie was at the kitchen table doing his homework. 'I hear you saved the game.'

'S'right, little brother.'

'So? How was she?'

Alex cuffed him hard. 'Save a game yourself, brat.'

Aunty Dorie looked up and smiled, having no idea what they were talking about. 'Are you going to the dance tonight, Alex?'

'Sure am.' It was the senior dance. Most of the sixteen-year-olds would be leaving school. With university an option only for the very bright or the very rich, not many went the extra two years of senior school.

'I hear the club looks really good. Some of the mothers have been decorating it today. There's a band coming up from Gabs, too. It's a new African band and they say they're excellent.' Aunty Dorie was shredding cheese as she spoke.

'I wish I could go,' Paulie said.

'All in good time, youngster.' Doris Baker was like a second mother. No, better. She wasn't religious. Alex and Paulie adored her.

'I'll run you up if you like.' The club was on the edge of town.

'No need.' Alex swiped a piece of cheese from where she was working and dodged a crack on the knuckles with the cheese grater. 'A few of us are meeting in town and going together.'

'Don't go getting drunk now.' It was a yearly ritual— drink-affected school leavers roaring around town after midnight, driving anything they could get their hands on.

Francistown was a frontier town, created during the goldrush days. It had not lost its pioneering spirit. The kids were allowed this one night of the year while the adults and the police turned a blind eye.

'Would I do that, Aunty Dorie?'

She smiled, wiping her hands on a cloth. 'Don't go sweet-talking me, mister. Besides, if you didn't I'd bloody disown you.'

Paulie guffawed.

'Get out of here.' She waved them away shaking her head.

She was not their real aunt. She was a friend of their parents and the boys had known her reasonably well before coming to stay in Francistown. She had no children of her own and had taken first Alex, then Paulie under her wing. Alex had always liked her but, when Michael-John finally succumbed to his Paget's disease at the age of five, she had been like a rock, supporting and loving.

He and Paulie went outside so he could show his younger brother how he had scored the try. Despite the age gap, the boys were close, Paulie nearly as big as Alex and just entering puberty.

'Did you do it?' Paulie asked, as soon as they were out of earshot.

Alex was dying to tell someone. Although he had balked at boasting about it earlier, Paulie was closer to him than anyone. He held nothing back. Paulie's eyes grew wider and wider.

'You mean you actually put your tongue down there?'

'Yep.'

'Yuck!'

At 8.30 he met five of his friends outside the local hotel. One of the boys had borrowed his dad's old truck. Colin Tigg, who was seventeen, had been chosen to buy the liquor. Beer would be available at the dance but a few teachers would be present, watching the intake. Acting on advice from the previous year's school leavers, they intended to have some hard stuff stashed outside. The barman, knowing full well Colin's age, sold him a bottle of whisky and a bottle of gin.

Alex had never tasted hard liquor before. 'What'll it be, guys—gin or scotch?' Colin held up the bottles. 'Let's get lubricated before the dance.'

No-one knew what to choose so Colin opened the gin and passed it around. Alex did not much like the smell but he took a large sip and swallowed, shuddering as the neat alcohol scorched his throat and set fire to his gut. 'Jesus!' His eyes were swimming with tears as he passed the bottle on.

Annie was at the dance. So were all the other girls. Normally he would have had eyes only for them. But when he walked into the clubhouse he felt as though he had been lifted up and swirled around by a hurricane. He stopped dead, staring. From the ceiling, turning slowly, was a ball of light. It flashed red and green and blue, shards of colour which lit up everything they touched. The hairs on his arms stood out and he had goose bumps all over his body. His stomach churned with excitement, a nameless excitement which he could not understand. He found it hard to breathe. Something tugged at his memory but what? The ball of light was so very familiar. But he had never seen anything like it before, of that he was sure.

'C'mon Alex, let's get a beer.'

'In a minute,' he mumbled.

He was in a trance. He could not take his eyes off the light. His mind escaped momentarily into memory and he could smell a pleasant tangy smell but it was gone as quickly as it came. He shook his head to clear it but the gin kept it foggy. The light drew him in, drew him back in time and sent him spinning out again.

What? What? Where had he seen that light? Shadows seemed to dance. Murmurs. Strange clicking language. Memory swirled in his head but it was too far off for him to capture and examine it.

'Hey, Alex, d'you want a beer or not?'

'Coming.'

The light was everywhere. Filling the room. Filling his head. It transfixed him. Wherever he was, dancing on the floor, sitting at one of the tables, talking, drinking beer, he could not get his mind or his eyes off the light.

Around midnight, with the gin wearing off, three of the boys went outside to try the scotch. Some of the girls joined them. 'Coming, Alex?'

'You go ahead.' He was at a table, staring, staring at the light. The beautiful colours made him want to hold them in his hand. They filled him with longing for something he could not identify and yet knew so well. His eyelids felt heavy. A campfire and a wrinkled old child. Warm sand. It was just out of reach, so close and yet so unattainable. His memory stretched towards his past but there was nothing there.

'He's drunk,' one of them laughed. And they left him where he was.

At 2.30 Doris Baker shook him awake. 'Alex, thank God.'

'Aunty Dorie!' He looked for the light but it had gone. He was alone in the clubhouse. Then he saw that she was crying. 'What's the matter?'

'There's been an accident. Down by the river. The police called us. We thought . . . oh Alex, thank God you weren't with them.'

'With who? What? What accident?' Where had the beautiful light gone? The clubhouse lights hurt his eyes in their plain brightness. The deep warmth of blue and green and red now overtaken by flat yellow. As flat as Aunty Dorie's voice. As sober as her words. As loud and brash as the clanging in his head. As terrible as the sudden fear in his heart.

'Kevin, Colin Tigg, the Davidson boy, Annie Carter and two other girls. The truck overturned. It's a dreadful accident.'

Alex struggled to his feet. 'Are they okay?' It didn't seem possible. They had all been laughing and joking earlier. What did she mean?

Tears flowed down her face. 'Annie and Kevin are dead. Two of the others are critical. The police say they'll be flown to South Africa as soon as it's light. Colin and one of the girls are in hospital here. Colin is in a serious condition. He might lose his sight. Oh Alex, we thought you were with them.'

He was trying to take it in. Annie dead! Kevin, his best friend! They'd been alive a few short hours ago. The truth hit him as hard as the flat yellow light. Again he heard briefly the murmured clicking. Again, the face of a wrinkled child. He had a sense of safety. It was not the first time. He'd felt it before. Safety. He was safe. The light had saved his life. Just as it had done once before.

School was out of the question. For their final week the entire senior class stayed away, in shock. The teachers understood. Exams were over anyway. Jamie Davidson died during the night, before he could be airlifted to Johannesburg.

People whispered it was just as well. The girl survived but was still in a coma by the time she reached South Africa. Wild rumours flew around the town about drunken orgies and drink-crazed teenagers. A man came up to him in the street and said, 'Jesus, kid, I heard you were dead.' Uncle Hugh, well into his cups, muttered, 'Bloody kids always have to overdo it.' Elderly ladies shook their heads in disapproval.

Aunty Dorie had the facts from the police. Colin Tigg and one of the girls had been in the cab. The other four were in the open back of the truck. Colin had one arm around the girl with him and, on a sandy corner of the road, they encountered a donkey. With only one hand on the steering wheel he swerved too wildly. The truck lost it on the soft sand, skidded and flipped over before rolling down the grassy verge. Kevin and Annie died instantly, crushed under the vehicle. Glass from the shattered windscreen showered the two in the cab. Colin had shards of glass in both eyes. The girl with him had escaped remarkably unscathed.

Kevin and Jamie were buried in a sad joint ceremony two days later. The following morning, Alex went to Annie's funeral. Listening to the Minister yet again, seeing another coffin lowered into the ground, he realised it might have been his coffin. It was a sobering lesson for a boy poised on the edge of manhood.

The wake was similar to the day before. Stunned and heart-broken parents, traumatised and bewildered siblings, shocked friends and relatives sitting around trying to be natural, trying not to cry. Alex found himself next to a silently morose man who savaged his whisky glass constantly and curtly refused food.

'What a fucking waste,' he muttered, to no-one in particular.

'What?' Alex didn't think the man was talking to him.

The man turned his head and looked at him. He had faded blue eyes under unruly eyebrows, a long nose and a wide mouth. Dressed in jeans and a brand new chequered shirt, he looked as though he were attending a party. 'I said, it's a waste. A young life gone. For what?'

Alex didn't know the man. 'Yeah.'

'Friends of yours were they?'

'Yeah.' A lump of misery rose in his throat.

'She was my niece.'

'Oh. Sorry.'

'Not a bad kid. Bit wild.' He gave a humourless laugh. 'What the hell, she was only sixteen, she was entitled to be wild.'

'Yeah.'

The man's voice was slurring slightly and he sounded aggressive, a bit like Uncle Hugh after a session at the pub. Alex wanted to move away.

'You in her class?'

'Yes.'

'So you're leaving school?'

'Yeah.'

'Don't say much do you?'

Good manners prevailed. 'Sorry, sir.'

'Ah that's okay, kid. I guess you're upset too.'

Again the misery and the tears which threatened. Alex bit them back. 'They were friends, sir, all of them. Kevin was my best friend.'

'Kevin? One of them kids from yesterday?'

Alex nodded. He lost his battle with the tears and brushed them off his cheeks impatiently.

'It's okay to cry, son.'

66

Alex took a deep breath. The man watched him silently. Then, 'My name's Jeff. Jeff Carter. Annie was my brother's kid.'

'Pleased to meet you, sir. I'm Alex Theron.' Alex put out his hand and found it gripped by a strong rough brown one. 'I'm from Shakawe,' he added, his voice shaking as Jeff Carter pumped his hand up and down.

'Shakawe! That's the back of nowhere.'

'Yes, sir.'

'Folks with Wenela out there are they?'

'No, sir. We have a farm.'

'A farm?' Jeff Carter looked surprised. 'I didn't think there were farms out there.'

'We're the only ones. My dad likes it there.'

The man laughed. 'What do you farm?'

'Cattle.'

He laughed again. 'What do they eat? Fish?'

Alex heard the sarcasm but was too young to know how to deal with it so remained silent.

Jeff Carter sensed he had embarrassed the boy. 'Shakawe, huh?'

'Yes, sir.'

'So you're going to work on the farm?'

He didn't know. Working for Pa was an easy option. He wanted to get out into the world, experience life. Pa had encouraged him to do just that. 'Learn what the world is all about, son,' his father had told him. 'If you want to work on the farm you can do it later. It's not going anywhere.'

'I might,' he told Jeff Carter. 'But first I want to . . .' he stopped. Just what did he want to do? He shrugged his shoulders. 'I don't know, sir, first I want to just . . .'

Jeff smiled. 'Experience life? Lose your cherry?'

He'd done that a couple of days ago. With Annie. But he was warming to the gruff man at his side. 'I guess.'

Jeff was watching him. 'How old are you, son?'

'Sixteen.'

'I can use an extra hand. Care to work for me for a while?'

'Doing what, sir?'

'Driving cattle. Can you ride, son?'

'Yes, sir. I've helped Pa drive cattle.'

'Where to?'

'South West, sir.'

Jeff put out his hand. 'Well then, whaddya say?'

Alex hesitated. He never doubted that what he wanted to do was own a farm like Pa. Mum had implored him to come home when he left school. 'Your father could do with help around here,' she had said. 'The Good Lord gave us sons so they could help out. It's your duty to come home.'

Her words made him feel guilty as usual. But at sixteen, they also made him rebellious. Jeff Carter was waiting for an answer. 'Yes, sir. I'd like that, sir.' Once again his voice shook as Jeff pumped his hand vigorously.

'Don't be too sure, kid. It's hard work.'

Alex was delighted. One day after school officially finished and here he was getting a job. His mother couldn't object too much. He could always say it was for the experience. He felt an overwhelming sense of relief that he now had the perfect excuse for not going home. 'Where do you live, sir?'

'Ghanzi.'

Uh oh! Shakawe might be the back of nowhere but at least it had the Okavango River. Ghanzi was much further south. Hot, sandy, dry desert country. 'Where do you drive the cattle to, sir?'

'Lobatse.'

Holy shit! Five hundred miles of fuck all. He had heard about these drives. They were reputed to be the roughest in the world. And the men were known to be some of the toughest in the world. Between Ghanzi and Kang, a distance of almost two hundred miles, there were only four places where permanent water could be found, the last of which was halfway. That left one hundred miles of nothing but sand and heat.

'You still on, kid?'

The big wide world. He had to start somewhere. Memories of three dead friends stirred in him. Life was to be lived, not stuck away at home with parents who inevitably made him feel as though he were somehow to blame for their disappointments. He might as well be dead too. Swallowing hard he said, 'Yes, sir.'

'Good boy. I'm leaving day after tomorrow. You can ride with me.'

'Ride?' He had visions of galloping halfway across the country.

'You betcha. Got a little Cessna single engine. Best little bird in the business.'

Alex was suddenly wary. The man sounded as though he were bragging. Instinct made Alex want to know more. 'You a trained pilot, Mr Carter?'

'Nah. Never got round to that. Anyway, what's to learn? Once you get it up in the air you've only got one option left.'

'How long have you been flying, sir?'

'Two months.'

Uh oh.

Aunty Dorie was uncertain. 'What about your parents, child? They'll be expecting you home.'

'Aunty Dorie, I've left school. I have to look out for myself.'

'Leave the boy alone, Doris.' Uncle Hugh was sober for a change. 'He's right. He's a man now. His life is his own responsibility.'

'But Hugh! Ghanzi? It's so far.'

'No further than Shakawe. Closer in fact.'

'Only for crows,' she retorted crisply.

Uncle Hugh chuckled. 'He'll be flying there won't he?'

'Yes.' She was still doubtful. 'But what about the cattle drive?'

'What about it? It'll make a real man of him.'

'If he survives it,' she muttered under her breath.

There was no way to let his parents know. Paulie would have to tell them.

Paulie was full of envy. 'Wow, you're lucky. No more school. You'll make lots of money.'

Alex thought so too. 'Never mind, you've only got three more years.'

'Five.' Paulie wanted to do the extra two years. He planned to go to the University College of Roma in Basutoland and study economics.

Alex thought his brother was mad. In the first place, Francistown did not offer the final two years of schooling, not having enough students interested in places. Paulie would have to move to Gaberones to finish his education. Then, with no university in Bechuanaland, and because of South Africa's race classification rules which made Paulie ineligible to attend university in that country, he would have to get his degree in the British Territory of Basutoland, a tiny mountainous region over a thousand miles east of Shakawe.

In that Basutoland was surrounded by South Africa, Paulie would have to travel to and from Bechuanaland on overloaded public transport specifically provided by South

Africa's white regime for use by the black population. Whilst travelling through South Africa, Paulie would be treated as a second-class citizen.

'Are you still determined to become an economist?' Economists were an emerging breed. Paulie had learned about them six months ago. Always interested in mathematics, he had not wavered in his intention to become one since then.

'Economists will rule the world one day.'

Alex laughed at him. But a part of him thought his brother was lucky. At least Mum did not put pressure on him to come home.

'Give Mum and Pa my love.' His heart did a little leap. He knew his parents would be surprised and he wondered if he was doing the right thing.

'Mum will be spitting chips.'

'Yeah. Tell her I'm sorry.'

'Alex?'

Paulie looked serious and Alex gave him his full attention.

'Do you think you could start calling me Paul? Paulie sounds so . . . damned young.'

Alex raised one eyebrow. 'Sure.'

'I'm going to ask Pa and Mum to do the same.'

'Pa will. Mum still calls me Ali.' He grinned, 'Unless she's mad at me.'

Paulie laughed. 'I guess she'll be referring to you as Alexander for a while then 'cos she's going to be good and mad when I get home and you're not with me.'

SIX

Paulie nearly fell out of the window when he left next day with Aunty Dorie who was taking him to the airport, he was leaning out so far to wave goodbye. Alex watched him go, a lump of fear in his stomach. Paulie was the last link with his family. From now on he was on his own. The future loomed ahead, unknown and strange. Until Paulie left it had looked exciting. Now he wasn't too sure. Still, it was too late to change his mind.

Jeff Carter told him to be at the airfield at six the next morning. Aunty Dorie drove him there. He carried with him all his worldly possessions: a small suitcase containing his clothes. 'That the lot?'

'Yes, sir.'

'Drop the sir, kid. Name's Jeff.'

'Okay.'

'Bung the case up here.'

Alex looked. The back of the aeroplane was haphazardly loaded with boxes of supplies.

'Yeah, that's right. Stick it on top.'

His stomach was doing backflips and handstands; he had

never flown in such a small plane. Saying goodbye to Aunty Dorie he wished he had gone home with Paulie. In his heart he knew the light aircraft would crash and his remains would be strewn over the hot desert to be picked clean by the jackals and the ants. Jeff Carter, who had seemed like a nice man two days ago, became someone hell-bent on suicide. And even if they did make it to Ghanzi, he would be worked so hard he could well die of exhaustion. This was a mistake. His first independent decision and he'd blown it.

The little aircraft shook so hard while Jeff went through his tests that Alex was convinced it would fall apart. Then they were taxiing to the end of the strip. Aunty Dorie seemed so far away. He craned his neck to watch her. Jeff lined up on the strip. 'Here we go.'

Too late. It was too late to do anything about it. He desperately needed the toilet. The aircraft lunged forward. Faster and faster, they sped down the grassy strip, past Aunty Dorie, past the huts on the side of the strip.

'C'mon, you bitch, get your nose up.' Jeff's face was set and anxious. The end of the strip was rapidly approaching.

This is it. We're going to crash into the fence. This is the end.

The aircraft gave a little shudder and hopped into the air. 'C'mon, c'mon!' Jeff pulled the stick back. Labouring under the weight of supplies, the plane dipped, then righted itself. Then, roaring with exertion, it shuddered and vibrated slowly higher, skimming the fence at the end of the strip by the merest whisker. Trembling and groaning, the little plane rose by degrees. Trees flashed underneath. Rooftops were close enough to touch. There was Aunty Dorie's house, so close he could see the dog in the garden. Over the town, away to the west, still climbing, the engine screaming, Jeff's

73

hands holding the controls tightly as they fought him in their effort to return the aircraft to earth.

'Jesus!' Jeff had perspiration running down his face. 'That was a close one. Guess I've got too much weight.'

Alex shifted his attention from his desperate attempt not to shit himself. 'Are you going back?'

'Back? No way, kid. We're winning.'

They were still climbing. The engine had lost its strained noise and settled into a steady roar. The ground beneath them was flattening out.

'Which way did we head out of town?'

Christ! He doesn't know where we are. 'West.'

'You sure? I don't recognise this.' He was peering sideways, out his window.

'We flew back over the field.'

'Huh!' Jeff sounded amused. 'Must be better at this than I thought.' He banked the plane slightly to the south. 'I might be a whisker too far north, though. Let's have a look around.'

'What are we looking for?'

'The road to Orapa will do nicely.'

They found the road a few minutes later. 'We'll just follow this. They're looking for diamonds in the Orapa area. De Beers grade the road every now and then. It's easy to see from up here.'

The roar settled into a nice healthy drone. The little plane had done it. After half an hour they had reached an altitude of 6,000 feet. Now all they had to do was find Ghanzi and land safely. Alex relaxed somewhat. Ahead he could see the south-eastern extremity of the Makgadikgadi Pans, stretching away into the distance, monstrous, swirling sheets of salty sand, glittering under the desert sky. Further north and west the Pans were covered with golden grasses lined and crisscrossed with thousands of game trails. But down here the endless white flatlands which, from the air, looked like ice, patterned in places by gigantic swirls from evaporated shallow lakes, looked hostile and empty.

Fifteen minutes later they saw signs of mining excavations and then, when the road turned north, they flew on towards the immense emptiness of the Central Kalahari. 'What do you follow now?'

'With a bit of luck we'll find Deception Valley. From up here it looks like a saucer. If I keep to the northern side, we'll get to Ghanzi.' Jeff grinned. 'If we get to the Tsau Hills we hang a left.'

'Don't you have a compass?'

'Sure.' He banged his hand against it. 'Rather do it by sight though, I'm not sure how to read the bloody thing.'

Alex changed the subject. He didn't want to know about Jeff's lack of flying experience. 'How far out of Ghanzi is your farm?'

'Not far. Half an hour by road.'

'What's Ghanzi like?'

'Pub, hospital, police station and general store. Not much else. You'll get to see it Saturday. All the men go in on Saturday night.'

Men! He was a man. The thought made him smile.

'Like a drink do you?'

'Beer. Not spirits.'

Jeff laughed. 'You'd know would you?'

'I tried gin the night of the dance. It made my eyes water.'

Jeff laughed again. 'What did you put with it?'

'Nothing. Just drank it straight from the bottle.'

'Jesus! You kids.' He was silent. Then, 'Did Annie have any?'

'Annie? No. She wasn't with us.'

75

'Poor little bitch.' He looked at Alex. 'Don't take this the wrong way, kid, I tell all my men the same thing. I have a daughter too. Same age as Annie. She'll be home for the holidays. You keep your hands off her, you hear.'

Where did that come from? 'Where does she go to school?'

'England.'

England! To Alex that was as good as another planet.

'Maddie's younger than Annie, know what I mean?'

'Not really.'

'Annie was . . . well, she'd been around hadn't she?' He saw Alex's face and added, 'She was a good kid but she knew more about life than Maddie.'

'Maddie?' It sounded like an odd kind of name.

'Madison. We call her Maddie. Well, the family does. No-one else.' Jeff frowned. 'She's a bit funny about it. You'll have to call her Madison.'

'Okay.'

'And keep your distance. I know what you young fellas are like. Your brains are in your cocks. Maddie's not like that, understand?'

'Yes, sir.'

'Jeff.'

'Okay, Jeff.'

Abruptly, he changed the subject. 'Done any branding, kid?'

'Sure. Lots.'

'Good. You'll be busy with that for a few weeks.'

'When do we drive the cattle?'

'When the rains start. Makes it easier.'

That could be weeks or it could be months. Alex had no idea when the rains came to this part of the country, if they ever did. It was December now and the rains would already have started at home. But looking at the flat brown country beneath them he could see they'd had no rain recently. Jeff read his thoughts. 'I've seen this country covered in wild-flowers. It's a beautiful sight. The Pans fill up. The wonder bush comes out. It's incredible.'

'Wonder bush?'

'Yeah. You'll see lots at home. Dead shrubs. They can stay like that for years. But give them a bit of rain and next day they're covered with leaves. Try it for yourself. Break off a branch and stick it in a jar of water. The next day I guarantee it'll be green all over.'

On and on they flew. He didn't know what to make of Jeff. He seemed friendly enough but, once or twice, had shown a harder side. Like when he warned him about Maddie. And that stuff he'd said about Annie. Alex hadn't liked it. Sure, Annie had been around but that didn't give the guy the right to put her down. Even if he was her uncle. *Especially* since he was her uncle. Alex would have expected more loyalty.

'There's Ghanzi.'

He looked. A couple of sandy streets. A scatter of tin roofs. A dirt road ran from the southwest, through the town and away to the northeast. Another headed south, presumably the one they would follow with the cattle. He hadn't known what to expect but he had expected more than this. Ghanzi had a reputation as the cattle baron capital of Bechuanaland. From the air it looked more like one of the small villages he passed through on the road to Shakawe. They flew over the town and continued westward.

'Aren't you going to land there?'

'They won't let me. I put her down there six weeks ago and bloody nearly knocked over the general store. Besides, I've just built my own strip. It's rustic but it works.'

77

He needed the toilet again.

Jeff adjusted a lever between the seats. 'Flaps,' he explained. 'They slow us down.' He pulled the handle further and the aircraft seemed to hiccough in mid-air. 'Oops, too much.' He pushed the lever back again. The plane settled down. 'There's the house.'

Alex could see a patch of brilliant green in the otherwise barren landscape. He wondered how the trees could possibly survive. From the centre of the green canopy he caught a glimpse of a red roof as they flashed over it.

Jeff banked around, standing the aeroplane on one wing. Dead ahead was a cleared strip of sand, marked on both sides with the occasional white painted rock.

Shit! He's going to land on that? The strip was no wider than a road and didn't look much longer than a rugby field.

Jeff adjusted the flaps lever again and the plane hiccoughed once more causing Alex's stomach to heave. Closer and closer to the ground, they were travelling impossibly fast. Jeff pulled back on the stick. The aeroplane floated down, landed on one wheel, floated up, floated down, landed on two wheels. Jeff pushed the stick forward and the nose went down. They were doing all right until he got busy with some pedals at his feet. The plane slewed left, slewed right, left then right again and shuddered and skidded, taking an agonising amount of time to stop, some ten yards from an anthill and very definitely off the left of the runway and into the veld.

'Here we are.' He saw Alex's white face. 'That was my best landing yet.'

All Alex could do was let his breath out noisily.

Jeff taxied back the way they had come and parked the plane next to an old petrol pump. 'Give us a hand, kid. The others will be a while.'

They had the aircraft offloaded and tied down before two Land Rovers roared up. 'Hey, boss, howzit?' Alex looked at the driver of the first as he jumped out. He was possibly the ugliest man he had ever seen.

'Howzit, Artie?' Jeff strode over and shook the man's hand.

Artie grinned at Alex. 'Who's this?'

'Alex Theron. He's just left school. Parents have a place up at Shakawe. He's going to help with the drive.'

Artie walked over and looked Alex up and down. 'Done much riding, fella?'

'Some.'

'Done any driving?'

'Yes.'

Artie clapped his shoulder. 'That's good enough for me. Name's Artie Black. You'll be working for me.'

'Pleased to meet you, sir.'

Artie laughed, delighted. 'There are no sirs around here, young fella. You left them behind at school. Call me Artie.'

Alex liked him instinctively. He was extremely short, coming just to his chest. He had an open, creased face and the largest grin he had ever seen. When he smiled his mouth split his face in two. His nose had been broken at least once, it was flat in the middle and bent to one side. Greying brows hovered just over his eyes. His thinning grey hair was cut short all over and stood straight up from his head like a brush. He had a massive chest, large shoulders, and muscles on his arms and hands Alex never knew existed. He was narrow at the waist with legs which bowed outwards before returning his feet to where they should be. One eye looked crazily sideways. A scar pulled one side of his lip up. But when he smiled, showing big yellowish teeth, his whole face lit up.

'Come on, young fella. You can ride with me.'

Alex slung his suitcase into the back of the Land Rover. Then he saw the girl beside the other vehicle. She was watching Jeff, smiling. Alex had never seen anyone so beautiful. She was about his age. Her dark hair fell like a curtain around a perfectly oval face. Skin the colour of milk, dark winged brows, clear untroubled eyes, straight nose, lovely smile, a long white neck, breasts . . . oh God, he'd never seen such perfect breasts.

'Eyes front,' Artie whispered. 'You're perving on the boss's daughter, fella. Not allowed.'

Alex dragged his eyes away. Then he looked back, he couldn't help himself. She was looking at him. He smiled at her. She tossed her head and stuck her nose in the air.

'Serves you right, fella. Come on, in you get. Time you met the others.'

As they drove away he asked, 'Is that Maddie?'

'Madison. And yes it is. And no you can't. Jeff would shoot the first man here who even thought about it.'

Too late!

He looked around with interest. From the air the ground looked like endless brown sand. But it wasn't. Brown grass, a foot tall, grew as far as he could see. 'Much goodness in this grass?' he asked Artie over the roar of the Land Rover engine and the wind whistling in his ears.

'Surprisingly good. We have good water here too.'

'Where?' He hadn't seen any.

'Artesian. We have bore holes every few miles. There's plenty of water.'

'Does it ever go green?'

Artie laughed. 'Sure. Every five years when we get good rains.'

Every five years! And his mother thought *they* were on the edge.

They skirted the main house and drove to a rambling complex about 300 yards away. Cattle yards, sheds, barns, workshops, a silo and a large bunkhouse formed a square. 'Here you go.'

His heart sank. It looked basic and dirty and hot. The bunkhouse was built of cement blocks and had a corrugated iron roof. A wide verandah ran around two sides. Artie saw his look. 'Jeff converted old stables. It's much better inside.'

Several men were sitting on the verandah, tilting back in their chairs, their feet on the railing. As Alex reached into the Land Rover to get his suitcase one of them called, 'Who's that, Art?'

'New hand.'

'Looks a bit wet behind the ears.' The others laughed.

Alex flushed with embarrassment but walked onto the verandah with his hand outstretched. 'I survived a flight with Jeff.' He grinned at the man who had spoken. 'Name's Alex Theron.'

The man laughed, kicked his feet off the railing and rose slowly. He stood several inches taller than Alex. His good-humoured face was long and thin, like the rest of him. 'That's more than I can say for most of us then. Jeff scares us shitless in that plane of his.' He shook Alex's hand. 'Welcome, Alex Theron. I'm Bob.' He waved his hand at the other two. 'This ugly bastard is Pat and that ugly bastard is Willie. Pat's Irish but don't hold it against him—he's likely to take your head off.' Alex shook hands with a burly blond man who he guessed to be about thirty and whose pale blue eyes and wide smile belied any inclination to tear anyone's head off, and then a small, wiry, slightly older man who, when he smiled a welcome, revealed two front teeth of gold.

'Done any riding?' Willie asked. His gold teeth flashed.

'Yeah. My folks have a farm near Shakawe. I helped Pa drive a few times.'

'Thank Christ for that. Last youngster Jeff brought out here thought a horse was something you draped clothes on. Done any branding?'

'A bit.'

'Well hey, man, welcome to Carter's Crazy Crowd.'

'Show him his bed,' Artie said. 'I've got to talk to the boss.'

'Come and have a beer,' Pat invited, then added, worried, 'you do drink beer don't you?'

'I've had a bit. Not much.'

'How old are you, sonny?' Bob asked.

'Sixteen.'

'Sweet sixteen and never been laid,' Willie sang. He had a good voice.

Alex began to relax.

'You'll meet the rest of the motley crew tonight. I guess you'll start work tomorrow. We're branding. Shitty bloody job but someone has to do it. Fucking hot out there, wear a hat. Well come on, boyo, come on. A man could die of thirst talking to you out here.' Pat shoved him through the door and into an armchair. 'Sit.' Alex had no option.

He was in what was obviously the general recreation room. Two refrigerators were side by side and, when Pat opened one, he saw it was groaning with beer bottles. 'Beer's in here,' Pat told him unnecessarily. 'Cokes and sissy drinks in this one.' He banged his hand against the closed door of the other. Cabinets next to the refrigerators held glasses, plates, cups, bowls, and cutlery. A table tennis table was at the far end, a pool table in the middle. Several dart boards were near the door and, judging by the holes in the wall, the inside of the door and on the floor, no-one took the game seriously. There were even holes in the ceiling.

At the other end, scattered in comfortable array, a variety of armchairs and settees and, in front of the refrigerators, a long wooden table for dining. With gingham red and white curtains and matching tablecloth, it was surprisingly homely.

Pat handed him a bottle. 'We don't use glasses. Beer gets too bloody warm. Come and see your room. You can settle in later. We're going for a swim.'

He was hauled out of the chair by Pat who appeared to get people to do what he wanted by physically pushing and pulling them around.

As bedrooms went, it wasn't much. A bed, a wardrobe and a chest of drawers. 'We decorate our own rooms if we want. You can buy stuff at the store in town. Some of us don't bother, we live in the main room anyway. Here, find something to wear and grab a towel.' Pat opened his suitcase, rummaged around, found a pair of swimming shorts, threw a towel at him from on top of the chest of drawers and looked as if he was prepared to undress him if necessary.

'Where's the bathroom?' Alex found the manhandling disconcerting.

'Down the hall. Hurry up, boyo. We'll wait for you on the verandah.'

The bathroom contained four showers, two toilets and two sinks. It had a cement floor but the walls were lined with square white tiles. Alex took a leak, changed into his swimming shorts, collected up his beer and joined the others on the verandah. Pat looked at him. 'Jesus, boyo you can't ride like that.'

'We ride?'

'Yeah, down to the waterhole.'

'Sorry.' He returned to his room, pulled his jeans on over his swimmers, put his boots back on and rejoined them on the verandah.

'You about ready now?' Pat asked heavily with good humoured sarcasm.

Willie walked four horses up to the verandah. 'This one's yours.'

The mare pranced sideways, tossing her head. Alex was a good rider and he knew a bit about horses. This one was trouble. The men were testing him. As he steadied himself to swing into the saddle she turned her head and snapped at his arse but he was ready for her and whipped up his elbow, jabbing her on the side of the face. The mare snorted and skittered sideways but he swung onto her and shoved his foot firmly into the other stirrup. 'What's her name?' he called, staying on easily as she churned in circles.

'Nightmare,' Bob called back. 'Stick with her, kid.'

'Okay, Nightmare,' he said through his teeth. 'Let's see what you're made of.'

Willie ran and opened a gate and the mare shot from standing to a full galloping run within three seconds. 'At least she doesn't buck,' he shouted back as he gripped his knees tightly and turned his toes inwards. He gave the mare her head.

Alex could never remember the details of that ride. Nightmare galloped at full stretch. Unfamiliar country whipped past unnoticed as he concentrated on using all his skill as a horseman just to stay on her back. He prayed she knew where she was going. After ten minutes he felt her tiring and, several minutes later she slowed to a canter, then a trot, and finally came to a trembling stop. He leaned over and patted her shivering neck. 'Good girl, Nightmare, good girl.'

The horse bucked and Alex flew through the air and landed on his back.

When the dust cleared and the ringing in his ears stopped, he looked up and saw Nightmare cantering home. He climbed off the ground, dusting his jeans. He was grinning from ear to ear. 'Okay, Nightmare. Strike one to you.'

The walk back took him fifty minutes. Bob, Willie and Pat were on the verandah, waving their beer bottles at him. 'Where'd ya go?' Bob yelled.

He limped up to the verandah. He tried dignity. 'Just for a ride.'

The men laughed uproariously. He tried bluster. 'To Johannesburg.'

The men roared. He tried humour. 'And back again.'

'You're okay, kid,' Willie slapped his back. Dust billowed out.

Pat wiped his eyes. 'At least she doesn't buck,' he mimicked. 'Here, boyo, have a beer, you've earned it.'

Alex took a swig. They had put cold coffee in the bottle.

SEVEN

By the time the other men arrived—tired, dirty, in a noisy confusion of faces and names—Alex felt at home. Artie had come back and given him a tour of the yards and sheds, explaining his job as they went. 'You'll be with Pat and the other new fella, Kel. You'll meet him later. Funny sort of bugger, doesn't say much. Young. Close to your age I'd say. Maybe you can get him to talk. Bit surly but maybe he's shy.'

'Where is he from?' Alex was pleased to know there was another person his own age around.

'Gaberones. His father is a friend of Jeff's. I don't think Kel likes it here. Jeff took him on as a favour but the kid is useless. Still . . .' Artie shrugged, '. . . maybe he'll come right.'

Nightmare was eating oats from a trough. 'Hear you've met her.' Artie grinned. 'You did the right thing, young fella: let her have her head. But she'll always buck, considers it her duty.'

'Has anyone ridden her?' Alex admired the horse. Relaxed and with no rider in sight to make her eyes turn mean, she was a beautiful animal. Russet red hair rippled and shone, flowing over powerful muscles.

Artie laughed. 'Ride her? Never. Most of them don't make it out of the yard. That young Kel, he lasted exactly two seconds. Nightmare pitched him onto the verandah. Didn't take too kindly to it neither. Some of the others had to hold him back. He was going to take a stick to her.'

Kel was one of the last to arrive back. Alex shook his hand and looked at him. He was a big boy, as tall as Alex and just as strongly built. At a time when men wore their hair cut short back and sides, Kel's hair straggled to his collar. He had a high-bridged nose and, looking completely out of place, a tiny, baby-shaped mouth. His eyes never quite met Alex's. He looked Alex up and down. 'I hear you're coming out with us tomorrow.'

'That's right.' Alex tried to lock eyes with him. There was something shifty in the way he would not make contact.

'Try to stay out of our way then. We're busy.' He turned and walked through to the bedroom section.

Alex flushed bright red. 'Don't worry about him,' Willie said. 'Couple of weeks ago he didn't know one end of a branding iron from the other.'

'Still doesn't,' Pat growled. 'I'd like to shove one up his arse, cheeky little brat.'

Willie laughed at Pat. 'The kid thinks his shit don't stink,' he told Alex. 'His father owns a couple of businesses in Gabs and one of his uncles is big time on the Joint Advisory Council. Seems Kel got some girl into trouble and his daddy sent him here till the dust settles. Kid's got a French fry the size of a baseball bat on his shoulder, he's a pain in the arse.'

Kel avoided Alex's company for the rest of the evening. In fact, he ignored everyone, preferring to sit on his own, reading.

The men turned in early. Most of them would be up at

four. 'Must write to Mum and Pa,' Alex thought as he got into bed. 'I'll get some writing things in town on Saturday.' He fell asleep as soon as his head hit the pillow.

It was still dark when Pat, in his unique manner, woke him the next morning. 'Up, boyo, work's awaiting.' He pulled back the sheet, grabbed his arm, forced him to sit, pulled him to his feet and propelled him to the bathroom. Alex was getting used to this although it was a bit much first thing in the morning.

Breakfast was whatever the men wanted to make of it. It just kept rolling out of the kitchen and being thumped on the table by a cheerful-looking black man who took it upon himself to sample everything and raise his eyes in appreciation. Toast piled high on plates. Great platters of bacon, swimming in grease. Fried eggs gone hard from being kept warm in the oven. Fried onion and tomatoes mixed together with chilli pepper. Baked beans. Sausages, crisp and split open. Last night's leftover vegetables, roughly formed into pancakes and fried golden brown. Steaks cooked to leathery slabs. Pots of coffee. Jugs of milk.

'Dig in,' Pat advised, shovelling more baked beans onto Alex's plate. 'Lunch is a long way off.'

Outside, dawn broke with a chorus of song. Weaver birds, swallows, doves and starlings competed with chattering guineafowl on the ground. It was desert country so the nights were cool but, as soon as the sun broke over the rim of the earth, it promised another scorcher. 'Got a hat?' Pat picked one at random from a peg near the door and rammed it onto Alex's head.

They rode six miles to where the cattle were penned. For as long as he lived, Alex would remember the beauty of that harsh land. Softened by early light, long shadows of grey covered the sepia coloured grass which sparkled with moisture. Filmy fingers of pink cloud lingered in the sky. The horizon was as sharp as a lithograph. Trees stood out like black holes against the pale blue sky. The air was sweet and cool, with the smell of soft dew. Riding alongside the other men, hearing the creak of leather and the steady rhythm of hooves, Alex felt his life was just beginning.

Riding back at sunset, covered with ash and dust and manure, sticky with perspiration, back breaking from bending, both feet on fire in boots which threatened to suffocate, arms burned crimson from the sun, eyes stinging as sweat ran freely, Alex believed his life was over.

He'd branded before. He knew it wouldn't be easy. But he had never worked so hard, for so long, in such suffocating flying sand, in air so desiccated it hurt to breathe, in heat which bore relentlessly down so his whole body was on fire. To help keep cool the men regularly threw themselves, boots and all, into a cut down water tank. But ten minutes later their clothes were dry. The water in the tank grew so warm it was like having a hot bath.

He worked alongside Pat and Kel. Pat grunted and groaned his way through the day, occasionally breaking out with 'Jesus, mother of Mary,' which didn't make a lot of sense although Alex was too hot and tired to say so. He quickly grew to hate the dumb, stubborn, fractious cattle. Kel sneaked off too often to the water tank, leaving Pat and Alex to bear the brunt of the work. At one stage, just before their half-hour lunch break, Pat called, 'Where the hell are you going this time?'

'To get wet.'

'Get back here.'

'Stick it up your arse.'

Pat shook his head and muttered to Alex, 'Bastard! Bloody bludging asshole. Jesus, mother of Mary.'

Alex made a beeline for the beer fridge as soon as he got back to the bunkhouse. Pat headed him off. 'Drink the sissy stuff first. Get some liquid inside you. You'll get as pissed as a fart otherwise.' He shoved two bottles of lemonade at Alex.

He could have sworn the first one sizzled all the way down.

Artie came in and pinned up next week's roster. None of the men was expected to work more than three days straight before having two days off.

'It's different in the winter,' Willie explained. 'There's not so many of us and the weather is great.'

'Why doesn't Jeff use blacks?'

'Oh he uses them. Just not for branding. They're hopeless at it.'

'My Pa uses them.'

'How many head does your Pa have?'

'Around 600.'

'Jeff's got more than 6,000.'

'How many have been branded so far?'

'A thousand.'

Shit!

No-one worked Sunday. Alex was rostered on for Saturday and, by the end of the day, felt he could never muster the energy to go into Ghanzi. Pat had other ideas and Alex simply lacked the strength to fob him off. They drove in a convoy of four Land Rovers.

It was light enough to see the town when they drove in. Not that there was much to see; one wide dusty street, rutted and practically deserted, a general store and several other buildings enjoyed as much space as they needed.

90

Overcrowding was definitely not a problem. The hotel, the Kalahari Arms, was in the centre of town, its solid brick walls giving it an air of permanence.

The bar was busy with men who, on Saturday evenings, drank as hard as they worked. 'How's it going, kid?' Jeff Carter bought him a beer and slapped it in front of him.

Alex had seen nothing of him since the day he arrived. 'Bloody hard work,' he replied.

Jeff laughed. 'Artie tells me you're doing okay.'

'Pat is good to work with.'

'He's a permanent.' Jeff looked over to where Pat was chatting up a tiny African woman. 'Good man. Got a background of course, most of the permanents do.'

Alex wondered why Jeff was telling him this. He felt uncomfortable, as though he were spying on Pat without his knowledge.

'Killed a man in Ireland.' Jeff saw his look. 'Ask him. He doesn't try to hide it.'

Alex looked across the room to Pat. He saw Kel saunter over and say something to him. Pat shook his head.

Willie joined Alex and Jeff. All three of them could sense trouble brewing. The woman was backing away from Pat and Kel uneasily.

'He's a pain in the arse that Kel,' Willie said. 'Always riding Pat. Someone should warn him off, Pat'll tear his liver out if he gets mad.'

'He's okay,' Jeff said. 'Bit mixed up maybe, but he comes from a good family.'

'Mixed up,' Willie scoffed. 'He goes out of his way to get up your nose, like he was morally obliged to do so. I'm telling you, boss, someone is going to teach that little shit a lesson one day. It can't come soon enough for me.'

Jeff shrugged. 'He'll just have to learn the hard way.' He left them to talk to Artie.

Willie saw Alex's troubled face. 'Jeff's all right,' he said, misinterpreting Alex's unease. 'Hard man but he's fair.'

'Is it true about Pat, that he killed someone?'

'Told you that did he? Yeah it's true enough. Pat'll tell you himself if you ask. Jeff should keep his mouth shut though. Not his place to talk about Pat's life.'

The argument had turned into a scuffle. Pat shoved Kel who swung at him. Pat easily deflected the blow and turned away, secure in his big competent body. Kel snatched a glass from the table and smashed it. He lunged at Pat with the jagged end. Pat sensed it coming, sidestepped quickly and brought his arm up and around Kel's neck, cutting off his air. 'Little boys should not play with dangerous toys. Time you cooled off, boyo.' Kel was marched outside with half the men following to watch. Pat tipped him head-first into a water trough.

'He'll have to watch his back now,' Willie said, worried. 'That Kel's shaping up as a nasty piece of work.'

Kel did not reappear. No-one knew how he made it back but, by the time they drove into the yard at the ranch, his boots were on the verandah where everyone left them.

Sunday. The day of rest never had such meaning. Alex wrote a long letter to his family. Then he went to see Nightmare. She started nervously when she saw the bridle and saddle. No-one had ever gone back for a second try before. But she stood still and allowed him to slip the bridle over her head and buckle the saddle tightly. Several men drifted over.

'Like to fly do you, fella?' Artie called.

'Nah, he just likes it when the pain stops,' Bob said.

Alex ignored them. Nightmare had caught him unawares before. This time he was ready for her. He swung into the saddle, deflecting her snapping teeth near his backside. Nightmare stood still, muscles in her neck flicking and rippling. Alex dug his heels into her sides. Nightmare rippled. He flicked the reigns. She rippled. He leaned forward to pat her neck. Nightmare bucked.

Jesus! She'd done it again.

The men cheered as he got up. Several more had arrived to watch the fun.

He approached her cautiously. He had broken one of his father's horses. He believed the way to do it was with patience and gentleness. He spoke softly and slowly held out his hand. Nightmare's teeth snapped so close to his skin he felt an electric shock. He swung into the saddle swiftly. Nightmare went back to rippling.

This time he just sat there. His legs gripped her tightly. When she gathered herself to buck he was balanced. She only bucked the once and he stayed on easily. Then she trotted around the yard.

'Hey, boyo, you've done it!' Pat was watching.

Alex didn't think so. Neither did Nightmare. She bucked five times in quick succession. He hung on grimly, his breakfast threatening to burst from his mouth. Nightmare snorted and tossed her head in disbelief that he was still there. Then Kel thrust a stick through the railing and jabbed her soft flank. Nightmare went mad, bucking and turning, pronking like a springbok, shaking and jerking. Alex wanted to get off for her sake, before she did herself some damage, but he couldn't. The horse finally stopped in trembling exhaustion.

He swiftly dismounted and examined her flank. A thin trickle of blood ran from where the stick had cut the soft skin. Pat was just on the other side of the railing. He handed him the reigns. 'Take the saddle off.' Then he jumped the fence and strode over to Kel.

'What the hell did you do that for?'

Kel looked spitefully smug. 'Do what?'

Alex could not remember ever having been so angry. He shot out his hand. Kel thought a punch was coming and jumped back but Alex snatched the stick and jabbed it straight into Kel's arm. 'How do you like it?'

Kel swung at him. The blow glanced off his jaw.

Alex had never had a fist fight in his life. He had sparred in fun a few times with Pa and enjoyed the odd scuffle at school but that was all. Kel had the instincts of a street fighter. He aimed a kick at Alex's groin. Alex avoided it but the kick deadened the top of his leg. The leg would not take his weight and he nearly fell. Kel was steadying himself for another kick and Alex did something he had never done before: he lost his temper. Using his good leg, he propelled himself straight at Kel who fell over backwards under the weight. They grappled on the ground, each one trying to get the upper hand. Kel grabbed a fistful of dirt. Pat shouted a warning and Alex closed his eyes a fraction of a second before the dirt hit them.

The dirty fighting tactics of Kel pushed Alex into a deep rage. His ears thundered with hot blood and strength surged into his limbs. A primitive instinct to kill, kill, kill rose powerfully inside him. He felt no pain, just a deep satisfaction each time his fist connected with Kel's face. Pat had to pull him off. When the mist cleared behind his eyes and he saw what he had done he was appalled. Kel lay half conscious, flat on his back. His face was a mess of blood and dirt. The surging rage left him as quickly as it had come as, weaving, he stared down at Kel. Sickened, he turned and lurched for the bunkhouse. He felt no sense of pride at Kel's defeat, he was disgusted. He sensed someone watching and looked up. Madison stood, a look of disdainful dislike on her beautiful face. She had seen the fight.

He threw himself under the shower. The aftermath of the sudden surge of adrenalin left him weak. Pat found him there and pulled him out, tossed him a towel, took him to his room and would have dressed him if Alex had let him. 'You did the right thing, boyo. That Kel has had it coming since he got here.'

Alex shook his head. 'No, Pat. I lost my temper. I might have killed him.'

The bed heaved as Pat sat next to him. 'I killed someone that way. Vowed never to lose my temper again.'

'It happened so fast,' Alex whispered, shaken at his loss of control.

'No-one blames you, boyo. Kel's bad news. Artie wants to sack him but Jeff says give him a fair go. Just stay away from him from now on, it's all you can do.'

The loss of common decent behaviour scared him. He never suspected he had that kind of violence in him. 'The man you killed, what did he do?'

'Beat up a woman.'

He bowed his head. All Kel had done was poke a stick at a horse. Pat knew what he was thinking.

'That horse might have killed you, boyo. It was the dumbest thing I've ever seen.'

Jeff found them there. 'Artie told me what happened. I'll let it go this time, kid. If you men want to kill each other be my guest, I don't give a shit. But if you ever pull a stunt like that again in front of my daughter you're out of here. Understand?' He left abruptly.

The fight subdued Alex. He had a gentle nature and had never knowingly hurt anyone or anything before. The violence which erupted so quickly left him deeply ashamed. Jeff's words burned in his head. He wanted to apologise to Kel but Pat stopped him. 'He's trouble I tell you, boyo. Just keep your distance.'

Bob, Willie, and then Artie, all said the same. Alex made up his mind never to lose control again.

Another week loomed. He worked Monday and Tuesday, had Wednesday and Thursday off and was rostered for Friday, Saturday and the following Monday. By Tuesday afternoon Alex doubted he would ever move again. Kel, his face a shameful reminder of the fight with a broken nose and a scar forming near one eye which looked as though he would carry it for the rest of his life, kept out of his way. Bob joined Alex and Pat as part of their team. The three of them worked steadily together. On Wednesday they went into Ghanzi where he was able to post his letter to his family. On Thursday he had another attempt to ride Nightmare who bucked him off twice before standing quietly.

'Open the gate,' he called to Pat.

'Are you sure?'

'Yes, I'm going to walk her around the yard.'

Nightmare rippled.

But she didn't buck. She walked nervously around the bunkhouse, the main house, back to the yards and through the gate, shying at the slightest thing. 'That'll do for today.' He jumped off. Nightmare swerved towards him and lashed out with her hind leg. He danced out of her way laughing. She tried to bite him when he removed the bridle. He covered her nose with his hand then gently stroked it. She shivered. She snorted. She bobbed her head. He blew softly at her flared nostrils. She stood stock still, breathing in his breath.

'She's loving it,' Pat said, safely behind the fence.

He turned his head to speak. 'All horses love it. My Pa reckons it's the way they kiss.'

'I think you might just do it, boyo.'

But Nightmare was not that easy. With his breath removed, she reverted to nasty. Her teeth narrowly missed removing a portion of his upper arm.

'I think she likes me.'

Pat shook his head. The boy was obviously crazy.

On Sunday he decided to ride Nightmare out onto the ranch. After a couple of attempts to unseat him, she settled down and allowed him to lead her out of the gate. He took her slowly, gently, holding her back against a trot. Her shoe clicked on a stone and she jumped violently sideways. He realised she was not so much wild, as nervous. He spoke to her constantly, patting her as far as he could without leaning forward. He knew her now. To lean forward in the saddle promised a short flight and a hard landing.

She was obviously keen to run. Once they were away from the houses, with the open range spreading as far ahead as he could see, he gave her her head. Nightmare sprang forward immediately, her powerful legs pumping under him as she strained to go faster. He moved with her, his body attuned to her every move. He allowed her to run herself out. By the time she had, he was on a part of the ranch he had never seen. The bunkhouse and homestead were well out of sight. This did not bother him. Artie had explained that all the boreholes were numbered and sited around two miles from each other. By following the boreholes it was easy to find your way back, providing the numbers decreased as you went.

Having run out her nervous energy, Nightmare was content to walk which gave him a chance to look around. The land stretched away on all sides, curving on the horizon, broken only by an occasional group of trees, the roots of which had managed to tap into underground water. They rested next to borehole number eight. He was around sixteen miles from the bunkhouse. He dismounted and removed the saddle, tethering Nightmare to a tree on a long rope so she could drink from the trough. He did not yet trust her not to run. The silence out here was total. It reminded him of home. In the heat of the mid-afternoon, not a bird called in the wide bluc sky, not a beast lowed to another, nothing stirred.

Then a horse whinnied. Looking around he saw nothing, but Nightmare was staring towards a clump of trees almost half a mile away. The horse called again and Nightmare replied. Curious, he saddled her again. She appeared anxious to get going and broke into an easy canter, her ears pricked forward. He could see nothing until they had almost reached the thorny acacias, then a horse stepped out of the shade, watching their approach. It was saddled and the reins were trailing on the ground. Then he saw Madison. She lay in a crumpled heap, blood trickling from her head, staining the white collar of her shirt.

He jumped down and went to her. She looked deathly white but a pulse fluttered in her neck. Alex had no idea what to do. He could not leave her out here while he rode back, but he was reluctant to move her. She needed help. Praying he was doing the right thing he took a deep breath, then grasped a leg and moved it gingerly so it bent at the knee. No obvious breaks. He did the same with the other leg. Even as he tested her limbs he admired her. He couldn't help it. She had the classic good looks of a movie star.

She must be concussed. He had to get her home. He walked around her, reluctant to move her. *Come on, Theron, she needs help.* He bent and picked her up. She was surprisingly light. Getting her into the saddle was difficult, she was floppy and kept sliding sideways. Finally he propped her forwards, her head resting on the horse's neck. He swung up behind her and took the reins around her body, pulling her back so she rested against him. No, that was awkward. He pushed one of her legs over so she was sideways to him and leaning into him. That was better. Grabbing Nightmare's reins he looped them around one arm. The horse was rather close. He hoped she would not bite.

The ride back took two hours. Her horse struggled in the heat with the extra weight. Madison remained unconscious for most of the time, waking briefly to mumble something unintelligible once or twice. She sounded delirious. Someone must have seen them coming. He was still over a mile out when a Land Rover roared up to meet him. Jeff was out of the cab before it stopped. 'What happened?'

'I don't know, Jeff. I found her lying out there.'

Between them they got her into the back seat. She moaned slightly. 'Bring the horse back.' Jeff drove away quickly but, he had only gone a few yards when he slowed down. The movement of the Land Rover must have caused her to moan again.

He led Nightmare back, riding Madison's horse.

That night he was invited to dinner at the Carters' house. He had never met Mrs Carter, not even caught a glimpse of her. When he did, he could see where Madison got her looks. She was what his mother would have called an English rose.

She greeted him warmly. 'Please come in, we owe you so much, I can't thank you enough.'

'How is she?'

'A bit disoriented but she's fine. I've been onto the doctor on the radio. He said she needs rest for a few days.'

'Did she say what happened?'

'A snake. The horse shied and she must have fallen and hit her head on a rock. She's got a nasty gash. Thank heavens it's under the hair line.'

Alex agreed privately. Nothing should be allowed to mar that perfect face. 'Should she have stitches?' Alex didn't know much about such things but if the gash was big she should probably be stitched, he knew that much.

'Done.' Jeff came into the room. 'Stitched her myself.' He held out his hand. 'Thanks, kid. We wouldn't have missed her until nearly dark. God knows what would have happened if you hadn't come along. We owe you a debt of gratitude.'

'Well . . .' he felt ill at ease in Jeff's house. The bunkhouse was homely and comfortable. Jeff's home was formal and English. 'I'm glad she's all right then.'

'C'mon kid. She wants to thank you herself.'

He was led up wide and curving stairs, along a long and carpeted hall. Ancestors on walls watched him disapprovingly. He hoped the soles of his shoes were clean. The carpet was cream-coloured. He looked surreptitiously back: no dirty marks. Her bedroom was as large as their lounge back in Shakawe. She lay in a four-poster bed, propped up on pillows. Her room was cream and pink with patches of rose. Feminine smells surrounded him. He felt big and intrusive in this softly lit room.

'Hello.' What else could he say? 'Glad you're okay.'

She looked up at him and he was startled to see her

dislike of him in her eyes. 'Thank you,' she said. 'I believe you found me.'

'Yes.' He felt grubby and smelly, although he had just showered.

'I'm very grateful to you.' Her eyes ripped him apart. To her, he was obviously the big lout she saw fighting the other day.

He could swear he could smell his socks. He felt a prickle of nervous perspiration under his arms. 'It was nothing.' *Please, Jeff, can we go?*

But Jeff sat beside her bed leaving him standing in exposed isolation, like the sole occupant of a stage.

'Knew this kid would be good when I saw him in Francistown. You're okay, kid. You can stay on permanent if you like.'

'Thanks.' All he wanted to do was get away from this room before sweat stained his shirt and his socks tainted the perfumed air.

She moved in the bed and her shawl slipped and he glimpsed white milky skin where her breasts began. He tried not to look but he couldn't help himself. She saw him looking. Dislike turned to frosty loathing. 'I'm tired, Daddy.'

'Okay, Maddie. C'mon, kid, let's have dinner.'

What a relief! To be out of the room. She hated him. He didn't blame her. He was ugly and clumsy and smelly.

Mrs Carter was a charming and gracious hostess and went out of her way to put him at ease. She asked about his family and seemed genuinely interested in his replies. Alex felt gauche. She thanked him profusely for finding Madison. He felt patronised. She insisted he have a second helping of the main course. He felt like an ill-bred glutton.

Jeff was his normal self. Alex knew, with no doubt in his

mind, that Jeff hated having him in the house. After dinner Jeff insisted he stay for coffee. Alex knew, with no doubt in his mind, Jeff could not wait for him to leave. When he said goodbye the Carters stood together on the verandah, smiling and thanking him. He knew, with no doubt in his mind, they would throw themselves into chairs and say, 'Thank God that's over.'

He gratefully returned to the familiar bunkhouse with all the other big, smelly men. He felt comfortable there.

Kel sneered at him. 'Getting into Daddy's good books won't get you into her pants.'

Anger rose swiftly but he stamped on it. Kel was told to shut up by several others.

Outside, the rumble of thunder. 'Rains are coming. Be driving the cattle in a couple of weeks.' Artie peered through the window. 'Time we got some decent rain.'

A couple of weeks! Would they ever finish the bloody branding?

Christmas came and went. The only concession to the festive season was an extra day off. His mother sent him a Bible and a shirt. The note accompanying the present said:

We do miss you, Alexander, Pa could do with your help. I pray every day for your safe return and trust the Good Lord that you see fit to come home soon. The farm is doing well thanks to Pa's hard work but he is not as young as he once was and gets very tired. I worry for his health. The house isn't the same at Christmas without you—families should be together to celebrate the birth of Christ. Are you saying your prayers? God bless and keep you.

Your loving mother.

Alex read the letter three times, feeling more guilty with each reading.

Paulie sent a card:

Guess what? I climbed on the roof and fell off. Now my left arm is broken. Pity it wasn't the right arm, then I wouldn't have to do holiday homework. Happy Christmas.

Alex wondered why his mother hadn't mentioned Paulie's arm.

There was a card from Pa as well.

We are all fine. Hope you're having a good time and look-ing after yourself. Have a good Christmas son.

Fondest love.

Pa.

It crossed Alex's mind then that while his mother's note filled him with the guilty realisation that he *should* go home, his father's words, and those of Paulie, made him *want* to go. 'I'll stay for the cattle drive,' he thought. 'Then I'll go home.'

Two weeks later Jeff came into the bunkhouse to speak to the men. 'Doesn't look like it's going to be much of a rainy season this year. So we don't wait any longer. Cattle drive starts in two days. Artie's got the list. Those not going will be fencing.'

He was relieved to find his name on the cattle drive list. Although he had seen nothing of Madison since that night in her bedroom, he could feel her dislike of him following wherever he went.

Artie and Pat stared at him in open disbelief when he said he wanted to take Nightmare. 'For Christ's sake, boyo, why?'

'She can run. She's strong.'

'She'll take your bloody arm off one day.' The horse tried to bite at every opportunity although she had almost ceased her attempts to unseat him.

In the end he won his argument and Nightmare became his main mount.

Those going on the drive were spared the last of the branding. The day before they were due to leave he was sitting with Pat on the verandah when Jeff's plane roared overhead. 'Where's he going?'

'Gaberones. He goes about once every six weeks.'

'When's he coming back?'

'You won't see him again until after the drive.'

'Madison gone too?'

'Haven't a clue, boyo, and you shouldn't be thinking about it.'

'She's beautiful,' he said softly.

'Forget her. There's plenty of others.'

'Not out here.'

Pat grinned. 'True, boyo, but you sure as bejesus can make up for lost time in Gabs. We get to spend a week there. You'll forget Madison then, boyo.'

Alex didn't think so.

Pat grabbed his arm. 'Pull yourself towards yourself, boyo. That one's off limits. She's on ice till her daddy lets go. If you're so desperate, try one of them little black girls at the pub. I'm telling you, boyo, I know one that fucks like a rattlesnake.'

Alex shook his head. The man was incorrigible. There was no point in telling him that sex was the furthest thing from his mind because . . . well . . . it wasn't. But what he really wanted was for Madison to like him. Pat wouldn't believe that. Besides, he had decided it was beer time and was man-handling him inside.

They were leaving at first light. Alex packed a few belongings into a bedroll. 'Travel light,' Willie had said. 'No-one out there to mind. We all smell the same. You can buy some new duds in Gaberones.'

He had saved all the money he had earned, barring the few pounds he spent in Ghanzi. 'Take it with you, fella. You'll be wanting to kick your heels up for a bit.'

He wrapped his money in a handkerchief and put it in his shirt pocket which buttoned down. He was excited about the drive. The men had told stories of the hardships, dust and heat and flies, lions and lack of water, but he was looking forward to it.

Most of the farmers in the area moved 600 to 800 head at a time. The farmer himself, or maybe his son, would ride with the herd, a handful of Africans would ride with him and twenty or so Bushmen would walk alongside the cattle, herding back strays. Jeff Carter did things differently. Perhaps because his farm was three times the size of others around and he had the men to use, he never sent Bushmen with the drive. Pat told Alex that Jeff didn't trust the Bushmen to stick with the drive for its entire thirty day duration. 'They meet up with clans and just bugger off,' Pat said. 'Jeff prefers to use his permanents. That way he knows they'll stick it out to the end.'

'Does Jeff ever ride with the cattle?'

'He's done it occasionally. Depends how busy he is.'

'Has Madison . . .'

'Will you stop that, boyo.'

They were all up at four the next day. Pat, Bob, Willie, Kel, two other men and Alex. They were joined in the horse yard by a dozen Africans who would make the ride with them. He saddled up Nightmare who, sensing something different, decided to be difficult. 'Told you, boyo,' Pat warned.

'She'll settle down.'

There was something wrong with his boots. He took them off and pulled them on again. His feet settled in comfortably this time.

He saw the supplies wagon pull away, drawn by four yoked oxen, looking like it had stepped out of the last century. Six spare horses trotted behind, tethered to the back of the wagon. Other horses ran with the herd. The wagon had pre-arranged places to wait. It would travel at the front of the drive the whole way.

The men rode the six miles to the holding pens. They were driving 2,000 head to a farm Jeff had near Sekoma. If the rains had come the cattle would have been driven all the way to Lobatse but they would need time to recover their condition after the long haul. The big double gates of the holding paddock were swung open. Cattle bellowed, whips cracked, voices shouted out.

Pat rode up to Alex. 'Come on, boyo, come on, we're not here to fuck spiders.'

Alex grinned at him and cracked his whip.

The animals streamed through the gates. The cattle drive was on its way. Alex pulled a scarf over his mouth and nose. Nightmare was as skittish as hell but he managed her easily. He cracked his whip again and she jumped but kept going. As the first of the cattle reached the road and dust swirled thick yellow in the rising sunlight, he looked back to the yards. The lone figure of Madison stood, watching them depart. In an exultant mood, he raised his hat and waved, but received no acknowledgement. He hadn't really expected any.

EIGHT

He rode with Pat and Bob on the left flank. He was pleased he was not riding at the back—within minutes, those who were had become dust ghosts. Nightmare settled down after the first hour although the other two were not prepared to ride too close alongside. Her snapping teeth were capable of removing a large chunk of flesh. Riding a safe distance from Pat he asked why the supplies were carried in a wagon, rather than a truck.

'We tried vehicles a couple of years ago. They don't carry as much. If they break down you have to ditch them and they're too fast. The guys driving them spend most of the day sitting around in the heat just waiting.'

'What if someone gets sick? A vehicle could get them to safety.'

'That's not just any old wagon you're looking at, boyo— no sir. There's a two-way radio and it carries enough medical supplies to deal with anything from a common cold to a dose of clap. Bob here did a first aid course a few years back. He would have to be forcibly restrained from chopping out your liver if he thought it would help. If anyone runs into real trouble Jeff can always bring the plane. Mind you,' he grinned, 'most of us would prefer to take our chances with Bob. We figure we're more likely to survive him than a flight with Jeff.'

That made him feel marginally better.

The cattle were allowed to take their own time, stopping frequently to eat the brown grass. By the end of the day they were still on Jeff Carter's land. 'We don't push them,' Pat told him, 'until we get to Takatshwane. Between there and Kang there's no reliable water and we're into deep sand. Then we hurry them up. They have to do a good twenty-five miles a day then. It's the worst part of the trip. A hundred miles of bugger all. They need their strength for that.'

They camped that night on the southeastern border of Jeff's land. 'We always camp here first night out.' Willie held his foot up for Bob to pull his boot off. 'Ahhhh, that's better.'

Willie preferred American style cowboy boots. He ordered them from a Sears and Roebuck mail order catalogue and, as soon as one pair arrived, he ordered the next. They could take up to a year to reach him by the time the wheels of finance had turned between Bechuanaland and America, followed by a sea journey to the South African port of Durban and thence the arduous trip by road to Ghanzi. They must have been hellishly hot but he stubbornly refused to wear any other. Everyone else (apart from Alex who was still wearing store-bought riding boots from Francistown) took their feet to a San shoemaker in Ghanzi who made their boots from the soft leather of gemsbok. They fitted like gloves and were unbelievably comfortable. Alex intended to get a pair on his return.

The wagon arrived ahead of them. The driver, a short stocky Bantu, had their food cooking, their bedrolls laid out and beers standing in water from the bore with a wet towel thrown over them to keep them cool. They were not icy cold but they went down just as well.

The conversation ranged from women to women and back again. 'Lost your cherry yet, boyo?'

Alex blushed. 'Yes.'

'Good for you. You'll get some action in Gabs. Plenty of women there.'

Willie laughed. 'This mad Irishman only thinks of two things.'

'What's the other?' Alex grinned at Pat who pulled a finger at him.

'Beer.' Willie whoofed as Pat jabbed his finger into his solar plexus.

'Wrong, I think of three things.'

'After beer and women, what else is there?' Bob asked.

'Ireland,' Pat said softly. 'I think of rolling green hills.'

'Out here? What! You trying to send yourself mad?' Bob shook his head. 'I never think of home.'

'Where's home, Bob?' Alex couldn't place his accent.

'I'd have to say Cape Town although I was born in England. Yeah, Cape Town. Prettiest little town in the world. Ever been there?'

Alex shook his head. 'I've never been out of Bechuanaland. We lived near Shakawe all my life. Until I went to school in Francistown I'd never been anywhere else.'

'All in good time, boyo. You'll get there.'

'Where are you from, Willie?'

Willie stared at his bare toes. 'I've really been around, man.'

'So where did you grow up?'

'Ghanzi.'

'But you've travelled?'

'Yep. Every year. Ghanzi—Lobatse—Ghanzi, via the Kalahari Cattle Highway.' He hitched himself higher. 'You see, kid, I'm happy where I am. Don't need to know about anyplace else.'

'Is Jeff from Ghanzi?'

'Jeff? Nah! He's from South Africa. Came here twenty years ago. When Britain was allocating farms Jeff was there with his hand out. Mind you, he's worked at it. Hocked himself to the hilt to buy out his neighbours. It's paid off too. He's the richest farmer in the area.'

'Why does Madison go to school in Britain?'

'There you go again, boyo. Get her out of your mind.'

'I can't.' He grinned and shrugged his shoulders. 'She just sort of sits there all the time.'

Pat laughed. 'Won't do you any good, boyo. She's out of reach.'

'Even if she weren't, she doesn't like me anyway.'

'Forget her,' Willie advised. 'Jeff would have a pup if he knew you were even thinking about her.' He reached for his guitar and strummed a few experimental chords while adjusting the tuning to his satisfaction. Then, with the camp fire crackling in the background, he entertained everyone for hours, the firelight glinting on his gold teeth as he sang cowboy songs in his strong tenor voice. Alex listened, content. The last song he sang, 'Oh Give Me a Home, Where The Buffalo Roam', had been memorised by the Africans. From the darkness beyond the fire they joined in, their rich voices harmonising as only Africans can. It was a stirring sound.

The next morning they had to get 2,000 cattle through a fifteen foot gate. As Willie said just before he cantered off to round up yet another stray, it was a bit like squeezing a soft turd through the eye of a needle.

'How many bloody gates are there?' They had been at it for two hours.

'Only one. It's the quarantine camp the other side of Kang.'

Alex was relieved. Nightmare was foaming at the mouth with exertion by the time the last stragglers went through.

'Think this is tough?' Willie grimaced at him. 'Wait till we get into the sandy country.'

The ride on the second day was action filled. While they were on Jeff's land the cattle could virtually wander wherever they liked providing it was in a forward direction. Stock routes, in some areas half a mile wide, ran alongside the road. Most of the farms were unfenced. When cattle were not being driven, neighbouring ranchers let their own cattle graze near the road. Technically, the land in these routes was privately owned. A gentlemen's agreement existed between all the ranchers but certain ground rules did exist. Now they were on someone else's land they were honour bound to keep the herd bunched. The cattle had to be discouraged from foraging until they reached each night's destination. However, as with most things to do with cattle, Alex discovered they had different ideas. Strong as she was, Nightmare was ready to drop by the end of the day.

That night, as the tired men sat in the darkness, they were treated to the spectacle of an awesome electrical storm. Forked lightning split the sky as it danced in crazy patterns from one end to the other. Sheet lightning accompanied it, lighting up the land briefly like a flare. Thunder rumbled continuously. In the distance, the lightning started a grass fire. Within a few minutes the wind had it blazing against the dark horizon and spreading swiftly so it resembled a distant explosion. 'We'll have to watch that tomorrow,' Bob said. 'It's okay for now but it'll depend on which way the wind's blowing. Might have to stay an extra day here.'

Competing successfully against the thunder, lions announced their presence. 'Bastards!' Pat said in disgust. 'We'll need extra men on tonight. Come on, boyo, let's take the first shift.'

Normally, the Bushmen on a cattle drive would build a *kraal*, an enclosure of thorny branches, to keep the cattle in one place during the night. They would light large fires to keep the lions away. Because of the size of Jeff Carter's drive, this was impractical. Men had to work double shifts.

Riding around the cattle on another horse to give Nightmare her well earned rest, bone weary, with his mind crying out for sleep, Alex watched nature's fireworks and listened to the snarling voices of one of her children. Lions were close. Shadowy shapes slinking just thirty feet away, waiting for a chance to rush in and grab one of the cattle. Each time sheet lightning flashed he could see them, crouched low and menacing. The cattle knew they were there and were restless. His horse wasn't particularly fond of them either and she danced nervously whenever she caught their scent. Pat shouted a warning and he wheeled the horse and, whip cracking, headed off a bold female who had sneaked in behind him.

He had thought he'd worked hard during the day but it was nothing to the vigilance required to keep the lions away. By the time he finished his extra shift and crawled into his sleeping bag he was too damned tired to worry about them.

In the morning the lions were nowhere to be seen but, wherever they went, they had managed to take four of the cattle with them. 'Not bad,' Bob said. 'Last year at this place they got twelve.' Although the air was filled with smoke, the grass fire had burned itself out. Added to the heat, flies, sand and dust, the smoke made the day more uncomfortable than a day had any right to be. The scarf he pulled over his mouth and nose kept the flies off and the sand out. But the smoke seemed to seep straight through, choking his straining air passages, making his eyes run, fouling his taste buds. He figured it couldn't get any worse.

He was wrong.

Made bold by desperation, the lions killed again and again. The cattle became as jumpy as hell, the horses likewise. Nightmare, to her credit, remained obedient but he could sense the tension in her. With hardly any sleep, the men grew cranky. Whips cracked more often, cattle who got in the way of them suffered open wounds and blood from the wounds encouraged the lions. It was a vicious circle. Alex's mind was so tired he could barely think straight, his body ached with fatigue, he hated cattle more than he hated anything in his life. He hated the desert, he even hated the other men.

The further south they went, the sandier the terrain became. After the third day they left the farming country behind and were into the desert. Keeping the cattle bunched became easier; there was hardly anything worth eating and the sand was so deep it made moving along it too difficult. The cattle tended to stick to the rutted road. Two men rode in front, five at the back, the rest flanking the herd. Alex, to his acute physical discomfort, spent two days behind and three on the left flank before being asked to ride ahead. They were the most miserable five days he had ever known. Even the sand got through his scarf. He had grit up his nose, in his eyes and ears, in his mouth, down his throat, between his fingers and toes, under his nails and in his groin. His clothing was stiff with dust and sand, his hair stood on end with it, his eyebrows and lashes were whitened by it, his hat the same. The sand was attracted to his perspiration-soaked clothing like a magnet. The glare from the sun on the white dunes was physically painful. And the lions became so bold they did not even bother to hide their presence during the day.

'I don't understand,' he said morosely that night by the fire, 'in all this whiteness, how come we're so dirty?'

They had not used water to wash for two days. They had another day to go before they would find water again, unless it rained and that did not seem likely. The sky had remained obstinately blue every day, tantalising them with thunder and lightning each night. But no rain. All the men looked the same: grime encrusted. Not healthy brown dirt, a kind of sludge grey grime which crept into the creases on their faces and stayed there.

'I hate this. Why did I come?' Pat, like the rest of them, was filthy.

'You say that every year about now.'

'Well why doesn't someone remind me?'

'We did,' Bob and Willie yelled at him. Tempers were at boiling point.

They were camped in the middle of nothing. The cattle had had no water and nothing to eat for two days. The horses were handfed and watered, they had to work. By pushing ahead tomorrow, with luck, they would reach the holding pen just outside Kang. It was unlikely there would be much grass but the water had always been good. From then, the terrain became more friendly. Most of the cattle were holding up well but Bob was worried about a dozen or so who were about to calf.

'It's tough on them,' he said to Alex. 'They're already weak. We put the new calves into the wagon but the mothers get frantic. It's against the natural way they do things.'

'Why don't you run them in winter?' Kel looked sourly at him. He had barely said two words since they left Ghanzi and always made sure he was riding somewhere other than where Alex rode. At night, around the fire, he seldom joined their conversation. Whenever he did open his mouth, it was to complain. 'Surely that would be better for the cattle and the men.'

Bob answered patiently. 'Less water, practically no grass and, believe it or not, it's so cold out here in winter the calves could freeze to death.'

Freeze to death! Bloody hell! It didn't seem possible.

The sand had even got into his bedroll.

The next day he was glad he had taken his turn at the back and side. He was even more relieved when a Land Rover appeared on the road ahead. Grinning, he turned to Pat. 'How's he getting through?'

'With great difficulty, boyo,' Pat grinned back. 'The boys will have their work cut out. Getting around a vehicle on this track is not easy.'

'Do we help?'

'Love to, boyo, love to.' Pat laughed. 'But someone has to stay at the front.'

They cantered ahead to greet the driver who stopped and got out, looking at the swirling tidal wave of 2,000 head of cattle making straight for him. He was watching the approaching herd with disbelief.

Pat tipped his hat back. 'Just sit tight, boyo. They'll go on round you.'

'They will?' The vehicle had South African numberplates

and was loaded with camping equipment and supplies. Tourists. The man shrugged and reached into the back of the cab. 'Well, if I can't go anywhere I might as well have a beer. Care to join me?'

Pat and Alex looked at each other. Then they looked at the beer which he had just taken from an ice chest, beaded with cold moisture. Alex thought briefly of the men working at the back. But only briefly. 'Would we ever.'

The girl in the passenger seat had long blonde hair, tiny short shorts and knee length brown boots. 'I'll open them.' She hopped out and flipped open the bottles using the bumper. Alex and Pat took a long, long look at her legs and arse. 'How long will this take?' she asked, handing them a bottle each. She walked around the vehicle arching her back.

'Not long enough,' Pat muttered to Alex. Then out loud, 'About two hours.'

'God!' she laughed. 'Could be well and truly drunk by then.'

The cattle were several hundred yards from them. 'We'd best be off.' Pat drained his beer in two long swallows and handed the bottle back to the driver. 'Keep your windows up and sit tight. Thanks for the beer.'

The holding pen in Kang was geared for men and beasts making the trip south. Water troughs were plentiful. 'This is where the fun starts, boyo.' They had cantered ahead and were waiting for the cattle.

Alex watched them come. A cloud of white dust with heads at the front and no legs. It was an amazing sight.

The cattle at the front caught the smell of water. The pen, five miles long and two miles wide, had no gates. A gap had

116

been left in the fence, some 200 yards wide. Alex took his position on one side, Pat the other. He had never seen a stampede but, watching the effect of 2,000 thirst-crazed cattle with their first whiff of water in three days, figured he was about to come close. Nightmare did the only thing a self-respecting nervous horse could do. She bucked.

He hit the ground crawling. The ground was shaking. Eight thousand hooves created an earthquake under his hands and knees. He crawled for safety, thirty miles an hour. Cattle on the outside flank jumped him. He kept crawling. The fence caved in. Two hundred yards was not wide enough. He kept crawling.

Later, about a hundred years later, Pat told him he thought he had intended to crawl to Angola. That was after he had pawed his entire body checking for damage.

Alex had been lucky. As Willie said, 'Cattle don't like squishy things between their toes.'

Nightmare looked suitably embarrassed when he found her. But he wasn't having any. 'Bad horse.' She was so embarrassed she forgot to snap at his backside when he mounted up.

The wagon had gone on into Kang to the trading store, bought cartons of cold beer from their coldroom and returned to the holding pen. The men's stampede almost matched that of the cattle.

Alex floated in a cement water trough, naked, an icy cold beer in his hand. The water was filthy but he didn't care. Neither did the others. A shower had been rigged from a water tank on stilts. He would wash the dirt off later. For now it was enough to get the grit out of his pores. Besides, he and Pat were to shower last. Their punishment for accepting beer from the tourists.

Kang had had some rain. There was a little grass in the holding pen. The driver of the wagon had been told there was good grass further south. 'That's the worst of it, boyo. From here on in it's a milk run.'

'Shaddup. Every time you say that we hit trouble.' Willie splashed water at Pat. 'You say that every year in Kang. Last year Perce had his appendix burst. Year before the trail flooded and we were stuck for a week. Then Ken had that bloody trouble with lions and damned near lost a leg.'

'Just trying to make it interesting,' Pat said mildly, wiping his face. He grinned at Alex. 'Don't listen to him, boyo, nothing's going to happen.'

Bob was immersed in water up to his neck with a fat cigar clenched between his teeth. 'Always wanted to ask you this, Pat: Why do you say "boyo"? It's Welsh.'

'So?' Pat looked aggrieved. 'Can't a man be a little international?'

Alex loved these men again. In the space of a few weeks they had become his family, especially Pat. Now the worst of the trip was over, good humour had been restored.

'It's because he's always taking a leak,' Willie offered. Bob and Pat pushed him under the water.

The wagon had escaped the worst of the gritty sand. Each man had a complete change of clothes wrapped in plastic. After a shower, the luxury of pulling on something clean made Alex groan with pleasure. He left his boots with everyone else's. That night, the men treated their feet to fresh air. The driver, who everyone considered had a cushy job, had to wash their clothes. He had to change the water five times before the worst of the dirt came out.

Alex ran his hand through his hair. It was getting long and starting to curl. The sun had bleached the top layer white.

He'd get it cut in Gaberones after they left the cattle at Jeff's farm.

The next morning he and Kel had to stay behind until the last of the cattle had left. It was their job to repair where the cattle had gone through the fence. They had only just started when an aeroplane roared overhead, dipped its wing at them before turning towards Kang. 'That's Jeff's plane,' Alex said, surprised.

Kel looked up briefly. 'Must be checking up on us.'

'I guess I would too if I had so many cattle.'

'Yeah, well you'll never know. Hand me the pliers and stop yabbering.'

They worked in silence for fifteen minutes. Then they heard a vehicle. It raced up to them over the bumpy ground. Jeff Carter jumped out. 'Show me your boots.'

A greeting died on Alex's lips. Jeff looked furious. He stuck out his foot.

'The underside, you idiot.'

Alex turned and lifted his foot. Kel did the same.

The little San bootmaker in Ghanzi, with his old fashioned tools and basic knowledge of shoes, produced plain leather soles. All the boots were the same. Alex had rubber soles on his boots which had a wavy lined pattern on them.

'You perving little bastard!' Jeff's fist crashed into his ear. With his back turned, he had not seen it coming.

He spun around, his ear burning. 'Jeff, what . . .' Jeff's fist crashed into his mouth. He felt his teeth move.

'Spying on my daughter. I'll teach you a lesson, you little creep. Climbing a tree to watch her through the window. I saw your boot prints.' Jeff was beside himself with rage.

'I didn't . . .'

'Don't lie about it, you bastard.' Jeff swung and his fist bounced of his shoulder.

Alex jumped backwards. 'Wait, Jeff . . . I didn't . . .'

Jeff came for him. Alex hesitated. He did not want to fight him. After Kel, he never wanted to fight again. Besides, Jeff had it all wrong. In the split second he hesitated, Jeff was all over him. Blows rained down on his head, his arms, his chest, his stomach. He fell to his knees. He was hurting, really hurting. Jeff kept hitting him. A hard blow to his kidneys made him cry out with pain. He toppled over onto the sand. 'Get up, you bloody animal.'

His body felt as though it were on fire. He could taste blood in his mouth. Perspiration stung the cuts on his face.

'Boss, I think . . .' Kel sounded scared.

'Shaddup,' Jeff snarled. 'C'mon, get up.'

He groaned and curled his body, trying to find the strength to move. But his body wouldn't work.

'Piss on you,' Jeff spat. 'You're out of here, kid. Don't ever try to come near me or my family again. I'll fucking kill you if you do.'

He felt fingers fumbling with his shirt pocket. 'What are you doing?' Jeff's voice.

'If you're going to leave him here he won't need this.' Kel held up his money.

'Put it back.'

'But boss . . .'

'Put it back. Next to perverts I don't like thieves. Put it back.'

The money was put back. Alex rolled up onto his hands and knees. He felt he was going to be sick. He tried to speak but his voice was a whispered croak. He heard the Land Rover start up and drive away. Kel bent over him and took the money from his pocket. 'Silly to waste this. You're not going to need it.' He did not have the strength to stop him. He fell on his side again.

'See ya, kid.'

Nightmare whinnied and he heard Kel snap her reins. 'Come here, you fucking bitch.'

He heard the creak of leather as Kel mounted his own horse.

He lay in the hot sand hurting all over. 'Pat will come back for me,' he thought. Then he lost consciousness.

When he opened his eyes the sun was high in the sky and shadows formed perfect circles around the short trees. Water. He needed water. Crawling and retching he reached the tank where, last night, he had showered. He pulled himself up. His whole body was aching. Leaning against the tank stand he took off his clothes. Every movement hurt. Standing under the cascade of lukewarm water he felt the inside of his mouth with his tongue. Several teeth were loose. His mouth felt bruised and water stung a cut on his lip. He explored his face with his fingers. A gash on one eyebrow, one eye felt puffy and half closed. His chest and ribs were on fire but, after gingerly pushing against them, he decided nothing was broken. A sharp stinging pain shot through his kidneys.

Jeff had been thorough. Alex's head felt fuzzy and he was unable to focus. But the water helped. He saw Nightmare standing ten feet away, reins hanging to the ground. Kel had led her away, what was she doing here? Perhaps she bit him? He hoped she bit him. God, the water felt good.

There was a roaring noise in his head. He was going to pass out again. He turned off the tap, took three steps and fell, face down, into black nothing.

He had no idea how much later, but a strange whispered clicking cut into his consciousness. Brief memories flashed but he couldn't place them. He rolled onto his back. His body shrieked with the pain of movement. Then, through eyes which felt as though he were looking under water, he saw a group of tiny Bushmen. They stood bunched together, maybe fifteen feet from him. They were pointing at his nakedness.

'!ebili. He has come back.' !Ka had seen the brown half melon shape on his left buttock.

Alex covered his front and reached for his clothes.

Another man, N!ou, a kinsman of !Oma who had died to save the baby Alex, pointed. 'See his hair. See if it comes back to the colour of the Moon.'

'It must be the little beetle. How he has grown. But he is hurt. Who could have done such a terrible thing?'

Like all Bushmen, !Ka abhorred violence of any type. Conflict in the clans, when it arose, was resolved by spirited debate, to be laughed over when the tension dissipated. If an issue could not be satisfactorily talked through, those involved in the dispute usually packed up and left the clan rather than remain and run the risk of physical violence.

!Ka walked closer to Alex. '!ebili is near the end of his strength,' he said to the others, ready to help if the need arose.

Dressing under the unwavering gaze of five little Bushmen was difficult. Pain accompanied every move and waves of nausea swept over him constantly. By the time he had gingerly lowered himself to the ground to pull on his boots, his hair was drying. The sun-bleached top hair sprang into curls. Why were they smiling at him like that? Their faces held nothing but gentleness. The one closest approached him, his hand held out, speaking in that strange clicking language. Memories stirred.

'Da,' said !Ka.

Alex stared at him.

The face of a thousand wrinkles creased further into smiles. 'Da,' he repeated, holding his hand out and bobbing his head.

'Da,' Alex said tentatively. He rose with difficulty and held out his own hand.

'Da, da.' The Bushman was chuckling gently as he grasped Alex's hand and held it.

!Ka turned to the others. 'See, he remembers.'

N!ou was not so sure. 'Tell him your name.'

The Bushman tapped his chest with both his hands. '!Ka. !Ka.'

Alex tilted his head and stared at him. Something was there. Something he should know. But the blows to his head would not let him think. He tried to move towards Nightmare and would have fallen if the Bushman had not jumped forward and held him.

'He is badly hurt. We must take him with us. Be will know what to do.'

'She will be very pleased to see the little beetle again.' N!ou, like all of their clan, knew how Be had become fond of the child of the Moon. 'She will make him better.'

!Ka tugged on Alex's arm. Pointing out into the desert and smiling, Alex realised the Bushman wanted him to go with them. He felt strangely calm. He had a sense of being saved. He pointed to Nightmare. !Ka nodded he understood. He helped Alex over to the horse. 'Don't bite him,' Alex gritted, through jaws which ached. Nightmare tossed her head. 'And for God's sake don't buck,' he muttered to himself as !Ka

123

shoved him on her back. Nightmare stood stock still in injured outrage.

Once in the saddle he slumped over her neck. !Ka took the reins warily. He had never had anything to do with horses and they were big enough to frighten him. However, the animal simply followed along behind him. The others walked on either side, chattering and clicking softly together.

In this manner they covered eight miles over the desert to where the clan were camped. Once again a child told Be that her husband was bringing in something strange. Once again, when she saw the injured Alex, she cried, 'Oh, oh, what have you done?' and once again !Ka had to sternly tell her how he had found the little beetle.

'*!ebili?*' she said, staring at Alex's bent head over the horse's neck. 'Is it really the little beetle?'

'He has the mark of the Moon here.' !Ka tapped his own rump.

'What has happened to him?'

'I do not know. But he is hurt. You will tend him.'

He was far too big for her to cradle in her arms as she had before but she was waiting beside the horse when he slid, with assistance from !Ka, from the saddle, and her arm went around his waist and she led him, on his rubbery legs, to her hut. 'Oh, little beetle, what terrible thing has happened?'

Alex heard her, saw her face, saw her concern. He knew he was safe with these people. Not just safe from harm. He knew they cared for him. He relaxed while her fingers explored his injuries. He did not mind when she removed his clothes. He felt the soothing, tangy tsamma ointment on his skin. Memories stirred again. But he slipped into sleep before they could come to the surface.

It was pitch dark when he awoke. Outside the hut, the

men of the clan were dancing. Alex crawled to the door and looked through. Women were sitting around a fire, clapping and singing. The men were smacking their heels on the ground and shuffling around the women. Several of the men were holding the one in front by the hips. The rattling of their leg adornments added to the singing and clapping. One of the women played a thumb piano, prongs of metal of differing lengths and tension which produced a series of eerily high twangs. The combined sound was one of extraordinary ethereal beauty.

He had no way of knowing that !Ka and his clan were conducting a curing dance on his behalf. The songs were medicine songs. The dancing men were aiming for a trance, where their spirits would travel outside their bodies to do battle with the spirits of the dead. This would give them the power to draw sickness from his body. Alex sat in the doorway of the flimsy grass hut and listened, enthralled.

One of the women noticed him and smiled, nudging the woman next to her. She also smiled at him but they did not stop their singing and clapping. They did not dare. To do so would leave the men vulnerable to evil spirits.

He realised his vision, from one eye at least, was clearing. The pounding headache was nowhere near as bad and the feeling he wanted to be sick had subsided to some extent. He felt his swollen other eye. It was completely closed. He guessed it would be black and blue. His kidneys were on fire. His ribs hurt. Weariness overtook him. He crawled further into the hut, lay down on the woven sleeping mat, and fell instantly into a dreamless sleep.

NINE

For two weeks he lay in the hut, his body slowly recovering from the savage beating Jeff had given him. Most of his cuts and bruises healed quickly but his urine was bloody and it hurt to pee. Be knew this should not be so and, after ten days with no improvement, took action. He submitted willingly when Be brought the medicine man from another clan. He never questioned their sometimes strange methods of curing. He uttered no sound as small incisions were made in his back. He did not query the wildebeest horns which the medicine man placed over these cuts or when he sucked the air from the horns and used a sticky substance to seal the small holes made in their points. He sat perfectly still when, after a few minutes the medicine man pierced these seals, gently removed the horns and poured out the clotted blood which had collected from his wounds.

He never discovered whether this treatment worked, or if he was on the point of recovery anyway, but he immediately began to feel better. Months later he was to learn that the tiny arrowhead used to cut his skin had first been smeared with the poison they used to such good effect when hunting. It was considered to be an essential element in the drawing of 'bad blood'.

Several days after the medicine man's visit Alex felt strong enough to leave the hut. His legs were still rubbery but he joined a group of men and women sitting outside. They smiled at him and returned to their conversation, leaving him alone with his thoughts. As their rapid-fire clicking language washed over him and he watched their gentle faces, he felt completely at peace.

!Ka was carving and whittling an animal bone and Alex watched with interest. !Ka saw him watching and put one end of the bone to his mouth and sucked in air, then blew outwards in an elaborate display of smoking a pipe. '*n/i!xu*,' he said.

Alex knew what the word meant. He just couldn't say it. '*N . . . tsk . . . i . . . pop . . . pop . . . u.*'

The Bushmen rolled on the ground laughing.

'*N*,' !Ka prompted.

'*N.*'

!Ka nodded approval. '*Tsk*,' he said, showing Alex how he withdrew his tongue from just behind his front teeth. '*N . . . tsk.*'

'*N/*,' Alex responded.

Several of the men clapped in encouragement.

'*N . . . tsk . . . i.*'

'*N/i.*' Alex was smiling. Getting his tongue from '*N*', through the '*tsk*' and rapidly into the '*i*' was difficult but he managed it.

'*N . . . tsk . . . i . . . pop.*' !Ka put his tongue against the hard palate, just where it rises to the roof of the mouth. When he removed it it created a hard popping sound.

Alex lost it and they had to start again.

Seeing his enthusiasm, !Ka began patiently and gently to teach Alex their language and ways. Alex was only too happy to learn; he was still basically a boy. !Ka and Be represented a safe world, a world without people like Jeff and Kel. In their company, and that of the others in the clan, he could stay a boy. He could never have verbalised this fact but he must have been subconsciously aware of it because when he was recovered enough to leave them he delayed.

As soon as he was well enough he went looking for Nightmare. !Ka had done his best but his knowledge of the needs of a horse was scant. In this hostile environment, Nightmare's seemingly unlimited capacity for grass and water taxed his meagre resources considerably. Even though he was, as yet, unable to converse in their language, Alex could see that. But he was reluctant to set her free; a bond had developed between him and the horse. Besides, having spent her life in the company of people and the safety of corrals, Nightmare would feed the lions as soon as he let her go.

Nightmare solved the problem for him by coming into oestrus.

In a barren land where only a handful of species had adapted in order to survive, there was no place for the wild horse. Their presence was unheard of. Not in the desert country, not in the flat cattle country, not in the Delta. Bechuanaland had no wild horses.

'Tell that to him,' Alex muttered to himself in surprise. The black stallion appeared from nowhere and, judging by the clan's reaction, they had never seen him before. He stood on a ridge, tossing his aristocratic head, his black mane flowing out like a woman's hair. His coat shone in the sunlight, so black it almost looked blue. He stamped his powerful legs and sand flew. He looked exactly as he was: proud, beautiful and free. Alex had never seen such a magnificent horse.

Neither had Nightmare. It was love at first sight. She reared and plunged against her tether.

'Sshhh. Easy now.' He spoke gently and blew softly on her nose. She quietened and stood still, rippling. With a lump in his throat he took off her halter. Nightmare trotted in a circle, came back to him and nudged his arm with her nose, looked over at the stallion, then, with sand flying from her hooves, kicking and bucking with joy, joined the stallion on the ridge. Both animals stood, side by side, tossing their heads, looking back at him, one a shining russet red, the other a glossy black. Then, with no signal between them, they wheeled and went racing away.

Alex ran to the top of the ridge and watched them go. He told himself it was the right thing to do and swallowed hard against the ache in his throat. 'She deserves to be free.' He watched until they were out of sight. They ran side-by-side, turning their heads often to look at each other. Alex realised they were flirting. Something inside him soared. Months later, after he learned a bit of the San language, !Ka would explain it was the spirit of his own freedom, a rare event since men were usually bound by thought.

He saw Nightmare occasionally after that—always in the company of the stallion. She never came closer than a hundred yards. It was as if she was checking to make sure he was still there.

Alex spoke Setswana fluently. It was the common language spoken by most of the Bantu tribes in Bechuanaland. He actually spoke Setswana before he learned to speak English, the result of playing with the farm children at home.

The language of the Bushmen however differed from place to place. Up north, near Shakawe, the Kung Bushmen spoke a different dialect from the desert dwellers. Alex knew a few of the northern Bushmen words—Pa occasionally hired them to work on the farm. They usually only stayed a few months before returning to their clans near the Tsodilo Hills but were always willing to befriend the young white child of the man who paid their wages.

As time went by, what had first seemed to be a jumble of clicks and pops began to make sense. He realised that the San used five different clicks which ranged from something which sounded like a kiss, to one used to spur on a horse. It took longer for him to learn that words having the same sound could actually mean distinctly different things, depending on whether the vowel was stressed in nasal, breathy or normal tones. In addition, a low or high tone could further change a word.

The clan had a great deal of fun at his expense, especially the day he got the tone wrong and implied that !Ka was smoking an elephant rather than a pipe. He persevered, however, and was soon able to make himself understood and follow the general direction of their conversation. But when !Ka mentioned finding Alex when he was a baby, Alex thought he had misunderstood the Bushman's words.

It took several months for !Ka, who patiently repeated the story over and over, to make Alex understand what it was the Bushman was trying to tell him. Even then, he believed !Ka must be mistaken. Surely his parents would have mentioned it. He had no recollection of the event although sometimes, like in his dreams, snippets of memory surfaced. Alex assumed they were nothing more than dreams.

However, if the story *were* true, a number of things fell into place: Why he had a strong feeling of belonging to !Ka's clan. Why, as a child, he often sought the company of the Kung who worked for Pa. Why the sight of their tiny creased faces made him feel happy inside. And why, when others cursed the Bushmen as lazy or primitive or dishonest, Alex always had to swallow anger.

He had been with the clan four months when !Ka told him they were moving on from the Kang area, going further southeast. Alex, with no hesitation, went with them.

He enjoyed their lifestyle, particularly in the evenings when smoke rose from their cooking fires and the softly spoken clicking language could be heard around camp as husband and wife discussed domestic matters, friends spoke of hunting, men argued over someone's laziness, yelling one moment, helpless with laughter the next, children played. He was a popular guest to their fires and was constantly being called over to sample food, or take a handful back to !Ka and Be. As he learned more and more of their language he developed a deep respect for their ways. They lived as one with nature. By learning their ways, he developed inside himself a profound contentment. The simplicity of their lifestyle left no room for pettiness, greed, envy or hate. At some stage he knew he had turned seventeen but he had no idea when and found it didn't bother him. Life, time and daily activities were controlled by the five seasons.

!Ka taught him how influential the seasons were and how they related to the necessities of his people. Alex had arrived in January, in the middle of *bara,* the main summer rains. It was a time of hunting for meat and a time when their major plant food was available. The clan ate enormous meals at this time, storing the excess in their bodies. This season was followed by */=obe,* a time for harvesting the nuts. Then *!gum,* the winter months of June, July and August. Food was still plentiful and the hunting was good. *!ga,* the time before the rains, was hardest. Water was difficult to find, even though the Bushmen had collected water when it was plentiful and stored it in ostrich eggs, buried in the earth to be dug up during *!ga*. It was in *!huma,* the spring rains before the heat of summer, when the clan replenished their depleted stores of water.

Alex was expected to pull his weight, something he did readily. He became a kind of unofficial clan architect, being especially adept at erecting the two types of dwelling they used. If they were not staying long in one place, a flimsy structure was erected so that, when they moved on, the landscape could return to the way nature intended it. This was done using a semi-circle of saplings, bent towards each other and tied together with dried reeds. Grass thatch or reed mats were then placed over the living frame. A fireplace had to be set opposite the open doorway to warm the inside and also keep away unwanted predators. When the clan left this kind of temporary dwelling all they took with them were the reed mats. The sapling ties would rot allowing the young trees to spring up into their original shape. Any thatch on the roof either blew or rotted away.

If a more permanent hut was required, a scaffolding of sorts became the skeleton framework, reinforced by horizontal ribs which were bound to the uprights by bark. Whichever kind of shelter was built, Alex soon realised that !Ka and his clan made certain it was invisible from a distance, inconspicuous from close up and would quickly return to the landscape as though man had never occupied a tiny space in it. It was almost as if they were apologetic for having disturbed the area.

He learned how to make a bow, how to set snares, how to fire arrows with deadly accuracy, how to make the poison to immobilise an animal. Be gave him a *kaross*, a blanket made from black backed jackal skins, which kept him warm at night. He discarded his western clothes in favour of the modesty pouch, made from animal hide and sewn with sinew worn by the men. And then, after he had been with the clan several months, he received his first gift from someone other than !Ka and Be.

Gift giving, as Alex had observed, was the way the clan networked. No-one kept a gift for more than a couple of months. It was always passed on to a trading partner. At some stage, that trading partner would reciprocate with a similar item. If the clan argued about anything it was either the distribution of food or another's tardiness in the business of gift giving. So when N!ou gave him a quiver and another man gave him a hunting kit, Alex knew he would have to get busy and make something to give back. By clan standards he was poor, not having a proper gift giving network. He set about to rectify this.

!Ka helped. He showed him how to make a quiver but explained, 'It is no good finding a tube of root bark unless you have killed a gemsbok.'

Alex asked him why.

'The scrotum is used to cap the quiver.'

But before he could kill a gemsbok he had to learn to make the poison and before that, where to find the pupa of the flea beetle. It was a long process.

In the end, and with much advice and teaching from !Ka, he proudly gave N!ou a quiver. By then he had received other gifts. His own quiver contained five arrows, some special sticks used to make fire, a sharp stick for holding meat over flames, a hollow sip-stick for sucking up any moisture that may have collected in the hollows of trees or a little below the surface of the sand, and a stick with blobs of gum and vegetable mastic stuck to it for making running repairs to equipment while out hunting. His hunting kit held a digging stick, a knife and a bark saucer so he could mix his own poison. All these items had been given as gifts. Alex in turn, learned how to make them so he could reciprocate.

Time passed. There was always something new to learn, something else which needed doing. Alex was in no hurry. The simple, day-to-day activities filled him with a great sense of contentment. Then !Ka, returning from one of his hunting trips, showed him a stone. 'You had one of these when we found you. It made you laugh.'

Alex held the diamond up against the sky. He remembered his excitement when he saw the round light the night of the dance. The same thing was happening to him now, a kind of shivery tingle which he could feel from his scalp down to the base of his spine. He could not understand it then, had no way of knowing why the lights seemed familiar. Now he thought he knew. The lights flashing off the diamond were spectacular. 'Where did you find this?'

!Ka pointed east. 'In the throat of an ostrich. The same way you found one.'

'Will you show me tomorrow?'

!Ka said he would.

Alex had a new name. They called him !Oma, after the one whose spirit had flown to save him as a baby. Although he could not possibly have been related, they enforced their traditional laws and told him he could never marry a woman called Be. With only about thirty-five names at their disposal for each sex, names were transmitted from grandparent to grandchild according to strict rules. By prohibiting him from marrying a woman named Be, they were protecting him from the sin of incest. Alex took the advice seriously. It was a serious issue. He doubted, however, if it was one which would ever affect him, although he would not insult them by saying so.

Having killed a gemsbok, Alex officially became a man in the clan's eyes. This was a significant occasion since a man who has not killed an animal remains a child and is forbidden to marry. !Ka, as Alex's surrogate father, took the event seriously and performed The Rite of the First Kill. A shallow incision on Alex's back was rubbed with charred meat and fat. The resultant scar, which Alex would carry for the rest of his life, ensured an inner force which compelled him to hunt and provided magic to bless him with superior hunting skills. No woman was allowed to touch his bow and arrows ever again in case they weakened his hunter's heart.

Alex, who had grown up believing that on attaining the age of twenty-one the key to the door of life would be his, felt a pride of achievement, a surge of masculinity and adulthood, which far exceeded anything he expected he might feel when he reached twenty-one. In the eyes of the clan he was a man. In the eyes of his own world it would be another four years before he became one. With his newly acquired status providing encouragement, Alex decided it was time to take his life into his own hands.

They were camped in the Jwaneng district, about as far towards the rising sun as they cared to travel. Further east lived the Bantu and the white man, both of whom the Bushmen shunned. From Jwaneng they habitually roamed north. By the time they were ready to move Alex felt confident he had learned enough to survive in the hostile desert environment. The diamond !Ka had given him made him want to find more. As much as he enjoyed being with the

135

clan, as much as he appreciated the serenity of their simple, non-capitalistic lifestyle and envied them for it, his own upbringing told him that finding more stones was the chance of a lifetime. He could not help himself. Diamonds would provide for his future and there was too much white man inside Alex for him to turn his back on that. !Ka had taken him to where he had found the stone. The area beckoned. The clan left without him.

The simplicity with which the Bushmen lived was never more evident as when they moved from one place to another. Each family had packed their permanent belongings into two leather sacks, each sack no larger than an overnight bag. Their farewell was casual, leaving no doubt that they would see each other again. Be placed her hand on his face and said, 'Go well, my son.' !Ka advised him where to find buried ostrich eggs in the event he ran out of water. Then the clan left and he was on his own, aware that the hollowness in his stomach was far greater than he'd ever felt before.

But !Ka had taught him well. 'A man should know two things,' he had said. 'He should know how to live with others, and he should know how to live with himself. When a man knows these things there is little else he needs.' So he headed east knowing he was bound to the clan by some unseen ribbon of love and this gave him comfort.

He carried the stone in his hunting kit and brought it out often, marvelling at the smooth whiteness of it. Holding it up, if he got it just the right way, reds, blues and greens, topaz and yellow and pure white flashed back. At some stage in the diamond's history it had fractured along a cleavage plane, leaving a perfectly flat surface. It had then split in a different direction inside the stone, creating naturally a reflective angle which absorbed and dissected the sunlight before radiating it back.

Alex assumed he would find others like it, not knowing that the beautiful colours were usually the result of a diamond cutter's skill. The stone he carried, like the one he found as a baby, had been damaged as it was forced upwards from the earth's mantle, altered by chemical changes and subsequently flawed as it was released to solidify in the earth's crust. Not that he would have cared. All he knew was he wanted to find more.

Alone in the desert Alex lived between two worlds. The one in his head was a white world which had his mind watching in bemusement at how he had adapted. The world in his heart was a San world, filled with new knowledge and capabilities he never expected to acquire. His head and his heart enjoyed these worlds, mixing them together and using the best of both. He was never lonely or afraid, never hungry or thirsty. The solitude and space filled him with peace.

The boy in Alex was having an adventure. The man moulded by !Ka made him self-sufficient. But the man emerging from his boyhood eventually started him thinking about where his life was going.

He wanted a farm of his own, he had always known that. He wanted experience—life, girls, parties, fun—he was young and the world awaited him. He wanted what the San had—simple pleasures, contentment, a sense of self-worth. He needed a goal yet he resisted that need at the same time as he accepted it.

'You can't have it both ways,' his white head told him. 'Why not?' his San heart challenged.

The conundrum confused him. He was poised between two worlds. The realisation that the next step he took would set him on his life's path scared him.

'Think,' his head said. 'Draw a list of plus and minus factors for each.'

His heart resisted the idea. 'Sit,' it told him. 'Sit and feel. What makes you smile?'

'Diamonds make me smile,' he thought.

'Why?' his head asked.

'So I can buy what I want.'

'What *do* you want?'

Round and round it went. Just when he believed he'd solved the riddle, the answer skittered away.

It took a horse to provide the solution.

He had been on his own for nine weeks, wandering the desert, looking for something he had no idea how to find, when Nightmare found him, using whatever instinct a horse has for such things. He went to bed one night totally alone and woke in the morning to find he had guests. The stallion, Nightmare and their foal. The young horse, possibly no more than two months old, had his father's deep black colouring. But when he stood in the sun, russet red glowed. He was like a diamond, his colour depended on the sun's angle. So Alex christened him Diamond. The horses hung around his camp for several days before disappearing. Nightmare was showing off her baby. He missed their company.

Loneliness crept up on him slowly. He found himself talking out loud. Young and fit, he thought about sex more and more and his body responded with a yearning he found irresistible. Watching the silver planes fly overhead, on their way to South Africa or Europe, he imagined the people in them and a strange hungry feeling came to him. With a sense of deep sadness, he realised it was time for him to go. His head had won.

It took him two weeks to find the clan. 'You are as my father,' he said to !Ka that night around the cooking fire.

!Ka nodded and smiled. 'You are as my son.'

'You have taught me many things. I have come to understand your ways and my heart tells me they are good ways. And yet I have other words in my heart.' !Ka had told him that the Bushmen thought and felt with their hearts. Their heads were there for only one reason: to give them a headache.

'And what is your heart saying?'

'I must go and be with my own.'

!Ka sucked on his pipe, saying nothing.

Alex waited.

'Come.' !Ka rose. 'We will talk with the others.'

He sat with the rest of the men around the fire. !Ka addressed them. '!Oma is listening to the voice in his heart. It is telling him it is time to go.'

Heads nodded. This was nothing new to them. Individuals came and went to and from the clans for various reasons, sometimes simply from a desire to move on.

'!Oma's heart is like that of the elephant-girl.'

Alex agreed, delighted with the comparison. It was exactly how he felt.

The elephant-girl was, according to San beliefs, sometimes married to an elephant. At other times she was married to the older brother of the Great God's only two sons. Alex had never been able to understand this. If the Great God had only two sons, how could she be married to one who does not exist? And why can't she make up her mind between a man and an elephant? He had asked !Ka more than once to explain but !Ka could not. The story was one he accepted but did not question.

!Ka, by comparing Alex to the elephant-girl, showed he understood the confusion in Alex. He set out to reassure him. 'Look, !Oma, can you see the backbone of the sky?' !Ka pointed upwards.

Alex looked up. The clarity of the Milky Way out in the desert always impressed him. It appeared to sit just over their heads. 'I see it, Father.'

'Can you see it tomorrow when you wake from your sleep?'

'No, Father.'

'Does that mean it is not there?'

'No, Father. It is always there.'

!Ka drew on his pipe. 'It will always be there, my son, even if you cannot see it.'

N!ou leaned towards Alex. 'Remember, *!ebili*, the solitary male buck is easy to kill. He is morose. He has no interest in others. He is very often fat. He forgets that which he saw as soon as he sees it. He does not smell like the rest so he cannot join them. I do not think that you are abnormal like the solitary one.'

Alex had his answer.

Be brought him his clothes. He had grown and filled out and he found them uncomfortable after the freedom of wearing nothing more than a duiker skin loin flap. Using pieces of animal skin, it took almost a week to stitch and sew extra space into his clothes. Be helped and was very proud of the result. He knew he must look very strange but did not care.

When he said goodbye there was a lump in his throat. As he set off into the vastness of the Kalahari, he wondered if he would ever see them again.

Nine days later he walked into Molepolole, a sprawling traditional village some thirty miles northwest of Gaberones, his heart thumping with excitement. Black children saw him and ran alongside, laughing and pointing. Not with malice but with insatiable curiosity. He was not like any white man they had ever seen. When he entered the general store and saw the face of the white man behind the counter, he realised he was about to speak English to someone else for the first time in almost eighteen months.

Marvin Moine had seen plenty of strange sights in his twenty-eight years. A South African, he had joined the regular army there when he was twenty. He trained as a mechanic and then, aged twenty-four, had been seconded to the Defence Research Unit which was testing new ways to render army vehicles impervious to the destructive forces of landmines.

An experiment had gone badly wrong and Marvin had been trapped under a deflector plate which had parted company with the remotely controlled test vehicle during an explosion.

The outcome of this was a permanent limp, a large compensation payout, an honourable discharge, and a revised approach to life. At twenty-six Marvin—his friends called him Marv—went, to coin his own phrase, 'walkies'.

His travels led him eventually into Bechuanaland. For Marvin, it was love at first sight. He worked for a spell up in the Okavango Delta, acting as general dogsbody to one of the safari companies. When the hunting season ended, he tried setting up his own service station in the small town of Palapye but he wasn't ready for that kind of commitment and he quickly sold it again. Eight months ago his wanderings had taken him to Molepolole where he was employed as a mechanic and store assistant by Jacob van Zyl who owned the general trading store, cum garage, cum bottle shop, cum chemist. Jacob had taken one look at Marv and, correctly, deduced he would have to go a long way to find another such transparently honest, hard-working and capable employee.

Before coming to Bechuanaland, Marv's walkies had taken him to some of southern Africa's most remote places. He had met and mixed with some of southern Africa's hardest characters. He took one look at Alex and tried to throw him out.

Alex's hair, wild and tangled, had been hacked off occasionally with a sharp knife but it grew to his shoulders in a mess of uncombed, sun-bleached curls. His beard also showed the effects of sporadic attacks with the same instrument. Clothing, lovingly patched by himself and Be, nonetheless looked ragged and makeshift. He had smeared tsamma ointment over his face to protect his skin and !Ka had wiped his own perspiration over his head to protect him. Alex had not seen much water on his trek, apart from enough to drink and, although it was June and not yet searingly hot in the desert, nine days without a wash left a lot to be desired. Not to put too fine a point on it, he stank as bad as he looked and he looked as bad as he stank.

'Please,' Alex said as Marv propelled him towards the door. 'I need work.'

Jacob van Zyl had been packing a delivery of soft drinks into his coolroom. He popped his head around the door, took in Alex's appearance and drew the same conclusion Marv had.

'Work, jong? What kind of work would a madman like you want?' He approached Alex cautiously.

'I'm not mad. I've walked here from Khutse. I need money. I'm strong, I'll do anything you ask.'

'Get off! No-one walks from Khutse. What do you take me for, an imbecile?'

'It's true. I've been living in the desert.'

'Ach man, you stink.'

'I'll take a bath. It's only sweat. Please, sir.'

Jacob stopped and looked into Alex's eyes. What he saw there startled him. Beneath the tangled hair, in spite of the rank odour and the grime, there was a soul, the essence of which was pure, free and honest. The sum of this boy, he decided, was worth a second look. Deep in the blue–green, a calmness and maturity, a wisdom and compassion, far beyond the youthfulness of those clear eyes. He motioned for Marv to let go of Alex's arm. 'How old are you, boy?'

'Eighteen I think.'

'What the plurry hell you doing wandering around like that? How come you don't know how old you are?' He looked over at Marv. 'What are you standing around here grinning like a loon for? There's work, there's work. Get your heap of bones outside and don't come back until my truck's fixed. Go on. What are you waiting for?'

Marv left, grinning widely.

Alex sensed that the store owner's bark was an act. He took a deep breath. 'I'll tell you the whole story if you like. It's a long one and I'm not mad. Honest.'

The man shook his head. 'I must be mad myself, taking on a boy like you. Get yourself out back, there's a Rhodesian boiler out there with a shower. Get those clothes off, I'll give you some new ones. You can pay me back out of your wages.'

Alex tried to take his hand. 'Thank you, sir. Thank you.'

The man shook him off. 'Get off me. Sus, man, you stink worse than one of them bloody bushmen.' He pointed the way around the back. 'What's your name, boy?'

'Alex Theron.'

'Theron. That's an Afrikaans name.'

'Yes, sir, my father is Afrikaans.'

'Well then boy, speak to me in Afrikaans.'

'I can't, sir. My mother is from Europe. We never spoke it at home.'

'Where's home then, jong?'

'Shakawe.'

The man laughed suddenly. 'My name's Jacob van Zyl. If you're a Theron from Shakawe I guess you must be Danie Theron's son—am I right?'

Pa! God how he would love to see him right now. 'Yes, sir.'

Jacob looked again. His appearance was enough to frighten the hardiest of souls. Yet the gentle wisdom in his eyes, the stance of the boy, his voice—all pointed to someone who respected himself and thus, deserved respect. Above all if he was Danie Theron's son he must be all right. 'You the boy who got lost in the Kalahari when you were a baby?'

It must be true. Why wasn't I told? 'Yes, sir.'

'Guess you got kind of used to them little yellow men then?'

Alex swallowed anger. 'Yes, sir.'

'Well, jong, I need a handyman. Enough work here for six months. After that you can bugger off—understand. I'm not running a bloody charity home.'

'Thank you, sir.'

'You can sleep on the stoep out back. It's enclosed at one end. There's a bed, that's all. Oh, and one more thing. Burn those bloody clothes, jong.'

Marv had his head under the bonnet of an old Ford truck. 'He's right about one thing,' he said as Alex passed him. 'You stink.'

The first free hour Alex got, he sat down and wrote a long letter to his parents. As he wrote, he realised how thoughtless he had been. They would be frantic with worry about him by now.

144

His mother's response, two weeks later, filled him with guilty anguish. Several lines were smeared, as though her tears of relief had fallen on the page. She blessed the Good Lord seven times in three pages. She admonished him and told him she loved him in the one sentence. And she made a point of telling him how much Pa could use his help.

All he had learned while living with the San, all the respect and assistance he had seen afforded to the elderly, all the deference adult children showed their parents, none of it quelled his rising irritation as he read his mother's letter.

She had the knack of stifling, annoying, and laying blame and guilt at his feet, even while she was saying she loved him. His inexperience did not allow him to blame her for it. It had to be his fault.

Alex worked for Jacob for seven months. Despite his gruff manner and his rough words, Jacob van Zyl was a gentle soul who, once Alex had showered, shaved, changed into fresh clothes and allowed Marthe, Jacob's wife, to cut his hair, took him under his wing and treated him as his own son.

As for Marv, he and Alex became good friends. Alex liked the way the older man danced to a different beat from most and was happily unconcerned about those who failed to appreciate him. He was certainly an acquired taste. Rough around the edges, he had a lived-in face and a habit of saying the wrong thing at the wrong time. Men reacted favourably to his practical nature but women simply didn't take to him. Alex thought this a pity because Marv had a lot of love and loyalty in him. His heart was in the right place and he was a big softie, it just took time to know him. Anyone who bothered discovered, as had Alex after several weeks, that beneath the Punchinello exterior there was a penetrating intelligence and a resourceful competence. Sadly, most people wrote him off as a buffoon, a fact Marv was aware of but seemingly unmoved by.

His injured leg gave him a good deal of pain on occasion but all Marv would say was, 'Must be going to rain, my leg's twinging.' Alex grew to like, respect and finally, love like a brother this big, hard, gentle person.

After seven months, and many imploring letters from his mother, Alex could not put off going home any longer. In any case, Jacob had no more work for him.

'About time you saw your parents, jong.' He knew Alex received letters from home.

'You're right, Jacob. It's time I went home.'

'That boy who robbed you. What are you going to do about him?'

Alex shrugged. 'Nothing.'

Jacob looked into his eyes. There was no malice in them. He wondered again at the maturity of someone so young.

Marv shook his hand. 'You'll be back. You and me are going to find diamonds.'

Alex had shown Marv the stone !Ka gave him. Marv was getting bored in Molepolole. Prospecting for diamonds in the Kalahari would do nicely for a while. 'Couple of weeks, Marv. See you then.'

Old man van Zyl grumbled and complained. 'Man must be mad. I take on a lunatic and lose the best mechanic in the country. That's all the thanks I get.'

Alex grinned and hugged him. Jacob had ridiculed their plan but then told them they could have one of the old Land Rovers rusting in his backyard. 'If you can get one of them old buggers to work it's yours. Hell, take two. They're just cluttering up the yard. I'm telling you true, man, I wouldn't ride to my own funeral in one. Bloody unreliable British junk. Bloody British. Bloody uncomfortable that's what they are.'

Marthe dabbed her eyes when he left. 'We'll miss you, Alex.'

'Don't be so plurry silly, woman. Miss him! Why would we miss a madman? You stop that nonsense now.' But Jacob's own eyes were damp when Alex said goodbye. 'You stay in touch you hear. And don't go running off to the plurry desert again. This old ticker couldn't stand another shock like that.'

He knew from his mother's letters that Paul was now in high school in Gaberones. He went to see his brother who was overjoyed by the visit.

'Boy are you going to cop an earful from Mum,' Paul said gleefully. 'Wish I could be there.'

'How are they?'

'Pa's fine. He hurt his back last year but he's okay.'

'And Mum?'

'When she came back from Ghanzi she was worse than ever.'

'She went to Ghanzi?'

'Sure did. Pa tried to talk her out of it but she went anyway. Tore a strip off your boss for taking on a minor. She must have given him a really hard time; he threw her off the property. Didn't stop her, though—she got the cops onto him.'

'She didn't!'

'Truly. She didn't believe it when he said you'd walked off the job. She's had posters all over Gabs and Francistown. Didn't she mention it?'

The guilt was back. 'No, she said nothing about it in her letters. Just the usual . . .'

Paul pulled a face. 'God, grief and guilt.'

'Yeah,' Alex said quietly. 'But this time I deserved it.'

Paul had shot up and was now slightly taller than him. The two of them looked alike, although Paul's hair was straight and dark like Pa's. He was still determined to become an economist.

'Bechuanaland is going to get independence. When that happens, I intend to be here,' he told Alex as they parted.

'Doing what?' Alex wished his own future was as clear.

'Shuffling numbers,' Paul told him seriously. 'Getting numbers to speak to me. It's all the rage.'

Alex laughed. 'What do these numbers say to you?'

'Any damned thing I want them to.'

'That's scary.'

'Nah,' Paul said with all the wisdom and experience of a schoolboy. 'It's the way the world's going.'

Alex stayed at the only hotel, down near the railway station, before catching the train to Francistown. When he walked into the bar he heard a voice saying, 'I'm telling you, boyo, you can stick that bloody drive. It's the last one I'm doing.'

He looked over. Pat had his back to him and was thumping the bar with his fist. Willie was half turned to him, grinning at Pat. Bob, facing him, raised his glass to drink and his eyes met with Alex. 'Jesus Christ!'

Willie looked up, Pat looked around. 'Jesus Christ, mother of Mary.'

Alex was grinning. He walked over to them. 'Meant to tell you this before, Pat, that doesn't make sense.'

Pat grabbed him and pawed his arms and shoulders. 'Where did you spring from? Why did you leave like that? You never even said goodbye.'

'I didn't have much choice.'

'Whaddya mean? Kel said you'd just up and left. Jeff was so angry he refused to talk about it.'

'Is Kel here?' He looked around.

'Kel? Nah! Jeff got rid of him. Bugger had been climbing a tree outside Madison's room. Jeff caught him at it. Bastard was wearing Willie's American boots so he'd get the blame.'

'What'd Jeff do to him?'

'Kicked him off.'

'That's all, just kicked him off?'

'Yeah, why?'

Alex told them what had happened outside Kang.

Pat had violence in his eyes. 'The bastards. They never said. Christ, boyo, you might have died. To think I wasted sympathy on that little shit Kel for what happened to his face.'

'Why? What happened to his face?'

'Fell of his horse. Got a bit banged up,' Pat said vaguely. 'It happened just after you disappeared. Little turd said nothing about Jeff laying into you.'

'Always knew Jeff had a mean streak.' Bob looked troubled. 'He should have said something.'

'Is he with you?' Alex did not want to run into the man. Ever.

'No. He's in Ghanzi. Madison's here, though.'

'What! On the drive!'

Pat laughed at that. 'Madam Madison? Oh dear me no, darling. Much too dirty. She's working here temporary until she leaves for Europe.'

'Where's she working?'

'Now there you're at it again, boyo. Haven't the past few years taught you anything?'

Alex grinned. 'Yeah. They've taught me that Madam Madison and her bloody father can fall off the edge of the world.'

'Well, that's a relief.' Pat stopped and looked at Willie. Willie looked back.

'What? What?' They were looking over his shoulder.

'Actually, boyo, she's just walked in.'

He spun around. At nineteen, Madison Carter was more beautiful that his wildest imagination could conjure. She had seen the men, smiled and waved. Then she was walking towards them. He watched her. Dark hair falling like silk to her jawline. Smooth skin, tanned lightly. Dark grey eyes. Those breasts, hidden under a snowy white blouse. Tiny waist. Slim hips. Legs that went on forever.

'Hi there.' She smiled from Pat to Bob to Willie.

'Hello, Madison. What brings you here?'

'Dad phoned. He said you'd be in town.' She looked pointedly at Alex.

He stared at her. Did she know what her father had done?

She stared back, a small frown marring the smooth perfection of her brow, as though she was trying to remember something.

God, she's beautiful.

'Like a drink, Madison? Beer's very cold here. Best in Bechuanaland.' Pat was babbling to cover the awkward silence.

He wanted to hate her. She tried to bridge the gulf growing between them. 'Dad would like to see you again. He owes you an apology.'

Anger at Jeff burned in his gut. With an effort he pushed it away. He had learned much from !Ka. He accepted that anger led to violence and violence led to sorrow and the way to avoid sorrow was to have no anger in the first place. But, while this belief was etched in !Ka's soul, it only sat in Alex's heart and he had to work at it. 'Your father can go to hell, Miss Carter.'

She flushed, angry and embarrassed. 'It was a mistake.'

'No. Half killing me was the mistake. He should have finished the job.'

'He didn't . . . Dad wouldn't . . . he said he fired you.'

Alex laughed cynically. 'Your father beat a sixteen-year-old kid half to death and left him in the desert. Like I said, Miss Carter, your father can go to hell.'

She was still staring at him. 'You're lying,' she said coldly.

He shrugged. 'Suit yourself.' Slowly and deliberately he raked his eyes down her body and then, with a small smile, turned his back on her. He knew it was madness. What had happened had not been her fault. And God she was beautiful. He turned back, ready to apologise.

'Dad was right about you.' Her voice was clipped and hard, hatred blazing in her eyes. 'You're nothing but a lout.'

'He's not a lout, Madison,' Pat said quietly. 'He took a terrible beating from your father for nothing. He was a kid. If anyone's a lout . . .'

'It's us,' Willie said quickly, before Pat could jeopardise his job.

She tossed her head. 'Well, I can see I'm not wanted here. Good night.' She turned and quickly crossed the floor, not looking back.

'What are you up to now?' Pat asked, grabbing his jaw and forcing his head away from Madison's exit.

'Between jobs. I thought I'd go home for a bit. It's been a long time.' It was hard to talk with his jaw being squeezed. 'Let go, Pat, before my teeth pop out.'

Pat let go. 'You're not going anywhere, boyo. Not yet. We're in town for two more days. You're with us.'

It seemed that Carter's Crazy Crowd knew every damned person in Gaberones. They lurched from one party to another, from one bar to another. Pat seemed determined to drink every house dry and bed every woman he met. On the second night Alex found himself at the home of yet another acquaintance of Pat's. He had been drinking most of the afternoon and was well on his way to being drunk when Madison walked in with a man. She came directly to him and, just as directly, got straight to the point.

'I've been talking to Dad. He said to tell you he's sorry. I'm sorry too. I didn't think he would do anything like that.'

He looked at her blearily, respecting her courage for coming to him. 'Forget it.' He wished he didn't feel so out of control.

'I can't. What he did was shocking. I can't stop thinking about it.'

'Do me a favour.' Why did she have to keep moving?

'What?'

'Please get me some coffee.'

He never did discover who she arrived with. He drank black coffee for several hours and sobered up. Madison seemed content to sit and talk with him.

His time with !Ka and the clan had taught him many things. Among them, not to put off something which causes you to quake with fear. As !Ka had reasonably pointed out, there is no use in worrying about that which may never happen or, if it is going to happen, that which you cannot prevent from happening. It is always best to face extreme fear with action. So he did. 'Can I take you home?'

Hesitation. 'All right.'

That hadn't hurt a bit. 'What about . . .'

'Forget him.'

152

!Ka had taught him something else: 'I shall eat' is not 'I have eaten'; 'I have eaten' is that which is in the stomach. But he forgot those wise words in his excitement at finally, finally getting close to Madison without her hating him.

He said goodbye to Pat and the others. 'Stay in touch, boyo.'

'I will.'

'Watch her. She's still her father's daughter.'

'She's over eighteen. Daddy can go to hell.'

'That's not what I mean.' Pat looked troubled. 'She's not a one-nighter. You tangle with her you're likely to find it's permanent.'

'Jesus, mother of Mary, Pat. I'm only taking her home.'

Pat raised his eyebrow knowingly. But all he said mildly was 'That doesn't make sense, boyo.'

She offered him coffee at her place but he had sobered up and, after the black coffee at the party, felt thirsty. 'Rather have a beer.'

She got two.

'How long have you been living in Gabs?' He and Marv travelled the thirty miles of dirt road between Molepolole and Gaberones most weekends. While they enjoyed the quieter aspects of the rural village, the action in the capital beckoned between Friday and Sunday. He wondered why he hadn't bumped into her.

'I've only just arrived.' She took a swig from her bottle. Her hair swung back as she tilted her head. It was the action of a tomboy, not the Madam Madison he remembered.

'Are you planning to stay here?'

'No.' Her hair swung forward, framing her face. 'I'm leaving for Maun next month.'

'What to do?'

'Working for Game Department. It's only temporary, just till I go to Europe, but I like it.'

'Is that what you do here in Gabs?'

She was looking at him with curiosity. 'You seem different from how I remember.'

'I'm older.'

'No, that's not it.' She swigged her beer and he watched her hair. 'I thought you were nothing more than a thug.'

'The fight you mean?'

'Yes.'

He asked for that. 'I'm not proud of it, I lost my temper, but he really did have it coming. I don't like fighting, Madison, but sometimes, like then, well there are principles involved.' He told her about Nightmare and the stick and then he found himself telling her about Nightmare and the stallion and all the time he spoke he was aware she was watching him and listening with interest, not dislike.

'You actually lived with the Bushmen?'

'Yes.'

'What are they like?'

So he told her that too. He talked about their gentleness, their respect for nature and each other, their love of children, their sense of loyalty and their understanding of how the world and their bodies work, despite having no education. She watched his face, smiling sometimes, nodding at others. 'You can't help but be influenced by them,' he said finally. 'Their way of life makes more sense than anything else I've seen.'

She put down her beer. 'Alex, you talk too much.'

He put down his. 'You make me nervous.'

She rose. 'Why?'

He rose and moved towards her. 'You're so damned beautiful.'

She laughed up at him. Her body leaned into his. Her breasts brushed his chest. Her face was turned up to his. He lowered his head. Electric currents threatened to stop his heart. It started gently, but her soft lips and the tip of her tongue weakened his legs and had blood pounding in his head. He tightened his arms around her and crushed her into him, and the kiss deepened and his heart was thumping wildly, so wildly he could hear it.

She pulled away. 'Alex, wait. This is too fast.' The intensity of his kiss disturbed her. 'That was no ordinary kiss.'

He pulled her back. 'No. This is right. It's been coming a long time.' He kissed her again, a long, lingering kiss, and felt her reluctance dissolve as desire flooded both their bodies and she kissed him back with a growing urgency that left him drowning in liquid warmth.

When at last they pulled apart he looked deeply into her eyes and saw the need in her, but he also saw apprehension. He realised that while he had woken the woman, the lingering child was unsure. He was not very experienced but instinct told him to take her gently from where she was poised or he would frighten her. His hand brushed her hair softly back from her face. 'Are you sure, Madison?' he whispered.

Her eyes were searching his, looking for reassurance. Doubt and confusion were being replaced by a myriad of surging emotions which she had, up till now, suppressed. 'Yes,' she whispered back finally.

He put out his hand and she took it, like a trusting child. He felt tremors of desire and nervousness in her fingers. He tugged gently on her hand and she came to him, her eyes never leaving his. He wrapped her in his arms and held her against him, allowing her to feel his intent, giving her one last chance to change her mind, but she stayed in his arms and her ragged breath told him she was as committed as he. 'Come,' he said, leading her towards the bedroom.

They stood facing each other at the foot of her bed. Gazing into her clear grey eyes which were rimmed with a blue so deep that the outer edges looked violet, Alex saw her trust in him and it touched him more deeply than anything he had ever felt before. Slowly, gently, he unbuttoned her blouse and she shrugged out of it so it fell to the floor in a whisper of silk. Her lacy brassiere joined it seconds later and he bent his head and sucked first one, then the other nipple so they hardened and she moaned with the unfamiliar sensations which burned at the very core of her sensuality.

Holding back his own need, Alex undressed her completely, his hands gentle on her burning skin, his tongue finding soft corners until he knew, by her trembling and tiny sounds of pleasure, that she was ready for him, that she wanted him as urgently as he wanted her.

In his eyes, Madison was perfect and he wanted to make this perfect for her and so he took her far beyond a state of readiness. He took her soaring in a sky filled with wonderful new feelings until the woman emerging in her reached a pulsating pinnacle of pleasure and she went spiralling down into a warm sea filled with wonder and contentment and, above all, a need as old as time itself to have his body joined to hers. When he entered her she cried out, a throaty deep cry of longing fulfilled, an animal growl of the sweetest of delight and she moved with him as though she were a part of him and they reached the pinnacle together, and together they plunged into the warm contented sea, and together they lay as one with their hearts and minds as joined as their bodies.

'Madison,' he whispered when he could. 'That was beautiful.'

'I had no idea,' she said softly, her breath still fluttering in her throat. 'I feel so alive, so free.' Her fingernails traced gentle patterns on his back, giving him goose bumps. 'It's like I've been flung off a roller coaster and suddenly find I can fly.'

He rolled off her and lay on his back, staring upwards. His limited experience with girls had not prepared him for the way he was feeling. For the first time he did not want to get up and go. The conversation girls seemed to need after lovemaking, something he shied from because it always seemed that they were seeking commitment, was now what he wanted. 'That was your first time,' he said. 'I didn't hurt you did I?'

'No.' He heard puzzlement in her voice. 'Everyone says it hurts but it didn't.'

'I'm glad.'

He gathered her up in his arms, a need in him to hold her close, to feel the softness of her against his body. She snuggled into him and they lay together in silent wonder, the magic of their shared intimacy around them like a cloak of fulfilment. Alex wanted to hold her like this forever.

Finally she stirred. 'Alex,' she said softly, hesitantly, 'can we talk about Dad?'

He was too full of new feelings to understand that *she* needed his forgiveness for her father's actions so that she could forgive her father herself. Her question should have alerted him that, in this regard, she was vulnerable; that for someone as proud as Madison, this vulnerability was intolerable and that her question was another form of trust. But Alex didn't want to talk about her father. The beating he received, the callous indifference to whether he lived or died, always made him angry. Besides, lying naked next to her, the only thing he wanted was to touch her again and again, hold her close to him, feel her heart beating against his.

'Forget it,' he said, harder than intended in the usual rush of anger. 'It's done. It's over. Nothing can change it. Just forget it.'

She sat up. 'Don't tell me to forget it.' She got off the bed and pulled on a robe. 'I'm trying to understand it.' She moved to the dressing table and attacked her hair with a brush so stiff that Alex could hear the crackle of electricity. 'He's my father,' she said between strokes of the brush. 'He did something terrible, something I would never have expected of him. Surely you can see why I want to talk about it.'

Alex rose and pulled on his clothes, cursing her father for having spoiled the mood. He spoke without thinking. 'Your father is pathological about keeping you pure. The thought that I had been spying on you through your bedroom window was too much for him. He lost control. That's all there was to it.'

She stopped brushing her hair and stared at him. 'What do you mean, pathological?' Her tone should have warned him.

'He told all the men to keep away from you. You are his princess. Most fathers want to protect their daughters but yours went overboard.' Anger triumphed over his attempt to stay calm and he took it out on her. 'If your father had his way you'd still be a virgin when you were fifty.'

A look of pure hate crossed her face. 'Is that why you seduced me?' She stood up, breathing hard. 'I trusted you and all the time it was to get even with my father.' A tear of rage slid down her cheek. 'You used me, you bastard. Get out. Go back to the gutter where you belong.'

He was shattered she believed that. 'Madison, that's not true.' He took a step towards her. 'I didn't use you.' He only just ducked in time to avoid the hairbrush she flung at him. 'Madison, for God's sake calm down.'

'Dad was right about you.' Her eyes blazed. 'You're not good enough for me.'

For Alex, whose emotions had run the gauntlet from elation to anger, that was the final straw. 'You're not so special, Miss Carter, and I was good enough for you ten minutes ago. I didn't hear you yelling rape.' He turned to go. 'To hell with you,' he grated over his shoulder. 'You're nothing but a spoilt brat. Who needs it.'

Slamming her front door he strode angrily into the night. It was a long walk back to the hotel. Her words, 'you're not good enough for me' burned in him. He'd covered a quarter of the distance before it struck him that someone like Madison would hardly give herself to someone she felt was beneath her, that her angry words were a cover for hurt. He considered going back to apologise then discarded the idea. He'd blown it. He called himself a fool for the rest of the way back to the hotel.

TEN

His train from Francistown left at midday and so, in the morning he went back to see Madison. He had to. He could not live with the knowledge that she believed he had used her. He got two words out. 'Madison, I . . .'

'Nothing,' she said coldly, 'you could say is of any interest. Last night was a mistake. I intend to forget it.' Her eyes glinted in anger. 'Take some good advice, Alex Theron, and stick with your own class.' She started to shut the door in his face then added, 'Don't kid yourself that last night meant anything. It didn't. I never want to speak to you again.' The door slammed shut, leaving him standing in speechless helplessness.

'At least I tried,' he thought as the train pulled out of Gaberones station. But he was saddened. Last night had shown him a different Madison Carter, or had it? Who was the *real* Madison Carter? He stared at the passing countryside as the train gathered speed. Whoever she was she hated him as much now as she ever did, that much was clear. He would never be able to get around that fact. 'Put her out of your mind, boyo,' Pat had once advised him. Slumped in his seat, with anger slowly replacing the bewilderment in him, Alex decided to do just that.

Shakawe was just as he remembered it: sleepy, flat, pale grey sand, an atmosphere as if time had somehow passed this way and decided not to stop. Wright's trading store, however, was proudly sporting a new roof. The same African woman was behind the counter. '*Dumela mma*,' he greeted her.

'*Duméla rra*.' She did not recognise him. Hardly surprising; last time he saw her he was still at school.

'How is the grumpy old elephant you married?' he asked in Setswana.

Once when he was too young to know better, she overheard him telling Pa that he liked the lady who worked in the shop but her husband, who was also employed there, was like a grumpy old elephant. He had been horrified when he realised she had heard his words, even though she had laughed so hard tears rolled down her cheeks. On his next visit to the trading store, while his mother discussed the purchase of some cloth with the woman, he had been down the back among the tiers of buckets, rolls of hosepipe and jumbled piles of boots when the most fearful apparition leapt out at him from behind a rack of dresses. Her husband, with a watering can on his head, a large dark-coloured raincoat draped over it so only the spout stuck out where his nose should be, and trumpeting in a fashion he supposed was like an elephant but in fact sounded more like a demented, adenoidal pig, chased him through the shop, out the door, off the verandah and into the dusty street.

Alex had not forgotten. As he stood quaking in the street he had watched the piggy-looking apparition remove the raincoat and watering can to reveal a grinning African face and his five-year-old heart swore revenge. The two of them had spent the next ten years trying to give each other a fright. When Alex was fifteen and home for the holidays, he

161

planned spectacular success with a bucket of water he'd rigged over the door of the outside toilet. The toilet, as everybody knew, was there for the convenience of customers but was used, almost exclusively, by Pig Face—as Alex now privately thought of him—and his wife. The only trouble was, old Mr Wright who owned the store had been caught short and used the toilet first. Alex was hanging around, dying for old Pig Face to take a leak before his mother finished her shopping, when he heard a bellow followed, minutes later, by the appearance of a very soggy and very angry Mr Wright at the door.

Pig Face knew the water was meant for him. Mr Wright was yelling blue murder about catching the little bastard who did this and Alex was trying to make himself invisible behind a heap of second-hand tyres. Pig Face opened a side door and ushered him out. 'No more,' he whispered. 'We're even.'

He had never given Alex away. The two of them had become firm friends.

The woman looked at him closely. 'Ah, ah, ah, young Alex. My, how you've grown.' She laughed and clapped her hands. 'What a big man you have become. Just wait until my husband sees you. He would not be able to scare you now.'

Alex asked if anyone was going in the direction of the farm. Not that it was likely—the only people who travelled along that road were the occasional tourists who came to see the Tsodilo Hills. Alex had been lucky enough to get a lift with two African school teachers from Francistown to Maun and then, after half a day hanging around Riley's Hotel in Maun, a delivery truck had brought him all the way to Shakawe. But the driver was anxious to return to Maun now and not willing to go out of his way.

The woman clapped her hands, delighted she could help.

'But your father will be here this morning. I am getting an order ready for him to pick up. He will be here soon.'

Alex felt a nervous flutter in his stomach. It would be so good to see his father again but he knew he had stayed away too long. He had considered letting his parents know he was coming but, in the end, decided against it; perhaps his mother would be so surprised she would forget to harp.

Alex sat on the verandah of the shop and waited for Pa. He thought of everything that had happened since he last sat there. The death of his friends at school, the friendships formed at Jeff Carter's, the beating, !Ka and Be and their small clan, Jacob and Marv, and finally, of Madison. He was nineteen years old and, it seemed to him, his experiences over the past two and a half years were all intricately weaving his future. Then, shading his eyes, he looked along the deeply rutted track which ran through the village of Shakawe and saw . . . nothing.

His future was not here, of that he was certain.

The hippo were in full-throated bliss in the river. He didn't hear the vehicle over their grunting arguments until it was nearly at the trading store. Alex did not recognise the truck but Pa was driving. He sat where he was, watching his father climb out. He seemed stiff, as though his back hurt. He had aged, there were lines on his face. He still wore the same old battered hat. Alex watched while Pa rummaged in his pocket for his pipe, stopping beside the truck to stuff it full of tobacco, jamming it between his teeth, lighting it with his hand cupped around the bowl. Every action seemed slower than Alex remembered. Satisfied the pipe was lit, Pa went up the steps past him, not even glancing in his direction.

'Pa!'

His father slowed, stopped, turned. 'Alex?' He was incredulous. 'Alex? Is that you?'

'Yes, Pa.' He stood. 'It's me at last.'

'Son!' It was a shout of pure joy.

They hugged and his father felt frail. Alex could feel the sobs Pa tried to suppress. For the first time, he realised what it must have been like for his parents. He felt deeply ashamed. 'How's Mum?' He pulled away, not wanting to dwell on the hurt he must have caused.

'Still the same.' Pa was beaming at him, his face split in two in his happiness. 'Where did you come from? How long have you got? Oh, son, there's so much to tell you.'

'No-one,' Alex thought, '. . . should have their love for another rewarded this way. What a prick I've been.' He pulled his father close again. 'I've missed you, Pa.'

His father wiped his eyes. 'Come on, son, let's load up and get home. Mum will be thrilled to see you.'

They had to stop at Ndete's tree for meat. Watching Pa fuss over the selection he wondered how many cattle had found their way to Ndete's wooden table to be cut up and sold to the inhabitants of Shakawe. He knew it was the African way but, after the butcher shop in Gaberones, and the hygienically refrigerated coolroom at Jacob's, and even the efficient distribution of meat among the clan, the sight of hundreds of flies clustered over the carcass and milling in the pools of blood on the ground made him feel slightly queasy.

Pa talked nonstop on the drive home. Familiar country passed and then they were on Pa's land, and the roan-coloured cattle, skinny and desperate, were pulling at the unappetising grasses which grew in clumps in the sickly-looking sand. The Tsodilo Hills sat, squat and mysterious in the distance.

The house looked just the same except the verandah roof sagged a little in the middle. And then there was Mum, coming out of the door to help Pa with the groceries. Her blonde hair was a little duller, she was plumper, but she moved lightly on her feet with the same swinging walk he remembered. He jumped out and went towards her. 'Oh Lord, thank you, Lord. My son. My son has returned. Thank you, Heavenly Father.'

Well, some things never change.

Within ten minutes he felt he had never left. Pa was still planning to fix the old shed. Mum pottered in the kitchen blessing the Lord and supervising whatever maid she currently employed. Alex went to open the door of his room. 'Don't go in there.' Mum was behind him. 'We have a guest. She's using your room. You'll have to use Paulie's. Still, if you'd let us know you were coming . . .'

'Who?' He cut her off.

'You don't know her. Chrissy Cameron. Remember Reverend Frith? He's back in England now but he suggested she contact us. Apparently they're cousins. She's renting the room.'

'Why?' He was intrigued. Why would someone rent a room out here?

'She's working here.'

'Here! On the farm?'

Mum smiled grimly. 'Don't be silly, Ali, where would we find that kind of money?'

'Where is she now?'

'She goes to the Hills every day. She's an anthropologist out from England. She's cataloguing the cave paintings.'

'On her own!' The Tsodilo Hills were the centre of much folklore and superstition. The Kung had told Alex how the spirits of the dead whispered through the crevices and caves, trying to trick the living into joining them. He had heard the sound once. The low moaning and rustle as a breeze went scurrying to places too small for any human to follow. It had given him goose bumps when he was twelve. It probably still would.

He lost interest in the intrepid anthropologist. 'I saw Paul in Gaberones.'

'He's doing well. With independence coming he expects to be offered a job in Gabs when they set up the new Ministry of Commerce and Industry. Of course he has to get through university first.' She spoke as though she hadn't heard him.

'I know, Mum. I saw him.'

'Can you stay, Ali? Your father . . .'

'Mum,' he said as gently as he could. 'I love you and Pa very much but I can't stay.' He put his hands on her shoulders and looked down at her. He had always thought her beautiful. She was still beautiful but her eyes seemed somehow empty. 'Please try to understand. My life is for me to decide.'

'The Lord decides, Ali,' she said primly.

'Old ones know so much more than you and me,' !Ka had said. 'And that is why, when the old ones speak, we listen. They are giving us the gift of their years. If we do not listen then they might as well not have lived and that, my son, would be a tragedy because, if they had not lived tell me, where would that leave us?'

'Oh !Ka,' Alex thought. 'What would your wisdom make of my mother?' But he kissed the top of her head and said, 'Of course He does, Mum, but I think He has other plans for me.'

'I'll go and see to dinner.' Her strangely empty eyes brimmed with unshed tears.

'I wonder what it's like . . .' he thought sadly, '. . . to live with a heart filled with disappointment and a head which believes the only truth to be had is that which you read in the Bible.'

He was sitting outside with Pa when the anthropologist returned. He had expected a stumpy old lady with a hearty personality. The willowy girl with the short-cropped bright red hair, amber eyes, tip-tilted nose and quite the most kissable mouth he had ever seen took him by surprise. When Pa introduced them she stuck out her hand and gave him an unexpectedly firm handshake. 'Hi there. The prodigal returns I see.'

Chrissy Cameron was actually Scottish. She had a lilting accent which went up and down at odd times. It was very attractive and so was she. When she smiled her eyes crinkled at the corners. When she laughed, which she did often, she threw back her head revealing a long white neck. Her carroty-coloured hair was too bright to be anything other than natural. Besides, her brows were a darker version, and the hairs on her arms were too. Her skin was finely freckled, or as much of it as he could see. She was liberally smeared with zinc cream. He liked her immediately.

Over dinner she talked about her work. 'I've nearly finished. Only a couple of weeks to go. I'll be sorry to leave here, it's so peaceful.'

'Where will you go, back to the UK?' Alex put a fork of beef stew into his mouth, savouring the taste. His mother's cooking was as excellent as he remembered.

'No, I'm based in Gabs. I'm on secondment from the Natural History Museum in London. My specialty is primitive art. When this country gets independence they intend to

167

have a combined museum and art gallery. My job is to list and photograph the rock paintings and then come up with some sort of display. The field work is nearly finished but I still have about two years' work ahead of me to put it all together.' She grinned across the table at him. 'Finding the stuff is one thing. Researching it takes forever.'

He was glad she was not leaving the country.

He changed the subject. 'Everyone's talking about independence. I thought Britain was going to hand this country over to the South Africans.'

'The South Africans thought so too,' Pa said. 'But the people here don't want that and neither does Britain. Seretse Khama is the man to watch, you mark my words. He's got a lot of support, and not only from the Bamangwato. The other tribes like him too.'

'A black man running the country. Never heard such rubbish. What does he know?' Mum was still smarting from Alex's request that she keep the grace short.

'I met him once,' Pa said. 'He's a moderate. Very committed to a peaceful handover. He and that farmer fellow, Quett Masire, apparently put forward a very detailed plan of action. They want elections next year. Elections! That's almost unheard of in Africa.' Pa shook his head. 'He's got my vote that's for sure.'

'How does he feel about South Africa?' Chrissy was taking note of Pa's words. Alex liked that. Pa had a lot to say when he cared to say it.

'He's against apartheid. He has no time for Verwoerd and his policies. He's also against Ian Smith and his plans for a Unilateral Declaration of Independence. But he's treading a fine line. He can't be seen to be actively against them. He's too reliant on South Africa and Rhodesia for food.'

'What's the future for whites?' Chrissy asked.

'We shouldn't have to worry. As you know Seretse Khama has an English wife. Okay, the British messed him around horribly but that's in the past. Seretse knows he must work with the current administration, not confront it. He's already said he will honour existing freehold land ownership. Residents will be invited to take citizenship when we become Botswana.' Pa put down his knife and fork. 'Lovely meal, Pets.'

'Botswana? That makes more sense.' Alex liked the name. After all, a person living in Bechuanaland was known as a Motswana, the people collectively were Batswana and their language was Setswana.

'You talk about elections,' Chrissy said. 'Will they be fair?'

'As far as I can tell,' Pa answered. 'There are three main players. The People's Party, the Independence Party and Khama's Democratic Party. Dr Motsete is also expected to run as an independent but he doesn't stand a chance. He's Malawian for starters.'

Chrissy sipped at her glass of water. 'What's Seretse Khama's background?' She put down the glass. 'Is he qualified to run the country?'

'I don't know much,' Pa told her. 'He was studying . . . law I think it was . . . in Britain. When he married Ruth it set off all kinds of alarms.'

'Why, because she's white?'

'Yes. His uncle, Tshekedi Khama, was acting chief of the Ngwato until Seretse could complete his studies. He felt that tribal customs had been compromised. After all, any son Seretse had would inherit the chieftainship. That's the custom. If that son were half white would the Ngwato accept him?'

'Would a half white son accept the Ngwato?' Alex commented.

'I see the problem,' Chrissy said.

'That's not all. Back then, South Africa was asking for Bechuanaland to be absorbed into the Union. They couldn't possibly accept a marriage like Seretse and Ruth's.' Pa smiled sadly at Peta but she looked down at her plate. 'With their apartheid policies and rules, Seretse and Ruth were breaking the law. The only course of action left to South Africa, if Bechuanaland became theirs, would have been to throw the two of them into prison. Imagine the outcry from around the world?'

'How did the problem get resolved?'

Pa got a twinkle in his eye. 'Britain did what the British do best. They exiled Seretse. They figured if he were out of sight the problem would go away.'

'But it didn't,' Chrissy said.

'Seretse solved it himself. He renounced his rights to chieftainship which reconciled him with his uncle. He worked tirelessly to convince the British not to hand Bechuanaland over to the South Africans. As soon as Britain made it plain that *they* would administer this country the problem of Seretse's marriage went away. Seretse came back here and now serves as vice-chairman of the Ngwato Council.'

'He's obviously cut out for public life.' Chrissy handed her plate to the servant with a smile of thanks. 'I wonder what motivates him; the quest for power or a sense of duty?'

'Motivates him!' Pa thought for a moment. 'The winds of change,' he quoted Harold Macmillan. 'The time has come. Britain has taken countries like Nyasaland and Bechuanaland to the edge. The people are now ready to jump. Seretse

Khama is the rightful chief of the majority tribe. He's intelligent and well educated. I'm only guessing here, Chrissy, but I'd say a sense of duty is probably what motivates him.'

'It can't be easy for him being married to an English woman. Do the people accept her?'

'They do now,' Pa told her. 'She's gone out of her way to learn the language and customs.'

Mum looked disapprovingly at Pa. 'It's disgusting. A white woman living like a native. It can't work.'

'It's been known to work,' Pa said quietly and with infinite sadness. 'It just requires a bit of give and take.'

Alex realised that a second conversation was taking place at the table. 'Is this why Mum's the way she is?' he wondered. 'All because Pa's great-grandmother married someone with a bit of black blood?' He shook off the idea. It had to be more than that.

After dinner Mum took her Bible into the lounge. Chrissy briefly joined the men on the verandah but excused herself saying she had to be up early. 'Sleep tight,' Pa said.

Alex saw her face soften as she smiled at him.

Alex didn't see much of Chrissy during his stay. **She** went out at first light and returned at dusk. She then **spent** several hours in her room working, only coming out for **dinner** and then going to bed early. The little he saw of her interested him. He liked the way she fitted in with his family, as if she were one of them. She treated his mother with gentle respect and sometimes sat chatting with her as she bustled around the kitchen. She clearly had a soft spot for his father. She often asked him questions and always listened intently to his replies.

Where Madison seemed like a constant challenge, Chrissy felt like a pair of comfortable slippers. 'No! That's not fair.' He laughed at the comparison. 'Chrissy is just so easy to be with.' He decided he wanted to see more of her. He put Madison out of his mind. She hated him. She believed he had made love to her, taken her virginity, for no other reason than to get even with her father. There was no way he could convince her otherwise. He thought of !Ka's words.

'When you choose a wife, *!ebili*, always remember that you and she will cry together over great sadness and laugh together over great happiness. These things are easy. Even strangers can do these things. It is the time between good and bad events that are hardest. The woman you choose should think like you, do like you and be like you so that when you are between the excitement of sad and happy times you and she can share the silence. If silence does not sit easily between two people they fill it with empty words. People tire of empty words and grow angry and tell lies. Test your woman with the silence, *!ebili*. See if she becomes angry.'

Ruefully, Alex realised that Madison didn't need silence to grow angry. The mere sight of Alex would probably do it.

He spent his days with Pa. Alex had to examine every corner of the farm, every part of the house. Pa dragged him from one end to the other. When he proudly showed him the cattle yards, Alex didn't have the heart to tell him he'd seen them before, that they had been completed before he left school. Mum, once she had recovered from his sudden appearance, acted as though he had never left. Pa couldn't bear to let him out of his sight. Alex realised he was lonely. 'It can't be easy,' he thought on his second day, 'living out here with a woman who spouts the Bible from morning to night.'

Pa, however, always loyal to his beloved Peta, only hinted

172

at dissatisfaction after Alex asked him the question he had been burning to ask. 'How did I get lost in the Kalahari, Pa?'

His father looked surprised. 'Who told you about that?'

Alex folded himself to the ground and waited while Pa took a little longer to join him. Then he told his father everything—the beating Jeff had given him, how he was rescued by the Bushmen, and how, after he had been with them a while and learned some of their language, he heard the story of them finding him when he was a baby. 'Why didn't you tell me?' he concluded.

His father looked pained. 'I wanted to.'

'What stopped you, Pa?'

Pa took his time, rummaging for tobacco, stuffing his pipe, lighting it with a match. Finally, 'When I first met your mother she was not . . . well, you know . . . religious. Well, yes she was—' he amended hastily, 'but not like she is now.' He puffed on his pipe slowly. 'We were very much in love,' he said dreamily.

Alex said nothing; !Ka once told him, 'If you break into a man's heart while he is looking backwards, you may never learn what it was he intended to say once he starts looking ahead.'

'That business with you in the Kalahari was peculiar. I've wondered again and again what happened to you.'

'How did I get lost, Pa?' He could hear the tobacco crackle as his father drew deeply on his pipe.

'Back then your mother and I went into the desert every year to hunt. We loved the bush and this yearly hunting trip was our holiday. We'd pack everything but the kitchen sink into the truck and take off for two weeks. It was great fun.'

'What did you hunt?'

'Buck mainly. We were after meat. We'd always come home

with enough biltong to last us months. You cut your teeth on biltong.'

Alex remembered the sun-dried strips of meat which, even if other treats were in short supply, were always available as snacks.

'Did you hunt lions?'

Pa shook his head. 'Never. I don't collect trophies, son. If you can't eat it, don't shoot it. That's my motto.'

Alex thought how like the San his father's philosophy was. But he said nothing.

'You were just over two but as adventurous as hell,' Pa continued. 'Independent too. You'd take yourself off to do whatever it was you wanted to do and, when we'd come to look for you, you wouldn't be there. You'd have gone off somewhere else. When you decided you were sleepy you'd just find somewhere quiet and lie down and have a nap.' Pa laughed. 'We once found you sound asleep in the dog kennel.'

Alex laughed too. He had heard that story before but it always amused him.

Pa frowned suddenly at his pipe. 'That day . . . the one you got lost . . . you'd climbed into the back of the Land Rover and fallen asleep. I had no idea you were there. I went off to try and shoot a springbok. I stopped several times before I picked up fresh spoor. As usual, once I found the spoor I tracked the animals on foot. The rifle was in the cab with me and I had no reason to look in the back. You must have woken up after I left, climbed out and started to look for me. I didn't see your tracks when I came back with the springbok because, well frankly, they'd have been the last thing I'd have expected to see. When I got back to camp your mother asked me where you were.'

'So you came looking for me?'

His father shook his head. 'Not right away. We searched all over the camp site in case you'd done your falling asleep trick. By the time we realised you must have been in the back of the Land Rover it was almost night. Your mother was frantic with worry.' Pa smiled slightly. 'Come to that, son, I wasn't all that unconcerned either. There are a lot of lion out there.'

Alex shivered at the memory of Her With The Bad Foot. !Ka had told him about his near miss.

Danie Theron continued. 'We backtracked my route. When we got to the place where I had stopped to track the springbok we found your shoe print. We also found lion spoor; there must have been fifteen or twenty in the pride and they were headed in the same direction as your prints. By this time the wind was whipping up the sand something fierce but we kept following your footprints. Then the sandstorm hit. I tell you, son, I've never seen anything like it. Your mother and I only just made it back to the truck. We couldn't move. That damned sandstorm blew all night and most of the next day and all we could do was huddle in the bloody truck. Your mother was in a terrible state. I didn't dare leave her. She was six months pregnant with Paul and I had to stay with her. By the time it was safe to leave the truck your footprints had disappeared but we kept looking and calling your name.'

Alex could tell by his father's voice that he was reliving the experience as though it were happening now.

'When we found your shorts and nappy snagged in a thorn bush, son, we both believed you were dead. It was a terrible moment. Your mother sank down next to them and I thought her heart would break.' Pa took a shuddering breath. 'We kept looking for you but there was no trace. The

175

decision to return home, not knowing your fate, was the hardest thing I've ever done.'

'I must have had a guardian angel looking out for me.'

'That's what Mum said when you were returned.'

'I don't understand, Pa. How come you didn't tell me?'

'Your mother was never quite the same after that. She'd been brought up by very religious parents. She sort of turned to religion as a way of easing the pain. When you were returned she saw it as some kind of miracle. She believed her prayers had been answered.' Pa looked over at him and smiled briefly. 'She had this kind of belief that if we spoke about the miracle something bad would happen to you again. I dunno. It was as if she believed that her faith had been tested and to speak of the miracle would be tempting fate. Something like that.'

'I guess I can understand that,' Alex said slowly.

'Don't tell her you know,' Pa said. 'She's still superstitious about it, especially since you vanished and returned a second time.'

'You love her very much don't you, Pa?'

'More than I ever believed possible,' his father said softly. 'Even if . . .' his voice trailed off and Alex let it go. It was his father's business, not his.

On his last day Alex cornered Chrissy before dinner. 'Can I look you up in Gabs?'

'Sure.' She smiled. 'I didn't know you lived there.'

'I don't. I plan to go back to the Kalahari. I'll be in Gabs on and off.'

'I'd like to see the desert.'

'Ever spent time with the Bushmen?'

'I think so.' She sounded doubtful. 'Are the Kung proper Bushmen?'

'There are all kinds of Bushmen. Some live a hunting and gathering life in the desert, some own farms, some, like those in Shakawe, are river Bushmen. The Kung live in the Tsodilo Hills. There are various tribes all over this country, all speaking different dialects. There's been considerable debate as to what classifies a Bushman. A lot of people think they are bound by a common language group; others say it's a cultural thing and only the hunter-gatherers are Bushmen or, as they are also called, San. Still others say it's a biological grouping.' He had her full attention so he continued. 'I tend to go on appearance. The Kung are certainly of Bushman origin although very few of them these days are full-blooded.'

'That explains a lot,' Chrissy said. 'I've met a few in villages near where I'm working. They're different, but not as unsophisticated as I expected.'

'Cross-breeding with Bantu tribes and exposure to tourists has caused that.'

'I'd like to meet some traditional Bushmen; I find them fascinating.'

'You'd have to go into the desert for that. Maybe we can go together some time.'

She gave him a number in Gaberones where he could contact her. She had already left for the Hills the next morning when he said goodbye to his parents.

'Don't leave it so long next time.' It was the closest Pa had come to criticising his long absence. He was rummaging in his pocket as he spoke. 'Here, I've got something for you. Mum and I bought it for your eighteenth birthday. I've kept it. Always knew you'd turn up again. Go on, take it.'

Pa held out his hand. A silver and onyx signet ring lay in his palm, square cut and solid looking.

'Gee Pa, you didn't have to do that.' Alex was not sure he wanted it; a signet ring was not really to his taste. But, there was Pa looking pleased and Mum was smiling and excited and he knew he would wear it to make them happy.

He slipped the ring on his finger. It fitted perfectly. 'Thanks,' he said, feeling awkward. He kissed Mum and hugged Pa and saw their pleasure at giving him the ring. 'Thanks,' he said again, meaning it.

'It might remind you of us, son, bring you home more often, what do you think?'

'I won't stay away so long again, Pa. I promise.'

Mum did a lot of praising and blessing and crying. 'Why do you have to go? Stay here and help your father.'

But he did not want to stay. He found her company a strain and the knowledge made him ashamed.

Pa drove him into Shakawe. 'You're doing the right thing, son. You have to make your own life. Don't mind Mum, she's only thinking of me but I'm fine.'

'Are you, Pa?' Alex thought, watching his father drive away. Then he realised his guilt was gone. And at the same time it occurred to him that he really did love his mother. He just didn't like her very much.

A local staff member of Wenela said he could take Alex as far as Francistown. He planned to see Aunty Dorie there, and maybe even spend a night with her, but he picked up another lift immediately into Gaberones. Tired, he arrived in the capital at six o'clock on Friday evening. He stayed at a friend's house and slept until midday Saturday. When he woke Marv was there, anxious to get out into the desert.

'Hold on, Marv. There's a girl I want to see tonight.'

'Where are we going?'

It was then that Alex discovered that Marv had absolutely no concept of privacy. Reluctant to hurt his feelings, Alex said, 'The hotel.'

'Great,' said Marv. 'They do terrific steaks.'

Chrissy sounded pleased to hear from him. 'My partner is with me,' Alex told her. 'Do you mind if he joins us?'

She said she didn't mind.

'Got any clean clothes?' Marv looked as though he had just crawled out from under a vehicle.

Their host came up with a pair of clean, but threadbare jeans. Alex tossed Marv a T-shirt. 'That'll do you.'

At 6.30, having cleaned the interior of the old Land Rover Marv was driving, the two of them went to collect Chrissy. Marv had showered and changed into the borrowed clothes, slicked down his hair with water so it dripped onto the T-shirt and placed a piece of toilet paper over a cut on his chin from shaving. As much as he liked Marv, Alex was wishing he'd take a hike.

Chrissy had the same reaction to Marv as did every other woman. 'Hello,' she said coolly when introduced.

Marv was grinning from ear to ear. 'Hi, carrot top.' He nudged Alex. 'Better watch this one, redheads have terrible tempers.'

The trouble was, he meant well. His heavy handed humour was without malice. He treated all women the same way—like one of the boys.

The evening looked to be ruined before it began, Alex could tell. Chrissy did not like Marv and Marv was oblivious of the fact.

To her credit Chrissy was not openly rude to Marv. As they walked into the hotel, though, she could not stop herself from saying, 'Marv, you have toilet paper stuck to your chin.'

Marv whipped it off so quickly his chin began to bleed again and he spent the next thirty minutes dabbing at it surreptitiously.

The evening wasn't as bad as it might have been. Using !Ka's wisdom yet again: 'No man, whatever his failings, is worthless. If you fail to find the worth of a man it is your fault, not his', Alex got Marv talking about the two Land Rovers he had put together from the wrecks in Jacob's yard.

This was Marvin Moine territory. He dropped his attempts at humour and got serious and technical. When he could see he had said something Chrissy had not understood, he patiently explained, using utensils, plates and napkins to illustrate his point. With the subject exhausted, Alex then asked Marv to tell Chrissy why he limped, knowing that Marv's reluctance to speak of the accident resulted in him appearing modest and brave.

'Okay, !Ka,' he thought, watching Chrissy's respect grow. 'I'm fresh out of ideas.' But it was a start.

They dropped Marv off first. 'See you later,' Alex said, revving the engine to drown Marv's 'How much later?' response, although he could do nothing about the lewd wink.

At her place she made coffee. 'He's the weirdest man I've ever met.'

He found a bottle of milk in the refrigerator and took it to her. 'He's different,' he agreed. 'Can turn his hand to anything, though.'

'He's okay. I just wish he wasn't so crass.' She looked up at him, ignoring the bottle he held out.

'Totally honest.' He looked back and carefully placed the bottle of milk on the counter.

'And loud.' She moved towards him.

'Very brave.' He put his arms around her.

'Even his name is weird.' Her face was inches away.

'Full of sincerity.' He tightened his arms.

'You don't really want coffee do you?'

They were content to take their time. They explored each other, paced their emotions, not reaching for blood-pounding, star-bursting passion. By the time he entered her he knew her body well. He felt as though he were wrapped in a warm cocoon of gentle intimacy. As he moved inside her he watched her eyes. They looked back at him unblinking, loving, friendly eyes which flooded him with warmth and happiness. He thought he had known her forever. Each of them was giving, not taking. And in the giving, each of them took more than they believed possible. There was no heaving and sweating finale. He came to her as she came to him, with the sweetest, intimate, loving tenderness. He stayed inside her and kissed her lips, her nose, her eyes. When he rolled off her he took her with him, held in his arms, his lips against her hair.

He stared up at the ceiling, listening to the words in his heart. Her hair smelled like fresh air on a soft autumn morning. Her breath against his neck whispered like the gentle Mantis breath. Her skin felt soft, like a duiker's underbelly. She filled his senses as fully as a day in the desert.

'Chrissy, Chrissy, Chrissy,' he whispered into her hair. 'I felt this coming at the farm.'

'I did too,' she whispered back. 'I felt as if I'd known you for a very long time.'

181

He held her from him and looked into her face. 'This isn't casual.'

'No,' she said slowly. 'It's more than that.'

The way she made him feel took him by surprise. 'I want to know you very well, Chrissy Cameron. Can you deal with that?'

They talked for hours. There were so many things to say. She had her job in Gaberones, he was about to go into the desert. They had to find a way to see each other. For now, it could only be at weekends. They made plans. They told secrets. She was twenty-four, he was nineteen. It didn't matter to him. She was university educated, he had left school at sixteen. It didn't matter to her. Her father was headmaster at one of Scotland's finest private schools. His father was a farmer scratching a living in a far-flung outpost in Africa. It didn't matter to either of them.

They made love again. Tender, caring, kissing, touching love. He had never known anything like it. It gave the term love-making an entirely new meaning. It was more than simple physical desire which made him want to touch her. It was a need to share his entire personal psyche with another, to trust another so deeply that his very soul was safe with her, to take to his heart her own eternal being and to nurture and protect it, never hurt or harm it. When he looked into her eyes he saw his own soul mirrored there. Leaving her was the hardest thing he had ever done.

He promised to return to Gaberones the weekend after next. She would visit him once he had set up somewhere to stay. As he drove away from her flat he felt a sense of loss, more deeply even than the loss he felt when he first went away from Shakawe to school. Coming so soon after his one night with Madison he was puzzled by his feelings. He had always held Madison in a kind of gut fluttering awe.

'Maybe that's it,' he thought. 'Madison was the unattainable dream. Chrissy is real.'

In bed, before drifting off to sleep through what was left of the night, he did what he often did and opened his soul to let his feelings flow. It came as no surprise when all thoughts of Chrissy left him warm, secure and happy, while confusion and hurt were all that came to him when he thought of Madison. Satisfied, he let sleep take him away.

He and Marv drove to Molepolole the next morning. Old Jacob van Zyl was delighted to see him again, he could tell by his greeting. 'I don't have any work, you young skellum. Clear off before I set the dogs on you.' As he spoke he was thumping Alex between the shoulders and his lined and weathered face was creased with smiles.

He raised his voice and called through to the back of the shop, 'Mother, come see who's here,' then, turning to Alex, 'you keep your eyes off her, jong. She's my woman. I know what you young-uns are like.'

Marthe van Zyl heard him as she side-stepped her considerable bulk through the door. 'Alex!' She beamed at him in pleasure. 'You come here and give me a kiss.'

'Now you watch it, Mother. Too much excitement will stop your heart.'

Alex laughed at both of them. 'You two haven't changed.'

Marthe waddled over, wiping her hands on her apron. 'Ach, silly old man. I don't know why I stay with him.'

Marv was prowling around the shop. 'What are you looking for?' Jacob yelled. 'You don't work here any more, remember? You resigned Friday.'

'Supplies,' Marv replied mildly. 'Of course if you'd rather we bought them somewhere else . . .'

'All right, all right. Grab what you want. I suppose you expect a discount.'

'With the mark-up you put on everything you can afford it.' Marv winked at Alex. 'About twenty per cent should do it.'

Jacob pretended not to hear. 'How long you planning to be out there?'

'Don't know,' Alex said cheerfully. 'Till we find the diamonds.'

'Ach! There are no diamonds in that god-forsaken place.'

'We're still going to look.'

'You're mad in the head that's what you are. Ach! What's the use. You young people don't want to listen to an old man. Listen, jong . . .' he thrust his face into Alex's, '. . . you'll come to no good out there. Them plurry Bushmen and them plurry lions, between them you'll come to no good I'm telling you true, man.'

'Leave the boy alone, you silly old man. Come on through to the back and have a beer. You too.' She beckoned Marv whose head shot up at the mention of beer. 'Are you coming, Jacob?'

He went to the front door and shut it. 'No point in leaving the shop open for them plurry blacks to rob a man blind.' The bolts shot home. 'I'm coming, I'm coming, hold that tongue of yours, woman.'

Jacob, once he'd stopped grumbling, offered them the use of his cattle post as a base. 'It's about a hundred miles west,' he said. 'I get out there every few months. You're welcome to use it. Place is open. There's nothing to steal that's worth stealing. Probably crawling with snakes,' he added, happily gloomy. 'You'll need to take cooking things, I don't keep them there.'

They still had some work to do on the Land Rovers. Finally, after two days of salvaging more bits from some and cannibalising parts from others, the two vehicles worked reasonably well. Marv did most of it, he appeared to be able to think like an engine while he worked. Jacob van Zyl, who had spent the three days encouraging them—'here, use this, it comes out of that one but it should do the trick'—waved them goodbye grumbling, 'Man must be mad. Letting those two hooligans take my best vehicles. Should have charged them.'

And Marthe, waving a chubby arm which wobbled and jiggled, said, 'Ach, put a pipe in it, Jacob. Those boys are all right.'

Alex felt wonderful. He had a partner. They had two vehicles. They were kitted up. Chrissy was in Gaberones. He was going back to the desert. They were going to be rich.

ELEVEN

It took nearly three hours to reach the cattle post. They travelled along sandy tracks which were barely there and which managed to conceal wheel-wrenching outcrops of hard white calcrete. Jacob had said, 'You'll know when you're on my place, there's a white rock at the turnoff.' He forgot to mention the calcrete. He also forgot to tell them there were dozens of game trails and sandy turnoffs, unsignposted, branching off the main track like legs on a centipede. Driving the front vehicle, Alex could only guess the way. Several times he was certain they had reached Jacob's turnoff, only to find the track petered out or returned them to the main one. They had been driving more than two hours when they pulled up at yet another white stone to confer.

Marv was getting worried. 'What if we can't find it? Do we go back to Molepolole?'

'We'll camp out.'

'What? Out here? Not bloody likely. What about lions?'

'What's wrong with you? You must have camped when you worked for the safari company.'

'That's different.'

'How?'

'Cover,' Marv said. 'I mean, look at it. No real trees, no water, no hills.'

'Well at least you'll see them coming.'

'Who? See who coming?'

'The lion, the hyena, the jackals or whatever the hell else it is you're worried about. What's the matter with you anyway?'

Marv snarled at a fly. 'I dunno,' he said, waving his hand irritably at the persistent creature, 'this seems so exposed.'

'Marv,' Alex said patiently, 'that's because it is exposed. It's semi-desert. What did you expect, main roads and hotels?'

'Course not.' Marv looked injured. 'There's just so much of it,' he added lamely. 'It goes on and on.'

Alex gave up, confident he could find the cattle post. They set off again. Half an hour later, they found it.

Like most farmers with land in this part of the Kalahari, Jacob van Zyl did not actually own the land. He leased it. Technically, the land belonged to the people of the Molepolole area and use of it was granted by the Chief. Not wanting to spend money on a dwelling, Jacob had thrown together little more than a shelter to provide protection from the elements for those times he slept over at his cattle post. He had even laid a concrete floor, a luxury compared to some. Marv had obviously expected more. He pulled up beside Alex and yelled across to him.

'Is that it?' He was incredulous. The structure was clad entirely in corrugated iron which had clearly seen better days before being put to use here. Windows were holes in the walls with chicken netting wired in place, presumably to keep out the likes of curious lion or jackal. There were stained and faded canvas blinds rolled and secured up near the ceiling to be let down against rain or wind. The metal door had a bolt which could be operated from inside or out with a large padlock closed in such a way that it performed no function whatsoever. Inside, at one end, there were a few shelves, a rusting kerosene refrigerator and a sturdy but severely scratched wooden table. Three chairs, two of which may once have belonged with the table and one metal framed with a red vinyl seat and back, were placed along one side of the table like watching sentinels. Marv shook all three. The vinyl and stainless steel chair held its own, the other two lurched on unsteady legs.

At the other end of the shack, three iron beds with tortured coiled springs dipping halfway to the floor upon which were mattresses of dubious heritage. Army issue blankets had been folded and placed on each. The pillows, coverless, looked rather like lumpy grey pancakes.

Outside, a Rhodesian boiler sat over a crude brick fireplace. Plumbed directly into it was an outlet pipe which ran along the ground for a couple of yards before rearing up totally unsupported, to a tap and shower fitting. It looked a bit like a snake charmer's cobra. Next to this modern outdoor convenience, a sparkling white porcelain toilet bowl with no lid, connected to nothing. It just sat there, gleaming white and unusable. Between the shack and the shower, a few bricks had been placed to form a *braai*, although judging by the signs of previous cooking fires, Jacob preferred to barbecue his food in a more traditional way, in a semi-circle of stones. Old corrugated iron tanks, thorn-ripped tyres, engine blocks and all manner of broken things mechanical lay all over the yard.

'Does Jacob ever intend to use this stuff?' Marv kicked his foot against a heap of irrigation pipes which were lying alongside a large and relatively new bulldozer. 'And what the hell is this doing here?' he added, slapping his hand on the cab of the machine.

But Alex thought it was brilliant. 'This is great. Water. A roof over our heads and a hot shower. What more can we ask?'

'I could think of a couple of things,' Marv murmured. He peered into the toilet. 'Surely he doesn't use this? Where do we go?'

Alex waved his arm towards the surrounding country. 'Use the cat box.'

Marv snorted that it was the biggest bloody cat box he'd ever seen.

They carried their equipment and food inside. Marv went to one of the blinds and let it down to see if it would work. Half a dozen large scorpions fell onto the floor and scurried away. 'Jesus Christ!' He let all the blinds down and spent the next half hour flushing out scorpions and jumping on them. Alex ignored him.

At Marv's insistence, they gave the shack a thorough cleanout. Alex had to admit, it was better once they finished.

'What now?' Marv asked.

'We should get some wood.'

They looked at the surrounding landscape. Sand, scrub grasses and stunted bushes of acacia thorn. But Alex knew there would be dead and fallen trees in the area. They took one of the vehicles and, sure enough, ten minutes later, found some ideal firewood. They chained the whole tree to the bumper and towed it back.

While Alex cut the wood into manageable lengths, Marv fired up the Rhodesian boiler and started a cooking fire. 'What's for dinner?' Alex called, swinging the axe. He was having the time of his life.

'Might as well eat these steaks before they go off.'

Soon the aroma of cooking meat was wafting around them. Alex lit a hurricane lamp and hung it on a peg on the outside wall of the shack. 'Want a drink?'

'Good thinking.'

He got two beers from the refrigerator which had obliged them by starting immediately, and had gurgled its way to almost freezing within two hours.

Food, and a couple of beers mellowed Marv out. He man-handled the thick trunk of the tree, which Alex had not bothered to cut, and stuck one end of it into the fire. The other end lay in the sand, pointing towards them. The log was about six foot long and nearly two foot wide. Marv sat back, satisfied.

'How do we start?' he asked.

Alex had been anticipating this question and also dreading it. For all his enthusiasm, he really knew next to nothing about how to find diamonds. Marv would expect him to know more. After all, he had lived in the desert for nearly two years. Maybe, Alex acknowledged guiltily to himself, he had displayed a bit too much confidence. But now he had to come clean. All he really had to go on were two stones, one of which he lost as a baby, the other found by !Ka. Both had been discovered in a dead ostrich's digestive system. Added to that, !Ka had told him he had seen similar stones in the area. He had also read a little about the subject during his free time when he worked for Jacob. Not a lot, it was true, there was very little literature available, but enough to get them started. They could learn as they went. More than anything else, Alex had an unshakeable belief that under the hot sand lay wealth beyond his wildest dreams.

The desert held no terrors for Alex. Sitting on Pa's

verandah it seemed simple enough. Go into the desert and look for diamonds. But he knew his knowledge was sketchy, to say the least.

Marv was watching him suspiciously. 'Anyone at home?' he asked heavily.

'Sorry. I was thinking.'

'You planning to answer the question?'

He decided to keep it simple. 'Uh Marv, if we see any dead ostrich . . .'

Marv wasn't that easy. He narrowed his eyes. '. . . that just happen to be lying around?'

Okay, simple didn't work. 'Rocks,' Alex said desperately. 'Rock formations,' he amended.

Marv breathed loudly. 'It took us three hours to get here, right?'

Alex nodded.

'That's about a hundred miles, right?'

Nod, nod.

'Did you see any rock formations?'

Shake, shake.

'Apart from the bloody calcrete I sure as hell didn't see any rocks. No, sir. Oceans of sand. Not one real rock. Not so much as a fucking pebble.' He took a deep breath. 'In fact, now I come to think of it, I didn't see any fucking ostrich either.' He stared Alex down. 'Is there any danger you might say something soon or am I having this conversation with myself?'

Alex didn't know it but he looked as shifty as hell. 'Look, Marv, give me a break. The diamonds are here, I know they are. !Ka confirmed it. All we have to do . . .'

'. . . is trudge around this oversized kitty litter box until we stub our toes on sparklies? Is that it?'

191

'I've read some books . . .'

'That's nice.' Marv's face was benign. He looked like a trusting child—Alex should have known better. Foolishly, he relaxed. Marv let fly. 'While you were at it, it's a pity you didn't take a fucking geology degree.' He shook his head. 'Jesus! Talk about optimism. You don't have the faintest idea, do you? Where do we start? Out there. What do we do? We look. What do we look for? Something that sparkles. Christ, Alex, we'd stand a better chance—' He stared at the fire suddenly. 'Holy shit!' He jumped to his feet. 'Will you just look at that.'

A family of scorpions had been using the thick trunk of the tree as a nest. Flushed out by the smoke and heat, the scorpions had made a mad dash for one end and found their escape cut off by fire. They had then clambered on top of the log and were running up and down seeking a way off but the log was well alight and they were unable to get past the flames so they could run to the other end to safety. With a look of deep loathing on his face for the scurrying arachnids Marv put the kettle of water on top of the log, tilting it forward so that when the water boiled it would bubble out of the spout, scalding them. If they jumped, they would burn up in the fire. Either way, they were doomed.

'That's not very nice.' Alex had no problem with scorpions. In his experience, unless you were very unlucky, they left you alone. Besides, right now he was pleased to see them. Marv had been warming up to what Alex knew from previous experience could be a scathing and lengthy attack on him. The appearance of the scorpions was a welcome diversion.

Marv sat back satisfied the scorpions could not get to him. 'Ever hear about that vet up in Maun?'

Alex shook his head.

'Packed his suitcase to go to a wedding in Johannesburg. Before he shut it, a scorpion crawled into his case and cosied up in his good trousers. The scorpion must have liked it there, all nice and soft and dark, and it stayed in his trousers. The guy had no idea it was there. Next day he got dressed and went to the wedding. Halfway through the ceremony the bloody thing bit him on the balls. It happened just as the priest asked the congregation if anyone knew of a good reason why these two should not be joined in holy matrimony would they please speak now. This guy suddenly let out a howl that nearly brought the roof down. The priest jumped out of his skin. The bride burst into tears. The poor bastard was leaping up and down trying to get his trousers off.'

Alex was laughing. 'What happened to him?'

'He was rushed to hospital and given anti-venom. He didn't die but it took three months for his balls to get back to their original size.' Marv looked soberly at the dancing scorpions. 'And that's why these guys have to go. We don't have any anti-venom.'

Alex suddenly thought so too. His own balls felt tingly.

'Six weeks,' Marv said suddenly. 'If we don't find anything by then, we quit. Agreed?'

'But Marv . . .'

'Six weeks. Not a second longer.'

'But . . .'

Marv folded his arms and got a stubborn look on his face. 'Six weeks and I'm being generous. It's the hottest time of year in this bloody desert and I'm out here sharing my life with scorpions and a maniac. Six weeks. That's it. And stop bloody saying "but Marv" all the time.'

'But Marv. All I wanted to say was thanks.'

'Oh!' Marv looked pleased. 'That's all right then.' He

watched a large scorpion commit suicide into the fire before asking, 'How much do you know, really?' When Alex went to answer he added, 'The truth. No bullshit stuff about ostrich.'

'It's not bullshit.' Alex helped himself to a cigarette, lit it, and blew smoke noisily upwards. 'Ostrich pick up small stones all the time. They need them to help digest their food. They're attracted to shiny objects. Their gizzards are always worth a look.'

'We can't shoot every bloody ostrich we see. C'mon, Alex, you must have more than that.'

Feeling a bit like he used to when his mother questioned him about one of her Bible readings, Alex gave him what he had. It wasn't much. 'Ever heard of kimberlite?'

Marv shook his head.

'They're great pipes of rock which came up through the earth's crust millions of years ago.' He drew on his cigarette. 'They brought a whole range of minerals with them— diamonds, garnet, ruby, sapphire and a lot of other stuff.'

'Stuff?' Marv's practical side did not accept 'stuff'.

Alex shrugged. 'Nickel, other rocks, stuff like that.'

'Yeah right. Stuff.'

Alex ignored the sarcasm. 'Because the kimberlite usually settles either just below or just above ground what we have to look for are either natural pans or kopjies. And,' he contin-ued loudly when he saw Marv about to interrupt, 'we also have to watch out for denser vegetation. When the kimberlite is exposed to sun, wind and rain it breaks down and the ground turns a yellowish colour. This stuff . . . er . . . ground,' he amended quickly, 'retains more moisture than areas with no kimberlite. So you get a higher concentration of vegetation.'

Marv looked sour. 'So what are we doing here?' He waved his arm. 'There's not a real bloody tree to be seen.'

'It's only a base, Marv. We can explore a number of areas from here. At least it's a roof over our heads.'

Marv grunted. 'Go on.'

'The main thing to look for, once we've found land where there might be kimberlite, is termite nests.'

'Jesus! There you go again. What have termites got to do with it?'

'Marv, termites have been here for thousands of years. I was reading about it. They need mud to provide humidity so the fungi they eat can grow. Sometimes they have to go as deep as 300 feet.'

'No way. Three hundred feet! No way, man.'

'Not all of them. But they do go deep. And they have to get rid of all the gravel and sand so they bring it to the surface.'

For the first time since he began to speak, Marv looked impressed. 'I get it. The ants do the digging for us.'

'They provide us with an indicator, sure. Small broken crystals only. If we find them we set up a grid and take samples of the surface. What we would look for is a concentration of broken crystals, mainly garnets and ilmenites.'

Marv was looking sour again. 'What are ilmenites?'

'Black things,' Alex said, a bit desperate, since he wasn't entirely certain himself. 'Manganese and stuff.'

Marv let the 'stuff' go this time. 'Carry on.'

'If we find a lot of indicators, we dig.'

'How deep?'

'How long is a piece of string?'

'Huh?'

'Haven't a clue,' Alex said cheerfully. 'It varies.'

'From what to what?'

'Anything from six inches to hundreds of feet.'

'Fucking forget it.'

Alex ignored that. 'Then we bring up samples and use the sieves again.'

'Again?'

'Yes, Marv. We've already used them once looking for indicators.'

'A little point you forgot to mention.' Marv leaned forward and rattled the kettle, making water slop out the spout. He needn't have bothered. The scorpions, in their mad leap for safety, had all burned in the fire. 'So okay, we use the sieves again.' He sat back again. 'I thought we needed water for sieving. We haven't got much to spare.'

'We can dry sieve. It's harder but it's possible.'

Marv hunched his shoulders. 'Okay, what happens then?'

'It'll take a while to get the action right but you sort of shake the sieve around and all the heavy stuff settles to the bottom. Then you flip it over and, voila, all the heavy stuff is sitting on top.'

Marv was unimpressed. 'You ever done it?'

'Ah . . . not exactly.' Alex puffed on his cigarette. 'Um . . . no, actually. But how hard can it be? We'll just rattle the sieves around till we get the hang of it.' He could see Marv's practical mind shift into overdrive. 'We can practise in the morning,' he added hastily.

'Yeah, right.' Marv's sarcasm was really getting into top gear. 'What do we look for? Do all diamonds look like the one !Ka gave you?'

'No.' Alex unbuttoned his shirt pocket and pulled out the diamond which he kept on him at all times. 'This one is quite rare. Most diamonds are octahedrons. That means,' he added quickly, 'eight sided.' He handed Marv the stone. 'See how flat the sides are. Most diamonds have perfectly flat faces. And they're usually very bright. Nothing else has the sharp shape of a diamond. They stand out.' He drew in the sand. 'They look a bit like this.'

Marv studied the sand. 'Okay, so we sift through the heavy stuff and pick up sharp shiny things. Things that look like two pyramids back to back, right?'

'Right.'

'And they'll be diamonds?'

'Maybe.'

'Waddya mean "maybe"?'

'They might be quartz.'

'How do we know the difference? I don't fancy rushing into Gabs with a shit load of quartz.'

Alex held out his hand. 'See this ring?'

Marv nodded. 'The one your parents gave you.'

'If we find anything that scratches this, it's a diamond.'

'You'd bugger it up!' Marv was scandalised.

'If it's not a diamond it won't harm it. If it's a diamond I'll buy another onyx stone for the ring.'

'That's a bit off,' Marv said. 'You've only just been given the bloody thing.'

'Can you think of an alternative?'

Marv couldn't.

That night Alex had been asleep for nearly half an hour before Marv was satisfied there were no scorpions in his bedding and settled down himself. He was very disgruntled. There was no obvious way of fixing the shower attachment to the tap and, when he went to take a shower the end kept flying off and hitting him on the head. The water had heated up too much, scalding him. He did not like the wide open land although he had no idea why. The endless flat country seemed altogether too dangerously exposed. Older than Alex

197

by nine years, he could not share the younger man's sublime confidence that nature, God, or whatever, would provide. Nor did he have much faith in them finding diamonds. Lethal scorpions were not to his taste. Alex, who hardly ever smoked, had sat in front of him and clearly enjoyed every drag of his cigarette, knowing full well that Marv was trying to give up. All in all, it had been a bad day for Marv. Conveniently, he forgot that he had been as keen as Alex when they discussed the idea.

In the middle of the night, unbeknown to the sleeping men, a small pride of lions paid a visit, perhaps attracted by the smell of cooking meat. They found the spoor in the morning. This bothered Marv not at all. It was scorpions he was scared of.

Their quest for ostrich, rocks, yellow earth or dense vegetation proved difficult. In fact they couldn't find any. Not the next day, or the next, or for the next week. They found termite nests—hundreds of them—but no pieces of garnet or ilmenites. After ten days of searching over a radius of some fifty miles, both men were more than ready to spend the weekend in Gaberones.

Alex planned to stay with Chrissy. Marv said he would stay with a friend. Taking only one vehicle they drove the three-hour journey, stopping briefly in Molepolole to say hello to Marthe and Jacob.

He had thought about Chrissy a great deal during those first ten days. It was a strange feeling, he had never considered serious relationships—he was young and believed he had plenty of time. But in their one short night together a stranger had crept into his heart and lay there, snug and right and happy-making. Nothing he ever experienced before could have prepared him. Love, he had to assume that was what it was, hit him so hard it took his breath away. On the way to Gaberones, he remembered how she made him feel, recalled her soft body next to his. By the time he had dropped Marv and pulled up outside her flat he was hot, hungry and horny. When she opened the door and flung herself into his arms, he forgot the hot and hungry.

Where their lovemaking before had been tender and gentle, now they tore at each other's clothes, trembling and panting. 'Hurry, hurry,' she groaned, raking her nails down his back.

They climaxed together, ninety seconds later. 'Jesus, Jesus, Jesus,' he whispered into her neck, stroking inside her in rhythm to the last achingly sweet spasms as they shuddered through his lower body.

She rocked with him. He could feel her own climax pulsating deep inside her. 'God, I've missed you,' she sighed a little later.

It was wonderful to be with her again. To smell the sweetness of her, feel the softness of her, hear the feminineness of her. He caught himself smiling at the ceiling. Lighthearted happiness and a cocoon of warmth washed over and around him. The knock on the door was the most unwelcome sound he had ever heard. 'Ignore it. Pretend we're not here.' She snuggled back against him.

'I know you're in there. Open up.' It was Marv.

'Oh bloody hell.' She flung back the covers and grabbed her gown. 'What does he want?'

He pulled on his own clothes. 'Damned if I know. I dropped him on the other side of The Village.'

Marv banged again. 'Open up.'

Marv's special knack of putting his foot in things did not let him down. 'What took you so long?'

Chrissy had daggers in her eyes. Alex wasn't terribly pleased to see him either. 'What are you doing here?'

'My friend is away. Can't get in. I'll just have to stay with you guys.' Marv looked quite comfortable with the thought.

'I use the spare room as a study.' It was the last thing she wanted.

'That's okay.' He sat on the sofa and bounced up and down. 'This'll do fine.' He grinned up at them. 'What's for dinner? I'm starving.'

As much as Alex liked him, Marv's presence ruined what would have otherwise been a wonderful weekend. Chrissy simply did not take to him. Alex sympathised—Marv took a little getting used to and didn't help the process by constantly getting in the way or saying the wrong thing. Whenever she turned around Marv was there. He poked and prodded around her flat as though he owned the place. When she put a record on, he took it off. 'That's terrible, haven't you got any Beatles?' When she went into the kitchen he was right behind her, sniffing and tasting. 'Needs more salt.'

She had prepared dinner for two which she managed to stretch to three by adding a salad. Marv ate his portion rapidly then said, 'You don't eat much, do you? I'm still hungry.'

They sent him out for ice cream. 'Can't you get rid of him?'

'How? He's got nowhere else to stay.'

'That's his problem. He's got a damned cheek just barging in here. I hardly know him.'

He put his arms around her. 'I'll suggest a roster. He can have one weekend in Gabs, I'll have the next. How's that? For now, can you bear with him?'

She leaned against him. 'Do I have a choice?'

He kissed her. Marv crashed back into the room. 'Forgot

the keys. Hey, stop the mushy stuff.' He was grinning at them like a proud parent.

The trouble was, Marv meant no harm. He honestly believed he was welcome there. Alex was his friend, therefore Chrissy was his friend. Had the tables been reversed, he would have done nothing less for Alex. It simply hadn't occurred to him he was in the way.

By Sunday afternoon Alex could see that Chrissy was one step away from exploding. Marv had drunk all her beer, eaten all her food, played her records too loud, dominated every conversation and, worse, in a lighthearted moment of playfulness, slapped her backside, fondly believing she would not mind. Alex suggested it was time for them to leave. The last thing Marv yelled back from the vehicle nearly broke her self-control: 'See you next time.'

Tight-lipped, she managed, 'I'll be away.'

'How does she know she'll be away when she doesn't know when the next time is?' Marv asked, as Alex drove away.

'Maybe you misheard.' Alex couldn't bring himself to hurt Marv's feelings, even though there had been times during the weekend he could cheerfully have wrung his neck.

'No, I heard it quite clearly. She said it. Women are strange creatures aren't they?'

Early February in the Kalahari is not a place for the faint-hearted. For the next week they sweltered and suffered. 'This is worse than up north,' Marv complained, wiping sweat. 'I thought it was supposed to be a dry heat in the desert.'

'So it is, mainly.' Alex found the conditions trying as well. The last of the summer storms were threatening but not producing. Black skies on the horizon built the humidity so the air felt like a steam bath. Foraging ants, looking for moisture, dominated the kitchen. Flies, which normally did not bother them, became sticky and persistent. Cockroaches appeared from nowhere. Stepping through the screen door sent hundreds of them scurrying for cover so the floor appeared to be alive.

They found ostrich. Live ones. In a moment of irrational discomfort and frustration, Marv shot one.

'What'd you do that for?' Alex yelled, frustrated himself.

'I'm sick of this. For two pins I'd pack it in. Anyway, we can eat it.'

'They're greasy and horrible. What a fucking waste.'

'Look, if you're so fucking good, fuck off and shoot a buck.'

'Think I fucking can't?'

'Fuck no. All you fucking do is fucking criticise.'

'Fuck you.'

'Fuck you too.'

'Fucking hell. Fuck, fuck, fucking hell.'

Suddenly it was funny and they were laughing. They fell onto the hot sand and howled. Wiping his eyes, Alex said, 'Sorry, man.'

Marv propped himself on his elbows. 'Ja, man. Me too.'

'Come on. Let's have a look at the bird.'

'We could make biltong.' Marv eyed the ostrich with some distaste. Aside from the back straps, the meat was generously marbled with greasy-looking orange fat. Even sun-dried, it was obvious the end result would not remove the oiliness.

'The ants would probably get it.'

'They'd be bloody welcome to it.'

Alex had eaten ostrich with the San. It was not their favourite food but, boiled for several hours with ground nuts and tubers, it was edible. This particular bird did not look very appetising. He remembered !Ka refusing to kill a certain male ostrich once, explaining he was too old to eat. At the time, Alex assumed the Bushman was showing his respect for such an old creature. It was something the San often did— !Ka had once told him, 'A very old animal is a very clever animal and deserves to be treated well.' But looking at this particular bird he wondered if perhaps !Ka had been referring to the taste.

Having examined the grit and stones from the dead bird's gizzard, they left it for the hyenas.

While the days were hot and humid from sunrise to sunset, as soon as the sun went down they felt cold. 'Sand is a pain in the arse,' Marv said.

'Why?' Alex threw a stick on the fire.

'It's so damned hot one minute it'll take your skin off. The next it's as cold as a witch's tit.'

'We could always go inside,' Alex said mildly.

Inside was hell and they knew it. The corrugated iron walls and roof, and the cement floor, heated up during the day until the shack was like an oven. The heat remained unbearable until around ten in the evening when, with loud cracking and booming sounds, the outside temperature cooled the iron and the shack went from oven to refrigerator in the space of fifteen minutes. Until this happened, the ants and cockroaches had a field day but, as soon as the cooling process began, they miraculously disappeared. Alex and Marv remained outside by the fire.

'How do you think Chrissy will take to this place?' Marv asked. Chrissy planned to visit them the following weekend. Despite his lack of sensitivity around women, Marv was a thorough gentleman. In his experience, women liked and were entitled to some creature comforts.

'Okay I hope. She's seen worse. Her job takes her to some pretty ropy places.' Alex was less worried by Chrissy's reaction to their living conditions than he was about her prolonged exposure to Marv. He had tried to talk Marv into going to Gaberones for the weekend.

'Rather be with you guys.'

Short of demanding he bugger off for the weekend, Alex knew of no other way to get him to leave them in peace. Innuendo was lost on Marv. He crossed his fingers and decided to make the best of it.

The next day they ventured further than usual. The by now familiar build-up of storm clouds occurred around two in the afternoon. This time, though, the wind picked up. 'Think we'll get it?' It was a rhetorical question. Marv always asked it.

Alex thought of his mother. Pa once said that there was always someone who had to be on the edge of the rain and Mum had tartly replied, 'Yes, but why is it always us?' He was beginning to understand her frustration. With clouds like that, rain had to be falling somewhere. Sometimes, like now when the wind picked up, he could actually smell it. But it was always just over there.

They were in one of the Land Rovers, parked on a ridge, looking out over a grassy plain, dotted here and there with stunted, flat-topped acacias. The wind was blowing a little harder and sand blew against the vehicle, sounding like a thousand pinpricks in a sheet of paper.

A sudden movement to his left and, where the ridge descended, and where there had been nothing a moment ago, stood the glossy rippling black stallion. Alex nudged Marv and raised a finger to his lips. The stallion was no more than twenty feet away. His head was turned from them. Alex didn't think he knew they were there.

Then Nightmare stepped over the ridge. Alex caught his breath. Her years in the desert had hardened her body. She was slim and muscular. A foal joined her and the stallion. Then another horse. Alex recognised it as the one he had christened Diamond. The foal had Nightmare's colouring. Alex knew he was looking at her entire family. She noticed the Land Rover and snorted with fright, stamping and tossing her head, poised to run.

Very slowly, Alex opened the door. 'What are you doing? Get back. That stallion will kill you.' Alex called softly to Nightmare. She stood still, rippling, bobbing her head. He called her again and she took a step forward. The stallion exploded towards him, eyes wide, ears back, teeth bared. Alex stood his ground. 'Jesus, man, get in the car,' Marv hissed.

The stallion was prancing just out of reach. He was half-rearing, his front hooves kicking out, missing Alex deliberately, warning him off. Nightmare whinnied and the stallion wheeled and retreated.

It took her ten minutes to cover the distance between them. She walked two steps, stopped, danced sideways, stopped, moved backwards, stopped, all the time snorting and blowing, neighing an inquiry. Alex spoke gently to her the whole time.

Finally, she was in front of him. If he'd reached out he could have touched her. She extended her head towards him, breathing noisily, her calls lowered and softened to that which was like clearing her throat. Alex lifted his face to hers and blew softly into her nostrils. Nightmare jerked once, then gave herself up to the sensual and wholly personal pleasure of contact with the only human she had ever trusted.

If she had been so inclined, she could have taken his face off. But somewhere in the back of her wild senses, she remembered him. Alex blew his breath and she breathed it in and knew he was her friend.

He raised his hand and gently stroked her neck. The stallion called and Nightmare jerked back but the wildness in her eyes was replaced by trust. 'Off you go, lovely one.' His voice, so close to her ear, startled her. Like the stallion, she wheeled, kicking sand. Then she flew down the ridge to join her family. They disappeared as quickly as they'd come.

Alex was breathing hard. The experience had moved him greatly—she was strong and proud and free, yet he had her trust. Standing face to face, breathing his scent into her, was a moment of the purest most perfect exhilaration.

'You fool!' Marv was standing next to him. 'What made you do that?'

'I knew her a long time ago. She remembers me.'

Marv snorted. 'Bullshit!'

But Alex knew she did. He looked at her tracks along the ridge. The wind picked up some of the disturbed sand, exposing a rock.

A rock! A real rock! A dark yellow real rock! He ran to it and dropped to his knees, brushing away sand. It was weird-looking rock, as though it had once melted then hardened again. Smooth, without the jagged edges. Ridges, rather like the landscape around them, covered its surface. 'Marv. Come see.'

He was clearing away more sand when his hand hit something sharp. With an exclamation he looked at his hand. It was bleeding. He brushed more sand. Marv whistled. Lying up against the rock, a perfect octahedral, shiny and bright, was a stone the size of his thumbnail. Alex picked it up and wiped the sand off which came away easily. The stone felt cold and smooth. It looked like glass.

'Is that what I think it is?' Marv's voice shook.

Alex sucked blood from his hand. 'I think so.'

'The ring. Use the ring.' Marv was literally hopping with excitement, all disapproval of damaging the ring gone.

Mentally apologising to his parents, Alex forced one of the points across the onyx ring. 'This is it. Holy shit! We've done it, Marv.' His ring was scratched from one side to the other.

They had shovels and sieves in the Land Rover. They worked until dark. But, by the end of the day, they had found no more.

They carefully mapped their way back to the cattle post. Marv was in such a state of high excitement he forgot to complain about the roaches and ants and even laughed when the shower head flew off and hit him on the head.

'What's the plan?' They were sitting by the fire eating sausages off twisted wire forks.

Alex swigged his beer. 'Go back tomorrow and keep digging. Bring back loads of sand. Sift like hell and pray we find more. There must be more there, Marv. There can't be one on its own.'

'Think it's a pipe?'

'Maybe. They're out there, I know they're out there. This find may not be it, but they're out there somewhere.'

'I didn't see any indicators.'

'Neither did I and I don't understand why. Mind you, some of the biggest stones ever found were picked off the ground.'

'Who does the land belong to?'

'It's tribal. The local Chief grants use of it for grazing. Judging by the lack of cattle out there it's not being used.

That might mean we can apply to lease it.' Alex hesitated, then added, 'Marv, if we find a big haul we'll have to inform the authorities. Technically, that land belongs to the people of Bechuanaland so we'd be honour bound to report it.'

'Ja, man, that's okay with me. Just so long as I get rich myself.'

'Actually,' Alex went on as though he hadn't heard. 'When independence comes life won't be easy for the Batswana. They've got cattle, that's it. Just think, Marv, if diamonds are found in large quantities Bechuanaland, or Botswana as it will be then, can get off to a flying start.'

'Ja, man. Just don't go forgetting about us.'

'Would I do that, Marv?'

'Who knows? You're a crazy bastard sometimes.'

Alex just grinned at him.

The next day was Friday. They drove both vehicles back to the rocks, following yesterday's tracks rather than their map. They worked all day, sweltering and sweating and swearing. But they found no more diamonds. The rocky ridge petered out within thirty feet of yesterday's find. At the end of the day, hot, tired and disgruntled, they returned to the cattle post, the backs of the Land Rovers sagging noticeably under the weight of sand samples which they had to sieve.

'It probably goes underground,' Alex said, groaning as he sank into a deckchair.

'We'll find another ridge,' Marv pacified him.

'God, I hope so. All this pain must be worth something.'

'There's more to come,' Marv reminded him.

Sieving, as they discovered once they got the hang of it, was hard work, particularly as they could not use water. They had two sizes of sieve. Marv used one with a wide mesh to sift out large pieces of gravel. The other, with a smaller mesh, Alex operated. By the end of the day, the circular motion of sieving had their backs and arms screaming for relief. Swirling the sand would have been easier if they had been able to use water. So too would the up and down movement needed to shake any heavier material to the centre of the sieve, and to the bottom. Water would also have washed their samples, making it easier and quicker to look through them once they had been flipped over onto the hessian sacks. The lack of water made every step twice as hard.

'We get a reprieve tomorrow,' Alex said. Chrissy was arriving the next day. 'Uh, Marv.'

'Ja, man.'

'Think you could give us a little private time this week-end?'

'How?'

'I dunno. Go for a drive or something.'

Marv nodded reflectively but otherwise did not react. He had a knowing look on his face which should have warned Alex. On Saturday morning, within minutes of Chrissy's arrival, he said pointedly, 'I think I'll go for a drive.' He left with a lot of waving and a cunning expression on his face.

Chrissy watched him drive away with her mouth open. 'What the hell . . .'

Alex was laughing. 'I asked him to give us private time. I didn't expect he'd do it the moment you arrived.'

She shook her head. 'How do you stand it?'

'He's okay. He means well.' He took her inside. 'Well, what do you think?'

She looked around. 'It's great. You have everything you need. I expected something a little more basic.' She peered through a window. 'Oh, for heaven's sake . . .'

Marv, having made it plain that his absence was so the two of them could make love, had driven half a kilometre away and killed the engine. She could see the Land Rover in the distance. Marv was sitting out there waiting. 'Surely he doesn't think . . .'

Alex was more amused than angry. 'I'm afraid he does. That's Marv for you.'

'That's outrageous!' Chrissy was not amused at all.

'Chrissy, he thinks he's doing us a favour, he's not trying to be rude. Marv just doesn't think the way most of us do.'

'Does he think at all?' she asked sarcastically.

Alex gave up and helped her carry the supplies she'd brought with her inside. There was no point in trying to explain Marv to anyone.

Twenty minutes later Marv returned, grinning and asking Alex loudly, 'Was that enough time?'

'If looks could kill,' Alex thought, 'Marv'd be a dead man.'

Somehow they got through the rest of the day. Alex wanted to show Chrissy where they'd found the diamond. Marv thought it was a great idea. 'Hang on, I'll get some beers.' Alex heard Chrissy's teeth grind. The next morning, knowing how desperately she needed a break from Marv's company, he suggested taking Chrissy for a drive. 'Great idea,' Marv said. 'Hang on, I'll bring some beers.'

Chrissy groaned.

They drove to a spot they found a few days earlier, about ten miles away. There was nothing special about it save the fact it had a few trees which were larger than most. The shade provided relief from the hot sun. Chrissy jumped out and stood stretching, her hands on the small of her back. Alex got down from the driver's seat and went round to the back of the vehicle. Marv, who had insisted he sit in the middle so she did not have to straddle the gear stick, followed Chrissy. Then he saw the lioness. She was lying in the shade, a scant ten feet from them.

'Shit! Don't move.'

Chrissy had walked a few steps away from the Land Rover. She looked back at Marv and, in doing so, caught sight of the big cat. 'Stand still,' Marv hissed at her.

Alex poked his head around the back of the vehicle to ask if anyone wanted a beer. What he saw made him go cold. Marv had his hand outstretched towards Chrissy who stood stock still, her eyes wide, staring at the lioness now on her feet, a mere couple of steps and a leap away. The three of them—Chrissy, Marv and the lioness—appeared frozen.

The lioness twitched her tail. *Christ, she's going to charge.* Alex tried to move forward but found himself frozen as well. His head screamed at him to move but his body would not do it.

'Look down,' Marv hissed urgently, through clenched teeth. 'For Christ's sake, Chrissy, look down, you're challenging her.'

But Chrissy was too scared to hear him, let alone obey his words.

The lioness flattened her ears.

A blood-curdling yowl came from Marv as he stood there. It started low, like a growl, but fear put a tremor in it and, as it grew louder it became a scream. Alex stood paralysed. The lioness, bunched to attack, looked at Marv. By now he was screaming a kind of yodel. His arms flew in circles. Suddenly Marv galvanised himself forward, rushing straight at the big cat, leaping and screaming like an animated windmill in desperate need of oiling. In the face of such a fearful display, the lioness decided retreat might be a more sensible option. She turned and faded back into the bush.

Alex's paralysis left him and he ran to Chrissy who was shaking uncontrollably. He caught her to him and held her. Over her head he saw Marv turn, grin, go as white as a ghost and then, bent double, run a short distance before vomiting out his fear. With a face still drained of all colour and pouring with perspiration, he walked to the back of the Land Rover and, with shaking hands, grabbed a bottle of beer and whipped the cap off using the back bumper of the vehicle. He drank half the bottle before he lowered it again. 'Holy shit. I don't want to do that again.' He was grinning at them.

Alex felt Chrissy stir in his protective arms. She moved back from him. She had tears running down her face as she went to Marv and held him. Marv looked uncomfortably over at Alex. 'Get your woman off me, man.'

Chrissy laughed and held him tighter. 'Thank you,' she whispered. 'That was incredibly brave.'

'Ah hell, Chrissy.' Marv grinned, delighted. 'It was nothing.'

Alex moved to them and put his arms around them both. The two people he loved had, in the space of a few seconds, become more important than anything else in the world.

The lioness had cubs in the shade. She came back for them and they watched her from the safety of the vehicle. Although totally confused and demoralised by Marv's charge, her mothering instincts made her return, snarling a warning. She stood next to her cubs, tail flicking. 'Let's leave her to it,' Alex said, starting the engine.

The lioness halfheartedly chased after the vehicle, restoring her self-esteem.

Suddenly, Marv could do no wrong. Chrissy adored him. 'I'm sorry if I appeared rude,' she apologised.

'That's okay.' Marv would forgive her anything; she was Alex's woman.

'You knew I didn't exactly like you, didn't you?'

'Ah hell, Chrissy, it doesn't matter.'

She put her arm through his. 'It does matter.'

'Well you like me now don't you?' Her touching him both embarrassed and pleased him.

She kissed his cheek. 'I love you to pieces.'

'Aw, Chrissy, cut it out.' He was just like a big kid.

Alex glanced sideways at them, smiling. He guessed Chrissy had just discovered what he always knew: Marv's loyalty was a precious gift. If his personality took a little patience, and his constant presence took a lot of patience, then patience was what they would give him in return.

For the next month the three of them were inseparable at weekends, either in Gaberones or at the cattle post. But the diamonds continued to elude them.

'This is a ridge, right?' Marv asked one day.

'It's a ridge, Marv. It's the ridgiest ridge I've ever seen.'

Marv treated him to one of his 'you're crazy' looks. 'Something has to be holding it up, right?'

'Right, Marv. It sure as hell isn't standing on thin air.'

Another look. 'So how come we can't find it? Where is the bastard? How many places can a rock hide?'

'Under there. Under tons of bloody sand. It's lying under our feet laughing at us. And the diamonds in it are winking at each other. They're saying, "Ha ha, you can't find us," that's what they're saying. And you know why, Marv? You want to know why? Because the desert doesn't want us to find them. Because it's the best kept bloody secret Mother Nature ever devised.' He knew he sounded desperate. In truth, he was getting desperate.

Marv gave him another look. 'It's there somewhere,' he muttered. Since finding the diamond on, what they now called, Nightmare's Ridge, Marv was as keen as Alex to keep looking. The six weeks' time limit he'd set was forgotten. But when, after two months of frustration, they'd still found nothing, Alex began to think of visiting !Ka. He knew he could find the clan. Chrissy wanted to go with him. The opportunity to observe one of the few remaining hunting and gathering people whose ways had changed little in thousands of years excited both her personal and professional interest. 'I'll need to take some time off work,' she said.

Marv, for once, decided to stay behind.

A week before they left, Chrissy began to look troubled. 'What's wrong?' Alex asked. Alex and Marv had gone to Gaberones for the weekend and the three of them were enjoying a cold beer at the tennis club.

'An old school friend is coming to see me. I can't go with you, Alex. She's arriving late next week. I tried to telephone but she's already left home. She's travelling somewhere in South Africa. I'm so sorry to miss this trip, I was looking forward to it.'

'I can pick her up at the airport.' No trouble to Marv. A friend of Chrissy's was a . . . 'I'll take her to the cattle post so she'll be there when you get back. She'll be as right as rain. She can help me dig.'

Chrissy still looked troubled.

'What? Won't she like the desert or something?' Alex could see she was having second thoughts, but he wanted Chrissy to come. He was looking forward to introducing her to the clan.

'Pru is a little different,' Chrissy hedged. 'She'd like the desert but . . . well . . . I'm not sure she'd fit in with us.'

'Everyone fits in with us,' Marv said happily. 'We're very nice.'

'Yes but Pru is . . . she's . . . dammit, I like Pru but she's bossy and opinionated and horsy and downright upper class and she'll try to tell everyone what to do.' Chrissy looked ashamed. 'Pru is an acquired taste. We go back a long way. But she's not everybody's cup of tea.'

'Don't worry about Pru,' Marv said kindly. 'I'll sort her out.' He rose. 'Who wants a beer?'

Chrissy rose too. 'Excuse me.' She went towards the ladies' toilet.

Alex gazed around. People were on the court, sprawled in chairs or talking at the bar. The afternoon had a lazy, laid-back Saturday afternoon feel to it. After the heat, sand and frustration of the desert, he was enjoying being back in civilisation.

'Hello.'

He looked up. He had not seen her approaching. 'Madison!' He rose hastily. 'Care to join us?'

She shook her head and silky hair bobbed and settled. It had always fascinated him. 'No. I saw you and wanted to . . .' She bit her lip. 'Look,' she said, almost angrily. 'I'm really sorry for the things I said that night.'

He could see what the apology cost her. 'It's okay, Madison, let's forget it.'

He had said the wrong thing as usual. 'That's the trouble with you, you bury unpleasantness and refuse to discuss it.' She calmed herself with an effort. 'Some of us *need* to talk things through, Alex.' She hesitated, then blurted out, '*We* need to talk, you and I.'

Chrissy was coming out of the ladies' room. She smiled and waved and stopped at a table to speak to several people.

Madison followed his gaze. 'Who's she?'

As always, Madison's presence felt like a challenge. Alex constantly had the feeling that he was on his back foot with her, especially when they were discussing her father. Chrissy was making her way across the room, a question in her eyes. 'Chrissy?' Alex said, loud enough for Chrissy to hear. 'She's the girl I'm going to marry.'

He hadn't meant to say it. He wanted to let Madison know that she wasn't the only girl who mattered, that was all. He was stunned by the sudden pain on her face.

'Well . . . con . . . congratulations,' she stuttered.

Chrissy reached them, her eyes shining. She had heard his words. He introduced her, wondering as he did what was wrong with Madison. 'Can you join us?' Chrissy asked her.

Madison backed away, shaking her head. 'No. I'm with friends. Just stopped to say hello. Must fly.' She practically ran from their table.

Alex watched her go, troubled. He would never deliberately have hurt her but he could not shake off the feeling that he had. But how? She didn't like him, he was sure of it. He simply could not fathom her.

'Who was she?' Chrissy picked up on his confusion.

'I used to work for her father.'

'The one who beat you up?'

'Yes.'

'Do you have feelings for her, Alex?'

Well. Do I?

Chrissy was waiting for his answer. He knew she deserved his honesty. He put his hands on her shoulders and looked deeply into her eyes. 'I used to think so,' he said sincerely, believing it. 'Then I met you.'

She searched his face for the truth and found it. 'Thank you,' she said softly.

216

Then Marv was coming back with the beers and saying, 'I thought I'd take Pru out to look for that lioness with cubs. What do you think, Chrissy? Would she enjoy that?'

He and Chrissy discussed ways to keep Pru amused and Alex listened to them but his heart was uneasy, especially when he caught sight of Madison driving rapidly away from the club. He knew she was hurt and angry and he knew it was his fault. All he didn't know was why. With an effort he put it out of his mind. Seated beside him was the girl he had just declared he would marry. It was a new thought but the mere idea of it made him happy.

Marv was saying, '. . . so all you have to do is enjoy yourself. I can take care of Pru, you'll see.'

Chrissy admitted to Alex later, 'It's Marv I'm worried about. Pru could eat him for breakfast and spit out the pips. I don't want his feelings hurt.'

And the disquiet came back into Alex's heart because he had hurt Madison. The more he thought about it, the less he understood it. He concluded finally that she believed he had used her to get at her father and that it was her pride he had hurt. 'She'll get over it,' he told himself.

When Alex and Chrissy left to find !Ka the following week she was still troubled. 'Pru must be some piece of work,' Alex commented. 'I've never seen you so worried.'

'Wait till you meet her, you'll know why.'

'Marv's a big boy. Anyway, we might be back by the time she arrives.'

'God, I hope so,' Chrissy said with feeling.

217

TWELVE

!Ka and his people were camped at the place near where they first found the baby Alex. In the way of things with the San people, they had returned to this spot only twice since that time, giving the land a chance to recover. There had been a dancing the night before and !Ka told Be in the morning, 'The little beetle is not far.' She did not question this, or ask how he knew. But the news circulated and, when the Land Rover drove into their camp, every cooking pot held extra food in anticipation of *!ebili's* return.

Alex, too, had sensed they were close to finding the clan. The season was *#obe,* the time after the summer rains but before the cold weather of *!gum.* He knew the smaller pans would be drying up and the clan would have moved to one of the main pans or permanent springs so they would have access to water through the long dry winter. !Ka and his clan would be living mainly on mongongo nuts, berries and summer melons. Hunting and snaring activities, while it still went on, rarely yielded much meat. The animals the clan hunted could still find water over a wide area and so locating them, an easy task when water was short, would be too difficult.

218

Alex knew of eight different camp sites the clan used during *#obe*. He discounted three, knowing it was too soon for them to return. That left five. They had to be at one of them.

The camp was invisible until they were almost on top of it. In fact, even though Alex knew what to look for, he nearly missed it. Children playing with a *zani* stick gave its presence away. Alex felt a rush of affection when he saw them. He had played the game with them when he was sixteen. It was a simple toy, a length of hollow reed with small soft guinea fowl feathers stuck to one end, a short strip of leather weighted with acacia gum fastened with sinew to the other, and a large feather bound to the centre. It provided hours of fun. If properly made, when tossed into the air it would float and spin back down, slowly drifting on the breeze. The object of the game was to be in a position to catch it on the point of a stick and toss it in the air again.

He slowed the Land Rover and watched but the presence of white people had all the children staring at the vehicle in fascination, the *zani* falling to earth, forgotten. Alex opened the door and got out. 'It is me, !Oma, child of the Moon, *!ebili,*' he called.

After some excited conversation and nervous giggling, one of the boys raced over. 'Come, *!ebili*, come and play the game with us.'

Alex took the proffered stick. Another boy handed him the *zani* and Alex tried to throw it into the air but it belly-flopped to earth. The watching children laughed so hard a couple of younger ones fell over. The *zani* was thrown up by one of them and all the children positioned themselves politely out of reach to give Alex a chance to catch it. He missed.

Shaking his head and laughing with them at himself, he

got back behind the wheel and drove the last hundred yards with the children running alongside. 'They seem to have known we were coming. Those kids were waiting for us.' Chrissy was astonished.

'They would have known.' He did not know how but, many times, he had seen the clan anticipate visitors.

'They weren't afraid of you. What did you say to them?'

'I told them my name.'

'But they're too young to remember you.'

'They don't have to. !Oma is a clan name, it immediately tells them I am one of them. They all know the story of how !Ka found the little beetle and they've all been told I have the mark of the Moon on my body. As far as they're concerned, I'm family. Besides, they probably heard the adults say I was coming.' He stopped the Land Rover outside the circle of huts. 'There they are,' he said softly, love and affection making his voice husky. 'My second parents.'

Be hobbled to him, her tiny wrinkled features stretched wide in a smile. !Ka rose with dignity and walked to the vehicle. The children danced and shrieked around them. 'Welcome !Oma, little beetle, child of the Moon.' Be and !Ka had aged. Their life was a hard one. It would not be too long before they would be unable to keep up with the wandering clan. For as long as they could, their age would guarantee the respect of the others. But as soon as they became a burden they would be left behind, in a hut, with as many supplies as the clan could spare. Lions would probably end their lives. It was something they accepted.

They sat in the shade of some trees, visited continually by others. Chrissy's bright red hair was a source of great amazement to the clan, especially the women, and they hovered around her, touching it continually.

'They are saying your hair is like a fire at night.'

'Is that good?'

Alex smiled at her. 'They say mine is like the Moon. They asked if you are my wife. They said the Moon and the fire make a good combination but they warn the fire must not burn the Moon and the Moon must not let the fire go out.'

'Tell them I will never burn their precious Moon and if the Moon lets me go out I'll beat him around the ears.'

'I will tell them nothing of the sort. You are a woman. You have no opinions on important matters.'

'I'll get you for that.'

The Bushmen had politely listened to this exchange. Alex spoke to !Ka who laughed gently. He turned back to Chrissy. 'I told him the Moon's light and the fire's light should produce many bright children.'

The anthropologist in Chrissy found the clan fascinating. Despite not speaking the language, and with no-one in the clan able to speak English, she left Alex with the men and went with Be to watch her prepare some melons for roasting. Her trained eye took in the simplicity of Be's 'kitchen' and cooking utensils. A small fire, an iron pot, several spoons carved from wood and a couple of bones sharpened at the tip. Smooth stones of varying sizes were stacked against the hut. Be saw Chrissy's interest and picked up two of them. Taking an unappetising looking root, she placed it on the larger stone. Then, with short, sharp movements, shredded the tuber.

Squatting next to Be, Chrissy observed that although the root was tough and the utensils rudimentary, the San woman's actions were economical, designed to conserve energy. She supposed this to be due to the extreme heat in which these people lived and worked. She would dearly have

221

loved to try shredding the food herself and held out her hands, hoping Be would understand. But Be, with a small, almost apologetic smile, put the stones back where they came from.

Chrissy had no idea what had just taken place, although her training and instincts told her it would be unwise to pursue the matter. Rubbing and grinding stones were of such personal importance to San women that, when they died, they were buried with them. Be's polite refusal to let Chrissy touch the stones was a measure of her depth of feeling for Alex. She could see that the little beetle had fondness in his heart for this girl with fire in her hair. Instead of being angry at the breach of etiquette, something she would very quickly have become normally, she had stepped briefly outside her own world to make allowances for Chrissy's ignorance.

As if to make amends, she showed Chrissy her mortar and pestle and encouraged her to handle it. Feeling the glass-like surface of the pestle, Chrissy wondered how many hands, over how many years, had worn the wood to form such a slippery and rock hard utensil.

Her knees were aching from squatting. She knew that Be could squat for hours. She tried to get more comfortable but her western style jeans would not allow her knees to rest against her shoulders like Be. Smiling, she stood up and stretched.

Be stood as well. Chrissy felt a rough hand on her arm. Shyly, Be traced her fingers down both arms, holding each wrist firmly for several seconds. When Chrissy looked at the San woman she was startled to see tears in her eyes. Be's finger ran along the veins in Chrissy's hands. Quite suddenly, with an exclamation which sounded almost like disgust, Be broke the contact and went back to her cooking fire.

222

Chrissy sensed that something unusual had happened. She would like to have asked Alex to explain but he was deep in conversation with the men. Another woman beckoned for Chrissy to sample some food. She was quickly absorbed by a demonstration some young girls gave her on making a necklace with ostrich egg shell and the strange incident with Be was forgotten.

That night they ate roasted melons, then a stew made up mainly of tubers which Alex found delicious. Chrissy ate tentatively, refusing a second helping, explaining that the melons had filled her up. Feeling unusually tired, she excused herself and went off to the hut which the Bushmen had erected especially for their visitors. The strangeness of these people, the fresh desert air, the different sights and sounds had worn her out.

Alex sat and talked to the men far into the night, drawing pictures on the sand of places the clan knew well, until they understood where he was looking for diamonds. !Ka nodded. 'I have seen the bright stones sometimes in this place.'

He drew deeply on his pipe. Alex had brought tobacco knowing the San loved nothing better than to smoke and talk. Finally !Ka spoke. 'When I was a boy the land was different. The seasons change it. In some places the wind has blown the sand so much the ground is as hard as our cooking pots. In other places the sand has gathered and become very tall. In these places you will have to dig very far to find what you seek.'

'How far will I have to dig?'

!Ka pointed his pipe at the hut, some thirty feet away, where Chrissy slept. 'As far as that. Maybe more.' He puffed on the pipe again, enjoyment evident on his face. 'I have not seen stones in this place for many seasons. But I have not visited where the ground is hard since I was a young man.' !Ka smiled at him. 'You know—for you have learned well—how useless such land is to us. The Mantis has seen fit to move the sands. Who knows! Perhaps he blows it away for a reason. You might know this reason, !Oma, for you have the mark of the Moon on you.'

'Indeed, my father. I will seek both the hard land and the deep sand when I return.'

'Go to the hard land first. When I was a boy I saw many such stones there. If you do not find your stones then go to the place where the Mantis sends the sand. It will not be too far. Follow the direction of the wind, my son. Stop where the sand is so tall you cannot find the land underneath.' He shook his head. 'I hope it will be worth such hard work.'

Alex smiled. 'I know you have no use for such things but the white man desires them very much.'

'What use does the white man find for these stones?'

'He makes ornaments for his women.'

!Ka was impressed. 'He must be very clever. We cannot use them, they are too hard for us to work.'

'He has made special tools to work the stones.'

!Ka sighed. 'He seems a clever fellow then. It has always been so, ever since he tricked us to give him our share of the animals. He is . . .' !Ka struggled to find the right words, '. . . he must be a restless man, for only restless men seek those things not readily available.' !Ka did not actually use a word for restless—the word didn't exist in the San vocabulary. The way he put it, a combination of words and sounds, took several minutes and described the antics of foraging ants, the wind and the seemingly pointless actions of the jackal who is hardly ever still.

Alex nodded. 'You are right. The white man is restless, like the jackal.'

'Restless men are not easily satisfied. Nor is the clever old man jackal.'

'No.'

'Are all white men like this?'

Alex smiled. 'Most of them.'

'Is this not foolish? Do they not take time to sit and talk? What is it that makes them so restless?' As with all Bushmen, and despite his belief that the jackal was a clever hunter, !Ka held the restlessness of this animal in the utmost contempt. His belief, that the distinctive black, white, cream and tan markings on the jackal's back had not been put there by the Great God, but burned there when !Ka's own ancestors had thrown the contents of a cooking pot over the animal when they could stand his agitated actions no longer, was deeply entrenched and never questioned. It was not the animal itself the San despised, just his constant motion.

'To answer your question is hard,' Alex said. 'The San do not understand the white man's heart, just as the white man does not understand the heart of the San.'

'That is very true,' !Ka said quietly. 'Is *!ebili* going to try and make us understand?'

Alex hesitated, collecting his thoughts. Then, 'When the white man is a child he is taught to be better than all the rest. He is encouraged to run faster, be stronger, be more clever than everyone else. This is where it starts. By the time he is a man he has learned to be restless because he is always seeking that which is just out of reach. He needs to show the others how clever he is. It is something he cannot help.' The men were listening intently. Alex knew his words would be repeated again and again. 'Your people say it is wrong to fight or boast or be selfish. You believe it is pointless to want more than you need. The white man does not believe it is wrong or pointless. To

225

him, these things make him strong. Do you understand?'

!Ka shook his head. 'Then tell us this, !Oma. Where will the white man go when he can go no further?'

Alex knew he had reached the extremity of !Ka's understanding. And he knew to speak of space exploration or new technology would not be believed and the men would be insulted to think he would lie to them. So he said, 'I think when the white man can go no further he will become so dissatisfied he will destroy himself.'

!Ka clapped his hands softly. 'Then, !Oma, the white man is not as clever as the jackal. Would it not be better for you to seek these stones slowly. If you find them as a young man, where will you go then?'

Alex stared into the fire a long time before he answered. No-one else spoke. They politely waited for him to find his words. 'I have but one life,' he said finally. 'I seek these stones so I can live my life according to my heart's wishes. You see, you have taught me your ways and yet I have learned the white man ways too. If I have these stones I can live both ways. I must do this for I have both ways inside me.' He paused again, wondering if he could make them understand. 'When the Great God created himself he said, "I am *Chi-dole,* no-one can command me," and he then made the food and the water so all men could live.'

'That is so,' !Ka agreed.

'Did he also make the food and water so the white man can live?'

'I do not know,' !Ka said soberly. 'I suppose he must have.'

'The white man has his own Great God,' another man said sternly. 'He does not share our God with us.'

'He does not share his land or his food with us either,' someone else said. 'Why is this?'

'Because he is restless,' Alex told the men.

'Are you restless, *!ebili*?'

Alex waited again. It was important to him that his friends understood. 'In my heart . . .' he said finally, '. . . I have the old man jackal. There is nothing I can do about that. He was put there by the white man's Great God for the reasons I have already given. The jackal makes me want my own lands.'

He had their complete attention. 'When I lived with you other things were put in my heart. If I find these stones I can buy my own land and the restless jackal will be satisfied. Then I can listen to the words of the San in my heart.'

Several heads nodded but !Ka puffed his pipe and said, 'Then beware, my son. Our ways leave you like a helpless infant in the white man's world. It is better for you to forget our ways. The restless, like the jackal, seeks his own company.'

'Yes,' Alex said soberly, realising he had failed to make them understand his need. 'But it must surely be possible to put the good from both ways together.'

One of the others leaned forward. 'Have you ever seen the lion cry tears of remorse?'

And Alex had no answer.

'*!ebili* is too silent' !Ka commented quietly. 'Perhaps he is wondering how to make the lion cry?'

It broke the sombre mood and had everyone laughing with delight.

'Tell us of this woman you bring here,' !Ka said, when the laughter died down.

So Alex spent some time telling them of the far away lands where she came from, where the rain is so cold it falls in white tufts like the soft belly hair of the springbok. He spoke of rolling green hills, of oceans and cities and men with strange customs. They listened enthralled. No-one had ever spoken before of such things in a language and a manner they could understand.

He was loving being back with these people, especially when he did not have to translate. He had pondered long and hard as to the ethics of bringing Chrissy here. !Ka's people had avoided contact with whites all their lives. Some of the children had, until today, never seen a white person. !Ka was too polite to say so, but Alex wondered if he had overstepped the courtesy mark by bringing her with him. But when, hesitantly, he tried to raise the subject, !Ka simply smiled and said, 'Are you happy, !Oma, now that you are with your own kind?'

'I am happy in the desert, Father. I do not like the towns.'

!Ka nodded. 'The desert has given you back your life more than once. She can be very cruel to those who do not listen to her. You are of the desert now, !ebili, and the desert is of you. Heed her voice.' Was it criticism? He did not know.

Then they talked of other things, of San things, of nature and spirits and seasons past, of life and death, of finding Alex in the desert and, of course, of the Moon. That same moon was long set before he entered his hut and fell into a dreamless sleep.

Despite earlier worries about Marv coping with Pru, Chrissy happily agreed to spend an extra day with the clan. She woke refreshed and eager to learn more about them. After all, it gave her an excellent insight into a way of life that was, until 10,000 years ago, the way of life of all humanity.

She had always believed that the hunting and gathering subsistence life of the Bushmen left them permanently hungry and in constant pursuit of sustenance. But when she was invited to go with Be and several other women to collect food for their meal that night, she was surprised when the group ignored a patch of melons and headed further away from camp with a purpose that left her in little doubt that they knew exactly where they were going and what they were gathering.

The women stopped in a grove of mongongo nut trees and began to fill their bags with nuts. Chrissy could see literally thousands rotting on the ground. Clearly, there was such an abundance of nuts the clan couldn't eat them all. Be showed her which nuts to take and which to leave. It was an enjoyable experience. The silence in the desert was broken only by the conversation of the women. Excluded from understanding their language, she nonetheless sensed they were discussing simple, everyday things—food, children, husbands—the same as women all over the world.

On the way back to camp, Be pointed off to her left and, when she looked, Chrissy was horrified to see a big, black-maned lion was keeping up with them some 300 feet away. The women were completely unconcerned and, after a few minutes, Chrissy realised that the lion was simply following them out of curiosity. Just before they reached camp, the lion vanished.

Back in camp, Alex explained and translated what appeared to be a violent argument.

'N!ou has killed a porcupine,' he said. 'They are discussing how the meat is to be distributed.'

'Was it poisoned?' She didn't fancy the possibility of eating contaminated meat.

'They don't often poison porcupines. They seal the holes in his burrow except for the entrance. Then they build a fire just inside it and wait. When the animal makes a break for it they club it to death.' He laughed. 'Porcupines are okay. It's when they do that to warthog that things can get tricky.'

229

'Why are they shouting at each other? They look as though they're about to fight.'

'This is normal. Fifteen, twenty minutes from now they'll be laughing.'

She watched them. Several men appeared to be on the verge of physical violence. Then someone interjected with a few words and the whole group was suddenly rendered helpless with laughter. 'That's amazing!'

Alex smiled. 'Sometimes I think they argue so they can enjoy a good laugh afterwards.'

'Why were they arguing anyway? If N!ou . . .' she stumbled over the click in N!ou's name, '. . . killed the porcupine, then the meat is surely his.'

He looked at her in mock horror. 'Sacrilege, sacrilege,' he said. 'The San don't operate that way, my darling girl. All food is to be shared. *How* it's shared depends on the size. Small game—hares, birds, snakes and such—is cooked by the hunter's wife and eaten by his family. However, if anyone else joins the family at their fire they *must* offer them some. If they don't then you'd really see an argument.'

'How about the porcupine?'

'Again, the hunter's wife cooks it. Once it's cooked portions are distributed to everyone else.'

'I'll bet N!ou's wife is pleased he didn't kill an elephant then.' She grinned at the mental image of the poor woman trying to stuff an elephant into her cooking pot.

'They don't hunt elephants. !Ka says the San believe elephants think like humans. They leave them alone.'

'I don't suppose such a belief has developed out of respect for an elephant's size?'

'You're thinking like a white woman.'

'I guess I am.' She told him about the lion she'd seen.

'They're certainly not cowards. The only one worried about the lion was me.'

'That lion has been around for years. They know it won't harm them. But you're right, they're not cowards.'

She looked up at him. 'I'm loving this, Alex. Thank you for bringing me.'

He put his arm around her. 'Thanks for coming. Seeing things through your eyes shows me how much they've taught me.' He kissed her ear. 'Now, to complete your education on the distribution of food, if N!ou had killed a large animal the food would have been cut up and shared three ways. About a fifth would be kept by N!ou and another fifth made into biltong. The rest would go to relatives in camp. It would then be up to them to share their portion with other relatives.'

'There's something I don't understand.'

'What?'

'If the clan has such clear cut rules about how meat is divided, why are they having a hell of a row over there?'

Alex laughed. 'Because, darling, having a hell of a row, as you so elegantly put it, is one of the most enjoyable pastimes there is. There are heaps of things to row about. N!ou, for example, has had an argument with his sister's husband. What they're yelling about is that he wants to give his brother-in-law less meat than anyone else. !Ka has the porcupine as a totem and is not allowed to eat the meat. He's shouting at N!ou for being so stupid as to kill an animal he is forbidden to harm. That man waving his arm about is saying his family is large and he should get more of the meat than the others.'

Once again, the argument ceased abruptly as the men rolled around with laughter.

'What made them laugh?'

Alex was laughing as hard as the men. When he could, he

231

explained: '!Ka has just reminded everyone of the time N!ou brought a warthog back and, when they went to cut it up, it came to life and put most of the men up trees.'

She laughed too. 'He's a very wise man.'

'He's the wisest man I know,' Alex agreed. 'But why do you say that?'

'He's diffused the conflict with humour.'

'They all do that. As much as they love to argue, they back right away from fighting. They all know they have the capacity to kill. They go to extraordinary lengths to avoid serious dispute. They'd rather leave the clan than resort to physical violence.'

'What makes them like that I wonder?'

'I can't answer that. However, it's learned right from infancy. They have no concept of honour, bravery or masculine superiority. The games they play as children lack the competitiveness of our games. When I stayed with them I made a rough football. It was just a springbok skin stuffed with grass and sewn up. I tried to teach the boys rugby. They simply didn't see the point of it and got more fun out of running, throwing and catching. Their games are about sharing, not proving themselves.'

The porcupine, boiled with a kind of wild spinach and the sauce thickened with ground mongongo nuts, was delicious. Chrissy tucked into it with the same gusto as Alex. She saw Be watching her and smiled, rubbing her stomach and nodding. Be smiled back but her eyes held Chrissy's and the smile never reached them.

Chrissy sat with Alex and the men for a while that night but she could see that having to translate all the time was distracting him so she said goodnight. After she left, Be said, 'The fire which burns bright on that one's head burns bright in her heart too.'

'Yes.' Alex smiled at her. 'It burns bright in my heart as well.'

Be nodded seriously. 'You should marry that one, !Oma. You should have children. You should do it quickly.'

Alex was delighted she approved. 'As quickly as she will agree, my mother.' He had just turned twenty but he knew what he wanted. Chrissy's interest in the San, the way she happily fitted in with the women, had impressed him. He knew he was in love with her.

'The fire runs through the veins as well, !Oma,' Be said.

'*!ebili* knows that fire' !Ka said sharply. 'Stop your talking, woman. You are making us all tired.'

Alex glanced at him, surprised.

'We have other things to discuss,' !Ka said. 'We want *!ebili* to tell us more about the places far from here.'

And they talked until the moon had set and the backbone of the sky began to fade.

He was sad to say goodbye the next morning. He knelt in front of !Ka and allowed him to wipe his perspiration over his head. He held Be's hand a fraction longer than normal. They were getting old and he wondered if he would ever see them again.

Chrissy, sensing his mood, was silent for the first half hour. In the end, though, she burst out, 'Please, please can we stop and wash your hair?' As she tipped some water over his head from one of the containers he heard her say softly, 'Seeing you out there with those people tells me so much about you.'

233

He straightened and shook his head, water flying everywhere. 'That I'm a mad Bushman?' He wiped his face and grinned at her.

'No.' She looked into his eyes. 'That you are a very special person.' She leaned towards him. 'I want to kiss you very badly.'

Alex was only too happy to oblige.

The closer they got to the cattle post, the more Chrissy worried about Pru and Marv. 'She only arrived yesterday,' Alex pointed out. 'She can't have savaged him to death yet.'

'Pru could make mince meat of the devil in the space of ten minutes.'

'But Marv is so friendly.' He looked over at her. 'Why are you so down on her if she's your friend?'

She grinned. 'I'm not really down on her. It's just . . . Look, Pru's childhood was a bit odd. Her mother probably never loved anyone in her life, least of all Pru. Her father is so damned vague he's possibly forgotten he even has a daughter. Pru was basically raised by the servants. Her parents travelled all the time, they never took her along and they never rushed home to be with her during the holidays. I remember one time she was very excited because her parents were going to be home. When she got there she found all the letters she'd written to them during the term in a drawer, unopened. When she asked her mother why she hadn't read the letters, Lady bloody Darlington-Brown said, "But, darling, they're so boring." '

'Ouch!' Alex said.

'Pru developed a facade. The only role model she had was her mother, whom she adored. The result, I'm afraid, is one very insecure girl who acts like a bloody duchess, who hides her insecurity behind biting remarks and who refuses to let anyone get close in case she gets hurt. I am the only exception. We've known each other since prep school and she trusts me.'

'Some people should never have children.' Alex shifted down a gear and swerved around a pothole. 'I take it she doesn't see much of her parents now.'

'On the contrary. She and her mother press cheeks and call each other darling and go to first nights together. She hunts with her father and just about kills herself trying to win his approval. It's so sad. All her mother ever does is criticise. Her father is so busy with whatever mistress is current he barely speaks to Pru. And she keeps knocking herself out just trying to get them to *see* her.'

Alex wondered what !Ka and his clan would make of such people.

It was four in the afternoon when they drove into the cattle post. There was no sign of Pru or Marv, although the two suitcases in the hut showed she had arrived.

They heard a Land Rover about an hour later. 'Here they come,' Alex called.

He didn't know what he expected Pru to be, an obvious misfit of some kind maybe. But he was not prepared for the Prudence Darlington-Brown who leapt from the vehicle screaming, 'Darling, thank God you're here. The company leaves a bit to be desired,' before throwing herself at Chrissy with almost hysterical joy. He looked at Marv. His friend sat in the Land Rover in abject misery. Two days with Pru had taken their toll. Marv looked like a whipped cur.

Chrissy led Pru to Alex and introduced them. 'He's a bit young, darling,' was her greeting.

Marv joined them. 'Welcome back,' he said to Alex with profound relief.

'Come, sweetie, we have so much to talk about.' Pru dragged Chrissy inside.

'How's it been?' Alex spoke out of the side of his mouth.

'Perfectly frightful.' Marv gave such a good imitation of Pru's accent that Alex laughed.

'She's attractive enough.' And she was. Tall, leggy, slim, blonde hair cut in a bob and a face to turn heads.

'Yeah,' Marv agreed miserably. 'If she could just keep her mouth shut.'

From inside the cabin came shrill screams of, what sounded like, totally forced laughter. Alex told Marv the little he knew of Pru. 'All this is an act,' he concluded.

Marv looked thoughtfully at the hut, his tender heart touched.

When the girls rejoined them they all sat around the fire drinking beer from bottles. Pru had calmed down somewhat although anything she said was peppered with 'dahling' or 'sweetie'. She spoke to Chrissy mainly, giving her news of people at home. She was polite and distant to Alex. It was to Marv that she directed most of her rudeness.

When he brought her a beer, 'Oh how perfectly lovely— my own slave.'

When he offered her a cooked sausage, 'Ugh, you've touched it with your fingers. No thanks.'

When she said she was cold and he fetched her cardigan, 'Not *that* one, the blue one. Go and find it, it's in there somewhere.' Marv patiently went back for the blue one. Pru didn't even thank him.

Alex could see Chrissy was getting cross. Come to that, he wasn't too pleased either. No-one expected Marv's sudden outburst.

'. . . so Mummy was absolutely livid. I mean she's put up

236

with Daddy's indiscretions for years, you know what he's like. Poor Daddy, he just can't help himself. But really, dahling, Janice is Mummy's best friend. She . . .'

'That's enough,' Marv snapped.

Pru looked at him startled. 'I beg your pardon, I was speaking to Chrissy not you.'

'I said, that's enough.'

'How *dare* you.'

Marv stood up. 'Don't you have a life?' He scratched his head. 'Your parents are about as interesting as a pet rock. Do you ever talk about anything else?'

Pru's mouth had dropped open. Wordlessly, she turned to Chrissy for support.

'He's got a point,' Chrissy said gently.

Still speechless, Pru turned back to Marv who grinned, shrugged and handed her another beer. 'Get that into you.'

She snatched it from him angrily.

Marv sat down again and looked at her reflectively. Alex could see he was trying to find the right words and braced himself for one of Marv's gaffes. 'You don't like yourself very much, do you?'

'Of course I do.'

Marv grinned again. 'Bullshit!'

Pru jumped to her feet. 'I don't have to listen to this.' She turned to go.

'Sit!' Marv barked the command as if he was speaking to a dog.

'I will not. Who do you think you are?'

Marv groaned and lumbered to his feet. He put his hands on her shoulders and made her sit down, then stood over her. 'Jesus, lady, I'm just a man who'd like to know you better. Do you have to make it so hard?'

Pru went wordless again.

Alex and Chrissy spoke together, trying to fill the awkward silence, stopped when each of them realised the other was speaking, started together again and finally fell silent themselves.

Alex realised suddenly that his friend found Pru attractive but wasn't sure how to get through the protective barriers she had erected, but Marv was having an inspirational night. He cut straight to the bone. 'You are beautiful, intelligent and, when you're not acting like a bloody spoilt brat, very nice. Give us all a break and just be yourself.'

Pru's mouth formed a perfect O.

Chrissy said quickly, 'I guess what Marv's trying to say is you're amongst friends. You're way out in the African bush, under the stars, surrounded by space. There ain't no-one here but us and we all like you *au naturel*.'

Pru stood up suddenly.

'Where are you going now?' Marv demanded.

'Inside.'

'Why?'

'To get a bottle of wine. I brought some with me.' She glared at Marv. 'If that's okay with you of course.'

'Bring four glasses.'

'Get them yourself.'

Shaking his head, Marv followed her into the hut.

Alex went to speak but Chrissy raised a finger to her lips. 'She's taking it in, it's having an effect on her,' she whispered.

'How can you tell?' he whispered back.

She grinned. 'He's still alive isn't he?'

They could hear Marv and Pru in the kitchen. 'I don't suppose you have anything as useful as a corkscrew?'

'Swiss army knife do? Or is that too basic for you?'

'Don't just stand there, open the bloody wine.'

'Yes ma'am.'

They came back outside bickering. Marv poured the wine and handed out the glasses. 'French,' he said briefly, having tasted his.

'Daddy says . . .' She stopped abruptly. 'It's from Bellet. Locals swear by it. Travels well.'

'You brought it all this way?'

'No I did not. I found it in a wine shop in Johannesburg. I thought Chrissy might like some decent wine for a change.'

'What's wrong with South African wine?' Marv asked, stung.

'Nothing.' She hesitated, then added, 'If you like vinegar.'

'South Africa has some excellent wines,' Marv protested.

'Really,' Pru said coolly. 'They must keep them well hidden.'

The barbs kept coming. Finally Alex and Chrissy could take it no longer, said goodnight and left them to it. 'They're worse than children,' Alex said once they were inside the hut. 'I don't know how much more of this Marv will stand for.'

'She's warming to him, trust me on this,' Chrissy grinned at him. 'No-one has ever stood up to her before.'

The two of them were still arguing outside when Alex drifted off to sleep. At some stage during the night he was woken by a crash and a giggle. Marv and Pru were at the refrigerator getting another bottle of wine, whispering so as not to wake Alex and Chrissy. But, like most people when their sensibilities have been overruled by the intake of far too much alcohol, their whispered conversation sounded rather like they were using microphones. Alex turned over and went back to sleep. At least they'd stopped arguing.

What seemed like seconds later he was jerked awake again by the most hideous noise. It took him some time to realise that Pru and Marv were lustily, and with no regard for the fact that neither of them could carry a tune, murdering 'Poor Little Buttercup'. If the composers of *Pirates of Penzance*, and many other excellent operettas, had heard them, Alex doubted they would have recognised it as their own.

Chrissy and Pru returned to Gaberones the next day. By the time they left, it was clear some kind of chemistry was happening between Marv and Pru.

Twice, she started to say something about her parents but, with a look from Marv, she changed her mind.

'What's going on?' Alex asked Chrissy.

'At a guess, Marv's directness has sliced straight through to Pru's soul,' Chrissy told him. 'He could be exactly what she needs.' She waved her hand at four empty wine bottles. 'I think she could do without the hangover though.'

Alex laughed. 'Did you hear them?'

'Hear them!' She pulled a face. 'They probably heard them in Gabs.'

'It *was* Gilbert and Sullivan wasn't it?'

'God knows!'

'Well I think it's great. I've never seen two people less suited to each other, yet look at them. She could be exactly what he needs too,' Alex replied. 'Marv is reaching out to the hurt in her. She's appealing to the mother in him.'

'She's appealing to a bit more than that,' Chrissy grinned. 'Get a load of the body language.'

!Ka had indicated they should be searching an area further southwest from where they found the first diamond. It was land they had not considered suitable and, as far as Alex knew, was beyond the Molepolole chief's area of tribal land.

Alex surveyed the landscape doubtfully. 'If we find anything I'll probably have to go to Mafeking to find out who owns the place.' They had set off to find the area as soon as the girls left.

Marv looked sour. He was suffering horribly from a hangover. 'Do that. It'd be nice to know we're not going to be arrested for trespassing.'

This was different country. Not desert, not grassy grazing land, somewhere in the middle. The ground was white, not the sandy yellow of further east. It looked like powdered chalk. And it was as hard as !Ka had promised.

'Jesus!' The pick hit rock and stopped dead, sending reverberations along Alex's arms. 'I hope !Ka's wrong. I'm not sure I want to find anything here.'

'You'd better hope we do, we're running out of money.'

Diamonds, at the best of times, are very hard to find. Geologists, using their knowledge of how the earth's crust and mantle formed, of the Cretaceous period eighty million years ago when a weakness in the crust caused such pressure in the mantle to build up against seams in the crust that molten rock was forced towards the surface, know what they're looking for. Despite the added benefit of technology, exploration budgets, aerial surveys and heavy equipment, they are not always successful. The carrot shaped kimberlite pipes, only a few of which carry diamonds with them, are inclined to be reticent about revealing their presence.

Not encumbered with this knowledge, Alex and Marv were just plain lucky.

On the third day, after two days of backbreaking nothing, vultures circling told them of a dead or dying animal. They found the ostrich, dead from a cause they did not bother to identify, a mile from where they had been working. Slitting open the gizzard, they sifted through its contents. And there they were. Not one, not two but six stones, the largest the size of a pea.

Returning to where they had been working Alex realised that, between there and the ostrich, the ground rose slightly. He stopped and looked around. In an oval of perhaps a hundred feet, the ground had a curious yellow tinge. 'Marv.'

Marv stopped walking and turned back.

'Is it me, or is this ground a different colour?'

Marv squinted around him. 'Maybe.' He shaded his eyes. 'Yes it is. It goes in a sort of circle.'

They looked at each other. 'This could be it,' Alex whispered.

'There aren't any trees. I thought you said the vegetation . . .'

'Nothing would grow on this ground, Marv.'

Marv's face split into a grin. 'What are we waiting for then?'

'You go and get the Land Rover. I'll stay here. We must have walked over this place several times and not noticed it. I don't want to lose it now.'

They worked the yellow ground for three days. While it was hardly diamond studded they found enough stones to keep them there. There were no anthills, no indicators, nothing textbook about the land but they found diamonds. They didn't even have to dig. Once they had found a few their eyes grew used to seeing the distinctive shape. 'I'd have walked straight past this,' Marv said. They were averaging fourteen stones a day, although nothing as big as the diamond they found on the ridge where Nightmare had been. Most were hardly bigger than a pinhead. The ground was so hard they discovered the best way to search was to use their stiff brushes, sweep the top layer of dirt into a pile then scoop the pile into the fine mesh sieve. Marv swept and scooped. Alex sieved. After three days Alex decided it was time to find out who the land belonged to.

Marv said he'd stay and keep looking. Alex took their precious store of stones with him. He wanted to know they were tucked away in a safe deposit box. There was no time to see Chrissy. He only just had time to organise a safe place for the diamonds and nearly missed the train. He called her from the railway station in Gaberones just before boarding the train for Mafeking. 'I'll be back day after tomorrow. See you then.'

'What are you doing? Why are you going down to South Africa? Can you stay for a while?'

'Don't think so. I'll tell you about it when I get back. Have you got a cold? Your voice sounds funny. Gotta go, train's about to leave. Love you.'

'Love you too. Bye,' she croaked, sniffing.

Discovering who owned the land proved impossible. As the administrative centre for Bechuanaland, Mafeking was responsible for maintaining and storing all legal documents, even though Mafeking itself was in neighbouring South Africa.

'Sorry,' the clerk said. 'Since the District Commissioner's Report seems to confirm that the people of Bechuanaland want independence, London has told us to be ready for a transfer of all records. We've already started crating. Land deeds were among the first since we figured land was hardly going to change hands while everything was up in the air. I'm afraid you'll just have to wait.'

'Until when?'

'That depends on when Britain finally accepts the new

constitution. Rumours are the move could take place as early as next February.'

'Next February! That's ten months away.'

'Sorry, sir. There's nothing I can do. I understand your frustration but please try to see our point of view. We've got records going back to 1895. If we left everything until the last minute it'd be one hell of a mess. As it is, we're up against the clock. We still have to keep the show rolling. It's not just a matter of packing up and labelling every damned thing that's been documented for the last seventy years.' The man waved his arm at his overflowing desk. 'That includes births, deaths, weddings, prison records, land ownership, court matters . . .' he took a deep breath.

'Yes, yes,' Alex said hastily to interrupt the flow. 'Thank you for your time.'

'I'd wait if I were you, especially if you want to buy land. The system's likely to change. It's going to be a black man's country. Not much point in you buying something if the new government takes it off you is there?' The clerk looked smug. 'You whites will be sorry, you mark my words. Those bloody kaffirs will take it all back. All the hard work you've done will be for nothing. Those lazy buggers will just sit under the trees. I'm telling you, man, give them ten years and it'll be like you were never there.'

His attitude annoyed Alex. 'That won't affect me, I was born there. Besides,' he added, to get the man's goat, 'I'm not white. My father was reclassified in this country. I'm coloured.' For the first time in his life he could understand why his parents fled into Bechuanaland. The clerk made it plain that in South Africa white was right and black was the most undesirable thing since smallpox.

The man was staring at him aghast. Alex stared back,

unblinking. Finally, 'You're having me on. You're not coloured, no way. Still,' he frowned severely, like a displeased headmaster, 'if you are coloured you've come through the wrong door. Blacks have to use the other entrance.'

Alex looked to where he pointed. The two entrances were side by side. Once inside the building, a flimsy partition split the enquiries area in half. But anyone wanting to be served had to go to the same counter. They were served by the same staff. All the partition appeared to achieve was to prevent black customers from distressing white customers by being visible.

He looked back at the clerk who was nervously watching him. 'I'm sorry, *baas*. I didn't see the other door.' He turned to leave.

'Hey!'

Alex stifled a grin and turned back. 'Yes, *baas*.'

'You stop that, you hear. It might seem funny but if the police get ahold of you it won't be funny. No, sir. They don't take too kindly to that sort of thing.'

Defeated, Alex returned to Gaberones. 'Why don't you ask Jacob?' Chrissy suggested. 'After all, the land is close to his. Maybe he knows.'

He asked Chrissy about her cold but she said it had gone. Pru was out on a one-day tour of surrounding districts. 'She's a bit taken with Marv,' Chrissy said. 'She's talking about staying here and finding a job.'

'I'll tell Marv. He hasn't said a word about her but I think he'll be pleased.'

It was late afternoon and they were lying in bed. He had a bottle of beer on his chest and his arm under her neck.

Chrissy was making suggestive movements on the bottle, encircling the neck and running her long tapered fingers down to the base. She was not touching him at all but the effect was the same.

'You're a witch.' He watched her fingers. 'I can feel that.'

She laughed, throaty and languid. 'How does this feel?' She put the palm of her hand on the bottle opening and slowly rubbed in a circular movement. 'Or this?' She licked her fingertips and ran them very slowly down the neck of the bottle.

Alex groaned. 'I've made a tent.'

Her fingers stroked the bottle. 'Is it as strong as this?'

He removed the bottle and leaned over her. 'Better. Want to see?'

The next morning he drove to Molepolole. He could have telephoned Jacob but he needed to show him on a map exactly where the land was. Jacob had a cavalier approach to land, especially if it bordered with his. Alex wanted to do this right. No slip-ups, no misunderstandings. There was too much at stake.

Jacob did know who owned the land. 'You plurry fool. Should have asked me first. That land belongs to the Chief.'

'Does he use it?' Alex knew that the Chief of an area had extraordinary powers. It was up to him to apportion land. If the land where he found the diamonds belonged to the Chief, depending on the nature of the Chief, it might short-circuit months of negotiating. It all hinged on whether the land was being used. If it wasn't, Chief or not, others could ask for the right to use it.

Jacob knew this too. 'Have you seen cattle on it?'

'No.'

'He was using it last year.'

'Where do I find him?'

Jacob pointed. 'See that big hut over there, that's where he lives.' Then, as Alex turned to go, 'Wait, jong. Tch. You young people. Just wait up. There's a *kgotla* meeting on at the moment. You can't just bust into that.'

The *kgotla* was the most important of all the Chief's functions. It was during this time, seated inside a crescent of poles and surrounded by villagers, that he attended to all the administrative and tribal law matters affecting his village. He also had to arbitrate in the most serious of family disagreements. Only the most insurmountable problems were brought to the attention of the Chief. The *kgotla* was like the High Court. Alex knew better than to interrupt.

Curbing his impatience he agreed to let Jacob get word to the Chief that Alex had something of importance to discuss with him. He returned to Gaberones to wait. It was three days before the Chief sent word that he could see him.

He used the time to enjoy privacy with Chrissy. Although they had been seeing each other for nearly three months, Marv had always been with them. Pru was hardly ever there—she seemed to have an insatiable thirst for knowledge about Bechuanaland which took her out and about every day. When she was in their company she treated Alex with indifference as before but it seemed that her life was being filled by all the new things she was discovering and she hardly ever mentioned her parents. Alex was pleased for her. He was also pleased to see the back of her each day.

With Pru out of the flat, they slept late, wandered naked around the place, bathed together, read the papers from South Africa passing sections back and forth, cooked breakfast together and made love often. Chrissy's company was a constant delight. She had a quick mind and sparred verbally with him, topping his puns with her own, telling funny stories, letting him into her past life so that, although he had grown to know her very well, within those few days, he felt he had always known her.

She came from Stirling in Scotland. 'It's like an overgrown country town,' she told him. 'Stirling castle dominates the city. You can see it for miles. It's a lovely sight, especially on a summer's night. There's a wonderful statue of Sir William Wallace who led an important battle against the English in the thirteenth century. Stirling is full of history.'

He loved to hear her speak. Her soft Scottish burr was like a song, lilting and calm. Calm was how he thought of her. He doubted she had ever questioned who or what she was. The serenity within her was a constant balm, delighting him with its soothing warmth.

On Monday, while she was at work, Jacob telephoned. 'The Chief can see you this morning. Eleven-thirty.'

He looked at his watch. It was an hour's drive to Molepolole and it was already after ten. To keep the Chief waiting would be an insult, resulting, more than likely, in a rejection. He rushed out of the flat, not stopping to write Chrissy a note. He knew she would understand.

The Chief of the village of Molepolole, which included much of the country west of the village, listened intently while Alex sought his permission to use tribal land. He heard Alex out in silence.

'It is true,' he said, not looking at Alex but at the forty or so men also listening, 'I am not using this land.'

Alex held his breath. As a resident of Bechuanaland, he was

248

entitled to ask for use of land. As a white, it was no foregone conclusion it would be granted. He could, if he had wished, make an offer to buy the land from the British administration. This would have been time consuming and, with independence being proposed, not necessarily granted. Going directly to the Chief was the best way he could think of to gain quick access.

'Do you have cattle?' One of the elders spoke to him.

'No, rra. I have no cattle.'

'Then why do you want the land?' the Chief asked.

This was the tricky bit. He did not wish to raise false hopes. Later, if their find was worth it, the entire village of Molepolole would benefit. But it was too soon for such announcements. 'I wish to buy cattle.'

The Chief smiled inwardly. This man was a fool. The reason he had not used the land himself was because there was no feed on it. His cattle had nearly starved. Besides, the area was bad lion country. He looked at the men listening. 'Does anyone object?'

There was a general shaking of heads. They all knew cattle would not thrive on this land.

'If I allow you to use this land, what will you give me?'

Alex swallowed a burst of anger. The Chief had no right to ask for anything. Keeping the anger from his eyes he replied, 'What would the Chief want?'

Shouted suggestions erupted from the crowd. The Chief held up his hand for silence. 'One beast every year and the land is yours. If you fail to use it I will grant it to someone else.'

Thanking the man profusely Alex made to leave but the Chief smiled at him. 'You may start to use the land as soon as you deliver the first beast.'

He took the problem to Jacob. 'I'll sell you one of my beasts. If you can't afford it you can pay me when you get rich.' Judging by his face, Jacob did not think Alex would get rich. 'By the way, someone was here looking for you the other day.'

'Who?'

'Don't know. Marthe spoke to him. She gave him directions to the cattle post. Young oke, about your age. Marthe didn't get his name. He was in a bit of a hurry.' Jacob frowned. 'He scared her a bit. She says he's been in an accident of some kind. Weird looking.'

Alex returned to the cattle post. Jacob promised to deliver one steer to the Chief on his behalf. It was early evening by the time he reached the shack. Marv didn't look too pleased to see him. 'Where the hell have you been?'

Alex filled him in. 'I'll have to go back either to Gaberones or Mafeking. Somehow, I have to get prospecting rights for the area. Nobody wants to help. Mafeking seem relieved to be getting rid of the files but Gaberones have nobody to take them over. They keep fobbing me off. The Department of Geological Surveys are supposedly the people to see but they're sitting on their hands because a new Department of Mines is in the pipeline. I keep hearing the name Segokgo but I can't locate the man. I tell you, Marv, it's impossible to get decisions at the moment. They're all waiting for the elections next March.'

'But the Chief has said we can use the land?'

'For cattle, yes. I didn't tell him about the diamonds.'

Marv shoved his hand in his pocket. 'Probably just as well.' He held out his hand. 'I've found these but they're not exactly leaping out of the ground.' He had perhaps twenty small diamonds in his hand.

'Maybe we're still looking in the wrong place. Okay, we know they're here somewhere but we haven't cracked it yet. Perhaps there's a bigger deposit further west.'

'The first stone we found was the best.' Marv dropped the results of his labour into an envelope. 'It's bloody hard work out there, man. Is it worth it?'

'Patience, my friend. Have faith.'

'Faith!' Marv looked sour. Then. 'I've been doing some thinking.'

'That could be dangerous,' Alex grinned. 'Just kidding. What are you thinking?'

'Where am I going? I'm twenty-eight and I've got nothing to show for it. I drift from one thing to the next. It's time I got serious.'

'What brought this on?' Alex thought he knew, he just wanted to hear Marv say it.

Marv looked shifty. 'Nothing.'

'Oh yeah!'

Marv grinned.

Alex thumped his shoulder.

'You talk about a farm. That's what I want too.' Marv rubbed his shoulder.

'You'd be a good farmer. It doesn't suit everyone but I think you'd find what you're looking for on a farm.'

Marv looked worried. 'I've blown just about all the compensation money the Army paid me.'

'So what? Your share of what we've already found will help buy you a farm. It's more than you'd have if you stayed in the Army.'

Marv looked marginally better. 'Did you bring any beer back?'

'Six cartons.'

251

Marv narrowly missed looking pleased.

'Brought you this too.' He waved an envelope at him. It was a note from Pru.

Marv nearly kissed him.

'Aren't you going to read it?'

A worried frown. 'What does it say?'

'How the hell should I know?'

Marv gave him a wide grin, then charged off to the shack to read the letter. He sauntered back outside, trying to look casual. 'She's staying in Gabs for a while. She's going to try and find a job. She loves Bechuanaland.'

'And?' Alex prompted.

'And nothing. That's it.'

'So?' he prompted again.

'So,' Marv said smiling widely. 'I'm going to Gabs this weekend.'

Alex thumped him again.

Marv gave him one of his narrowed eyes looks. Then, 'By the way, a fella came looking for you a couple of days ago.'

'So Jacob said. Who was he?'

'Nice guy, bit odd-looking, though. Kel someone. Said he knew you a few years ago. He was really interested in what we're doing here.'

Kel! Alex hadn't thought about him for years. Why would he go out of his way to look Alex up? What was that bastard up to? Whatever he told Marv, it wasn't anything to do with an old friendship. 'You didn't tell him!'

'He asked a lot of questions. I didn't think you'd mind. After all, he said you knew him.'

'Marv you didn't show him where we're digging did you?' Alarm bells were ringing. Good old trusting Marv would be putty in the hands of someone like Kel.

'He came with me one day. Asked if he could. What's the matter? Did I do the wrong thing?'

Alex ignored the question. 'Did he mention how he knew I was in this area?'

'He said he'd been living in Molepolole. Said he'd heard you were trying to organise a meeting with the Chief.'

'Jesus, Marv! Did you say anything about prospecting rights?'

'Of course.' Marv looked at him confused. 'Why wouldn't I?'

Alex scrambled up. 'That bastard is going to try to get in first. He's had it in for me ever since our fight. I made him look stupid and he can't seem to forget it. I've got to get back to Gabs. You get back out there at first light and keep searching.'

Alex had a bad feeling in the pit of his stomach. Kel, he knew, was related to some highly placed and influential people in Gaberones. If anyone could short-circuit the process of prospecting rights, he could. And if anyone would try to beat him to it out of nothing more than spite, Kel would. The information Marv had handed him on a plate would be dynamite in Kel's hands. Everything was falling apart.

It was ten-thirty at night when he pulled up outside Chrissy's flat. Her lights were still on. He used his own key to get in. Chrissy was working at her dining-room table. She looked up, startled, when he opened the door. 'Oh, it's you.'

He was hyped up by the threat of what Kel could do to him. 'Who did you expect?'

She laid down her pen. 'I don't know,' she said tersely. 'You seem to think you can come and go as you like.'

'Chrissy.' He stepped into the room. 'I'm sorry I left like that. Jacob called. I barely had time to get to Molepolole. The Chief wanted to see me.'

Pru, who was reading a book, discreetly went into her bedroom.

Chrissy glared at Alex. 'A note wouldn't have taken more than thirty seconds.'

'I didn't think. I'm sorry.'

She rubbed a hand across her eyes. She looked tired. 'You'd better start to think, Alex. I'm not used to being taken for granted. I don't like it.'

'Christ, Chrissy, I said I'm sorry.'

'Fine. Just as long as you know how I feel.' She looked up at him, her face softening. 'Why have you come back so soon?'

He explained swiftly, glad she wasn't still angry.

'So you think he'll try to stop you?' she asked when he'd finished.

'He's a funny sort. He's got a cruel streak. I messed up his face a bit. I guess he is still looking for revenge.'

'And I guess you don't forgive him either.' She smiled slightly.

'I thought I had. No, dammit! I had. If he stayed out of my life I'd have forgotten all about him. But this, Chrissy, what does he want from me? This brings it back. The money he stole, the fact he lied to the others about the beating, the fact he was the one up the tree in the first place and deliberately implicated me.' He could feel himself getting angry. 'Well fine. If he wants a fight he'll get one. He's the one looking for it and I won't back away. I beat him once physically, I can beat him mentally too. He's the one asking for it. I could have died out there.'

A look of sudden pain crossed her face. She rose and came to him, her arms going around his waist as she leaned on him. 'I'm glad you didn't,' she said softly.

He kissed away the last of her resentment and, in doing so, his anger went with it. But not his determination.

He was at the Department of Geological Surveys at 7.15 the next morning. The office, according to the sign over the door, opened at 7.30. At 7.27 a Motswana woman arrived and unlocked the door, closing it firmly behind her and locking it again. At 7.45 Alex banged impatiently on the door. No-one appeared. The door was finally unlocked at 8.05. The same Motswana woman apologised. 'We are running late today.'

Behind her, stepping through the door of an inner office, he saw Kel. Alex stared, horrified at his face. He had obviously been in a terrible accident. The right side was caved in, as though the cheekbone had collapsed. A scar, showing a botched stitching job, ran across where the bone should be, pulling the eye down so it looked droopy. His nose bent towards the scar, and his right upper lip was pulled out of shape. The overall effect was one of a permanent sneer. Kel looked over and saw Alex and his already twisted features altered as the good side stretched wide, pulling the other towards it. Alex realised with a shock that Kel was grinning.

'Too late, Theron,' he said, waving a piece of paper in his hand aloft. His voice was blurred, as though he had just come from the dentist and his mouth was still frozen. 'That find is mine. You should tell your friends to keep their mouths shut.' He turned back and called to whoever was in the office, 'See you later, Uncle Ben.' He swaggered past Alex, his lips pursed, trying to whistle but failing.

Alex watched him go, angry that he had been tricked by the man but full of compassion that Kel had to live with that mess of a face. When he asked to see the head of the department, 'Uncle Ben' told the Motswana woman to inform Alex he was too busy to see anyone.

THIRTEEN

He did the only thing he could think of doing: he went to see the Chief. But Kel had second guessed him and had been there before him. It was immediately obvious that the Chief preferred to believe Kel, whom he knew well, to this callow youth who had deliberately lied. The man looked at Alex contemptuously and growled in Setswana, 'What seek you at the river, jackal, when you say you don't drink water?' Alex's heart sank. If he'd been mildly annoyed, the Chief would have admonished him in English, as a courtesy to his visitor. Angry, he would probably have spoken Setswana. But to quote a proverb showed Alex that the Chief was furious beyond words and didn't care about etiquette.

'I am sorry.' To deceive the man as he had was, he knew, foolish in the extreme. Rural and tribal the Chief may have been but he did not retain his position for no good reason. Alex had hidden the truth because he did not wish to talk about riches which might not be there. The real purpose for his wanting use of the land would have become known sooner or later. He just hadn't expected it to be this soon.

'Another will use the land. You are not to go back.'

'Chief . . .' Alex pleaded, his hands outstretched.

The Chief pulled the animal skins on his shoulders around him firmly and stood tall, staring at Alex through knowing and angry eyes. 'You offer us but one beast. Another offers us riches. That land is tribal land. You would take our riches and say nothing. You would become wealthy and leave us with nothing when that thing you seek is rightfully ours.'

He knew it was no use. To try and explain to the Chief how he intended to share the wealth and provide work for the people of Molepolole would fall on deaf ears. Kel and his family had seen to that. Still, he tried to warn the man.

'*Sedibana pele gaseikanngwe* [the well ahead is not reliable],' he said, startling the Chief somewhat; white men speaking fluent Setswana were not rare but ones who knew their culture well enough to quote their proverbs were. 'I hope I'm wrong,' he continued, 'but I fear you have been misled. The people with whom you do business are not honest.'

'Like you have not been honest?' Cold dark eyes flicked contemptuously at him. 'Are you telling me that I am a poor judge of people?'

Alex gave up before he upset the Chief further.

Even Jacob's place was tribal trust land. The Chief told him he must leave there as well. He returned to the cattle post and broke the news to Marv.

'How much do you think we'll get?' Marv had worked non-stop but had little to show for it. They stared at the collection of stones he had managed to find.

'Enough to get us started. Not enough to keep us going.'

Marv was satisfied. 'I'm definitely going to buy land and farm. It's time I settled down. Somewhere up near Francistown. My share should bring enough for me to put down a deposit. What about you?'

'It's all I ever wanted. I like the Tuli area up there. It's good cattle country.' He looked at Marv seriously. 'Do you think I'm too young to get married?'

'Yes,' Marv said promptly.

Alex was unconvinced but he said no more about the idea forming in his mind.

They heard a vehicle approaching. Marv shoved the stones in the ashes of last night's fire. They assumed it would be Kel.

Alex had not anticipated just how far Kel would go to get even. A second vehicle was behind the first. White policemen jumped out. 'They're going to search this place,' Kel told him smugly. 'If you have any diamonds here they'll be confiscated. You have been denied access to this entire area, therefore any stones you have are mine. I am now the occupier of this land.' He waved his licence in the air.

'Let me see that.' Alex might have guessed. The licence had been back-dated by two months. Legally, Kel could demand all the diamonds they possessed.

Marv might as well have pointed his finger at the fire. He sat down on the bricks at the side, leaning protectively over the cold ashes. But neither Kel nor the policemen knew Marv the way Alex did. They took no notice of him. They trashed the kitchen, emptied the refrigerator, overturned the beds, slashed the mattresses, let down the blinds and made the acquaintance of the resident scorpions with whom Marv had learned to live. Alex and Marv had to submit to a body search which Marv objected to so strenuously he was threatened with arrest. Judging by the looks which passed between the three policemen, however, they believed they were on a wild goose chase. It was Kel who urged them on. When they left empty-handed he was angry and disappointed. 'You'll be watched,' he told Alex, his eyes glittering. 'As soon as you try to sell those stones you'll be arrested.'

As they drove away Marv muttered, 'That must have been some beating you gave him. Did you do all that damage to his face?'

'I don't know what happened to his face,' Alex told Marv. 'I didn't do that to him.'

Alex felt sick. He'd had such dreams. There were riches here, he could feel it. Riches for the emerging country of Botswana and enough for him and Marv as well. And now Kel and his well-connected family would reap the benefits. He held no illusions that the villagers of Molepolole would see any of the profits. People like Kel did not operate that way, despite their promises.

It took several hours to repair the damage and tidy the mess in the shack. There was nothing they could do about the mattresses. They retrieved their hidden diamonds, wrapped them in an oily cloth and stuffed them through a slit in one of the Land Rover seats.

They stopped in Molepolole to explain what happened to Marthe and Jacob. Marthe cried and blamed herself for directing Kel out to where they were. Jacob said, 'Now, mother, how were you to know?'

'He's right, Marthe,' Alex said. 'Marv fell for his line too.'

When they tried to pay Jacob for the ruined mattresses he refused. 'Don't you go insulting me like that, boy. Them plurry things were on their last legs anyway. I've been meaning to replace them for yonks.' He also said they could keep the two Land Rovers.

They would have to sell their diamonds somewhere other than Bechuanaland. South Africa was out; if they sniffed the possibility of diamonds, indeed if Britain realised there was wealth to be had, independence would be put on hold. Alex believed his country should be independent.

They decided to take their diamonds to Southern Rhodesia. That country was thumbing its nose at Britain and rumbling about a Unilateral Declaration of Independence. It was full of mavericks, people who couldn't care less about world opinion. Surely they could sell them up there.

Chrissy, once again angry at Alex's disappearing act, was barely civil to either of them. Marv and Pru made themselves scarce, saying something about going to a movie at the club.

Chrissy wasted no time. 'You're not the only person in the world, Alex Theron. The rest of us exist. We have needs.'

'Look, I've told you what happened. I went straight to the Chief and then I had to get back to Marv. I'm sorry.'

'Apologising is not enough. All I ask is that you stop and think.' When she got angry the tip of her nose went white. 'I have no intention of sitting patiently here while you run around pleasing yourself.'

'Okay, okay.' His hands went into the air. 'What can I say? It won't happen again.'

She turned her back. It took him a few moments to realise she was crying.

'Chrissy!' He had no idea his actions had hurt. He went over and put his arms around her. 'Sorry, darling. Really I am.'

She mopped at her eyes. 'Okay,' she sniffed. 'Just stop and consider my feelings once in a while won't you.'

He turned her to face him and held her, feeling contrite and confused. He could not imagine why she was so upset. He could appreciate her annoyance but the hurt was something he could not fathom. He kissed her gently. Her lips quivered under his. She felt like a fragile butterfly in his arms.

'Let's have dinner out.'

She gave him a lopsided grin. 'You don't have to do that.'

'Yes I do. I'm an inconsiderate clot.'

A full grin this time.

He cocked his head at her. 'Well?'

'Well what?'

'I don't hear you denying it.'

She laughed and hugged him. 'Okay.'

'Okay what?'

'You're an inconsiderate clot.'

They both laughed. Peace had been restored.

Over dinner at the hotel he outlined his vague plans. 'Marv and I have to sell the stones. We'll go to Southern Rhodesia. Hopefully that will raise enough for Marv to put down a reasonable deposit on some land. We'd hoped for more. He'll have it tough for a few years until his farm starts to pay.'

'What about you?'

He looked doubtful. 'I just don't know, Chrissy. You know I want to farm but it's a lonely life unless you have someone to share it with.' He tried to lock eyes with her but she looked down.

'You're too young to tie yourself to a farm. Try something else for a while.'

He knew she had fobbed him off. He tried to hide his disappointment. 'I'm not qualified for anything.'

She looked at him in amazement. 'Of course you are. You're one of the very few people who have an understanding of the Bushmen. You even speak their language. That has to be invaluable for an emerging country like this. You're here, you were born here, the country will need people like you. You can do anything you like.'

'Politics, you mean?'

'Not politics as such, no. Bushmen affairs is more like it. You could be their voice.'

261

'Do they want a voice, I wonder?' In the year and a bit he lived with !Ka and his clan not once had he heard them complain about their way of life. They lived a happily isolated existence, undisturbed by development and technology. As far as he could see, since they lived in areas which nobody else wanted, they could remain this way for as long as they liked. And yet, as Bechuanaland became more settled fences became more commonplace and professional hunting killed more animals on land the Bushmen considered to be theirs. Perhaps their way of life was threatened.

He knew they were psychologically and socially prepared for change. They had not chosen to live in such arid areas. They lived there and adapted out of necessity. Others, although at home in the desert, regularly visited towns or farms for work. Still others became farmers themselves and never ventured deep into the Kalahari. Clearly, the Bushmen were adaptable but time was against them. They needed more than a voice. He saw what Chrissy was getting at and began to get excited. They needed a plan. A plan for survival in their ever changing environment.

He floated an embryonic idea. 'When I lived with them it crossed my mind that commercialisation of their skills, provided it did not affect their way of life, might work.'

'Such as?' She was smiling at his sudden enthusiasm.

'The things they make out of necessity using skin, bone, even ostrich eggs, are unique. African curios have been around for a long time but hardly anyone knows about the Bushmen handicrafts. They could be made commercially. Then nothing needs to change. The San could stay where they are, keep their traditions but improve their standard of living.' The idea took hold. 'Their way of life is hard. !Ka expects to die when he's about forty-five. He accepts that, but he would be delighted to think he might live longer.' He banged his hand down on the table. 'Chrissy! It's a brilliant idea.'

'You'd have to be careful. If you introduce money into their way of life you'll set off a chain reaction. Somehow, and I can't see how at this stage, they need to preserve their culture but improve their living standards.'

'Their biggest problem is health. If their craftsmanship could fund clinics . . . don't you see, Chrissy, they could trade handicrafts for health. It's exactly the sort of deal they'd like. Something for something.'

'Hey, slow down. You'll have to work it through.'

'You bet.' He was alive with new thoughts. Ideas flooded him. He spoke around the steak in his mouth. 'We'll get finance. We'll export to America and Europe. We'll . . .' Chrissy's eyes grew round. He was about to ask why when a hand thumped him between the shoulder blades so hard he choked.

'Hello, boyo. Jesus mother of Mary, you've turned into a man.'

Pat, Willie, Bob and Artie stood over him, grinning.

'He must be a man. That's a helluva woman he's with. Pardon me, ma'am, my name's Artie. This here's Pat. This is Bob. Willie you don't want to know.'

'You always say that. Why do you always say that?' Willie was grinning and flashing his gold teeth.

Chrissy was smiling but bemused. 'Pleased to meet you, gentlemen.'

Pat liked that. 'Gentlemen! She called us gentlemen. Miss, you can stay.'

'My name's Chrissy.' She glanced at Alex who appeared to have lost his tongue. 'Say something.'

'Something,' he croaked. He had only just dislodged the piece of meat from his throat.

'Boy's choking.' Pat manhandled his back and shoulders. 'There, boyo, that should do it.'

Artie kicked out a chair and sat down. 'Jeff's over there. He wants to see you.'

'I don't want to see him.' He dabbed at the tears streaming from his eyes. 'Jesus, Pat, you nearly killed me.'

Pat picked up extra chairs and set them down at the table, sinking into one and indicating the others should join them. 'Shove up, boyo. Finish your meal, there's a good boy. We've got some serious catching up to do. You drink, Chrissy? Good.' He didn't wait for her reply. He shouted to the barman. 'Hey, Max, about five bottles should do for a start.' He picked up Alex's wine glass and drained it, pulling a face. 'There, that's got rid of the sissy stuff.'

Alex had recovered. He quickly shovelled the last piece of steak into his mouth, chewing rapidly in case Pat felt the need to thump him again. Swallowing, he said to Chrissy, 'I'd finish that if I were you. Otherwise Pat will finish it for you.'

The barman sent them five quart bottles of cold Castle beer and six glasses. Artie was telling Chrissy about the cattle drive. '. . . six of the biggest lions I've ever seen. The bastards . . . oh, excuse me, Chrissy . . . them bloody lions took three or four head of cattle each night. The fuckers . . . oh, excuse me, Chrissy . . . the bastards had a go at the horses too. Jesus, I hate lions.'

Pat, who had drained Chrissy's wine, was pouring beer for everyone. 'C'mon, c'mon, drink up. It's hotter that a whore's knickers in here. Don't let it get warm. The beer, boyos, not the knickers. Oh, excuse me, Chrissy.'

264

Willie was trying to tell Alex something about seeing Nightmare. 'I swear to God, that bitch looks meaner than a black mamba. But by Christ, she's fucking beautiful. Oh excuse me, Chrissy.'

Bob sat, large and silent, drinking and smiling and nodding approvingly each time someone apologised.

Chrissy was looking slightly overwhelmed.

Alex sensed Jeff standing beside him. 'Didn't Artie tell you I wanted to see you?'

'He told me.' Alex locked eyes with him.

'Well?' Jeff thrust out his jaw.

Looking up, Alex found it easy not to hate him. !Ka had said, 'If you have hate in your heart, your heart knows it is wrong. Then, two things happen. Your heart will be so full of hate it will not be able to tell you anything else. And when the bad spirits see that your heart is occupied elsewhere, it will try to enter your heart. A man is easy prey at such times. Better not to have hate in your heart at all.' Alex saw the sense of what !Ka said. Why bother to waste his life hating? There were so many other more pleasant things to do.

He shrugged. 'I didn't want to see you.' He spoke quietly, his eyes still looking straight into Jeff's.

Jeff looked angry. 'I don't like you, kid. You're too damned smug. But I owe you an apology. I'm sorry I beat you up like that.' He turned on his heel and walked away.

'He's been itching to say that for years,' Bob said quietly.

'Should've gone out of his way to say it then,' Pat said. 'Instead of waiting.'

Alex shrugged. 'Doesn't bother me. Apology or not, I don't want anything to do with him.' He stopped, then added, 'Or his bloody daughter.'

'Good for you, boyo.'

Alex knew the thump was coming. He flexed his arm and deflected it.

'She's in Europe anyway,' Willie put in. 'Gone off to get finished.'

Chrissy was getting used to the onslaught of these men. Willie's revelation, however, put her back where she started. 'Finished?' she managed in a strangled voice which Alex knew meant she was trying not to laugh.

'Yeah, finished. You know.' He struggled to explain. 'Where to learn to arrange flowers and things,' he said finally. 'You know, what knife to use, stuff like that.' His tone clearly implied he thought it a waste of time.

'Oh!' Only Alex knew what an effort not to laugh she was making. The others took the explanation seriously.

'I hope they finish off her bad temper,' Pat said. 'She's like a bear with a sore head these days.'

'Excuse me.' Chrissy rose and walked quickly to the ladies' toilet.

Pat wasted no time. Gripping Alex tightly on his upper arm he said, 'She's a little beaut, boyo. Where'd you find her?'

'She was staying with my parents. She's an anthropologist.'

'A who whatta?' Willie looked puzzled.

'An anthropologist, you oaf.' Artie poked fun at him. 'She digs up things and tells us where we've been. Hey, Alex, she found any dinosaurs yet?'

Alex wished he could join Chrissy in the ladies' toilet.

Pat whistled softly. 'There's that bastard Kel. Jesus, he doesn't get prettier does he?' He looked at Bob. 'Sorry, boyo, that wasn't a dig.'

'What happened to him?' Alex asked. He couldn't help himself. Despite his intense dislike of the man, sympathy stirred in him when he looked at his face.

'A combination of things I guess,' Bob said. 'It happened on the cattle drive just after Jeff beat you up. Kel was trying to lead Nightmare back and she reared up, pulling him off his own horse. He hit the ground face down.'

Alex remembered regaining consciousness and seeing Nightmare, her reins trailing, and wondering how she got there. He even remembered wishing she had bitten Kel. 'What did he land on—a rock?' The ground was soft sand. It couldn't have done all that damage.

Pat looked uncomfortable. 'Now don't you go taking this the wrong way, boyo.'

They were hiding something. 'Let's have it, Bob.' Alex stared him down.

Bob glanced helplessly at Pat but all the big Irishman said was, 'The boy's got to find out at some stage. Might as well hear it from us.'

'That fight you had with him,' Bob said reluctantly. 'Kel claims it must have resulted in a hairline crack in his cheek-bone because when he hit the ground the bone collapsed and a sharp sliver went straight through the skin.'

'Jesus!' Guilt flooded through Alex.

'He had it coming,' Pat said loyally.

'He was a bit of a mess when he reached us,' Bob continued. 'He had this bone sticking out and the whole right hand side of his face was caved in but he wouldn't let me near it. Mind you, I wasn't sorry about that. I didn't have a clue what to do anyway.'

Artie interrupted. 'I wasn't on that drive but I back Bob one hundred per cent. He did what I'd have done. You can't force a man to have medical treatment if he doesn't want it.'

'So what happened?' Alex glanced over at Kel but the man was leaning on the bar and had his back to them.

'He kept on insisting he'd be fine. He wouldn't even take antibiotics. Two days later he developed septicaemia. His temperature shot up, his face swelled and he was in agony. We were at least two days from anywhere and the bloody radio was flat. We couldn't get in touch with anyone.'

'Bob did a great job under the circumstances,' Pat said. 'Kel had a change of heart and was begging us to help him. Two of us held him down, Bob cut off the bone that was sticking out and then stitched him up. It wasn't much fun. The whole cheek was full of pus by then and Bob had to cut away some skin.'

'No anaesthetic?' Alex asked shakily.

'I had a bottle of ether. I'm a bit wary of that stuff. Too much can kill a man. Kel felt most of it.'

'Jesus!' Alex said again. 'The pain must have been indescribable.'

'He's lucky he didn't die,' Pat said sourly. 'Stupid little sod brought it all on himself.'

'He tried to sue Bob,' Artie said. 'Didn't get to first base. A doctor at the hospital here said there was very little else Bob could have done.'

'So much for gratitude,' Willie put in. 'At least he's alive.'

'You might as well hear the rest of it,' Bob said quietly. 'He blames you for it. He was threatening to sue you too until Artie pointed out that every man on the ranch would testify that he provoked the fight. He swears he'll get even with you.'

Alex looked back at the bar but Kel was nowhere to be seen. He felt sick. True, the fight had been instigated by Kel and he couldn't be blamed for Nightmare pulling Kel off his horse. But somehow he still felt responsible for the fact that Kel had to go through the rest of his life looking like a monster. Then he remembered something !Ka had said once when a troublesome member of the clan had packed up and left and Alex had expressed relief to see the end of him: 'What a man carries in his heart today, he will wear around his shoulders tomorrow.'

Kel had got what was coming to him and there was nothing Alex could do about it. Chrissy returned to the table and the conversation moved to more pleasant topics.

It was well after midnight when they got back to the flat. There was no sign of Pru and Marv. 'Must be a hell of a movie,' Alex said.

Chrissy wound her arms around his neck.

The little book of his school years had taught him many things about women. But it had not prepared him for the depth of feeling in him whenever he and Chrissy were together in bed. Her nearness almost always caused him to fill with protectiveness. He was always warm and happy. She brought out a tenderness which surprised him. 'I love you, Chrissy,' he said, lying in the dark with his arm under her head.

The sheets rustled as she turned into him, sliding an arm over his chest. 'I love you too.' She kissed his nipple, then sucked it gently.

He felt desire stir. He pushed her away. 'If I get this Bushman scheme up and running I'll be happy to hand it over to someone else. Then I'll farm. How do you feel about . . .'

Her hand found his manhood and she circled the head with her fingernail, slowly and gently, round and round. 'Ah God, Chrissy.'

'Fuck me.' Her voice was deep with want. 'Fuck me, Alex. Push yourself into me. Fill me up with this. Fuck me, darling.' He wanted her answer but the low urgency of her voice took the question clean out of his mind. He had never wanted anyone as much as this. He rose over her. Her hand guided him into her. 'Ah yes, ah, ah yes. That's beautiful.' She thrust against him, her voice lust-filled, saying things he had never heard a woman say before. Part of him was shocked. But it was exciting. What she was saying was filthy and yet it wasn't. She used words he'd only heard whispered between schoolboys. Yet it seemed right. She wrapped her legs around him, crying out, demanding he get deeper.

Her climax shook through her body, pulsing inside her, bringing a cry to her throat. Their bodies were slippery with sweat. Her hair felt wet beneath his fingers. The intensity of their lovemaking left him gasping and breathless. It was a while before he remembered the question he tried to ask. Something held him back from asking again. He sensed she had deliberately avoided the question. Perhaps she was not ready. Perhaps she didn't love him enough.

He and Marv left to sell their diamonds the next morning. The road to Francistown was just over 300 miles of dust and boredom. They watched the endless flat, scrubby country for mile after mile, each man busy with his own thoughts. There was very little traffic but the occasional impala or duiker danced across the road, leaping for safety at the last possible moment. Alex let his mind drift. Chrissy. Marriage. Bushmen. Diamonds. Kel. Jeff. They all crowded his thoughts in a woven tapestry of confusion and uncertainty. He felt he was going nowhere. What had he achieved? What was wrong with Chrissy? He could have sworn she felt the same way about him as he did about her. Why, if she loved him as much as she said she did, did she head him off each time he tried to talk about their future?

They drove straight to Aunty Dorie's. He hadn't seen her since he left school.

Aunty Dorie was overjoyed. She sat them down at the large kitchen table and made a meal, the like of which Alex had not eaten for years. As she bustled around she talked non-stop. Uncle Hugh had passed on two years earlier. 'He's at peace now, God rest his soul.' The dog had died two weeks after Hugh. 'Bad tempered bugger he was but I miss him.' Alex was not sure if she meant her husband or the dog.

'Your parents were here last month. Your mother's not real well. Got some kind of heart condition. Your Pa's quite worried about her.'

Alex felt a pang of guilt. 'What does the doctor say?'

'Oh, him.' She dismissed the man derisively. 'Some doctor! Said she's got to take things easy. Silly bloody man. You'd think he'd give her pills or something wouldn't you?'

'Is she in any pain?'

'You know your mother. Wouldn't let on if she were. She says all sin will be atoned, whatever that means. She reads the Bible all day as though it were her salvation.'

'When I get back from Rhodesia,' he thought, 'I'll go and see them.'

Overflowing plates were put in front of them. 'There, that should fill you two up.' She sat opposite watching them eat. 'You know, when Alex flew off to Ghanzi I was real worried about him,' she told Marv. 'He seemed so young to be going off like that.'

Alex rolled his eyes at her, unable to speak. Marv seemed similarly afflicted.

271

She smiled at Alex fondly. 'I see your appetite is as good as ever.'

He nodded, his mouth still full.

'You going to try and see any of your friends while you're here?'

He swallowed. 'Are any of them still here?'

'The Tigg boy. He's not going anywhere. He's blind. The rest seem to come and go.'

Alex thought of Colin Tigg. He had been captain of the rugby team. Big and friendly and likeable. He had planned to become a mechanic when he left school. Alex hadn't thought about the accident in a long time. 'What's he doing now?'

'Drinking himself to death,' she told him bluntly. 'Doing a good job of it too by all accounts.'

Alex found he didn't want to see him. What was the point? Colin had been full of life, full of promise. Drinking himself to death seemed like a pretty good option. Alex believed he was going to live forever. But blind? He thought he'd probably do the same as Colin.

'What brings you here?' she asked as they washed down the breakfast with hot, strong coffee. No-one made coffee quite like Aunty Dorie. You could stand a spoon up in it, she liked to say.

'Marv is looking for land up here. Do you know of any?'

She inclined her head. 'There's always land for sale. You'd best be asking down at the Lands Office. It'll be closed by now. You two are welcome to stay the night. I could do with the company.'

The Lands Office was just opening its doors for business when they arrived the next morning. Yes there was land for sale. Four thousand acres divided into eight paddocks. The fences needed attention. There was no house on it. The Shashe River formed one of its borders.

'Sounds good. Where is it?' Marv looked keen.

'About two hours west of here.'

'Bit far out,' Alex said.

'It's a good road, sir,' the clerk replied. 'Good land. It's got permanent water. It's selling cheap because of the fences.'

Marv was doing a 'Can I talk to you outside?' number with his head. They went into the street.

'Uh, Alex?'

'Yes.'

'How much cash you got?'

Alex was practically broke. 'About fifty quid.'

'I've got 300. You good for a loan?'

'Don't you want to see the land first?'

'Nope.'

'Bit risky.'

'Are you good for a loan or not?'

'Of course.'

The clerk at the Lands Office looked harassed. 'A deposit on a deposit. I don't know. It's very irregular. I'll have to check with the seller.'

'Just to hold it,' Marv said. 'I'll be back next week with the rest.'

The clerk looked as if he were about to refuse. Alex intervened. 'Come on, man. You'll have to make these decisions when independence comes. Mafeking is miles away, what do they know. Bloody officials, I tell you, man, we'll be back with the balance before you know it.'

Elevated to a position of authority, the clerk took the decision Alex handed him. Then he grumbled over having to

273

write a receipt, stamped the Deed of Sale by mistake, counted the money three times before his tally agreed with theirs and, to Marv's horror, put the money into his pocket.

Alex dragged him out of the Lands Office before Marv could protest.

'What if he takes our money?'

'So what if he does, I've got the Deed of Sale. It's stamped and it states the money's been paid in full.'

'That's dishonest.'

'Only if he's dishonest.'

The Plumtree border was fifty miles to the north. From there, another eighty miles to Bulawayo in Southern Rhodesia. Having no contacts, they took their stones to the first jeweller they came to. A dark and musty-looking shop in a side street. The gold leaf sign on the window said 'Kramer's for the Finest'.

Before the Second World War, Solomon Kramer had been a diamond cutter in Odenwald, Germany, working with his father who taught him everything he knew about this rare skill, the intricacies of which, known to only a few, are a closely guarded secret.

A survivor of Spandou prison he returned to Odenwald after the war. His mother, he discovered, had died in 1942. Of his father, two sisters and brother, he could learn nothing. He reopened the old shop but his heart wasn't in it. In 1951, believing a better life awaited him somewhere away from the bitter memories and what still amounted to open prejudice, he went to Africa and set up a jewellery business in Bulawayo, living behind the shop as he was accustomed to doing in Germany.

Wealth became Solly's goal, his insurance against having to go without ever again. The rich were not his customers, they were his victims. He fleeced them unmercifully, insulted them to their faces, treated them with profound indifference and made them spectacular pieces of jewellery. They adored him. He, in turn, despised them.

Solomon had two weaknesses: his wife, Clara, a tiny woman ten years his junior who, as a result of her time in a concentration camp, could not bear him children. The second was honest, open-faced young people, in whom he saw himself, before that Austrian madman had intervened. He took one look at Marv and Alex and his heart sank. He knew they would cost him money.

'Goot mornink, gentlemens.'

Alex looked around the shop, at the beautifully crafted clocks, crystal and silver, display cases full of rings, necklaces, brooches and watches, and knew he had found quality. He was relieved to find the shop empty of customers. 'Do you buy stones?'

Solomon's interest quickened. 'Does an elephant shit in heaps?' He had read the remark in a book and had been dying to use it since then. 'Only if they're worth it mind.'

'I mean real stones. Diamonds.'

Solomon's heart missed a beat. 'Where'd you steal them?'

The look on their faces told him they were honest. 'We didn't steal them. We found them. In the Kalahari.'

'Why bring them to me?' He showed no interest in looking inside their cloth bag.

He pretended to rummage behind the counter while Marv said in a loud whisper. 'Tell him everything.' Solly wanted to cry. They were babies these two. A tiny soft corner of his heart melted.

'Go on,' Marv whispered. 'Tell him.'

So Alex told him everything.

'Let's see them.' Neither his face, or his voice, revealed the disgust Solomon felt for Kel when Alex stopped speaking. He was glad these boys had got away with something. It was good to see the honest and innocent win a few.

When he examined the stones he knew they were first class, gemstones. Most of them were free of carbon spots, small fissures or particles of other materials which had grown with the stones. They were of the finest colour, that is to say they were transparent and colourless. More than half of them would weigh nearly a carat, he could tell at a glance. One or two went higher. This was good. He knew he could charge much more for a single large stone than he could for smaller chips and stones amounting to the same weight.

And then there was the quantity. These boys did not know it but their stones were almost equal to half a 'parcel' which the Diamond Trading Company made up for sale to invited clients ten times a year. He was a little out of touch but he guessed the value of the stones to be around 150,000 English pounds on the open market.

'I'll give you £10,000.' But his heart wasn't in it. Sure, he wanted to make money, he wasn't here to go broke on account of these babies, but he had the contacts and he had the skills to make a clear profit ten times that amount, at least.

'Gee, that's not much.' Marv's disappointment was a tangible thing. 'I can't buy the farm on my share of that.'

Solomon hid a smile. Babies. Both of them. 'Drive a hard bargain, boy, you'll break a man.'

'Huh!'

Solomon chuckled. He really liked these boys. There

wasn't a bent bone in their bodies. 'I tell you what. Let's cut the bullshit. I'll give you £25,000, it's my final offer and you're making me a pauper yet.' Then his heart skipped another beat. Alex produced the diamond they'd found first. Solomon realised it had to go to twenty, twenty-five carats and mentally revalued the worth of their stones.

'Fifty thousand,' Alex said.

Good, good, the boy's not a fool. He stared at the large diamond. It was the biggest he'd ever seen. He could retire. He and Clara could travel. These boys were young and strong. They could find more stones. He raised his hands in horror. 'Fifty! What do you take me for? A bank yet? I'll give you forty thousand.'

'Done!' Alex put out his hand.

'All right already, all right. What can a man do? Fifty.' Solly cringed inside. What made him so nice? Damn but he loved these boys.

'But you said . . .'

Solomon averted his eyes while Alex nudged Marv.

'Can you pay us in cash?' Marv was hopping from one foot to the other in excitement.

Solomon shook his head. 'Does a vulture eat shit?' He had *not* read that in a book but he liked the sound of it. 'Come into the back. Come on, come on, I won't bite.'

They followed him through a beaded curtain into his little office. Books, figurines, clocks, heaps of paper and an Olivetti typewriter vied for space on the desk. Solly rummaged and produced a box of cigars. 'You boys smoke?' He was relieved they said no thanks. They were Havana's best. He pulled a bunch of keys from the desk drawer, examined them, selected one and inserted it into the door of his safe. 'You boys don't want to hit me on the head now?'

'Why would we do that?' Marv was aghast at the idea. Solly hid another smile. He loved them.

Solly kept all his money at home. Clara said he was mad but he remembered how the Germans had simply helped themselves to bank assets and safe deposit boxes. Anyway he had never trusted the banks. He had two safes. This one in his office, an up-front showpiece in which he kept a few stones and anything up to £10,000. In the event of a robbery, thieves would be well pleased with such a haul. In the back, under the floorboards of his workshop, he kept another. Solly's wealth was stored there.

He counted out £5,000. 'You boys wait here a minute. If anyone comes into the shop call my wife, she's through there,' he pointed to a closed door. 'Don't touch anything.' Solly went through the door and carefully closed it behind him.

Marv's eyes nearly popped out of his head when Solly returned with the rest of the money.

'Why do you keep so much here? Aren't you worried someone will rob you? I mean, we might be anyone.'

Solly looked into Marv's wide open face. 'My boy,' he lied, 'I think humans are nicer than that.'

They were not exactly rich but they had enough money each to make a pretty good start in life. Knowing nothing of the value of diamonds, nor of the different qualities found in them, Alex was surprised at how much they had been paid. He had not expected so much.

They drove back to Francistown and Marv bought his farm. They camped there a week, walking the fence lines, planning dam sites, finding a suitable location to build a house, pegging out cattle yards.

On the fourth day Alex said, 'Won't you be lonely living here on your own?' Marv hadn't mentioned Pru once since they left Gaberones.

Marv grinned and shook his head. 'Who said I'll be on my own?'

Alex grinned back. 'You old dog, you've been holding out on me.'

'Not really,' Marv admitted. 'I haven't asked her yet.'

FOURTEEN

Marv and Pru's wedding was treated by a large percentage of the Gaberones population as an excuse for a monumental piss-up. Most of them knew Alex, a handful had met Marv and no-one at all had laid eyes on Pru until a few days before the event. Not that this mattered. Hard working, hard living, hard drinking men and women, pioneers in a land poised on the brink of independence, many unwelcome in South Africa because they were believers in majority rule, most of them were warm, openhearted lovers of a happy ending. The material things in life had no real relevance to these people. They were larger than life for the most part, basic in the extreme, loyal to their friends and generous to a fault. God help anyone who got off side with them but it seemed like heaven smiled on those they called friends. Alex was considered one of them. Marv fitted in perfectly. Even Pru was enough of a character to be welcomed immediately, they liked her open manner and blunt way of speaking. That two of their numbers had decided to marry met with their wholehearted approval.

The change in Pru was just short of a miracle. In the two

months she had known Marv she was a completely different person. She had always been candid; God help those who asked for her opinion because she just came right out and gave it, irrespective of whether feelings got hurt or not. That hadn't changed. It was part of her personality and, very often, her directness put a different perspective on something which was both refreshing and plausible. However, the facade she had developed to protect herself had gone and with it, the snobbery, the barbed remarks and the continual references to her parents. For the first time in her life, Pru believed in her own worth. Chrissy and Alex tried to figure it out.

'We know it was the night they got pissed together, right?'

She nodded. 'At some stage that night they got fed up with arguing and started relating to each other.'

'They're both square pegs in round holes. Maybe that's it.'

Chrissy thought about it. 'He's the only person she's ever met who's had the guts to tell her to shut up. That certainly got her attention. Then he said her parents were boring.'

Alex grinned. 'A pet rock wasn't it?'

'Trust Marv.' She grinned back. 'He kept asking her about *her*. He kept forcing her to talk about herself. Even when they were arguing he kept bringing the conversation back to her. By the time they were into their fourth bottle of wine she was probably too relaxed to be anything other than herself.'

'And she liked it?'

'Think about it. She's been pushed away and criticised, ignored and shut out all her life. There she was out in the middle of the desert, under the stars in a strange land with a man who appeared hell bent on listening to her, valuing what she had to say and, above all, was not toadying to her.' She smiled. 'Instinctive is not a word that immediately springs to mind about Marv but, by letting her know that he found her

281

attractive and interesting but wasn't about to let her walk all over him, he was acting instinctively.'

Alex nodded. 'He certainly got it right.'

She agreed. 'Marv will love her for the rest of her life. She knows that. That's heady stuff for a girl who has spent twenty-five years trying to get noticed.'

'They're good together, that's for sure.'

'They're perfect together.'

He nearly said more but changed his mind. He had a plan.

Pru's parents had wired that they couldn't attend the wedding. Pru showed the telegram to Chrissy. CAN'T MAKE WEDDING (STOP) OTHER COMMITMENTS (STOP) DADDY IS SENDING PRESENT (STOP) BEST WISHES (STOP) MUMMY.

'A present!' Chrissy was horrified by the impersonal message.

'She means money,' Pru said curtly. 'It's too vulgar to mention in a telegram.'

Chrissy hugged her. 'Are you upset?'

Pru frowned at the message. 'I'm cross.' She screwed up the telegram and threw it across the room. 'To hell with them,' she said quietly. 'I've got Marv.'

It was a beautiful day in May. An endless blue sky, not a whisper of breeze, with a hint of autumn in the air. Pru looked a dream in white silk. Marv was distinguished and proud. The ceremony was simple and short. Alex, standing next to Marv in the church, only had eyes for Chrissy as she followed Pru down the aisle.

A small party of invited guests, and a very large number of the Gaberones crowd who believed it their moral duty, toasted the future of Mr and Mrs Moine at the Notwane Club afterwards.

Marv's family had come from South Africa—mother, father, a sister and two brothers. When his mother, with her arm around Pru, said, 'Isn't it lovely, now I have two daughters,' Alex thought Pru would burst into tears of happiness.

The next day Alex drove Chrissy out of town to a place he had found several years earlier. 'This place is the next best thing to being in the desert,' he told her.

She looked around. 'It's got a kind of serenity.'

Trees, taller than most, threw shade on areas which appeared to have been cleared at some stage. Gaps in the bush allowed a view off to the west. In the wild hard land that made up the eastern edge of the Kalahari, the little glen had a softness, as though the hand of God had gently passed by, bestowing a calming effect on the rugged wilderness.

'Come.' He held his hand out to her and she took it. He led her up a slight rise, along a shaded grassy path.

'What is this place?' Old ruins of several buildings lay in crumbling neglect.

'This is Kolobeng. David Livingstone built his mission and school here.'

'My God!' She rubbed her hand softly across a fallen, hand-hewn rock. 'Are you sure?' she whispered. 'It feels like angels walk here.'

He could see the place was having the same effect on her as it always did on him. The enormity of where they were standing always filled him with awe.

'I wasn't always sure. But a couple of months ago I found something else.' He tugged on her hand and she followed him. 'Just down this path there's proof.'

The tiny graveyard was overgrown. Little wooden crosses

leaned sideways. No writing remained on them. There was no clue as to who was buried there. Then he pointed out the granite headstone. Like the others, it was leaning crazily sideways but, unlike the others, the stone had been carved. He moved towards it.

'Wait.'

He turned his head. 'Come on, I'll show you.'

'No,' she whispered. 'No, Alex. Come away, please.' She had gone white.

'What's wrong?' He squeezed her hand.

'Can we go somewhere else?'

So they drove about a mile, to a shaded spot where a permanent creek crossed the road and grassy banks provided excellent picnic places. He had packed a hamper and borrowed a blanket and he led her to a flat piece of ground which gave them a view of the creek through the trees but was sufficiently off the road so anyone passing would not know they were there. He fussed over her, poured some wine, sat down next to her and said, 'Talk to me, Chrissy. Why do you shy away whenever I talk about our future?'

'That little grave. It was a child wasn't it?'

He wondered if she was stalling again but she had seemed so affected by the sight of the cemetery that he let it go. 'It was one of Livingstone's children. You can read the dates. A girl. About three.'

'Poor little thing. To be left out there alone like that. It doesn't seem right.'

'You said yourself, the place has serenity.'

'I know,' she said sadly. 'It's just so wild and lonely.'

'She's happy . . . you can't feel sadness there, just peace and love. Good things took place there. The land reflects it.'

'How do you know?'

'!Ka taught me to respect my instincts.'

She smiled at him. 'I felt peace there too. It just seemed wrong to disturb the place.' She shrugged and looked down at the rippling water in the creek. 'I don't know, sort of like sacrilege.'

He handed her a glass of wine. 'Okay, sweetie, time's up. Talk to me.'

She looked at him for a long moment. 'You have the most beautiful eyes,' she said finally.

Now she *was* hedging. 'So do you.' He would not let her off the hook. His eyes locked on hers.

'I love you very much.' She sipped her wine.

'I love you very much too. That's not what I mean.'

She dropped her gaze.

He reached over and cupped her chin in his hand. 'I want to marry you, darling,' he said softly.

Her eyes refused to meet his. 'I'm too old for you.'

'Five years?' He grinned. 'I like older women.'

She smiled. At last, she looked directly at him again. 'I won't marry you, Alex. One day you'll know why. Please, can we leave it at that?'

She had sadness in her eyes. He felt it strongly. It made him afraid. 'Why, darling?'

She jumped up and went and stood near the water, her arms folded. 'I have my reasons.' She did not look around as she spoke. 'They're very good reasons and you will know about them soon. I promise.'

He rose and went to her, putting his arms around her. She leaned into him. 'You do love me?'

'Yes,' she said softly. 'Yes, Alex. I love you more than I thought possible.'

!Ka had taught him, 'When you want to hunt the buck,

you find a place to sit and let him come to you. That way, he will not know you are there. If you try to go to him you will lose him because your impatience will scare him away. It is better to wait a long time and have meat in your cooking pots than to wait a little time and have none.'

!Ka's wisdom was seldom wrong. 'Okay, Chrissy. I can wait.'

She turned and held him. 'Thank you,' she whispered. 'You have no idea how much I love you for that.'

He kissed her and tasted the salt of tears.

FIFTEEN

Alex looked around the table at the serious black faces. They had listened courteously as he outlined his plan. Timon Setgoma particularly had paid attention, nodding approval at several points. Alex was glad of that. Timon was attached to the newly formed Ministry of Local Government and Lands and, as such, was very close to the Minister, the Hon. Lemmie Makgekgenene.

This meeting, the culmination of eighteen months' work, would see the make-or-break decision on his proposals. He had worked long and hard, learning as he went. When he started he believed it would be easy—working to help his San friends would be fulfilling and enjoyable. He did not anticipate the frustrating delays, the hurdles which had to be jumped one by one or, in one instance, disapproval of his scheme so intense and from such an influential individual that the scheme nearly failed in its infancy. There were times along the way he nearly gave up but Chrissy had encouraged him to continue.

Immediately after Marv and Pru's wedding, Alex and Chrissy, at his suggestion, moved into a three bedroomed house in

The Village. With independence around the corner, expansion of Gaberones sprawled in every direction in anticipation of the flood of expatriates and the migration of rural Batswana to the country's new-look capital city. The original village of Gaberones was immediately, though unofficially, called 'the village' to set it apart from the brash new developments scarring the surrounding bushland. Alex found a lovely old double brick building with large rooms, high ceilings and an established garden. Chrissy agreed to the move, claiming she had never been happier. Alex gave her the space she obviously needed and rarely mentioned marriage but, in his heart, desperately hoped that by living together she would change her mind about marrying him.

He set up an office in one of the bedrooms and went to work. Britain had still not accepted the new constitution which had been put together by Seretse Khama and Quett Masire, but the entire country was buzzing with excitement that an acceptance was just around the corner and that it would lead, in time, to full independence. Until Britain did accept the constitution, however, policy decisions simply were not being made. Bechuanaland, despite feverish expansion activity, was in limbo.

He went into the desert and found !Ka. It was important to Alex that !Ka understood the principles of the project and accepted them. !Ka's reaction had been typical.

'When the clever old man jackal wakes from sleeping he looks to the sky. When he sees the vulture he follows it for he knows it will lead him to food.'

Alex had nodded.

'The vulture is a hunter, like the jackal.'

'Yes, Father.'

'The vulture does not always wait for death to come

before he feeds. He has nothing in his heart and very often hunger in his belly.'

Alex nodded again.

'The jackal has a plan in his heart which fills his belly.'

Alex could see where !Ka was leading him but he said nothing. To ruin !Ka's punchline would have been unforgivably rude.

'Am I a vulture or a jackal?' !Ka asked, smiling.

That was !Ka's approval. In his own round-about way he had compared the San with the clever old man jackal who filled his belly by using the skills of others, rather than the vulture who cared not for the suffering of others and sometimes went hungry. It was not a definite yes but Alex knew that !Ka, like most of the San, would at least give his scheme a try.

Convinced it was only a matter of time before Bechuanaland gained independence, and wanting to be ready with a full feasibility study when that happened, Alex returned to Gaberones and got to work, using his own funds to finance the scheme. Finding a starting point was easy. The San were limited in skills which could be used commercially so any project had to revolve around existing talents, at least in the early stages. Artifacts could be made by the clans as they went about their daily existence and would not affect their way of life dramatically. They made all manner of things as part of their gift-giving culture. Up until now, however, they used only those materials which came to them in the course of their day-to-day struggle to stay alive. When a buck was killed, the meat filled San bellies, the skin was used for clothing and the bones and horns made into utensils. The Bushmen never took more than they required and this trait had to be preserved at all costs.

The first problem, therefore, was how to provide the San with materials in general, and animal skins in particular, so that their respect for the balance of nature was not altered in any way. Not only would this have disastrous effects on nature itself, but by encouraging them to take more than they needed for their own survival, it would eventually destroy the clans' unique culture as well. The second problem was how to remunerate them. The wandering people of the Kalahari had no use for money. Introducing cash into their lives would also destroy their way of life as they came to learn how a money economy worked. Their gift-giving and bartering systems were deeply entrenched into their culture. If it were undermined by capitalism, Alex knew other values would quickly fall. So his scheme not only had to put forward viable suggestions as to how best to supply the clans with materials to make curios, but how best to pay them as well.

Initially the problem of supplying skins led him up a couple of blind alleys. When he first started work on the project he intended that the clans use traditional materials to make their artifacts. Game Department, keen to assist, agreed to give him first refusal on any animals culled in the newly formed Chobe and Moremi Game Reserves. This guaranteed a steady supply of skins certainly, but skinning, cleaning, salting and drying them before transporting them vast distances to the Kalahari was a major problem. He was attempting to address this difficulty when he discovered that, in any event, the importation of curios made from skins prepared roughly in the bush would be refused by most other countries.

Realising he had a lot to learn and still keen on using skin from game animals, he investigated the possibility of farming impala, springbok and duiker near Lobatse. The abattoir in Lobatse would buy the animals, sell the meat, send the skins to South Africa for professional tanning and these could then be imported back into Bechuanaland and used by the clans. No go! The Bechuanaland Protectorate Abattoirs, together with the Livestock Producers Trust, were negotiating with the European Economic Community for a ninety per cent levy abatement on beef exports. The EEC, with its strict requirements in health and hygiene for exported meat, would not allow the abattoir to be used for anything other than cattle.

Next, he investigated the possibility of having a small abattoir built which would process meat from farmed game animals. He visited a similar enterprise in South Africa, only to discover that while an abattoir's needs are modest, an abundance of water is essential. The Lobatse abattoir was already stretching that town's water supply to the limit. A second abattoir there was out of the question. To site an abattoir anywhere else in the country was impossible. Water to handle the anticipated population explosion was already causing the town planners headaches. He looked briefly at the Okavango Delta as a possibility but quickly rejected the idea. It had the water certainly but it was just too far from anywhere and the road system was rustic to say the least. While he was still tackling this problem he also learned that, in any case, so far, no-one was successfully farming game animals with the possible exception of gemsbok. In a farm environment, the animals refused to breed.

Reluctantly, he came to the conclusion that the only economically viable supply of skins would have to be cowhide, of which there were considerable quantities. The Lobatse abattoir shipped all wet skins to a South African tannery. He investigated the idea of buying wet skins and setting up a tannery within Bechuanaland. The idea had potential and he drafted a proposal giving facts and figures which he might

291

include with his feasibility study but if not, could be an addendum to the main project and earmarked for inclusion once the scheme was up and running.

Then he hit an unexpected snag which almost halted the entire project.

The tannery, he decided, should be sited in Molepolole. Nicely situated between the desert where his craftsmen lived, the abattoir which would supply wet skins, and rail links with South Africa where the finished products would be sent, Molepolole was perfect.

The Chief of Molepolole had other ideas. He was still angry that Alex had lied about his reason for requesting the use of land in the desert. He didn't trust Alex and didn't care who knew it.

For centuries, the eight chiefs and five sub-chiefs within Bechuanaland enjoyed ultimate authority, recognising no-one above them. They were rulers, judges, makers and guardians of the law, holders of wealth, dispensers of gifts, leaders in war, priests and magicians. Such was their power that even the zealous, and often misguided missionaries who arrived in the nineteenth century realised the way to convert the masses was to first convert the Chiefs.

The Molepolole Chief, using his considerable influence, vetoed the plan, spread rumours about Alex and, before long, had several other Chiefs on side. Their argument was valid. The new Botswana should direct its energies and aid money to the bulk of the population, not to a handful of nomadic little Bushmen who probably didn't want help anyway.

In desperation, Alex went to see Her Majesty's Commissioner, Sir Peter Fawcus. He was a very busy man and Alex had to wait ten days before an appointment could be made.

'I've heard about your scheme,' Sir Peter said briskly before Alex was even seated. 'Like to discuss it fully with you some time.'

Alex opened his mouth to speak.

'Not today,' Sir Peter went on. 'Too much to do.'

'The Chief . . .'

'Don't worry about him. You go ahead. Things are changing.'

'But . . .'

'The world has only just become aware of the San. Mark my words, young man, you'll get your aid money.'

'But . . .'

'Now if you'll excuse me.' Sir Peter rose, smiling slightly. 'I have another appointment.' He pressed a button on his desk, held out his hand and, as his secretary came through the door said, 'Show Mr Theron out, there's a good girl.'

Alex shook his hand. 'The Chiefs . . .' he tried again.

Sir Peter frowned at him.

'Please come with me, Mr Theron.'

He was out of the door two minutes after entering the room.

'I got six bloody words out,' he exploded to Chrissy that night. 'He thought I was worried about aid money.'

'He said things were changing didn't he?'

'That's supposed to make me feel better?'

She patted his arm. 'He probably couldn't say too much but I've heard the Chiefs will lose a lot of their power. Keep the faith, darling, you're getting there.'

If it hadn't been for Chrissy he'd have dropped the project there and then.

Marketing formed another major part of his study. African curios were gaining popularity around the world but no-one had ever heard of Bushmen artifacts. He spent months collecting as many San items as he could. Reed mats and baskets, clay pots and vessels, decorated ostrich eggs, bows, arrows and spears, drums, thumb pianos, beaded and woven bracelets and anklets, necklaces, animal skin products of all types, and items made from the bark of trees filled his office. 'What are you planning to do with all this?' Chrissy asked.

'I'll need a catalogue. It will have to be professionally done. Paul knows someone in Johannesburg who specialises in catalogues and who will, for a small fee of course, come up with a layout. I've arranged to meet him.'

'It'll cost a bomb.'

'I know. But I have to have it.'

Before he could commission the production of a catalogue he needed to work out prices and before he did that, he had to negotiate with the clans some method of paying them without corrupting their ways with actual money.

'Clinics,' he said to Chrissy. 'I know there's venereal disease among the San. It was brought back to this country by men working in the South African mines. It's almost an epidemic in the adults.'

'I'm surprised they haven't figured out a way to get rid of it. They're pretty cluey about most things.'

'This is different. They don't understand how it came to them. It's an introduced disease and therefore alien. !Ka believes it is yet another way the white man has tricked them, and in a way he's right. As well as that, because it's a foreign thing he says the desert cannot provide something which can help them. That's the way he thinks.'

'Would they go to a clinic?'

'It won't be easy to convince them at first but, once they see how they can be helped I think they'd go.'

'What if our modern medicine takes away their natural

resistance to other things. I mean, there's virtually no heart disease or cancer among them. Antibiotics would surely upset the natural balance.'

'I know.' He scratched his head, worried. 'But where do I draw the line, Chrissy? Today they're dying of gonorrhoea, tuberculosis, rheumatic fever and leprosy. Trachoma is a huge problem. Their teeth are generally bad and God help their children if measles ever catches up with them. The kids have no resistance at all to measles.'

'Okay. But I think you should get advice. If you start fiddling with nature anything could happen.' She thought for a moment. 'Why don't you go to the University of the Witwatersrand. They have an Institute for the Study of Man in Africa which is headed by the same man who is Chairman of the Kalahari Research Committee. Someone told me about him the other day. If he can't help you he can probably put you in touch with someone who can.'

'What's his name?'

'I don't know but I can find out tomorrow.' She frowned. He noticed she did that whenever she was deep in thought. It made her look sort of serious yet like a little girl at the same time. She stopped frowning suddenly and looked at him. 'How about water? That's a constant problem for the San. You told me there's subterranean water all through the Kalahari. Couldn't bore holes be put down or water pumped to them in some way? Then they might even be able to plant their own crops.'

He shook his head. 'Water's a good idea but it brings about the same problem. They're hunters and gatherers. If they start planting their own crops they'd stop wandering.'

'I'll get that name for you tomorrow. I think you'd better get yourself down to Pretoria and talk to this man as soon as possible.'

He was not able to see Professor Tobias as he was on a lecture tour in Canada and the United States and not expected back for four months. But he made an appointment to see an Associate Professor in the same medical school at the university who told him, 'The Bushmen need protection. Some disruption, and some influence from outside is inevitable. You've virtually said it yourself. Death by any means is nothing more or less than death. But death by starvation because a man has gone blind when his sight might have been saved is downright neglectful. And as for water changing their way of life, we have found that the nomadic Bushmen prefer their hunting, gathering ways. There's nothing wrong with giving them an option for when times are hard. I'm sorry Professor Tobias is not here. He would be more helpful. But I know he would tell you that any scheme which enables the Bushmen to integrate with others yet retain their own cultural coherence should be encouraged.'

She smiled at him. 'In that feasibility study of yours, you might like to include some suggestions as to how the Bushmen can govern their own affairs. No-one else should be allowed to interfere. They're extremely moral people and quite capable of developing a governing system which can straddle their own culture as well as the laws of Bechuanaland. Inflicting our rules on them will not only confuse and anger them, but will ultimately bastardise their own codes. Then you've got a real problem.'

Alex chewed on the inside of his lip. 'Are you sure about this? I mean, is it a good thing? It seems to me that every action has a counter-action. I want to help them, not go down in history as the man who destroyed their ways.'

'They have to change, young man, just as everyone else has had to change. They can't be preserved in a time warp. Just remember to keep any changes in line with their ethos. In my experience, they'll be quick to reject anything they have a problem with anyway.'

'They are like that aren't they? They have a sense of who they are and it gives them self-respect.'

She smiled again. 'A public relations exercise wouldn't go astray. People need to understand them. Your study should provide for that.'

'Thank you,' Alex said, rising. 'I appreciate you taking the time to speak with me.'

She rose as well. 'What are you proposing to do for the farm Bushmen?'

Alex grinned at her. 'Give me a break, lady. I'm not qualified at all for this. All I want to do is help my friends.'

She stared at him seriously. 'Young man, you are probably more qualified than anyone else I know. You think like them. Take your scheme and go for it. Formally trained you may not be, but at least you are doing something. And that, young man, is more than anyone else has done.'

'She may have a point,' he thought, as he left the building. 'I just hope I'm doing the right thing.'

His time with the clan showed him they were content. In their own eyes, they didn't need help. But Alex could see what they couldn't. They were losing more and more of their traditional hunting and gathering lands to game reserves and dry land farming. Cattle breeders, experimenting and testing, were coming up with hardy beasts able to survive in the desert. In an ever-changing world, the inevitable losers would be the San unless something could be done.

Payment, in the form of medical clinics and water wells, was only the beginning. Alex knew that, ultimately, the San would probably develop a cash economy, the same as everyone else.

As soon as that happened, the old ways would start to change. It saddened him to think that in order to help them, he was also helping to destroy their unique culture. But he could not sit back and wait for progress to destroy it. The San had to be ready.

In June 1964, just a month after Alex started work on his project, Britain accepted the new constitution. Four months later, considerably out of pocket having paid for preliminary work to a catalogue which included the taking of hundreds of colour photographs, and having purchased a mailing list of all the major craft and curio shops in South Africa, Britain, America and Europe, Alex went back to see Sir Peter Fawcus.

'Awfully busy today, young man. Tell you what, go and talk to the Social and Economic Development Committee, they'll put your mind at rest about aid.'

This time Alex was ready for him. 'It's not the bloody aid money, sir, it's . . .'

'Yes, yes, you'd like some reimbursement I'm sure. Can't say I blame you.' He pressed the button, rose and put out his hand, 'Show Mr Theron out, there's a good girl.'

Jesus! He'd done it again. This time he'd only lasted thirty seconds. But as he left the building he realised that Sir Peter Fawcus, for all his briskness, had once again hit the nail right on the head.

Expecting another frustrating delay, he telephoned the Social and Economic Development Committee for an appointment and was amazed when they not only agreed to see him the next day but also mentioned that Sir Peter Fawcus had been in touch with them about his plans and had recommended they hear him out.

Up till that point, Alex had not discussed his project fully with anyone other than Chrissy. He had mentioned it in passing to many but, in the feverish activity affecting everyone in the lead up to independence, no-one had the time to stop and listen. Therefore, he had no real yardstick by which to judge the validity of his proposals, he simply had an urge to help the San. So it came as some surprise to him when the Social and Economic Development Committee not only listened carefully to his plans, but agreed to refund most of the money he had spent to date and urged him to proceed with the production of a catalogue, mail it out and come back to them with the responses. Encouraged, Alex decided to include the tannery suggestion in his feasibility study despite the Chiefs' lack of support.

Suddenly Bechuanaland was flush with money and brimming with projects. Britain was embarrassed by the impoverished land they had administered, halfheartedly tried to improve, failed with, and then gladly handed back. Doubtful as to how a country with a Gross National Product of less than fifteen million pounds could survive, the British government found they had all sorts of aid money available for all sorts of projects.

It wasn't only Britain's money either. The World Health Organisation, whose mandate was to improve the health of all countries and control disease by the collection of information, training, and guidance of all kinds, chipped in to the tune of five million pounds of general aid money, and quite coincidentally specified that special clinics be set up for the San. The Museum of Primitive Art in New York was good for 80,000 American dollars, no strings attached. They had their sights set on the Bushmen rock paintings but carefully didn't mention it. The National Assembly continued to contribute and the United Nations, with a nod and a wink, or in some cases, a vigorous shove in the back, directed dozens of organisations' aid packages to Africa's newest, about-to-be independent country. Alex's project, the Social and Economic Development Committee told him, was high on the list for special funding. Not, as he was quick to realise, because anyone gave a damn about the San people, but because they wanted to be perceived as giving a damn.

A month after he had been given official approval for his scheme a row blew up between the Chiefs and the new administration. The Chiefs were losing power and they didn't like it. Any attempt Alex made to have land allocated to his tannery failed. Alex tried again to find land in Molepolole. Angrily, the Chief told him the land was no longer his to give and referred him to the District Council. The District Council did not think it was theirs to give either and sent him to the Land Board. The Land Board had not been set up long enough for them to know if it was theirs to give and suggested he try someone in Central Government. And Central Government, with its mind on other things, claimed never to have heard of his scheme.

Finally a House of Chiefs was formed, legislation relating to tribal land falling under their mandate. Or so Alex thought. After several months someone was considerate enough to inform him that, while the House of Chiefs would examine his request for land, they could only make recommendations which Parliament was not obliged to act on.

And so the wheels of impending independence ground on, delaying him at nearly every turn.

Independence had not been a matter of going to bed one night in Bechuanaland and waking the next day in Botswana. From June 1964, when the proposed constitution was accepted by Britain, events behind the scenes worked towards full independence but progress was slow. The first house-to-house census was conducted and, by the end of 1964, voters had been registered in thirty-one separately defined constituencies. Shadow ministries were created and, in February 1965, the seat of government was transferred from Mafeking to the new capital Gaborone, changed from Gaberones, the colonial administration's incorrect name for Chief Gaborone's village. The following month full internal self-government became reality and in the first ever elections, Seretse Khama and his Bechuanaland Democratic Party won a sweeping victory, taking twenty-eight of thirty-one seats.

On 30 September 1966, the independent Republic of Botswana's flag was raised for the first time. Three weeks earlier, as he worked late at night in his office, South Africa's Prime Minister, Hendrick Frensch Verwoerd was stabbed to death by a white parliamentary messenger, sparing him the pain of seeing the emergence of yet another independent black country, this one rather closer to South Africa than he would have liked. The murder barely raised a ripple in a Bechuanaland gearing itself for the most important day ever.

After eighteen months of thinking, planning, setting up markets, working out distribution details, talking to the clans and producing an eighty-page document in support of his proposals, Alex's cock, as Marv would say, was on the chopping block. The external funding had stopped. Now it was down to the Botswana government to accept or reject the project. And it was down to him to get them to back it.

'. . . so you see, if this plan is implemented the San have a place in the new Botswana which does not jeopardise their lifestyle. They want to be involved. They want better conditions. And they're happy to contribute their skills in exchange for this. We could open a Bushmen curio shop here in Gaborone to sell their craft.'

'I see you have put a great deal of work and thought into this scheme.' Timon Setgoma flipped his hand towards the eighty-page feasibility study. 'What's the bottom line?'

Alex passed him a single sheet of paper. Timon adjusted his glasses and read it thoroughly before passing it across the table to the head of the Kweneng District Council. He in turn read it before passing it to the man next to him who was in charge of the Kgalagadi District Council. Alex held his breath. Their support was vital. Although their responsibilities lay mainly in providing schools, health facilities, water supplies and in maintaining roads, the activities he was proposing would affect many people in a fairly large proportion of their territory. Both men gave the sheet of figures a cursory glance before passing it back to Timon. Alex realised neither of them would voice an opinion until they learned what Timon thought.

'The San are not commercially orientated,' Timon said.

'Only because they've never had the chance.'

'Money will ruin their culture.'

'They already sell spears and things to buy tobacco. They won't expect much money. They've indicated to me that clinics and a better water supply will be more than enough payment.'

Timon stabbed his finger at an item on the sheet. 'Why do you need so much money to set up a tannery?'

The bargaining had begun.

Three hours later he emerged from the meeting dazed, elated and charged with excitement. It had gone better than he'd hoped. Financial support for his scheme would be forthcoming but not without some concessions.

The head of the Kgalagadi District Council wanted the tannery in Ghanzi where, it seemed, half his extended family were out of work. Timon Setgoma overruled his demand and Alex got a tannery site in Molepolole but, to appease the head of the Kgalagadi Council, Timon promised that distribution of skins to predetermined pick-up points throughout the desert would be the responsibility of a small cartage company in Ghanzi which just happened to belong to the councillor's half-brother.

To assist the San, and to ensure that money did not have to change hands, the government would buy skins from the abattoir and finance the tannery. The Bushmen therefore did not have to purchase leather. Instead, skins would be labelled and recorded in a register. Anybody participating in the scheme would be allotted three skins at any one time. The finished products had to equal in bulk, the equivalent of these three skins, with a reasonable adjustment made for waste. Artifacts sold had to cover the cost of the subsidised leather and contribute to the running of the tannery. Anything left over would go into a special fund and be used, alongside a small amount of aid money, for clinics and water supplies.

The rest of the curios, those made from anything other than skins, were, for the moment, the responsibility of the Bushmen. 'One thing at a time,' Timon said, when Alex argued. 'We're prepared to subsidise skins. If this scheme works, we'll look at beads and paints and all the rest you have in your recommendations.'

'What about the other side of it?' Alex asked. 'The self-administration aspect and the public relations campaign?'

Timon removed his glasses and looked at him. 'Mr Theron,' he said patiently. 'We are an emerging country. We've only just got our independence. Do you, in all faith, imagine we're likely to hand the smallest shred of control to anyone else?'

Alex was frustrated and looked it.

'We take your point, Mr Theron,' Timon continued. 'You've got some good recommendations in here. But for now the Bushmen will have to accept that, like the rest of Botswana, they are at the receiving end of . . . well . . . let's just call it an experiment.'

As for the proposed Bushman curio shop in Gaborone, he was advised to wait until market acceptance and demand had been established through existing outlets outside Botswana.

'Besides,' Timon said, smiling slightly, 'Botswana at this stage is hardly a tourist mecca. I think the curio shop is a little before its time.'

Alex thought that was fair enough.

He was put in overall charge of the project and given an office in a building occupied by the Town Council. It was cramped and dark but it gave him access to a secretary, photocopying, telephones and a mail box. He still had a lot of work to do before the project was actually operating.

Chrissy and Alex saw Marv and Pru occasionally, either visiting them at their farm or, more often, when they came down to Gaborone. Marv had taken to farming as though he were born for it. With his practical nature and mechanical aptitude, there was nothing he wasn't prepared to tackle. The house had been extended twice already in anticipation of starting a family which, while everything else was working well for Marv and Pru, was something which seemed to be causing some difficulties.

'It's not as if we're not trying,' Marv confided to Alex.

Marv had quickly learned the jargon of the cattle world and had a canny knack of buying the right beasts at the right prices. His life, as Alex observed with no rancour, was happiness from the moment he woke in the morning to the moment he fell asleep at night. He loved his cattle, his farm and his wife, not necessarily in that order. All he needed to make his life complete was a child.

Paul, freshly graduated from university in Basutoland, had returned to Gaborone and was immediately taken on as an economist by the Ministry of Finance. The Minister, Quett Masire, was also the country's Vice President.

Alex and Chrissy saw quite a lot of Paul. With his economist training, it was Paul who worked out the figures for Alex's feasibility study. Paul believed the scheme had a great deal of potential.

'I'd put in a good word for you at work but it would look a little obvious,' he said.

Kel and his Uncle Ben had tried to get finance for their diamond project from the Ministry of Finance. 'Dr Masire had them thrown out,' Paul told Alex gleefully. 'I think they're running into financial trouble.' Alex, very involved in his own scheme, was pleased to discover that the only emotion Paul's news evoked was indifference.

Chrissy's work had taken longer than anticipated but she was almost finished. The museum had a special room for her photographic display of the Tsodilo Hills rock paintings. The brief description, explanation as to materials used, cultural significance and dating of the paintings which were displayed under the photographs did not do justice to the months of patient research she had undertaken for each. She had been asked to stay on and help in the museum and art gallery. So far she had declined to accept. Alex did not push her. He knew her well enough by now to know she would make up her own mind in her own time.

He had ceased all attempts to get her to marry him. Her promise, that one day he would know the reason why she would not, had so far not been fulfilled. They lived together as man and wife, they laughed and fought together as man and wife—it seemed to be enough for Chrissy. So Alex told himself it would have to be enough for him as well.

The last time he broached the subject was after Marv had telephoned bubbling with excitement with the news that, finally, Pru was pregnant.

When he told Chrissy, she simply shrugged and said, 'That's nice.'

'Nice! It's terrific news. Marv's over the moon. They've been trying for a year.'

'Well good for him.'

'What's the matter with you? You almost sound as though you're jealous.'

'Don't be ridiculous.'

'That's it, isn't it? You're jealous. For Christ's sake, Chrissy, we could have a kid too.'

They had the usual argument about getting married. She cried the usual tears. He felt the usual fear that she didn't love him. They made up as usual. He never mentioned it again. He didn't understand her; he'd seen her with other children and knew she liked them. On infrequent visits by Pru and Marv he had listened to her sharing Pru's excitement about the baby, but he sensed that if he pushed her she might leave him. She never said she would, it was just a feeling he had. He never wanted her to leave, he loved her too much. But her refusal to discuss it made him scared.

He never ceased to marvel at his good fortune for having met her. Together, they were a complete unit of loyalty and love, tenderness and happiness, laughter and agreement. Sometimes he would glance up and she would be watching him, a small smile on her face, and he would blow her a kiss and go back to whatever he had been doing, secure in the knowledge his Chrissy was with him.

He learned to read her face. He knew, for example, when she was tired and wanted to go home. He knew when she wanted to make love by a softness which crept into her eyes, and when she didn't by the way she held her shoulders. He could tell whether she liked someone or not by the tilt of her head. The tip of her nose going white was a sure sign he was in trouble, a smile in her eyes when he was forgiven. She was his friend, lover, confidante, sounding board, loyal and staunch supporter and constant companion.

She liked to read in the bath and would shut the door and lock it. 'I need to be on my own,' she would say. When she did that he would be unable to settle to anything until she came out. At parties he was continually aware of where she was and to whom she was talking. It wasn't jealousy; he trusted her and respected her need to speak to others. He just needed to know where she was for, if he lost a sense of that he experienced a nameless panic. Sometimes his sixth sense about her let him down and, when he thought she was on the other side of the room, she would suddenly appear beside him and take his hand. He did not understand the fear in him. It was not, he conceded, like him at all.

But he stayed scared. There was something about her that seemed transitory. Once or twice, when she was unaware he was watching her, he could see that whatever thoughts she was having caused a look of deep sorrow on her face. He never asked what she was thinking. He was too scared of her answer. They were close but there was a barrier she had erected. And this barrier caused his uncertainty which in turn made him vulnerable. He was never completely sure of her.

They were sitting together on their verandah, looking over the lilac carpet of fallen jacaranda flowers in their garden. 'I've decided to accept that job at the museum.'

'Great. I was beginning to think you might leave.' His words did not reveal the relief he felt.

She put out her hand and stroked his arm. 'I never want to leave you,' she said softly. Tears slid down her face. She often did that. At first it worried him but now he was used to them. She always explained them away as sentimental foolishness, an explanation he accepted since she cried nearly every time they spoke about their relationship.

'Don't cry, Chrissy love.' He said it automatically.

The tears stopped as quickly as they started. 'Will you have to travel as much now the study has been accepted?'

'At first I suppose I'll have to get out there and talk to the clans again. That will take time, you know how the San are. Half of them have probably forgotten all about the project by now. After all, in some cases it's been a year and a half since I first mentioned it to them. I'll try to talk !Ka into coming with me, the others will listen if I have him there. And then there's the problem with the tannery. I've been shown five sites and the bloody District Council are arguing over which one is best. I have to make a final decision on that this trip. Once everything's up and running I guess I'll be away a couple of times a year, that's all.'

She nodded. 'It's suddenly happening so fast. You go away the day after tomorrow. I'll miss you.'

'I'll miss you too.'

Again the tears. 'Don't miss me too much, darling. Concentrate on what you have to do.'

He had a government Land Rover at his disposal. He set off two days later. Chrissy waved him goodbye. 'See you when I see you. Stay well.' Her smile did not reach her eyes.

Alex was busy for the next four weeks. He went to Molepolole and selected a site for the tannery, staying on there for five days to hold discussions with the District Council, a lengthy process where the ramifications of every stage of its construction had to be talked about fully, from who would lay the concrete floor to who would paint the walls to who would supply the light fittings. Council members tended to push relatives forward, irrespective of their skills. To head them off when clearly a cousin or nephew was unqualified required a great deal of tact and arguments flared quickly if a council member felt he was getting less than his fair share of the spoils. Alex knew that if he appointed a building contractor who was an unpopular choice with the majority of council members, he could expect sabotage at the very least.

The Chief, still smarting from losing most of his authority and still angry with Alex, went out of his way to make progress as difficult as he could. By and large, however, his constant sniping and whining was ignored or overruled. All he achieved was unnecessary delay at every turn.

Alex stayed with Marthe and Jacob during this time. Jacob was as outspoken as ever. 'Why are you wasting your time with this, jong? Them plurry Bushmen won't thank you.'

'This attitude,' he thought sadly, 'prevails everywhere. The Bushmen are vilified by white and black alike. Perhaps it's their small stature and childlike features which make people think of them as being of no consequence, or maybe it's because they were hunted and forced out of traditional homelands. People write them off as cowards but they went in peace, rather than stay and fight. That's their way. They have to be the most misunderstood people on earth.'

But all he said to Jacob was, 'I don't want them to thank me. I just want to help them.' Someone had to. Before they disappeared forever.

Once the clans roamed the whole of southern Africa. In the thirteenth century, with Bantu tribes fleeing south to escape the slave traders, the peace-loving Bushmen had been hunted and herded out of their lands. They moved away to the south, finding places along the way where they could live. With the coming of the white man, however, the Bushmen found themselves, once again, hunted—this time with guns from horseback. With nowhere else to go, they headed west, into the sand and rock country of the Kalahari and Namib.

There they found the peace they so desperately desired. No-one else was interested in such arid places. 'Until now,' Alex thought. 'Thanks to technology.'

Once the talks with the District Council were concluded he made his way across the Kalahari towards Ghanzi, stopping at each of the places selected as pick-up points for leather, giving each person a register for the skins, teaching them the system required by the government and checking, where possible, that the local clans were still keen to participate. He was not surprised to discover that some of the clans had either changed their minds or were indifferent. Their wandering, non-hierarchal lifestyle made them reluctant to make decisions which might affect anyone other than the individual concerned and they could not yet grasp the concept of reward. Polite to the nth degree, the clans listened and nodded, then went about their own lives as though Alex had never spoken to them. He was not overly concerned. He knew how these people networked and how they loved to talk. The word would spread eventually. Although he searched for !Ka along the way, he was unable to locate the clan but he believed he had !Ka's approval of the project and that would help get the entire scheme off to a good start.

Reaching Ghanzi, Alex stayed at the Kalahari Arms, hoping to run into Pat. Some of Jeff Carter's men came into the bar on Saturday evening and from them he learned that Pat, Willie, Artie and Bob had just left on an early cattle drive. 'Jeff wants to do more drives than usual this year,' the man told him. 'He's mad. He's pushing us too hard.'

Alex didn't want to talk about Jeff. 'Who owns that land just west of town with the old shack on it?' The cartage company he'd had forced on him was nothing more than a man with a truck. He needed a depot for the skins.

'Jeff Carter.'

'What about the fenced plot out along the Maun road? The one with the road sign just in front of it?'

'Tribal.'

'Where does the Chief hang out?'

'You'll find him in the pub most afternoons.'

Alex made contact with the Chief of Ghanzi who was more than a little drunk. 'You want to build a depot! For them Bushmen? Thieving little bastards! The land's not mine to give any more but, if it were, I'd not let them have it.'

In the end he found the perfect piece of land which had

been earmarked for a new District Commissioner's house in the days before independence. The project had been shelved and then the land forgotten about. In that it already belonged to the government, getting it for his depot was easy.

Negotiations with the 'cartage company' were nearly as complicated as they had been over the tannery. The man who owned the truck had been told that the depot would belong to him and became stubborn and uncooperative as soon as Alex advised him otherwise. Then he made unreasonable demands about his truck which, on inspection of the vehicle, did not look as if it could make the journey from one end of Ghanzi to the other, a distance of half a mile. Alex had to agree to a major mechanical overhaul before discussions could proceed. He had been away nearly a month when Paul telephoned him from Gaborone, on a radio phone. His voice sounded tinny and disconnected. 'Can you come back. Chrissy isn't well.'

They were cut off before he could get the full message.

There was no hesitation on his part. If Paul had taken the trouble to call him then he knew that whatever was wrong with Chrissy was more than a dose of flu. He dropped every-thing and made the long trip south, sleeping briefly in his vehicle. It was hot and cramped but better than running the gauntlet of lions who would have been attracted to the area by the cattle drive. He actually passed the drive as it was camped out for the night just before the deep sandy country, but he didn't stop. It was midnight, the day after Paul's call, when he pulled into the yard of their house. Lights burned inside. Paul's vehicle was in the yard. Another car was there, one he did not recognise. He rushed up the steps and into the house.

Paul met him inside. 'The doctor's with her.'

'What's wrong with her?' There was the deepest fear in him.

Paul handed him a glass of scotch. 'Sit down.'

He knew it was bad. The look on Paul's face told him it was serious. But he wasn't prepared for the kick in the guts when Paul told him how bad. 'She's got leukaemia, Alex. She's known about it for some time. She didn't want you to know.'

Alex felt the scotch burning his throat. He felt weariness in his arms from the long trip. He felt the grittiness of lack of sleep in his eyes. But he had no idea that tears were streaming down his cheeks. He just knew a lump had appeared in his throat that hurt, and a cold was creeping through his gut and down his legs, and a scalding rage was setting fire to his heart.

He turned his head slowly, seeing Paul through a red haze of anger. 'No,' he whispered. His Chrissy. His bright-haired, milk-skinned, warm, loving Chrissy. She who filled him with smiles of happiness. His gentle girl who cried so suddenly and so unexpectedly. 'No.'

The doctor came from the room looking grim. He stopped Alex from going in. 'She's deeply asleep. I've given her something to help.'

'How long has she known?'

The doctor looked at him sharply. Alex knew him slightly— a man born in Basutoland who had made his life in Botswana with a Motswana wife. He was a good doctor. 'Several years. Didn't you know?'

'No,' he whispered miserably, wondering why he hadn't guessed. 'I had no idea.'

'It was pretty far advanced when we discovered it. She's refused most treatment. She went into remission for a while

313

but it came back stronger than ever. She's done well to last this long.'

'How long . . .' the words hurt his throat, '. . . how long has she . . .' he could not bring himself to ask.

'Not long. Just a few days.'

Oh God! Oh God, Chrissy! Why didn't you tell me, darling? But she had. In a thousand different ways. He just hadn't been listening.

The doctor was leaving, telling Paul he'd come back in the morning. Paul was walking the man to the door. Then he was coming back into the house, arms outstretched, sorrow on his face. Alex went into his brother's arms and cried, broken and ashamed he had not guessed. Hating himself for pushing her to a marriage she would not live to fulfil and to children she had known she could never bear. Terrified of a life with no Chrissy. A large black hole of sorrow loomed in front of him, gaping and unknown, threatening and so very full of pain.

Paul led him to the sofa and sat with him, his arm around his shoulders, pulling his older brother close, trying to comfort the boy, and then the man he so idolised. 'She didn't want you to know. When she learned I had contacted you, weak as she was, she really chewed me out.'

Why didn't I know? Was he so insensitive he could not see that which was right under his nose? 'When Chrissy makes up her mind about a thing, nothing changes it. She would have been very cross.' *Sick and cross. My darling, my poor darling.*

'I'm sorry.'

'No. You did the right thing. I have to be here.'

Paul rose and poured him another scotch.

'How did you find out?' He took the glass from Paul. 'Thanks.'

'She called me. She was frightened. When I got here I

could see that something was obviously very wrong. She's lost a lot of weight. She didn't even want me to call the doctor but I had to. Her appearance scared me.'

Frightened! His girl was frightened and sick and cross and he was not here for her. It was all he could think of. 'Oh God, Paulie!'

'Do you want me to stay?'

'No.' He stirred himself, tried to take control of his emotions. 'No, I need to be alone with her.'

Paul nodded that he understood.

After his brother left he went to the door of their bedroom. A lamp lit the room softly. He stopped at the door, looking at the bed. Her bright red hair was a flickering fire on the white pillow. Her face was as pale as the linen. Dark circles, like smudges of charcoal, under her eyes were the only things to break the whiteness of her face. Her cheekbones stood out, high and fine in a face which had grown terribly thin since he last saw her. Her lips were white.

Misery engulfed him. The soft rise and fall of her chest taunted him. Soon it would stop. Soon she would not breathe any more. Soon the gleam of mischief would leave her eyes. Soon the intelligence he had come to respect would be no more. Soon. Too soon.

He undressed quietly. Naked, he padded through to the bathroom, taking a scorching hot shower. There was a need in him to hold her but, before he did, he needed to be clean. Cleaner than he had ever been. So clean his body touching hers would do her no harm.

She stirred and mumbled as he got into bed next to her. Gently, so as not to disturb her precious sleep, he put his arm under her head. Slowly he pulled her into him, curling his body around hers, cradling her in his arms, gently kissing her hair, her forehead, her closed eyes. And as he held her he was shocked at the deterioration of her little body, and his tears fell on her hair and he tried to swallow around the terrible ache in his throat, as his heart broke with the loneliness yet to come, as he willed his own strength to help her, to enter her body and make her well again, Alex knew a pain so deep, so intense he trembled with it. Holding her, trembling with hurt, feeling her breath against his neck, he knew he was losing the one thing that meant more to him than his own life. And, oh God, how it hurt.

Chrissy never woke up. She died in his arms that night. The terrible pain which he had kept in check so as not to wake her burst from him in heartbroken, racking sobs as he held her lifeless body in his arms. He held her until dawn. As the sun broke over the rim of the earth and sent long fingers of light into their room he looked at her face and he understood, at last, that she had gone and would never be coming back. Her spirit had flown away, leaving the shell which had contained it.

He knew about death. !Ka taught him about the Hare and the Moon and the argument they had long ago about rebirth. He also taught him about the inevitability of death. His mother told him of life after death. Everyone had a story, a theory. But no-one prepared him for this. No-one warned him that when a vibrant young person dies their body looks like a wax figure. No-one told him how to cope with the knowledge that right here in his arms was the girl whose voice he could still hear but would never hear again, breath he could still feel but would never feel again, warm smile he could still see but would never see again.

She had gone. She had left him. She felt nothing. She saw nothing. He wanted to laugh at her, she looked so silly. He was angry with her. He felt like shaking her. His ears were ringing, loud bells which pealed through his head. He had no idea he was crying. A red mist rose. He thought he was laughing. Someone was, he could hear it.

Paul and the doctor prised Chrissy out of his arms. Paul helped him dress. Then he stood aghast while Alex rummaged through Chrissy's clothes, stripped off her nightgown and dressed her, slowly, lovingly, talking to her as though she could hear. 'What about this pair?' he asked her, holding up some pink panties. 'Yes. I like them too.'

'Alex!' Paul tried to lead him away.

'No!' It rang from him, an anguished cry of sorrow. 'She needs my help can't you see that? Here, Chrissy love, what do you think of this? It's your favourite blouse. Come here, darling, I'll help you.'

Alex Theron had lost his mind.

SIXTEEN

Paul had taken charge that terrible day. It was Paul who telephoned Chrissy's parents in Scotland and broke the news to them. When they pleaded that she be sent home for burial, it was Paul who arranged it. All through that long bitter day it was Paul, Paul, Paul. He forced coffee into Alex, cup after cup of it, but the sandwich he made for his brother remained untouched. Alex knew if he took so much as one bite he would be sick.

He followed Paul around as though he could not bear to be alone. But when Paul tried to order the coffin he grabbed the telephone from his brother's hand and flung it against a wall, smashing it to pieces.

'It has to be done, Alex.'

'I know, I know. Just not here, okay? She'll hear you.' He was sobbing so hard he could barely speak.

'I'll go and arrange it.' Paul gripped his arm hard. The pain of it was comforting. 'Do you want to come with me?'

Alex shook his head. He had to stay with Chrissy in case she was frightened.

When Paul returned he found Alex sitting on the floor at

318

the foot of the bed where Chrissy lay. His brother seemed to have retreated into a deep and unreachable place.

'I think it would be best if she goes to the church tonight. The flight leaves tomorrow morning.'

Alex appeared not to have heard him. But, two hours later, when they came to take her away, two dispassionate men who spoke softly and moved too quickly, the haste with which they were prepared to take her out of his life shocked Alex out of his silence. 'No!' he yelled.

'It's better this way.' Paul tried to lead him out of the room.

'No. She's not going anywhere. Not tonight.'

The men looked at Paul for guidance. Paul looked into Alex's eyes and saw the desperate, lonely pain and waved the men away. 'Come back tomorrow,' he told them. So the men laid her gently in the coffin and went away, their own hearts aching for the silent despairing man whose eyes were wild with disbelief and pain.

It stood in the lounge for one night, this gleaming horrid box, for though he could not bear to send her to wait in a lonely church, neither could he stand the sight of it. She was in there. Lying on her back which he knew she hated, her hands folded on her breast, her eyes forever closed. Everyone who came to pay their last respects said, 'But she looks lovely, as if she's sleeping.' He wanted to scream at them all, 'She looks dead, nothing but dead, you fool,' but he held his peace and said nothing, nodding dumbly. That night, though, when they had all gone away—all those caring, sympathetic eyes which filled him with rage, those sad grieving eyes which overwhelmed him with guilt, Paul's loving, worried eyes which drenched him with pain—he sat on the floor and rested his head against her coffin.

'Chrissy, I love you.' But she had no words for him.

319

Restless, he prowled the house all night. Her book, open at page 145. Now she'd never know how it ended. Her reading glasses, resting on the open pages. Her shoes, kicked off and lying against each other under the bed. The clothes she was wearing that last day, thrown on the floor as, sick and frightened, she had crawled into bed. The indentation of her head on the pillow. A sandwich on the bedside table, stale and deserted, one tiny bite taken out, he could see the marks of her teeth. In the bathroom, some dirty clothes. He picked up her shirt and held it against his face and he could smell her. Red hair on her brush. 'Oh Jesus, darling, why didn't I know?'

And his heart broke again and again. But when they came for the coffin the next day he stood in the doorway and watched it go. 'She's not in there,' he slurred to Paul, waving the bottle of scotch at him. 'She's fooled them all. She's flying.' And he laughed at his clever Chrissy who was flying without him and then he cried.

He heard the aeroplane that took her away. It flew directly over the house. He did not bother to look up. 'Why didn't I know?' he cried to the doctor the next day who had come to see how he was doing.

'She was very determined not to let you know. She had great strength. I'm surprised she managed to keep it from you, though. The last couple of months weren't easy for her.'

'Why?' he whispered. 'I could have helped her.'

'Mr Theron,' the doctor said, his voice full of sympathy, 'your young lady knew that if you discovered the truth she could no longer pretend it wasn't happening to her. This way, she gave herself many moments during the past few years where she could pretend she was well. I saw her a few months ago. She was talking about the job you're doing for the Bushmen. She was full of enthusiasm and do you know what she told me? She said, "In a few years it will be good to see the scheme working." She believed she would see it. These are the moments I'm talking about. If you had known she was ill she could not have deceived herself. Your grief would have been a constant reminder of the fact that she was dying. Don't blame her.'

'I don't blame her,' Alex said quietly. 'I blame myself.'

'You couldn't have stopped it.'

'No. But I could have helped.'

It all seemed unreal: the empty house loudly echoing his solitary footsteps as he paced and prowled in lonely despair but which he preferred to the intrusion of well-meaning voices; her clothes and toiletries which mocked and tortured so he hated them but he could not bring himself to throw them away.

Alex did the only thing he could think of. He went into the desert and found !Ka.

Be took one look at his face and she knew. 'The fire in your girl has gone out.'

'Yes,' he cried in anguish. 'How did you know?'

'It was already growing cold when you brought her here. She did not know it then but the little arrows of sickness had already been brought by the spirits.'

!Ka tapped his arm. 'We could not do the curing dance. She had a sickness we cannot make better.'

'Yes,' he said miserably. 'And now she is gone.'

'Look up *!ebili*. Can you see the backbone of the sky?'

But it was no use. !Ka's wisdom could not help him this time and, three days later, feeling abandoned and alone in his pain, Alex returned to Gaborone and tried to throw himself into his work. But it was no use. The shell worked; he walked, talked, ate, drank and laughed but the impetus to carry on, the enthusiasm he had brought to his project, had gone. There were days when he was too hungover to get out of bed. Timon Setgoma had him removed from the scheme. Too much aid money had been spent on it to allow it to stumble along in the hands of a man who had lost his mind.

Three weeks after that terrible night when Chrissy left forever, a memorial service was held in Gaborone. Paul told him her parents wanted it. They wanted to meet her friends, get a feel for the last few years of her life. Marv and Pru came down for it, Pru heavy with child. She took charge of the arrangements for which Alex supposed he was grateful. He began to drink heavily. He didn't understand why a service was being held at all. But he kept that thought to himself and watched himself circulate among friends and listened to them saying how sorry they were and heard himself make the right responses. He watched while he comforted her parents who appeared to be as bewildered as he.

'Why didn't you let us know she was sick?' her father kept asking. 'Why didn't you tell us?'

'It'll be all right, you'll see.' He missed the worried look which passed between Paul and Marv. He thought how well he was doing. He thought he'd given the kindest answer. Why hurt her parents? Why tell them she lived with her illness right under his nose and he didn't see it?

They all turned out for the memorial service. A crowd who loved to laugh and have fun. A crowd too young and strong to ever die. A crowd struck dumb that one of them had traitorously fallen under the weight of illness. They were no help to Alex. They were too busy with their own shock.

They patted him awkwardly and mumbled about him coming over for dinner and moved away as quickly as they could. Alex preferred their company. Paul, Marv and Pru, Chrissy's parents, even Mum and Pa who had made the journey from Shakawe, they made him feel. And he didn't want to feel.

Pa's sympathy was unbearable. The pain he felt for his son made Alex's pain worse.

'Do you have to drink so much, Ali? It won't help you know.'

Paul dragged their mother away as Alex shouted, 'How the hell would you know?' and felt sadistic pleasure at the sudden look of shock on her face.

He didn't want to feel or think or do. He needed company but, as soon as he had company, he needed to be alone. Then he heard himself agreeing to return to the farm with Marv and Pru. He didn't have the strength to say no. Besides, at night alone in the house, the pain was too intense. He was sick of thinking and remembering and crying. He was sick of prowling the rooms, touching her things. Without knowing it was happening, a watcher was born who lived inside his head and observed. This watcher, whose impartial eyes observed an Alex who had gone cold, who moved and spoke like the old Alex but who was dead inside, this watcher never judged, simply watched and listened.

While Alex helped Marv with the fences and nodded dumbly when Marv told him hard physical work would take his mind off his grief, the watcher listened. He was there watching when Pru went into labour and Alex drove a calm and matter-of-fact mother-to-be, and a father-to-be who had fallen apart at the seams, two hours to the hospital in Francistown. He—or the watcher, he didn't know which— saw himself do all the right things. And then he listened

323

when, three months later, he explained to Marv why he was leaving. He did that rather well, too. 'I just have to get away. Leave Botswana for a while. I'll be back.' The voice was his, but the watcher knew if he didn't leave, the happiness and love between Marv and Pru and their newly born baby son, Alexander James, would send him truly mad.

So he left. He left Botswana. Then he left Africa. Life became a blur. Too many hotels, too many bars, too many girls who left him empty inside and aching, too many bottles of scotch. Sometimes he could not remember which country he was in. They all looked the same. Europe at her quaint best. Doll's houses lining canals and streets. Ducks in picturesque ponds. Bright green fields and hills dotted with fat black and white cows. Guttural voices and faces which smiled a welcome. Snow-capped mountains. Blazing blue Mediterranean seas. Grapevines. Fishing boats. Blue rivers. Brown rivers. And always, always the welcome oblivion of one amber liquid too many.

Sometimes he remembered snippets. Brawls mainly. He wanted to be left alone but they would not leave him alone. Young and free and convinced everyone was their friend, they badgered him with their conversations. Flat nasal Australians, broad twangy Americans, broken English'd Dutch or Germans or Spaniards or wherever they came from, they would not leave him alone. Mainly he went with the flow, allowed himself to be picked up by their lives and taken along for the ride. After a while, when they realised he had nothing of himself to give, they dropped him. On some occasions, when self-pity and pain were almost too great to bear, he lashed out at them. Verbally, he shouted abuse so he could watch their happy faces turn to bewilderment. Physically, he shoved them away roughly so he could fight them, lose himself in physical rather than emotional pain.

Once or twice the real Alex lifted his head and saw what had become of him. But grief hadn't finished with him and the pain was too much so the real Alex slunk away and the watcher returned.

He worked sporadically. Odd jobs he could not recall asking to do. He picked grapes somewhere, probably Spain. He painted boats. Greece, he thought. He shovelled pig shit and had no idea where except it was icy cold and the people spoke a funny lilting language and they all had blond hair. Hard physical labour which had him sweating out last night's whisky, only to top up again tonight. Mindless jobs which didn't require him to think. And the watcher in his mind noticed how well he was doing.

One day, nearly three years later, for no reason he could think of, he stopped watching himself. He woke in a strange bed, in a strange flat, in a strange land and the first thing to hit him was he felt pain. Pain in his head. Pain from too much scotch. But he, Alex, was feeling it, not the mind who had watched Alex. It was real and it was inside his own head. He stirred in yellow and ivory striped sheets and wondered whose they were. He cursed when he found one eye was swollen shut. He ran his tongue over teeth which felt like cat fur.

Stumbling, he guessed his way to the bathroom. He stared at his reflection in the mirror. Bloodshot eyes, a couple of scars, hair which needed cutting, a face which needed shaving and one very black eye stared back. But he could see himself. He realised he hadn't seen himself for a very long time. This time, for some reason, he did not retreat. This time he faced himself head-on. He ran cold water and splashed his face. His hands trembled. He could smell his own body odour.

The bathroom was feminine. He took a shower, a long hot shower. He found a razor and shaved, cutting himself several times. He wrapped a towel around his waist and wandered the flat. *Nice view.* Rolling hills and a castle. He wondered where he was, which country. He remembered he had been in France. When? How long ago? He went into the small kitchen and made himself coffee. The label was in English. He supposed he could always turn on the television and see what language it was in but he found it didn't matter to him. Snow was falling outside. The flat was warm. *Good.* He hated the cold.

He went back to the bedroom and stared at the bed. Had he and the owner of the flat made love? *No. Not made love. Fucked.* He hadn't made love to anyone since Chrissy died. *Chrissy!* He had blocked out her name. *Chrissy!* He could see her face. He waited for the darkness to cover his heart. *Chrissy!* But there was only light.

Had he fucked whoever owned the bed? He could not remember. He had just decided to get dressed and leave when he heard a key in the door, then light footsteps coming into the bedroom.

'Good, you're up. I bought you some clothes, you don't appear to live anywhere.'

He stared. 'Good Christ, Madison!'

She smiled grimly. 'The very same.'

He shook his head to clear it. 'Where am I?'

'My flat.'

'Yes but where?'

She raised her eyebrows. 'Don't you know?'

'I guess not.'

'Stirling.'

'Stirling? You mean Scotland Stirling? How'd I get here?'

326

She threw packages on the bed. 'Bought you some clothes. Yours were disgusting. Get dressed, we'll talk over breakfast.'

'Did you get me a toothbrush?'

'It's in there somewhere.'

He listened to her accent, South African upper class English, not another like it in the world. It made him think of home. He wanted to ask how he came to be in her flat but she turned on her heel and left the room, closing the door behind her.

He dressed in clean new clothes. She had thought of everything. He found aspirin in her bathroom cupboard and swallowed three, gagging as they stuck in the back of his throat. Then he joined Madison in the kitchen.

'I don't remember anything.'

'Hardy surprising. You're a helluva mess.'

'Yeah.'

She was doing something with oranges and a juice extractor. He could smell the tanginess of citrus. His mouth watered. When was the last time he wanted anything other than scotch?

'Here.' She handed him a full glass.

He drank it straight down. 'Like more?' She held out her hand for the glass.

'Please.' The last of the fur in his mouth had been washed away.

She turned back to the sink.

'How did I get here?'

'With great difficulty. You're a dead weight.'

'You carried me?' No way, she was too small.

'Practically.'

'Did we . . . you know . . . did we do anything?'

'Do me a favour!'

'Where did you sleep then?'

327

'On the sofa.'

'Sorry.'

'It's all right. It's quite comfortable, really.' She handed him another glass of orange juice. 'I found you in the street outside a bar. You'd been tossed out.'

Chrissy's parents. He remembered. He had gone to see Chrissy's parents. He couldn't recall what happened but he knew he left their home with a feeling of deep sadness. The words 'We blame you,' rang in his head.

'I guess I was a bit of a mess.'

She answered with a directness typical of people who came from a country like Botswana and had no time for coyness. 'You were covered in vomit and blood. You hadn't bathed in God knows how long. You had no coat, no jacket. You'd have frozen to death in the street.'

'And you picked me up?'

'Yes,' she said crisply. 'Much to the amusement of the occupants of the bar.'

He could imagine it. The small amount he was beginning to remember told him it hadn't been a very nice place. 'Thank you.'

'Consider us even.'

He let that pass. 'What are you doing here? Last I heard you were in Europe at finishing school.'

She grunted, half amused, half angry. 'They threw me out.'

He laughed. 'What'd you do, use the wrong knife?'

She laughed back. 'A couple of us decided to abseil from the third floor.'

'They threw you out for that?'

'No.'

'What then?'

'I hated the bloody place and I hated the bloody people.

When the headmistress had me on the mat and told me that nice young ladies don't climb out of windows, particularly in their nightdresses and especially not in full view of the townsfolk, I sort of let fly.'

'Let fly?' he was grinning. He felt his mouth widen and his spirits lift. The last time he felt this good was so long ago, too long ago.

'Sort of.' She smiled at him. 'I . . . uh . . . well I kind of implied that she ate too much, was of the canine variety and she could stick her manners and rules someplace no-one had ever been.'

He laughed out loud, he could just imagine her exact words. It felt good to laugh. 'So you stayed in Europe?'

'No. I went home.'

'But now you're back.'

She avoided his eyes. 'I felt like a break from Africa. Been working my way around Europe.'

She was hiding something, he could tell. But he didn't care. He was too happy at being happy again. 'I've been drinking my way around it.'

'I heard what happened. I'm sorry.'

'Yeah well. It was a long time ago.' Suddenly that's how it felt. The crushing weight of grief was lifting.

'You must have loved her very much.'

'I did.' He did not want to talk to Madison about Chrissy.

She placed toast and Marmite in front of him and sat opposite. 'Haven't got anything else, sorry.' The homely smell of toast and melting butter had his mouth watering again.

Her accent made him homesick. Suddenly he wanted to go home. He wanted to smell the bush again, feel the freedom of being the only person for miles, listen to the wind whispering through the sand dunes, talk the clicking language of the San.

329

He wanted to taste the tangy tsamma melon and feel the juicy tenderness of Botswana beefsteak in his mouth. 'I'm going back.'

'How?'

'I think I've got money there. I'll send for some.'

'You think?' She was incredulous.

'I might have already sent for it.'

'You don't remember?'

'I don't remember much at all. It's like I've been asleep.' He frowned. 'This is weird, Madison. To suddenly wake up and you're here. It's the strangest feeling.'

'I guess it must be.' Again, she was avoiding something.

'I need to get home. I need to be myself again.' He looked at her. 'Do you understand what I mean?'

'Yes.' She passed him more hot toast and sat opposite him. 'Anything's better than what you've become.'

'Thanks a lot,' he said drily.

'You'll see changes. Gabs has grown a great deal.' She nibbled a piece of toast. 'Do you know the date?'

He was insulted. 'I'm not that far gone, Madison. It's January seventeenth, 1969.'

She pounced. 'Eighteenth, actually. Saturday the eighteenth.'

'Oh.' He had finished the toast. 'Feel like a walk?'

'Where to?'

He stood up. 'I'm still starving.'

She laughed at him. 'You're not so sick.'

'Not any more. I've just woken up. It's a nice feeling.'

She handed him some money. 'I found this in your pocket. Nothing else. I burned your clothes by the way.'

He counted the notes: eighteen pounds. Enough for breakfast anyway. 'I have to find a bank.'

'It's Saturday.'

'Don't they open Saturday in Scotland?'

'In the mornings. It's 1.15 in the afternoon. You'll have to wait until Monday. You're welcome to stay with me but I get the bed, you have the sofa.'

'Fine with me.'

'And don't get any ideas. I'm helping because I know you.'

'Madison?'

'What?'

'You're full of shit.'

For a brief moment the watcher was back, wondering what she would do and not caring very much one way or another. But when she threw back her head and laughed, it was Alex who was relieved. The watcher was on the way out.

After the weekend she left him to himself, alone in her flat with his thoughts, while she went to work as a receptionist at a doctor's surgery. He thought of Chrissy and the terrible ache in his heart was gone. Instead he found himself smiling at a memory. He thought of Marv and Pru and the baby Alexander James who had caused him such pain. He would no longer be a baby. He thought of Paul and of his parents. By mid-week his mind was clear. It was time to go back.

The bank arranged to ascertain his account balance in Gaborone. 'Come back the day after tomorrow,' the teller told him. 'We'll have an answer by then.'

That evening Madison smiled when she saw his determination to go home. 'I miss it too. I'll probably go home soon. Mummy is lonely.'

'Why?'

'My father died last year. He got caught up in a stampede at Kang.'

'I'm sorry.'

'Are you?' Her smile was wry.

'Yes.' He found he was. 'There's no point in trying to hide the fact that I didn't like him. I didn't. You know what happened. I'm sorry he died like that and I'm sorry for the pain it would have caused you and your mother. That's all.'

'He always regretted what he did to you.'

'You wanted to talk about it that night we . . .' he left it hanging, wondering what she would say.

'The night we made love.' She smiled briefly. 'It's okay, Alex, you can say it.'

'I wasn't using you. I know you think I was but it wasn't like that.'

She took two beers from the refrigerator, then put one back when he shook his head. 'I know that now.' She popped the can and drank straight from it. Lowering it she grinned at him. 'I probably knew it then as well. I was just too bloody full of myself to admit it.'

Alex laughed. Then, 'I still don't want to talk about your father. There's no point.'

She swigged her beer and he watched her hair. 'I don't either.' She put her beer down. 'We had a sort of falling out a few years back. I thought I knew him but . . .,' she shrugged. 'Let's drop it.'

He stared at her. 'You're different somehow.'

'Older and wiser.' She grinned. 'Had to happen.'

'Do Pat and the rest of them still work at your place?'

'Artie has gone, he's returned to Rhodesia. The rest are still there although I don't know for how long. Mummy's got the farm up for sale.' She looked at him. 'What will you do when you get back?'

'Probably go back to Shakawe. I expect Pa could do with some help on the farm. He's not getting any younger. Mum's been trying to get me home for years.'

She nodded. 'That Bushman scheme of yours is off the ground. It's doing very well from what I gather.'

He was glad to hear it. 'Anyone found diamonds yet near Jwaneng?'

'Kel?' She laughed. 'He went broke.'

'Good.'

'Sent most of his family broke as well.'

'Good.'

'You're a charming little dear, aren't you?'

He shrugged. 'I guess I don't like bullies and cheats.'

She looked angry but said nothing.

'That wasn't a dig, Madison.'

'You'll never forgive Dad, will you?'

'It's over.' He saw she was waiting to hear more. 'You're right, I'll never forgive him. I've tried but I can't.'

'He was always sorry about it.'

Again, he changed the subject. He did not want to fight her. 'What will you do when you get back?'

'Try to get back my old job with Game Department. I liked that work.' She seemed pleased to talk of something else.

He realised how hard it must have been for her, loving her father as she did, to learn of his darker side. One day they might be able to speak of it together. Not today. 'Will you work in Gabs or Maun?'

'Wherever they send me, I don't mind.'

Alex discovered he didn't mind where he went either. The desert, the Okavango, Gaborone, Francistown, he loved it all. The freedom of space, the open people. He looked out through her window: a wintry scene in Scotland. It was beautiful but it wasn't for him.

The bank informed him he had 8,000 rand in his account

in Gaborone. The teller seemed surprised he didn't know that, with independence, Botswana had moved into the Rand Monetary Area. Alex remembered there had been talk of it. He did not bother to enlighten the man as to why he needed to have the figure converted into pounds.

'Four thousand approximately,' the teller said.

Four thousand. More than enough to fly home. More than enough to get him back to Shakawe. He had money in Francistown too, unless he'd spent it on alcohol.

He arranged a transfer of 5,000 Rand. The Botswana High Commission in London told him over the telephone that a passport to replace the one he had lost along the way would take two weeks to arrange. It seemed like a very long time.

His body showed the ravages of neglect. He felt white and flabby. He spent the two weeks trying to get into shape. He jogged for an hour every morning and evening. He swam daily at the local swimming baths. He ate plain food with lots of fruit and vegetables. He avoided alcohol completely.

Madison appeared happy enough for him to stay with her. They spent most evenings either talking or playing scrabble. She was easy to be with but he was wary of her. There was something she was not telling him. He tried once to find out what it was.

'How come you have a place in Stirling?' It seemed strange to him that she lived where Chrissy had lived.

She was making a salad and did not look up as she spoke. 'Guess I had to end up somewhere. Stirling seemed as good a place as anywhere.'

'Why not London or Edinburgh?'

'I spent time in both.' She was paying close attention to a tomato.

'Madison, look at me.'

She looked up, eyes wary.

'You've known pain too, haven't you?' he asked softly.

She bit her lip, went to say something, changed her mind, shrugged, then said, 'I'll tell you about it some time.'

He left it. He knew about pain.

Chrissy stayed at the forefront of his mind. She lay in his memories, warm and loving. There was sadness but it did not consume him. Instead, he invited the memories. Madison remarked on it one evening.

'You've been talking about her a lot in the past few days.'

'Do you mind?'

She shook her head. 'Of course not. It's good for you. You've bottled it up for so long. Grief has to be expressed.'

'It's no longer grief.'

'Yes it is. But it's only grief. The anger and guilt have passed.'

'What are you? Some kind of shrink?'

She smiled. 'When Dad died I felt he'd somehow betrayed Mummy and me. I was very angry about it and that made me feel guilty. I've been there.'

Yes she had. He put his hand across the table and took one of hers in it. 'I'm sorry. I have been very self-absorbed, haven't I?'

She removed her hand. 'Very.'

'Ouch!'

She put some scrabble pieces on the board. She had turned his word ZOO into ZOOLOGICAL and picked up a triple word score bonus. 'Bitch!'

She laughed at him and he grinned back.

Madison drove him to Glasgow airport. She hugged him goodbye and said, 'Go well, Alex Theron.'

'Stay well, Madison Carter.'

It was an old African greeting and farewell and it made both of them friends. So he kissed her cheek.

He changed terminals at Heathrow and returned to Johannesburg in a bright orange and white Boeing 707 with a flying springbok on the tail. Air Botswana then took him to the land of his birth in a blue, black and white DC3 which shook and rattled but did nothing to stop the rising tide of feeling as he stared down at the barren brown land beneath him. The cluster of low buildings which did for an airport terminal at Gaborone never looked better.

He stepped out of the aeroplane and breathed in the heat and dust of Africa. He looked out across the flat-topped acacia trees to the hills near Kgale Mission. He took in the evidence of new building, sprawling outwards, the ever-increasing suburbia of Gaborone. The braying of a donkey. The greeting *'duméla rra. A o sa tsogile sentlé?'* The low fence running up to the terminal. Paul just the other side. He was home. He was home. He was home.

Paul looked tanned and slim and healthy. Next to him, despite exercise and plain food, Alex still felt white and flabby.

'I'm taking a month off work,' Paul said, delighted to see Alex. 'We'll go home. Mum and Pa will love it—both of us there together.'

Paul lived in the newly established Extension 11. Alex was glad he did not live in The Village. He did not want to see the old house. Gaborone, as Madison had warned, had changed and grown. New streets, new houses, a shopping mall. 'Expats are pouring in,' Paul explained. 'There's an estimated 20,000 and it's growing every day. This is a boom town.'

'How about Francistown?' Alex didn't much fancy the idea of a boom town.

'Hasn't changed. Sleepy as hell.'

'Good.'

Paul had a swimming pool. Alex spent the next few days relaxing around it, trying to get some colour back into his winter white body.

They headed north at the weekend in Alex's Land Rover which Paul had kept in his garage. A couple of suitcases and Paul's dog, Ralph. They called in and saw Marv and Pru. Marv had put on weight and patted his girth self-consciously. 'She feeds me too well,' he said, his arm around Pru.

Pru was expecting their third child. 'One every two years,' she said, 'that's the ticket.'

Alexander James, or 'AJ' as he was called, was a shy three-year-old. His sister, Christine Priscilla, a chubby one-year-old baby.

The farm was doing well. Marv had extended their house as the babies came. 'Can't keep up with them,' he complained happily. He proudly showed them around. The original rectangle had been extended at both ends so the house was now U-shaped, with scaffolding and trusses where a further extension was planned. Marv seemed to be in his element; his farm was flourishing, as a father, he was a natural. With AJ, he was stern but fair and had a lot of time to play games or read to the youngster. With the baby Christine, he was an unashamed bumbling pushover. She had him around her little finger and he knew it. Disciplining this little dimpled charmer was left to Pru. Alex immediately referred to her as Chrissy and, after an awkward silence, everyone else did the same.

Marv and Pru hadn't changed. They were as in love now as they had been when they married. Their mirth bubbled out at the slightest thing. They touched each other constantly and the love on their faces when they looked at each other, or at their children, left Alex feeling mellow and gentle. He was glad of that. He had been afraid of jealousy.

They spent three days with Marv and Pru. The dog, Ralph, befriended Alexander James to such an extent that Paul left him with the boy. 'Bloody traitor,' he muttered, as they drove off while Ralph stood next to AJ with his tail wagging madly. 'To think I rescued him from death row.'

'Dog's gotta do what a dog's gotta do,' Alex chanted, feeling relaxed and happy.

Paul was right. Francistown hadn't changed much. Aunty Dorie insisted they spend a night with her and produced enough food to feed a small army. 'Your mum's real sick,' she told them. 'She'll be glad to see you both.'

Paul admitted the next day that he hadn't been home for several years. 'Just got caught up with things.'

'Makes you feel guilty, doesn't it?'

Paul sighed. 'Yeah. If it were only Pa then . . .' He let it hang in the air. Both knew they would go home more often if only their mother were not so strange.

'Does she go on at you about coming home and helping Pa?'

'No.' Paul glanced at him. 'I have a profession. She saves that for you.'

'You know all that stuff about our having black blood?'

Paul laughed. 'Only a South African could get hung up about black blood. It's ridiculous. Look at you—blond, blue-eyed—any black blood in us is long gone.'

'But it's the key to it. That's why she's like that.'

'She went to the Kirk every week to listen to the Dominie yelling fire and brimstone about the inferior blacks. She grew up with it.'

'If Pa had stamped on it early . . .' It was the only time in his life he felt critical of his father.

'If Mum told Pa to jump in a fire he'd do it, you know that.'

Alex grimaced. 'Sad isn't it? When I get married I'll make damned sure my wife and I are on the same wavelength.'

'Yeah,' Paul agreed. 'Me too.'

Maun was still the same except safari lodges were springing up to the east of town. 'It's big business now. Brings a lot of foreign exchange into the country. The Delta is becoming a great tourist attraction.' Paul's job with the Ministry of Finance and Development Planning was diverse. He had just completed a feasibility study on the financial benefits of tourism and professional hunting if they were promoted more vigorously.

'I've recommended that the government spend rather more than they're doing now. The Okavango has to be Botswana's best kept secret. It needs more promotion.'

'What about the ecology of the place? Can the swamps handle it?'

'Ecologists are swarming all over the swamps.' Paul grinned. 'One lot suggested dredging the river. Another guy is studying blind worms. Someone wants to cut down the trees along the river, someone else wants to plant more. One poor bastard lost a leg trying to prove that crocodiles were not aggressive. It's mayhem.'

'So what will happen?' They were driving along the Panhandle, along the road they both hated so much as schoolboys. Alex watched the scenery, not wanting it to change so much as a leaf.

'What will happen is what usually happens. Nothing.' Paul grinned again. 'Even the tsetse stays.'

'Why?'

Alex well remembered this dreaded fly which thrives in the southern Okavango. It has a bite as painful as a horse fly and carries the disease known as sleeping sickness in man or rinderpest in animals. Hosted, with little to no adverse effect, by warthog, buffalo, bushbuck, kudu and others, the tsetse is deadly to cattle and can also prove fatal to man. For years attempts to eradicate the fly were made. When it was discovered that it could not live in temperatures over 40°C large areas of bush were cleared, giving the fly nowhere to shelter. The tsetse moved on. Fences were built to contain the host wildlife and huge belts of animals were deliberately wiped out. The fly population decreased significantly. DDT and Dieldrin were sprayed on the large trees favoured as the tsetse fly's resting places. Total eradication became a real possibility. The cattlemen wanted the fly gone. The Okavango was the only place of permanent surface water in the entire country. Why would Paul recommend a halt to the eradication program?

'Money, my friend. Or, to be more specific, foreign exchange. Believe it or not, the wildlife has more potential for foreign exchange than the beef industry ever could. If we get rid of the tsetse, cattle will come back. If that happens, farmers will want to fence their properties. The wildlife will either move on or, worse, die of starvation. So, while the government has the know-how to get rid of the tsetse, they're not doing it.'

Paul cursed as he swerved to avoid a pothole. 'Oh sure,' he continued, having shaken the Land Rover to the point where an array of items had fallen off the back seat, 'the government wants to keep everybody happy. So they spray regularly and keep talking about how tsetse numbers are reducing. But we now have the means to completely eradicate them.

Endosulphan. Sprayed every twenty-one days, after six applications the fly density has been reduced by 99.9 per cent. But we sure as hell aren't telling the farmers.' He glanced at Alex. 'The wonderful world of economics,' he laughed. 'Wars, disease, politics, you name it. Any man-made or natural disaster you care to mention, and I include politicians deliberately. They're all controlled by the bottom line.'

'That's kind of cynical,' Alex said.

'Show me an economist and I'll show you a cynic.' Paul raised both hands and the Land Rover headed towards the bush. 'What's even more depressing,' he went on, grabbing the steering wheel, 'is the hidden agenda. We call it number crunching. More often than not the bottom line is given to us *before* we start a feasibility study. In other words, we get a brief like, "Do the study, show us the numbers, but get them to say what *we* want them to say". To hell with the truth. Profit is truth.'

Alex cocked his head. 'Enjoy your work, do you?'

Paul grinned and raised his eyebrows. 'It's a living.'

They stopped in Shakawe and picked up supplies. Their parents, not knowing they were coming, would need the extra food. Pig Face was still there. He was stacking tins of baked beans on the shelves and nearly jumped out of his skin when Alex came up behind him quietly and said 'Boo'.

The road to the farm was more rutted than they remembered. 'Jesus, you'd think they'd grade it once in a while,' Paul said, as they bottomed again on the high ridge of sand in the centre.

'For all the traffic you mean?'

Paul laughed. 'Must be at least one vehicle a week on it.'

The farmhouse brought a lump to his throat. But not as big a lump as when he saw Pa sitting on the verandah in his

341

favourite chair smoking his pipe. Pa rose stiffly and stared at them. 'Pets,' he called suddenly, excitement making his voice high. 'Pets, come and see. The boys are home.'

Alex jumped the garden gate. His mother ran out of the front door and down the steps. He embraced her and his father together, then stood back while Paul did the same. They all had tears in their eyes. 'Praise the Lord, you're home.'

His eyes met Paul's over their parents' heads. She hadn't changed.

Pa was grinning like a fool. 'Welcome home, welcome,' he kept saying.

'How long can you stay?' Mum asked.

Alex looked at her. She had lost some weight and the lines around her eyes and mouth were deeper. 'Paul's got a couple of weeks,' he told her. 'I thought I'd stay on for a while.'

'Oh, Ali. Thank God, thank you Lord.' He folded her into his arms. Over her head he saw Pa brush tears away from his eyes.

'It's the right thing to do,' he thought.

They all sat on the verandah talking. Pa quietly happy, Mum bubbling with joy. Her conversation was still peppered with praise and prayer but Alex realised after half an hour that she had not actually quoted from the Bible once. She seemed more content somehow.

He noticed some attempt had been made to start a garden and commented.

'Mum did that, didn't you, Pets?'

'We had a lovely garden once,' Mum said wistfully. 'We never had enough rain though. Everything died eventually.'

Alex could not remember a garden. A few bougainvillea

struggling to grow against the fence and a line of frangipani at the back where the water from the house drained was all.

'We've got a new well,' Pa said. 'It gives us all the water we need.'

'The good Lord provides.' Mum rose. 'I'll go and see to dinner.'

'Is Mum well?' Paul asked once she had gone.

Pa tapped his pipe on his shoe. 'No,' he said sadly. 'She's got something wrong with her heart.'

'Pa,' Alex said. 'Should you be living way out here? Why not move to a town? Then at least you're close to a doctor.'

Pa stared out at the Tsodilo Hills. 'Mum won't hear of it,' he said finally.

'She seems . . . better. Know what I mean, Pa?' Alex wasn't sure how much his father would say.

'Better?' Pa smiled sadly. 'In a way I suppose she is. She's made peace with her God. Now she's just waiting for the call. You boys . . . well, make the most of your stay.'

Sobered by his words, both Alex and Paul went out of their way to listen to her, praise the food and answer her questions. It was too late for either of them to love her unconditionally but they loved her enough to go out of their way for her.

She seemed to be calmed by their interest. But Alex felt something was not quite right. In her calmness there was an eerie emptiness.

After dinner she asked them both to join her in the lounge. Expecting a Bible reading, they joined her with some reluctance. Pa, as usual, had gone onto the verandah to smoke his pipe.

'I have something to tell you both,' she said, once they were settled. Her eyes glinted strangely although she was smiling. 'Your father is trying to kill me.'

343

In the silence which followed only the clock on the mantelpiece could be heard.

'Mum . . .' Paul said uneasily.

She held up her hand. 'I know you find it hard to believe. He's an evil, evil man. He's black you see. Black men are not like us.'

Alex sat stunned. What he'd taken as contentment earlier was insanity. His mother was totally mad. And like many unhinged people, she was able to conceal her affliction until suddenly, wham, she hit you with it right between the eyes.

She was crying. Neither Alex nor Paul knew what to do. They held her until her sobs subsided. When she looked up, her insanity was gone. She smiled as though nothing had taken place. 'I'm going to sit here and read my Bible for a while. I'll join you later.'

Shaken, they went outside. Their father, from the darkness, said quietly, 'Well boys, now you know.' Then sensed, rather than heard, that Danie Theron was crying like a little kid.

Two days later, as she worked in the kitchen, Peta Theron finally found her peace. They heard a crash and a scream from the servant and had run to investigate.

'Her heart, her heart.' Pa rushed to her side. 'It's her heart. Pets. Pets, darling.'

Paul picked her up and carried her to the bedroom. He lay her on the bed. Her face had gone grey.

'I'll call the doctor,' Pa said, wringing his hands. 'You hang on there, Pets, the doctor is coming.'

'I'll call him.' Alex could see it was no use. 'You stay with Mum.'

The doctor was busy in his bush clinic some ten miles the other side of Shakawe and his wife was unable to reach him.

It took him nearly four hours to arrive. By the time he did, Mum had been dead for three and a half hours.

Paul went back to Gaborone two weeks later. Alex and Pa settled into a comfortable routine, Alex taking on the harder tasks, Pa content to supervise or assist. They didn't talk much. Pa had long ago got used to sitting by himself on the verandah while Mum read her Bible. Alex had his own thoughts to occupy his mind. The days turned into weeks. The weeks into months.

He and Pa repaired fences, dipped cattle, dug a new dam, fixed the verandah roof, drove some cattle into South West Africa and built new water troughs. Before he knew it, he had been on the farm eighteen months. His body responded to the hard work. He became fit and slim and brown and strong. And after that time, he knew he had to get away.

'Farm's looking good, son. I couldn't have done it alone.' Pa knew. Pa always knew.

'I've enjoyed working with you, Pa.'

'I've enjoyed having you here, Alex. But Shakawe is not for you, I know that. When are you leaving?'

'You don't mind?'

Pa smiled, a slow, sad kind of smile. 'Of course I mind. A man likes to have his sons around him. But I'd mind even more if I felt you were staying on just to please me.'

Good old Pa. Poor old Pa. All alone now, with his pipe. At least Mum had been company of sorts. 'I'll stay until the new calves are born, help you with that.'

'Thanks, son.'

'Pa?'

'No, son, I won't sell.'

'Okay. Just a thought.'

Pa, standing at the gate wearing his old clothes and his old hat, puffing on his old pipe, waving his old arm goodbye, his Pa who had once been fit and strong, his Pa who the young Alex wanted to be like, his old Pa. Now he was old and alone. It was the saddest thing he'd ever seen.

SEVENTEEN

When he left Shakawe Alex had no real plan of action. He was twenty-eight years old, his bank balance was far from healthy and he had no formal training, no qualifications and no idea what to do next. Another man might have been worried but Alex possessed the wisdom of !Ka. 'In the desert it is foolish to plan ahead for the desert has a heart which beats differently to ours and the desert is always the master.'

Alex's future was like the desert. He could not predict what would happen next, had no interest in controlling it and would roll with whatever punches it threw at him. He knew he was drifting aimlessly but, like !Ka, preferred to let fate take control.

There were only two things he was sure of. At some time in the future, he would have his own land. Not in Shakawe, he was sure of that now. But he knew that his own land, his own cattle, his own home, promised a deep contentment, and that this contentment was the future he wanted. But not yet. He had no money.

Marv had been blunt. 'You pissed it all against the walls of Europe.'

He knew he had. Yet he did not regret one drop of it. Each to his own. It had been Alex's way to recover and he did not question it.

The other thing he knew for sure was that he was over the hurt of Chrissy. He had planned to make her a part of his future but it didn't happen and he had recovered. When she died, his future became a black hole. Perhaps that was why he reacted as he had. A man with no future is a man without hope. At least, that is how he looked at it now. But he was healed. Perhaps his money wasn't all he had pissed against the wall. The pain, guilt and despair were gone. He no longer missed her, simply remembered her. His future was no longer a black hole, it had become a grey area, a blank page, waiting for him to lift his pen.

Fate, or perhaps !Ka's desert heart beating a different rhythm, intervened.

He was staying with Paul in Gaborone. The capital was growing so fast he could not find the Ministry of Local Government and Lands which had moved from its original cramped offices in The Village and was temporarily situated somewhere in the new shopping mall waiting for the completion of the government's administration complex, where it would finally reside. Alex wanted to find out how the Bushman project was progressing but while wandering The Mall looking for their offices, he saw a familiar figure coming towards him.

'N!ou.'

The little Bushman was barely recognisable in his western-style clothes. '!ebili.' His face creased into a smile of welcome. 'It has been too long.'

Alex was overjoyed to see him. 'From where do these fine clothes come?'

N!ou looked none too pleased at the compliment. '*Ntsa*,' he said in disgust. 'I am not allowed here in my own clothes.'

'Why are you here at all? Where are the others?'

'They wait for me in the bush. I come here to do business with the man who replaced you.' N!ou shook his head. 'He is not like you, *!ebili*. He will not go into the desert. He makes us come to him.'

'But he must know you have to walk here.' Alex was stunned that such an inconsiderate person was running his curio scheme.

N!ou shrugged. 'He knows. It makes no difference to him. I must come when *bara* is hottest and then I must come when *!gum* is coldest. We all have to do that, all the elders. If we do not make the trip he will not send us the cow hide.'

'That's terrible. Who is this person?'

But N!ou did not know his name. 'It does not matter, *!ebili*. I am finished my business now. We will go home again.'

'Where do the others wait? Can I take you?' Alex was grateful that Paul had kept his Land Rover. Scratched and dented as it was, Marv had done a good job on the engine and it remained a sturdy and reliable machine.

N!ou's face split wide open at the thought of travelling in a vehicle.

The clan waited for him along the Molepolole road. They were gathered in a deep, dry river bed and hid at the sound of the Land Rover approaching. 'Come out and see who is here,' N!ou called to them. One by one, heads popped out from behind bushes. !Ka and Be were not among them.

They had made a temporary camp on the river bank. They were all anxious to get back into the desert for although the nearest village was some ten miles away, cattle grazed nearby and, where there were cattle, there were people. The Bantu often accused the San of stealing their cattle and the clan would rather move on than stay and face a possible confrontation. They were not, however, in such a rush that they couldn't stop and talk to *!ebili*.

N!ou was now the leader. He told Alex that Be and !Ka had been left behind many seasons earlier. By now, they would be dead. Swallowed up by the animals, covered by the sand, their bodies would be in death as they had been in life: part of the harsh landscape. 'I'm sorry I didn't see them again,' Alex said softly. Their death was no surprise to him. By San standards they had lived a full life.

N!ou rummaged in his gemsbok skin travelling sack. 'They wanted you to have these,' he said, handing Alex several items.

Alex stared at them. A finely hand carved pipe, stained at the bowl and with teeth marks on the stem. A necklace made from ostrich egg shells. He was fairly certain he had never seen either item before. He turned them over in his hands, head bent, fighting tears.

In their gift-giving tradition, he knew these possessions had probably changed hands a number of times before finding their way to Be and !Ka. They would have been of no sentimental value and, if they had lived long enough, Be and !Ka would have passed them to someone else. What touched him so deeply was the gesture itself. !Ka and Be did not collect things. If an item had no use it was discarded. But here, in his hands, these crudely made little artifacts represented love. !Ka and Be loved him enough to think of giving him something that belonged to them, however briefly. They loved him enough to step outside their own ingrained traditions and make a sentimental gesture. They would never have understood why it meant so much to him, they just loved him enough to know it would.

For as long as he lived, Alex knew he would never receive a more valuable gift. 'Thank you, N!ou, for taking such good care of these,' he said huskily. 'You have fulfilled your promise.'

N!ou, pleased to have finally got rid of two items of excess baggage, simply nodded.

Knowing N!ou did not comprehend either the gesture or his feelings at receiving the pipe and necklace, Alex changed the subject. 'Have you seen the horses?' He had thought of Nightmare often over the past few years. Against all the odds she had survived to live free and wild. He had never once regretted letting her go.

'There is a bad spirit at work,' N!ou said. 'We have never seen his mischief before.'

'What kind of mischief?'

'A small rock which travels very fast. It breaks the bones of animals and men.'

'What have you seen?'

'The horses were all killed by this rock. This many.' He held up six fingers. 'Some of them were killed here,' he touched his head. 'And some here,' he touched his heart. 'What could do such mischief yet be so small?'

Alex thought he knew. 'The stick that sounds like thunder,' he told N!ou.

N!ou nodded. He had heard the thunder once or twice. It was always in the company of white men and, whenever they heard it, the clan sought deep cover. They had no understanding of rifles but instinct told them it was an evil thing that brought death.

'The thunder sends the rock to kill?' he asked Alex, struggling with the concept.

'Always,' Alex said. 'It is best to run from such things.'

351

'It seems to me, *!ebili*, that it is best for us to run from all white men, as we have always done.'

'Do not run from me, N!ou.'

N!ou smiled. 'Ah, little beetle, but you are not wholly a white man.'

Alex was profoundly touched.

The clan were heading for Kang to pick up more cow hide. They told Alex that the curios scheme had made some improvements to their lives. Boreholes were being sunk which helped in their constant search for water. A small bush clinic had saved the life of one of their children. Impressed as they were by this miracle, N!ou made it clear that they had more faith in their own remedies and would not go out of their way to seek help from the white man's magic. They still wandered. They still lived as hunter-gatherers. Alex was relieved. As much as he knew the San had to change, it saddened him to think that, by adapting to the modern world, their way of life would ultimately have to go.

Sitting with N!ou and the others, Alex's future suddenly crystallised. One moment he felt aimless and uncertain, the next moment he knew exactly what he wanted. Perhaps it was the clan's own sense of who they were and where they belonged. Alex had no idea. He was suddenly filled with a purpose. He would take control of his life, aim for his goal, and this time nothing would stop him.

'You know the stone I had when you found me as a baby?'

N!ou nodded.

'We have talked many times around the fire about such stones. You have heard me say why I want them.'

N!ou nodded again.

'Where can I find these stones?'

N!ou, like !Ka, could not understand Alex's preoccupation

with the glittering stones he sought. Wealth had no meaning to him. Nor could he comprehend the importance of such wealth to Botswana. He barely perceived that Botswana was a country in which he lived. To N!ou, whose world was the vast Kalahari Desert, who only ventured into towns when the curio scheme required it, who had never seen a television set or even heard a radio and who believed the slim silver birds which flew overhead were his gods sending messages to each other, these stones could not be eaten, used as tools or worn. Therefore, they were of no use.

'!Ka has told you before,' N!ou hedged.

'My father indeed led me to some. He did not expect me to find them, did he?' For some time now, Alex believed that !Ka had deliberately misled him as to the true whereabouts of the diamonds.

N!ou thought for a long time and Alex waited patiently. Finally, '!Ka was like your father. When he saved your life you and he were bound. That is our way. It was his task to see no harm came to you, that is what the Great God wanted when he brought you together with !Ka.'

'Yes,' Alex said soberly. 'I know that. !Ka never understood why I searched for the stones. Even when I tried to explain, he worried they would bring bad things to me. He hid from me where I would find them.'

'He had his reasons. I think you understand these reasons, *!ebili*. Always remember, he had love in his heart for you.' N!ou thought again and then seemed to reach a decision. 'Go to the place where we camped during the first *bara* when you lived with us. Look for the three tall trees where we bury our ostrich eggs in the sand. Turn your face to where the sun rises in the morning and walk until the sun is above you and your shadow flows around you. You will find these stones in this place.'

353

Alex returned to Gaborone with determination in his heart. 'Six months,' he told himself. 'The diamonds are there, I can feel it.'

De Beers Botswana had been searching for diamonds in Bechuanaland since 1955. Operating under the harshest of climatic conditions, with field staff constantly suffering food shortages as a result of terrain more suited to horses and donkeys than supply vehicles, De Beers firmly believed, as indeed Cecil Rhodes had believed, that the central districts of the Kalahari were rich in minerals, especially copper and diamonds.

Twelve years later De Beers announced the discovery of Orapa, a diamond pipe considered rich enough to merit further development. Other pipes had been found before but none with the same immediate potential, although they were impressive enough to keep De Beers looking.

In that Orapa was announced one year after independence, speculation regarding the true discovery date was rife. Certainly, if Orapa had been found before independence, Britain may well have stalled the independence process. Had De Beers struck a deal with the proposed government? Having spent an estimated five million rand on prospecting, it was whispered that De Beers believed they stood a better chance of recovering their money quickly from the fledgling Botswana government, rather than the more experienced British.

Alex knew all this. He also knew that production at Orapa had already commenced, that Orapa was now the second largest known pipe in the world, that De Beers were also prospecting in other parts of the country, including the Jwaneng area, and that this might be his last chance to find diamonds in the Kalahari.

He mentioned it to Paul that night.

'I can arrange an interview if you like. I know one of their chaps. I play tennis with him. Pretentious little sod until you get to know him but he knows his business.'

'I suppose I have to get permission from somebody,' Alex said glumly. 'Bloody bureaucracy.'

Paul laughed at him. 'What do you expect? Botswana's changing. The old days of camping where you like and helping yourself are over. The maverick era is finished. The Department of Geological Survey has to approve all prospecting applications. You'll need a licence too. De Beers might help you there, they sometimes issue sub-licences.'

'Okay,' Alex grumbled. 'Set up a meeting will you?'

'An interview, chum. A meeting is between two equal players. You'll have your cap in your hand.'

They were sitting, as they did most evenings, by the pool, feet dangling in the water. Alex enjoyed his brother's company, they had a lot in common. 'I've been meaning to ask you,' Alex said. 'Who took on the curio scheme? I understand it's doing well.'

'It was,' Paul stated flatly. 'Until three months ago. I'm not sure you want to know who's running it now.'

There was something in Paul's voice which alerted Alex. 'You're joking!'

'I'm not. Your old pal, Kel. Timon Setgoma was handling it himself but he carries an enormous workload and he just couldn't keep doing it. Kel pulled strings with his relatives and the job went to him. I didn't mention it to you because there's nothing you can do about it. Timon and Kel are as thick as thieves.'

'Why would Kel take it on? He has no interest in the San. What makes him . . .'

'I think you know,' Paul said quietly. 'He wants to ruin it.'

'Jesus!' Alex said, disgusted. 'When is he ever going to let go of that grudge?'

'He blames you for his face.'

'I know he does.' Alex slid off the side of the pool and into the water. 'I'm not responsible for his face.' He ducked under the water, resurfaced and pulled himself onto the side of the pool again, dripping. 'Kel only has himself to blame for that.'

'Yeah!' Paul copied Alex and then sat next to him, equally wet. 'You'd think he'd learn but I've heard he's been in a couple more fights. He's not popular, hardly anyone likes him, he's a vindictive little bastard, and he blames all his misfortune on his face. He even blames you for the fact that he sent his family nearly broke trying to find diamonds. He thinks you deliberately misled him as to their whereabouts.'

Alex suddenly realised just how determined Kel was. 'The guy won't rest until he ruins me.' He thought for a moment. 'Well he's not going to ruin that project. Somehow I have to get him off it before he does serious harm.' He turned to Paul. 'I've got to find diamonds. I've got to get some money together. Then maybe I can find a way to buy him off the project. Timon is a reasonable enough man. Surely he'll soon see through Kel.'

'One would think so, but Kel is pissing in his pocket something fierce at the moment. He's one of the few friends Kel has and I suspect that's only because Kel is buying the friendship. It's the only kind he can get.'

'Poor bastard,' Alex said, sympathy stirring. 'What a way to live.'

'Save your sympathy for someone more deserving,' Paul advised. 'He could look like Robert Redford and no-one would like him any better than they do now. Girls give him a big miss. There was a rumour going around last year that he raped a girl. I heard his family bought off hers but the rumour persisted and the girl's family left Botswana. There's a screw loose somewhere.'

'There always has been,' Alex thought to himself. 'Whatever's wrong with Kel has nothing to do with his face.' Kel worried him. Not for himself, he believed Kel was too cowardly for a confrontation. But the man was obsessed with hurting Alex and, it seemed, not above doing it through Alex's friends. To ruin the Bushman project was the act of a person who could think of nothing else but revenge. Alex had to find a way to get him off the project.

The next day, with nothing much to do, he went down to The Village. It looked pretty much as it always had except the old District Commissioner's house had been pulled down to make way for an ugly block of flats. The house he shared with Chrissy hadn't changed. But in the garden, two jacaranda trees she'd planted near the gate were now so huge their branches met to form an arch. 'Chrissy would have liked to see that,' he mused without rancour.

He went to the Notwane Club for lunch. And there she was. Madison.

'When did you get home?' He felt absurdly pleased to see her.

She had been playing tennis. The little white dress did its best, but failed to hide her superb figure. 'Couple of months after you. I missed Africa too much to stay away any longer.'

He bought her a beer. 'What have you been up to?'

'I've been helping Mummy. She had to run the farm on her own.'

'Are you going back to Ghanzi?'

She shook her head and he watched the silky black hair swing. 'The farm's been sold. My mother is moving to Gabs. I start back with Game Department next month. How about you?'

He told her about his plan. 'I want my own farm. This is the only way I can think of getting enough money.'

'Diamonds,' she mused. 'Are you sure you'll find them?'

He nodded. 'I am this time. Marv and I found a few but we were looking in the wrong place. They're there, Madison. This time I can feel it.'

She grinned. 'I've heard of gold fever. Diamonds must have the same effect.'

He sipped his beer. 'The San have told me where to look before but I don't think !Ka actually wanted me to find them. He worried that I would become restless.' He could see she didn't understand. 'Restless men destroy themselves,' he explained. 'At least, that is what !Ka believed.'

'What changed his mind?'

'He's dead,' Alex said, stating the fact simply the way !Ka might have done. 'Another man has given me new directions. He probably believes the same as !Ka but he doesn't love me the way !Ka did.'

She touched his arm sympathetically. 'I'm sorry.'

He smiled at her. 'I'm sorry too,' he admitted. 'But !Ka would not want me to grieve. He taught me so many things and I came to love and respect him.' He smiled again. 'I'm trying to accept his death the San way.'

'What way is that?'

'The inevitability of death is no surprise. What is the point of sorrow over a departed one when that person has lived a full life? Instead of grief, isn't it better to wish them a happy passage into the spirit world?'

She looked into his eyes. She saw only calm peace. 'Looks like you're succeeding,' she commented.

'I have to work at it.'

'When do you leave for the desert?'

'Couple of days. I've got to see De Beers. I need a prospecting licence.'

'Alex?'

He saw the request written on her face. 'No.'

Her eyes narrowed. 'What do you mean, "no"?'

'No, you can't come with me.'

'Why not?'

Stubborn. Alex knew stubborn when he saw it. 'I've got hardly any money. I'll be living rough. It's summer. The desert is no place for a woman.' *Shit! I should never have said that.*

'The kitchen sink syndrome!' she said sarcastically. 'Somehow I expected better than that from you.'

He held up his hands. 'Sorry, Madison. It's just that it's hell in the desert in summer and it's bloody hard work. Besides . . .' he grinned at her, 'I can't see you eating snakes.'

'I love snake. Spit roasted with a little red wine marinade they're delicious.'

He laughed with her. Then, 'There is absolutely no way you can come with me. That's final.'

The next morning Alex went to see Paul's contact at De Beers. 'Be humble,' Paul advised. 'Tim's okay but he likes to be on top.'

'Fuck him,' Alex growled, irritated at the need to grovel, and suffering slightly from last night's reunion with Madison. She was the first woman he ever met who could drink him under the table. But he was sufficiently humble for the man to make an offer.

'We would be prepared to finance an expedition,' Tim Boland told him. 'But not south of Jwaneng. If you insist on looking there you're on your own.'

Alex didn't like him. From his meticulously combed hair, to his immaculate shirt with broad blue and white stripes and exaggeratedly large white collar, to the sharp creases in his grey trousers, he represented bureaucracy, authority and expatriate self importance, all things he didn't like about the new Botswana.

'Your guys are looking in the wrong place. Diamonds are there but further south.'

'What makes you so sure?' Brown eyes raked over Alex's faded khaki shirt and trousers. A professionally detached smile slid from the side of Boland's mouth and drained away in his cheek.

Alex knew he was about to sound gauche. 'The San told me.'

The man shrugged, dismissing the Bushmen's store of knowledge. 'Our geologists tell us differently.'

'They're wrong.' The arrogance annoyed him. !Ka's experience was worth a zillion geologists. Then he smiled inwardly at his own arrogance. 'Well, I believe they're wrong anyway,' he amended. *Be humble.*

'Please yourself.' Papers were shuffled. 'If you insist on looking south of Jwaneng I can probably arrange for some equipment and a licence, that's all.'

Alex tried to thank him but he shook his head. 'Forget it. I'm not giving you much.'

'Why are you helping me at all?' Compared to the qualified men Tim Boland had at his disposal, Alex must have appeared to be nothing more than a rank amateur.

'Why?' Manicured fingernails tapped the glass-topped desk

360

and suddenly a real smile escaped, giving him a boyish look. 'I'll tell you why. You know nothing about diamonds, you know nothing about kimberlite pipes, you know nothing about prospecting. You've probably never heard of ultrabasic rocks, I'll lay odds you don't know the chemical composition of diamonds and you probably think adamantine lustre is what Eve got after sex.' He took a breath and carried on. 'In short, you're enthusiastically ignorant, blissfully untrained, confidently inexperienced and persistently stubborn. Frankly, you're just the kind of lucky bastard who *will* find diamonds.' Tim Boland laughed suddenly. 'Don't mind me. I've been in this business a long time. I've seen brilliant men work all their lives and find nothing. Then along comes a happy-go-lucky sod like you and stumbles over another Kohinoor. You'll get as much equipment as I can spare. If you're determined to kill yourself out there you might as well have some comfort.'

He rose. The interview was over. 'Just one thing,' he went on as they walked towards his office door, 'if, by any stroke of luck you find anything, don't even think of not letting us know. We'll find out. Then we'll find you. Then we'll shit on you from such a dizzy height we'll flatten you. Anything you find will belong jointly to De Beers and the Botswana government. You'd do well to bear that in mind. You find it, we'll pay you well. That's the deal.'

'I don't want to steal anything, I never did. I just want to make enough to kick start a farm. Then I'm out of your hair.'

'I hope you find something, son, I really do. I've heard about you. You certainly don't give up.' Boland favoured him with another real smile. 'I guess you'd also like to prove yourself right and the professionals wrong?'

Alex laughed. 'Probably. I believe the Bushmen. I think they're smarter than you.'

'So do I, son,' Tim Boland said quietly. 'But for Christ's sake, don't tell the boffins I said so.'

Suddenly Alex liked him. He liked him even more when, two days later, he picked up the licence and equipment. Tim Boland had been as good as his word. The items provided by De Beers consisted of basic tools and a fully equipped tented camp kit. He had three big tents, two canvas washstands, tables, chairs, a kerosene refrigerator, canvas camp stretchers, gas lights, cooking utensils, mugs and plastic plates. '!Ka would disown me,' Alex thought. It was luxury.

In addition to camping equipment, Boland had thrown in axes, shovels, sieves, mosquito coils, gas cylinders and water containers. He also supplied over 200 professional sample bags, tagged and ready to use, plus a couple of strange metal pots called soil splitters onto which the bags fitted. Soil samples taken were tipped into the pot and a special zigzag-shaped bar directed fifty per cent of the sample into the bag and the rest back onto the ground. Each bag held no more than twelve pounds of soil. Compared to the hessian sacks he and Marv used to heft around, this made the task of sample handling so much easier.

By the time he had packed the Land Rover with camping equipment there was barely enough room for Alex to squeeze in behind the steering wheel. Paul, who helped him, stood back. 'There's one glaring omission,' he said wryly, looking at the overloaded vehicle.

'What?' Alex literally punched the last tent into the back and slammed the door shut.

'Food.'

'Don't need food.' Alex looked at his watch. It would take

about six hours to reach the place N!ou told him to look.

'That makes you reasonably unique,' Paul said mildly.

A vehicle pulled up outside the front gate. They heard a door slam and then light footsteps. 'Looks like you could use some extra space,' she grinned, leaning over the gate.

She was dressed for the bush. Khaki shorts and shirt, a bush hat and snake boots. She also had a look on her face Alex didn't like. 'I told you, Madison, you can't come with me.'

She gave an elaborate shrug. 'You can't stop me.'

He walked to her. 'You'll only get in the way.'

'Thanks for the vote of confidence.'

Paul cleared his throat. Alex remembered his manners and introduced Madison to Paul. 'Excuse us a minute, Madison, we'll be right back.' Paul dragged Alex inside.

'Are you insane?' he said, when they were out of earshot. 'She's stunning.'

'She's a woman.'

'Ten points for noticing.'

Alex grinned. 'I mean, you idiot, the Kalahari is no place for her.'

'She looks pretty determined.'

'Yeah!' Alex looked worried. 'That's Madison for you.'

'Want to know what I think?'

'No.'

Paul told him anyway. 'If you leave her here, my dear brother, when she is so obviously keen to go with you, then a man in a white coat will come and take you away.'

Alex sighed. 'She'll get in the way.'

Paul smiled. 'So? Let her. I can't think of a more delightful obstruction.'

Madison poked her head around the door. 'Am I coming or not?'

'Very well,' Alex snapped ungraciously. 'Come if you must. But don't say I didn't warn you.'

Behind him Paul muttered something about blind as well as stupid but Alex ignored him.

He pushed her hard. He wanted her to get fed up and leave. He genuinely believed she was not physically equipped for such hard labour in such trying conditions. But she doggedly refused to give in, toiling alongside him in the heat and sand.

'Admit it, Madison. You're done in.' She was lying flat on her face in the scant shade of a thorn tree.

She raised her head. Sweat scribbled crazy lines down the grime on her face. 'No.' They had water but only for drinking.

'Why are you doing this?' He was leaning back against the tree, more tired than he ever remembered. They had been digging and sieving for five days.

She managed a crooked smile. 'Fun,' she croaked. He realised she was more than exhausted; she was dangerously close to being dehydrated. He dragged himself up and got her some water. 'Sit up.' Sitting behind her he put his arms around her and she leaned back into him and drank from the cup. Her hair tickled his nose. 'Better?' he asked.

'Thanks.' She didn't move away so he sat with his arms around her and rested his chin on her head.

'You're crazy, you know that?'

She moved away finally and turned to face him. 'It's too hot to sit like that.'

'Give in yet?'

'Why do you expect me to give in?'

He thought about it for a while. 'Because you're Madison Carter, I guess.'

364

'What's that supposed to mean?'

'Don't get mad.'

'I'm not mad.' She clipped her words when she was angry, he'd learned.

'Look, Madison, you grew up wrapped in air-conditioning and cotton wool. You didn't have to lift a finger if you didn't want to. You don't have that tough edge because you've never needed it. This is killing you and you're too stubborn to admit it.'

She scrambled up and stood, hands on hips, glaring down at him. 'Get off your arse, Theron, there's work to be done.' She tramped off to where they had been collecting sand.

He shook his head and followed her. She had to be crazy. But he bent his back to the task, merely commenting, 'The cats are back.'

She didn't even glance to where the lions lay. They arrived every afternoon, one male and three females, and took refuge from the heat under the vehicles. From there they indolently observed Alex and Madison, never approaching them, simply watching. They were like oversized house cats and just as elegantly indifferent.

'Sorry,' he said. He knew she would ignore him until he apologised.

'You . . .' she said through gritted teeth, '. . . have a hell of a lot to learn about women.' She passed him a sample bag.

'Oh yeah?' he replied, hot and irritated. 'I suppose you think you can teach me.'

She flung the sample bag down, making him spill the sand he was pouring into it. 'Grow up, Madison, for Christ's sake.'

'Piss off,' she hissed at him. She turned on her heel and headed towards her tent. The big black-maned lion growled a warning as she passed. 'And you can piss off too,' she growled back. The tent flap snapped shut as effectively as a slammed door.

Alex stared down at the spilled sand. Something glinted up at him. Bending, he picked it out of the sand and held it to the sky. It was a small, worn garnet crystal. He pushed his finger through the sample. 'Christ!' he shouted. 'Madison, come and see this.'

Working a planned grid, they began to find indicators in all their samples. At first, no more than a dozen in each but, as they worked their grid further away from the tents, there were hundreds and then thousands of broken and worn garnets and ilmenites appearing in each sample.

'We'll have to dig inspection pits,' Alex said, after counting five consecutive samples, each carrying in excess of 1500 indicators.

'How deep?' Madison wiped sweat.

'Until we hit the gravel.' Alex pulled a face. 'It won't be easy but that's where the diamonds are.'

'That could be thirty feet down.'

'We have to try.'

She groaned.

'No-one's forcing you to stay.'

'Will you stop that,' she yelled at him. 'Have you any idea how bloody insulting it is to have you continually trying to get rid of me?'

'Have you any idea how bloody frustrating it is to watch you work yourself into a stupor each day out of nothing more than pride?' he yelled back. 'For God's sake, Madison, I'm not trying to get rid of you, I care about you. You've earned your keep. If I find anything you'll get half.'

'Is that what you think?' She bit off each word. 'That I'm in this for the money? Is that it?'

'Why else would you be suffering out here every day? It's why I'm doing it.'

Her eyes glinted angrily. 'My job starts next week. I'll leave at the weekend. I don't want half. Keep your bloody money, it's all you care about.'

'That's not fair. Look, I'm sorry. I can see how exhausted you are.' Angry eyes stared through him. 'Ah, to hell with it. Do what you like, you will anyway.'

He knew their constant bickering was due to frustration at not finding diamonds and the intensely uncomfortable living conditions. Even so, he could have done without it and looked forward to Saturday when she returned to Gaborone.

They didn't fight all the time. In the cool of the evenings, watching the stars or, on a couple of occasions, stunning light-ning storms, they found peace with each other and their envi-ronment. Madison, he discovered, was one of those rare people who didn't try to fill silences with words. She was comfortable with her own thoughts and happy to leave him to his. And she never asked what he was thinking. He liked that.

'A man's thoughts belong to him alone. To ask what he thinks is very rude. He may not wish to tell you and then he must lie. Lying makes him uncomfortable. Good friends should not do this to each other.' Out here, under the stars, it was easy to remember the words of !Ka. He often shared those memories with Madison and she listened. In the silence of the desert, he could feel her interest.

Two days before she left, they found diamonds. They were sit-ting facing each other, sifting through samples. More to keep their minds off the heat than anything else, Alex asked, 'Why did you fall out with your father?'

She rattled her sieve. 'You don't want to know.'

Alex looked at her head bent over the sieve. She had one of his handkerchiefs tied around her head, keeping her hair back from her face. She looked like a gypsy. 'Yes I do.' He found he did. He was learning a great deal about her but he had the feeling she was hiding something.

She carefully put down the sieve. Raising her eyes to his he saw fear. 'What is it, Madison?' he asked gently.

'It's between him and me.' She ran her fingers through the sand in the sieve, took a deep breath and said, 'Oh to hell with it, you might as well know.'

'Only if you want to tell me.'

Her eyes searched his. 'I tried to tell you once before. The day you told me you wanted to marry Chrissy.'

He remembered. 'You were as jumpy as a cat that day. I couldn't figure out what was wrong but I had the feeling I had hurt you somehow.'

She gave a lopsided grin. 'I probably had it coming. I behaved like a bitch that night we . . . well, you know.'

'Made love?' He looked at her soberly. 'You were bloody horrible afterwards.' He hesitated. 'I did hurt you, didn't I? Talk to me, Madison. What did I do?'

Her eyes were still searching his. She wanted reassurance but he didn't know why. So he said, 'I would never knowingly hurt you. Back then, that night, it was just so good. I'd always been attracted to you but I always seemed to make you angry. When we had that fight after being so . . . well . . . close I just figured I'd never be able to please you.'

She worried a chipped fingernail with her teeth. Spitting a piece of nail onto the sand she said, 'I was a spoilt brat.'

'True.' He grinned to soften the truth.

She glared at him. 'I was Daddy's little princess.'

'Is this confession hard to make?' He was teasing her.

She swiped at him, deliberately missing. 'If you don't shut-up I'll bloody-well brain you.'

'Sorry.'

'No you're not.'

'Okay, I'm not sorry.'

'Truth, Theron. Stick to it.' She rubbed impatiently at the perspiration on her forehead. 'This is just as hard as I thought it would be.'

'You just told me to stick to the truth. Why don't you try it?'

'I'm not sure how you'll take it.'

'I'm a big boy. I'm not violent and I'm a nice guy. Just spit it out.'

She looked at him seriously. 'My father believed that no-one was ever good enough for me.'

'And you went along with it.'

'Until that night, yes.'

'What changed your mind. I mean, why me?' It was a question he had often asked himself.

'When he admitted what he'd done to you my life fell apart. I'd always idolised him. I knew he had faults but what he did to you . . . well . . . they were the actions of a stranger.'

Alex waited, saying nothing.

'I still didn't like you much. Daddy saw to that. I never realised until that night just how much he'd influenced me. When you were talking about the Bushmen it suddenly struck me that my father was wrong about you.'

'You grew up.'

'In more ways than one,' she said crisply.

He opened his mouth and she added, 'Don't you dare

369

apologise.' He snapped his mouth shut. She grinned at him. 'I didn't intend to go to bed with you. That sort of just happened.'

'Okay, I don't apologise but I'd like to know—do you regret it?'

She thought about it. 'Hell no,' she said wickedly. 'Compared to stories other girls told me, I was lucky.'

'Thanks,' he said drily. She was making fun of him and he didn't mind. Two could play that game. 'As virgins go, you weren't bad either.'

He held his breath but all she did was throw back her head and laugh. She had an earthy laugh, as though she had just been told a very funny dirty joke.

'Touché!' she said finally.

'So what happened with your father?' he asked. 'Did he find out about it?'

The fear came back to her eyes. 'Yes and no,' she said finally. 'He didn't find out, I told him. You see, Alex, I got pregnant that night.'

If she'd kicked him in the guts his reaction would have been the same. *Pregnant!* 'My God, Madison, why didn't you tell me?'

'I couldn't. I'd behaved so badly. I thought you hated me. I told Daddy.'

'Jesus!'

'I didn't tell him who the father was, just that I was pregnant.'

'What did he say?'

'He threw me out,' she said bitterly. 'Just when I needed him most.' She gave a hard laugh. 'That was when I realised I didn't really know him.'

He wanted to reach out and take her hand but he sensed she would resist. Proud and brave, she would hold herself to

370

herself until her story was told. Then she would look at his face to see his reaction.

'Mummy helped,' she continued. 'She has money of her own. She said I should go to Europe as planned. Everyone would think I was at finishing school. A couple of weeks before I left I saw you at the club.'

'And you tried to tell me.' He remembered how she had said that he and she must talk. At the time he believed she meant she wanted to talk about her father.

'It was a spur of the moment thing.' She managed a small smile. 'I've often wondered what you'd have done.'

Alex knew that in some strange way she needed reassurance. He also realised she would see through a lie. The truth, once he started to speak, came easily.

'I was half in love with you before that night. After our fight I believed you hated me. Then I met Chrissy.' He looked at her quizzically and she stared back, giving no clue to her thoughts. 'This may be a little hard on the ego, Madison, but, compared to you, Chrissy was rather easy to love.' *Have I gone too far?* She was still staring at him. 'I don't know now what I'd have done quite frankly. All I can say for certain is that I would not have turned my back on you.'

'Thank you,' she said with great sincerity. 'Thank you for not lying.'

He asked the question burning in his heart. 'Where is our child now?' It was an odd feeling, to know he was a father.

A tear slid down her cheek, following a crazy sweat pattern. 'I miscarried at ten weeks.'

The enormity of what she had gone through hit him. Brave, frightened, alone and far from home, she had faced the consequences of their actions. 'Madison,' he said softly, 'I am so sorry.'

She bit her lip. 'What about?'

He knew what she was asking. 'Everything. I'm sorry you had to go through that alone. I'm sorry you lost the baby. I'm sorry about your father.' He stretched out his hand and gently brushed the tear off her face. 'I wish I had known.'

She gave him a watery smile. 'When I recovered I went into finishing school as planned. I swore I'd never tell you.'

He picked up her hand. 'I'm very glad you did.'

She smiled at him. 'We have work to do.'

It hit him then how vulnerable she was. Vulnerable, and needing to know that their friendship was still intact. 'You're a bloody slave-driver.' He grinned at her.

'Compared to you, chum, I don't even come close.' She picked up the sieve and shook it. 'I think I'll get a job in the salt mines of Siberia for a holiday.'

He took the sieve from her. 'I didn't think you had it in you. I was trying to spare you the hard work.'

'How?' She snatched back the sieve. 'By making me work harder?'

'I didn't expect you to last. You've got more grit than this bloody desert.'

'Yeah well . . .' she rattled the sieve. 'I'm not just a pretty face you know.'

He laughed. 'Lady, you sure as hell aren't pretty at the moment.' When she smiled he added, 'I'd like to talk more about all this. I'll even talk about your father if you like. I can see now why you needed to speak about the beating.'

'I'll say this for you, Theron, your reactions could use a little oiling.'

He pulled a face at her. 'Okay, so I'm a bit slow. How about tonight? We can thrash it around then.'

'Your fire or mine?'

'Hell, if it's that hard forget it.'

They laughed together and Alex felt a rush of pleasure that, after all this time, he and Madison were friends. He emptied a bag between them and there they were, just as N!ou had said, just as Alex had always believed them to be. Diamonds! One was the size of a cherry.

As if in a daze he picked it up. 'Look,' he whispered.

She reached out and took it. He noticed how dirt encrusted her hand was, how broken the nails. He looked past the stone and saw her grimy, sweat-streaked face, rumpled and stained clothes. She was smiling at the stone and her teeth were startling white against the grime of her face. Mosquito bites stood out on her arms and neck. He stretched out his arm and placed his hand around hers. He saw her eyes focus off the stone and onto his face. 'Madison.'

The force with which it hit him nearly took his breath away. He was in love with her. 'Madison.'

She turned her head away, frowning. Then he heard it too. Vehicles were approaching. They stood side by side, waiting. Two Botswana Police vehicles lumbered up to the camp.

'Mr Theron?' A young, fresh faced English policeman who, even out in the desert, looked crisp and cool, came to meet him.

'Pa,' Alex thought. 'Has something happened to my father?' he asked.

The policeman shook his head. 'I don't know anything about your father. I'm placing you under arrest.'

'Arrest! Why?' Madison demanded.

'Not you, Miss Carter. Him. Trespassing and illegal prospecting with intent to steal government property.' The policeman looked back at his vehicle. The other man in it, and both men in the second vehicle, looked impassively back. He was doing all right on his own, let him get on with it. The young policeman shrugged and turned back. 'You are not obliged to say anything but it is my duty to warn you that anything you do say will be taken down and may be used in evidence against you.'

Alex relaxed and even smiled. 'You're mistaken, officer. I'm afraid you've made this trip for nothing. I have a licence.'

'May I see it, sir?' The policeman looked politely disinterested.

'Sure.' Alex moved to the supplies tent. 'It's in here.' But on opening the metal trunk in which he kept his papers, he could find no licence. 'That's funny.' He rummaged some more.

'What's the problem?' Madison called.

'I can't find it.'

'Nor will you, sir.' The policeman had moved up to the tent. 'We ran a check through the Geological Survey files. No licence was ever issued.'

'I tell you I have one. Ask Tim Boland at De Beers. He arranged it.'

'Mr Boland is no longer with De Beers. He's been PI'd.'

'PI'd! Why?' To be declared a Prohibited Immigrant was the ultimate disgrace.

'I really couldn't say, sir. Now, if you could get your things together, we'll escort you back to Gaborone.' He left the tent and went to speak with the other officers.

Alex was still not worried. 'I'll sort it out,' he told Madison. 'Leave the camp as it is, I'll be back in a few days. Paul can help. He knows I have a licence.'

Paul could not help. 'There is simply no record of the licence.'

'I had one. You saw it.'

374

'I know.' Paul frowned. 'This doesn't look good. No-one at De Beers has heard of you and Tim Boland is somewhere in South Africa. He was accused of racist behaviour although before he left he swore to me that he was innocent. We can't find him, though we won't stop looking. Your defence depends on him.' Paul shook his head. 'The timing couldn't be worse. He's the only one who can sort the whole mess out but it would appear he's so angry about the whole thing and feels De Beers should have backed him more that he's just dropped out of sight.'

'Who accused him of racism?'

'His gardener. Trouble is, it's been confirmed.'

'By whom?'

'A cousin of Kel's who says he witnessed Tim kicking his gardener and calling him "a dirty kaffir". And that's only part of it. Kel has an uncle in Geological Surveys. My guess is he's removed all trace of your licence. You've got a fight on your hands, Alex, and your hands are tied. A major kimberlite pipe has been found in the area near your camp, just a couple of miles away. Tim Boland put men south of Jwaneng because he believed in you. The entire area is officially off limits as of last week. Without Tim's word, De Beers don't believe your story. Kel has really got you this time.'

The court case was considerably more than just a minor infringement offence. The government of Botswana was prosecuting Alex for being in a restricted area and with attempted theft of government property. Kel's influential family had whispered words into the right ears, words fed to them by Kel. When Alex Theron was sentenced to five years imprisonment with hard labour, the nation and the government believed that justice had been done.

EIGHTEEN

Alex knew it would be hard. The prison in Gaborone was old and basic. Felons were punished. They were not, as they might have been in a more developed country, rehabilitated. Hard labour meant just that, bloody hard, back-breaking work. Food was African style. Stiff mealie meal porridge, covered by a thin gruel over which it seemed the cook had perhaps waved a chicken before ladling it onto the porridge. Spinach or cabbage were the only vegetables. He rarely ate red meat. He never had fruit.

He shared a cell with a man called Pule, a harmless enough individual who was severely intellectually impaired and who was serving three years for stealing chickens from his next door neighbour who had happened to be a policeman. He was company of sorts.

The accommodation was basic: two rows of cement block cells, facing each other across a narrow passageway, with small high windows and grille doors. Each cell was open to the elements. True, each had a roof, but the passageway did not and the windows had no glass. Dust, rain and wind blew through them as well as the doors.

The prison authorities, used to years of white dominance, suddenly had a white man at their disposal to do with as they wished. The temptation to get even with the arrogant 'whitie' proved too much. Alex was given the toughest, dirtiest, most demeaning jobs of all. He was also denied all visitors. Letters made it as far as the general office wastepaper basket where they lay in tattered fragments. So Alex never knew that Madison had tried to visit him, or that she had written to him on countless occasions. Paul, too, had tried to see him but, like Madison, had been unsuccessful.

The daily routine never varied. The guard banged his stick loudly on the cell door at five each morning. Alex had ten minutes to wash and use the bucket toilet. Dressed in prison clothes he was ushered to an assembly courtyard and fed tin mugs of sweet tea with chunks of dry bread. Then, once the other prisoners were marched to spend their day working in the quarry, in road gangs or in the acres of vegetable gardens, Alex had to clean cells, sluice out the shower blocks and empty the bucket toilets and clean them before reporting to one of the guards that he was ready to go to work. Mostly he worked in the vegetable gardens. Half the population of Gaborone bought their fresh vegetables from this lucrative enterprise. But while the other prisoners weeded and planted and picked, Alex was issued with a shovel, crow bar and mattock and sent to work at creating new beds.

Used to digging and swinging heavy picks, he nonetheless found the hard infertile ground took every ounce of strength. Rest breaks were not allowed. He toiled non-stop until midday.

Lunch was more tea and bread. Calls of nature had to be regimented to food breaks. More than once a day some unfortunate was caught short. If Gaborone residents ever wondered why the prison vegetables tasted richer than most, never in their wildest dreams would they suspect the real reason.

Work continued until four in the afternoon. By then Alex was ready to drop. Dehydrated, head aching from the sun, back breaking, hands blistered, he stumbled out of the fields half mindless with pain. Then the complaints started. A toilet bucket hadn't been properly cleaned, the showers needed more soap, a cell needed re-sweeping. While the other inmates rested and thought up more jobs for the white man, Alex—his body screaming for relief, with taunts and complaints ringing in his ears—somehow found reserves of strength to carry on. Objections on his part, he quickly discovered, brought more work. He had to grin and bear it.

Supper was the main meal. After food all prisoners were locked in their cells. There were no books, no games or cards to fill the evenings. Tired as he was, Alex's mind needed stimulation and this was denied. The world seemed to have forgotten him. No-one bothered to tell him he was not allowed visitors, so he began to think no-one cared. Alex wrote to Pa but his letters were torn up and tossed into the wastepaper bin by the warden. When he received no replies he assumed Pa was too upset or too disappointed in him to bother. Alex, despairing and exhausted, truly believed he was on his own.

Paul, Madison, Marv, Pru and Pa all tried to see him and were turned away. Marv had driven up to Shakawe to collect Pa and bring him to Gaborone. The warden, in the presence of Pa's sadness, told them, 'It is not my decision. Until I am ordered otherwise, your son cannot have visitors. I'm sorry.'

Madison met Paul in the entrance of the prison's administration office. Alex had been inside for nearly two months and still no visitors were permitted. She came storming out of the warden's office shouting, 'You're breaking the law yourself. I intend to report this.'

Paul, who was waiting to see the warden, grabbed her arm and dragged her away. 'You're only making it worse.' Her loss of temper impressed him but he knew it would do no good.

She ran a hand through her hair. 'I've tried to see the Chief Justice but he's too busy to see me. My mother's lawyer tells me an appeal will be useless. God! I've even tried to see President Khama but I didn't get to first base. We've got to help him. He must be going mad in there. He should at least be allowed visitors.'

'I've got a private detective trying to find Tim Boland in South Africa. The man has disappeared. Not even a whiff of him so far.'

They walked to their cars together but, after twenty minutes, they were still talking in circles.

A couple of weeks later he telephoned her. 'I have a plan.'

When she heard what it was she cried, 'No, never, no way.'

'Have you got a better idea?'

'Break him out.'

'And then what? Where would he go? Botswana is his life.'

'I can't,' she moaned.

'You can,' he said, remorseless. 'And you will.'

Loathing was in her voice. 'I feel sick already.'

But in the end, as he knew she would, Madison agreed.

'It'll be okay. I'll be in the next room.'

'Can't we break into his house or something? Look for the licence?'

They were in Paul's lounge where he was outlining his

plans. Madison, he could see, might refuse to cooperate at any moment. 'He's not likely to keep it there. Besides, we're trying to prove Alex is innocent. We can't do that by breaking the law ourselves.'

'You have no idea what you're asking me to do. I can't stand the man. The mere thought of just talking to him makes me ill. But this . . .' she spread her hands. 'I can't do it, Paul.'

He reached over and took her hands in his. 'Madison,' he said gently. 'We already know Kel will go out of his way to disrupt, spoil or destroy anything he thinks Alex cares about. You spent three weeks in the desert with Alex. Don't kid yourself that Kel doesn't know about it. He'll assume you're Alex's girlfriend. If he thinks there's the slightest chance of getting you into bed he'll jump at it. If you can get him to boast about stealing the licence we've got him. It's worth a try. I'll be here all the time taping you. If it gets rough I'll step in, I promise.'

'We don't know for sure he stole the licence.'

'Who else would? His uncle works for Geological Surveys so he would have known where Alex was looking. Kel could easily have taken it when you and Alex were off digging somewhere. And there's something else: it's a little odd, don't you think, that the duplicate has also gone missing from the same department?'

'Paul, Kel scares me.'

Paul looked grim. 'I know,' he said tightly. 'He scares me too. He actually went into the Kalahari to find those wild horses so he could shoot them. Not because it was Nightmare who caused him to fall off his horse and land on his face, that would be too simple. No, he shot them because he knew how much they meant to Alex. Apparently he was bragging about it. He's certainly unbalanced but don't worry—I'll be right in the next room, I won't let him near you. Please, Madison, it's all we can do.'

She took a shuddering breath. 'When?'

'Two weeks from now. The party at the tennis club. I know he's going.'

'Oh Christ, Paul, Christ, I hope you know what you're doing.'

He patted her hands and sat back. 'I'd do it myself but he doesn't find me attractive.' He grinned at her.

There was work to do beforehand. A rumour was deliberately leaked by Paul to someone he knew would repeat it to Kel: Madison Carter had let slip she found Kel attractive.

It was cocktail party season. Everyone in town was making the same nightly rounds. Several times during the next week Madison and Kel were at the same party. Safely in the company of Paul, she let her eyes rest on Kel until he looked up, then she would look quickly away.

'Step it up a bit,' Paul whispered.

So, the next time Kel glanced her way she smiled at him before turning away.

'Great!' Paul said out of the side of his mouth. 'As a sex siren you'd make a fabulous grandmother.' Then his eyes went wide.

She did something with her body. Nothing much. She shifted her weight to one leg, one hip went out, her back arched and her backside jutted provocatively. She had her back to Kel but the invitation was as clear as if she'd shouted it to him. 'Nice one, ducky,' Paul said in admiration.

'Call me ducky again and it's off,' she muttered, her head coquettishly to one side.

'Cool it. He's about to blow a fuse.'

She threw her head back and laughed, glanced coyly at Kel over her shoulder and said crisply to Paul, 'Okay, buster, show's over. Let's leave.'

On the way back to the house she shared with her mother Paul asked, 'Where do you women learn that stuff?'

'It's in our genes.'

'It's dynamite.'

'I know,' she said cheekily. 'It's meant to be.'

It was Wednesday night, three nights before Madison had to try and trick Kel into boasting about his involvement in sending Alex to prison. For Alex, the day had ended like all the others. Shut in his cell, and groaning with weariness, he stretched out on the mattress on the floor.

Pule sat on his own mattress talking to himself. The guard was moving along the row locking doors. Alex closed his eyes. Every night was the same. The stench in the cell could not be taken away by the strongest disinfectant. The mattress crawled with fleas. *God, will this ever end?*

Alex and Pule's cell was the third last in the row. The guard reached their door but someone called to him from across the passage and he went over to speak to them. Then he moved to the cell next to Alex and locked it.

He's forgotten to lock us in. He listened carefully. The guard moved further away. Excitement mounted in Alex. He opened his eyes and looked at Pule but the man was oblivious of the fact that their door had not been locked.

Alex thought rapidly. He knew the guard would not be back until morning. *I've got to get out of here.* It would be risky but not impossible. The prison was not a high security one. Most of the inmates were happy to be there. They got three meals a day and a roof over their head. The warden lived inside the prison grounds, his house and garden protected by a high netting fence and several large dogs. Guards patrolled the perimeter but Alex had heard them complain that there were not enough of them.

The front of the prison was out of the question. The entire fence and main gates were floodlit. The southern boundary was also too dangerous. The warden's dogs might raise the alarm. The northern perimeter bordered with a suburb of Gaborone. That left the eastern boundary. It was further away than the others but it provided more cover should something go wrong. Between there and the cell block was the vegetable garden and quarry.

The lights went out at 8.30pm. The guards changed shift at 11.00pm. They usually spent ten minutes or so chatting before the new shift spread out to patrol the fences. That was when he would try it. He'd never get a better opportunity.

Madison grinned at her reflection in the mirror, wondering if it would be appropriate to smear something black on her face. Wearing a black tracksuit, dark blue sneakers and a beret, she thought she looked like a cat burglar. She felt quite calm; the thought of breaking into Kel's house bothered her nowhere near as much as the thought of his hands on her.

Two things had combined yesterday to give her the courage she needed. A messenger from the Russian Embassy had hand delivered an invitation to her for a reception the following evening. She knew Kel would have been invited. The invitation said between 6.00pm and 10.00pm but, if past functions at the Russians' were anything to go by, the evening would go on much longer than 10.00.

The other catalyst was a girl at work. She had heard the rumour Paul started, that Madison was interested in Kel, and tried to warn her about him. 'Keep away from him. He's not normal.'

'Whatever do you mean?' She played it cool. She didn't know the girl very well and she might have been a friend of Kel's.

'He likes to do things that are . . . well . . . not usual. He's got a cruel streak. Please, for your own sake, keep away.'

Madison had shrugged. 'I'm a big girl.'

But the comments worried her. Her own instincts told her that Kel was strange. Not just unusual in the sense that he was an individual—some in-built sense warned her he was dangerous. This was why she was so opposed to Paul's plan. If something went wrong and she was left alone with him, Madison felt strongly Kel might harm her in some way.

The idea of breaking into his house to look for the licence had always been her first preference. Being the person he was, she felt sure he would keep it there to gloat over. But she knew Paul would try to stop her. So she had not told him. As she left the house, however, she told her mother and said, 'If I'm not back by eleven go to Paul for help.'

Her mother tried to talk her out of it. 'What if you're caught? You'll be breaking the law.'

'My mind's made up, Mummy. Kel will be at the Russians'. It's my only chance. On Saturday . . .' She could not bring herself to dwell on Saturday. 'I'll be fine.'

'What if he catches you there? I don't like this, Madison, it's a crazy idea. Please, darling, think of something else.'

'I've tried. I can't think of anything. I must do this Mummy, it's Alex's only chance.'

Pamela Carter rose. 'Then I'm coming with you. I can stand guard.'

Madison shook her head. 'I need you here. If something goes wrong you're the only one who knows where I am.'

'Then get Paul to go with you.' Pamela was getting desperate. Her daughter was one of the most stubborn people she knew and, once her mind was made up, nothing usually changed it.

Madison shook her head again. 'He won't approve. He's set on his own idea.'

Pamela Carter saw the determination on her daughter's face. 'Eleven,' she said, crisp in disapproval. 'Not a second later.'

Madison drove to Kel's house, having first checked that his car was among those parked outside the Russian Embassy. He lived in a quiet, leafy cul de sac. She parked her car several houses away and walked, the heavy bulk of her torch comforting. A dog barked and she jumped. 'Steady,' she told herself. 'Remember the alternative.'

A security light over the front door flooded the garden but, slipping through the shadow of trees, she made it around to the back. The servants' quarters were in darkness. *Good.* They were rather close to the house. The back door was locked. *Damn!* She'd hoped for a door with glass panels but Kel's back door was solid wood. That left one of the windows.

Moving in darkness because she did not want to alert any servant who might still be awake, she felt her way along the back of the house. The kitchen windows were shut and burglar-barred. She knew the front windows had burglar bars as well. That left the front door with its glass panels but it would be tricky; half the houses in the street employed guards at night. Breaking in with the security light exposing every move was dangerous.

Something landed at her feet with a plop. She stifled a

385

scream and then relaxed as the furry, slinky body of a cat wove in and out of her legs. Where had it come from? High, from the sound of its landing. She risked a brief flash of her torch. The laundry window was open and unbarred. 'We're in business,' she muttered, swallowing the rising tide of fear.

The laundry window was small and she barely managed to squeeze through. Kel had not bothered to lock the door between the laundry and the kitchen. She was still not prepared to use the torch, worried it would look suspicious if seen from outside, but the security light at the front threw light back into the house and, as her eyes adjusted to the dark, she found she could see quite well. *Where to start?*

She knew the layout of the house. It was a Type-2. Government housing only had four designs and, although Kel worked on the curio scheme and not directly for the government, his family had obviously pulled enough strings to get him this one. She checked the two spare bedrooms in case he used one as a study. He didn't. In fact, one was devoid of any furniture. The main bedroom had curtains pulled. Excellent. She shut herself in and, once she was sure no chink of light could be seen from outside, switched on the torch. 'Phew! What a mess.'

Talking to herself softly, for she found it helped to tame the wild beating of her heart, she went through his cupboards. But all she found was a jumble of clothes, some packets of photographs, a couple of books and a pair of handcuffs. 'Just what do you get up to, you creepy little shit?'

In the next moment she thought she knew. Playing the torchlight around the room she found a second pair. One end was secured to a brass rail at the head of the bed. The other dangled, open and ready to use. Madison shivered and wondered if this was what the girl at work had meant by 'not normal'.

She found nothing of interest in his bedroom. *Okay girl, let's try the spare bedroom.* She had to do it without the torch for the curtains had been left open. But the cupboards and dresser were totally empty.

Moving to the third bedroom took her further away from the light outside but she still couldn't risk using her torch. The built-in cupboard door squeaked as she opened it, making her jump. Feeling with her hands along the shelves, she hit the jackpot. Papers. Piled haphazardly on shelves. She took a bundle into the main bedroom and, sitting on the floor with the torch balanced on her leg, she went through them. Nothing. Most of them were letters threatening court action if Kel didn't pay his debts. Returning them to the cupboard she collected all the papers from the next shelf: bills, bank statements and a couple of girlie magazines.

The bottom shelf had only a few things on it but she took them to Kel's bedroom anyway. And then, she found the licence. Made out to Alex Theron, signed by Tim Boland, stamped by De Beers and dated. She shoved it into a pocket in her tracksuit pants and let out a shaky breath. Shining the torch on her wrist she saw it was 10.25. *Good.* She'd be home before her mother would start worrying.

The cat was back inside and scared her half to death by meowing loudly as she passed through the kitchen. 'I'm not cut out for this,' she muttered. Should she leave by the laundry door or the window? She decided on the window. No point in alerting Kel that someone had broken in. With difficulty, she wriggled through it. On the ground she turned to close it back to where it had been before.

'Hello, darling.' The voice in her ear was so unexpected she screamed. Hands went around her arms, gripping hard.

'Leaving so soon?' The torch dropped from her hand, breaking glass loudly.

Holding her arms behind her with one hand, Kel
unlocked the back door and forced her inside. The kitchen
light flooded the room and she blinked, unable to focus.
'Missed you at the Russians',' Kel said conversationally. 'I'd
rather hoped you'd be there. That little show you put on for
me last week got my attention. So I left early. Then I saw your
car just up the road. "Oh, ho," I thought. "What's that little
minx up to?" Something told me you might be here. And
here you are. How nice.' He had locked her arms behind her
back painfully. 'Let's go to my room.' She was pushed ahead
of him and shoved so hard she fell on the bed.

'Let me go,' she spat at him, fear in her throat.

He locked the bedroom door and put the key in his
trouser pocket. 'I don't think so, darling.'

She stared up at him, breathing hard. She was so frightened she couldn't move. He shrugged out of his jacket and
threw it across a chair. He removed his tie with quick flicking action and tossed it over the jacket. All the while he
stared at her thoughtfully. 'Couldn't keep away could you,
darling. Come for a bit of this?' His hand went down and
cupped his genitals, and he made an obscene thrusting
movement.

She was like a mesmerised rabbit, unable to move, staring
at him with wide, frightened eyes, hearing the blood pounding in her ears. He moved to her slowly and stretched out his
hand, running his finger lazily from her chin, down between
her breasts, down her stomach, down between her legs where
he pinched so hard she cried out in pain.

'Don't you like that?' He pinched again, harder. 'You could
learn, darling.'

388

'Leave me alone,' she screamed at him, mobilised at last into words.

'Keep your voice down or I'll gag your mouth, bitch,' he snarled, eyes glittering.

Madison was suddenly deathly afraid. He was not just repulsive, he was evil. He was enjoying hurting her. 'What are you going to do?' Her voice trembled with fear.

He laughed. 'Do?' He pushed his face down into hers. 'I'm going to fuck you, darling. I'm going to give you what you want. You're going to get it front and back. But first, darling . . .' he stood away from her and unzipped his trousers, '. . . first we're going to see how well you whistle.'

'No!' It was wrung from her. Released from paralysis, she came off the bed like a panther, swinging wildly at him. 'No!' she screamed again. Her clenched fist connected with his face.

The punishing backhander lashed out, knocking her back onto the bed. 'Right, you little bitch. Don't say you weren't warned.' Then he was astride her, pinning her down, sitting on her stomach wrestling one arm up and back. She felt the cold metal of handcuffs close around her wrist. Pushing himself off her he went to the cupboard and got the other pair.

This can't be happening. She opened her mouth to scream and he hit her again, an open-handed slap which made her ears ring and snapped her head sideways. Then he was pushing something into her mouth, shoving it so far back into her throat she was gagging.

The fight went out of her. He handcuffed her other hand to the bedhead and stood looking down at her suffering with callous indifference. She was heaving, trying to get her breath through the prickly, woolly gag. 'Do you promise not to scream?' he asked finally.

She nodded, desperate for air. The gag was removed. He had used a sock. She dragged oxygen into her lungs, choking and coughing, tears of fear and pain running from her eyes, down through her hair, staining the pillow. Through eyes wide with terror, she watched him remove his shirt. 'Like what you see, baby?'

She could not keep the revulsion from showing. His deformed face was shiny with perspiration. His eyes gleamed with a strange madness. Saliva of anticipation wet his lips. The scar on his right cheek stood out, stark and red, pulling his features awry. 'Can't take your eyes off me can you, darling?' The bed rocked as he sat down to take off his shoes. He spoke without looking at her. 'Don't worry about the face; the rest of me is just fine you'll see.' He spun around and stared down at her. 'Alex Theron did this to me,' he said softly, bitterness twisting his features even more.

She found her voice. 'No he didn't. I was there, remember?'

'Yes he did,' he spat out.

She realised it was no use. He had convinced himself that the way he looked was Alex's fault. But she tried anyway. 'You asked for that fight. It was all your own fault.'

He stood suddenly, his hand going to his belt. 'Your boyfriend will pay for the way I look. We'll see how he feels about you when I'm finished with you.'

'He's not my boyfriend.' She tried to sound angry but failed. She was too scared. 'He's never been my boyfriend.'

He undid his belt. 'Yeah, right! I suppose that cosy little jaunt into the desert was so the two of you could count stars.'

'We were looking for diamonds.'

He leaned over her, light glinting on his deformed face. 'Theron has to pay and you, my dear, will be the price.' He straightened, smiling a ghastly smile. 'Just lie back and enjoy, my dear.'

At 10.50 Alex rose quietly. Pule was deeply asleep on his mattress. On bare feet, he moved slowly to the door. Pule stirred and mumbled, then rolled over. The bolt slid back with a slight sound but Pule was snoring and did not move again. Alex let out his breath. He half expected that he had made a mistake, that the guard had in fact locked the door. He shut the door behind him. 'Stage one,' he thought.

He had to make it through the avenue of cells. Alex knew if he were seen by one of the occupants the alarm would likely be raised. The brotherhood of inmates did not extend to a white man. However he made it down between the cells and stood in the darkened archway at the end, his heart beating loudly.

Five minutes later he heard the crunch of shoes on gravel and a guard passed him on his way to the office. A minute after that a second guard made his way into the building. *Is this all?*

He heard the sound of loud conversation coming from the room the guards used. He was just about to move from cover when a third man appeared. Alex shrunk back into the shadows. He waited another minute. No-one. *Now. It's got to be now.*

Expecting a shout, or worse, a shot, he ran into the open towards the vegetable gardens. Light from the front of the prison enabled him to see where he was going but it also meant he could be seen. He dashed along a line of silver beet, aware that the damp earth would give a clear indication as to which way he had gone but unwilling to stop and cover his tracks. Then he was across the dirt road which ran up to the warden's house and into the quarry. *Another hundred yards.*

He cursed his stupidity for not bringing a blanket to protect himself from the barbed wire. *Too late.* He reached the fence and climbed the wire netting easily. Then, ignoring cuts on his hands and feet from the three strands of wickedly sharp barbs, he vaulted over the top, landing hard and rolling. He'd done it. He was free.

The telephone rang in the next room, loud and insistent. Kel frowned, looked at Madison, shrugged and said, 'I'm expecting this call. It's important. You just wait there, darling. I'll be back in a minute.'

On her own, her arms painfully handcuffed over her head, Madison realised just how much trouble she was in. She was at his mercy. When he finished with her he could probably do with her anything he liked. He'd have to. He could not risk her going to the police. Her mother would raise the alarm but it would be too late. Tears of helplessness rolled into the pillow under her head. Paul had been right. *What a dumb thing to do.*

She heard him in the next room, shouting into the telephone. 'Can't it wait? I'm in the middle of something important.'

Silence while he listened.

'Jesus, Uncle Ben, this can wait until tomorrow.'

More silence.

'No. No. Don't come over here. I'll come to you. I'll be there . . . Uncle Ben . . . Uncle Ben . . . oh, fucking hell.'

She heard him bang down the receiver. Two minutes later he returned to the bedroom, a roll of adhesive bandage in his hand. 'You'll just have to curb your impatience, beautiful.' He smiled, his plump little lips wet and slack. 'The wait will be worth it, you'll see.'

He wound the bandage so tightly around her ankles that her shinbones jarred painfully together. Then he placed five separate strips over her mouth, each one overlapping the other. She tried, but it was so effective she could not even move her jaw. After pulling his shirt back on he went out, closing the door carefully behind him.

How long did she lie there? She had no idea. Minutes ticked by, rolling into one long, painful experience. Her jaw ached from her attempts to loosen the gag on her mouth. The pressure of her shinbones forced together became an excruciating throb. Her arms screamed to be free, wrists chaffing against the handcuffs.

She heard the doorbell ring and Kel's footsteps as he went to open the door. 'I could have come to your place.' He sounded angry.

'Boland has been found.'

'So what?' Kel was smug. 'He's still got to prove it.'

'Don't you see, you young fool. Whether it can be proved or not, it places us in a bad position. I have a reputation to protect.'

'Look, Uncle Ben, what's the problem? I've got the original here and you've destroyed the copy. There's no way . . .'

'Here! You've got the licence here? You idiot. Go and get it.'

'Well no, not here exactly. It's in a safe place.'

Why is he lying?

Madison suddenly realised he must know what she came for. What he didn't know was whether or not she had found it. And he wasn't about to let his uncle know he'd made a mistake. 'I'll get it in the morning.'

'Make damned sure you do. Bring it to me. I'll destroy it.

And that's the end of it. You've had all the help from me you'll ever get. Your mother . . .'

'Leave her out of it.'

Madison heard Uncle Ben pacing. 'I've helped you in the past because she's my sister. Stealing Theron's licence was because she begged me to help you. I destroyed the duplicate for her, not you. Everything I've done, I've done for her. Backing you up against Boland was for her. If it ever comes out that my son lied about Tim Boland's racism he's likely to be PI'd himself. God knows why but your mother loves you.' Uncle Ben stopped pacing. 'But no more, kid. This latest plan goes beyond human decency. I want no part of it. If you go ahead with it I'll . . .'

'You'll what, Uncle Ben? Come on, you'll what? Report me? I don't think so, I know too much about you.' Kel laughed threateningly. 'Don't think I wouldn't take you with me.'

Madison heard a sharp intake of breath. 'You little bastard. You're rotten right through.'

'What's the matter with you? You won't be breaking the law. All you'll be doing is paying two men for looking the other way.'

'What's stopping you from paying them? And why so much?'

'I'm paying the men in the desert, remember? They're not cheap. They know they're in a restricted area. If they're caught they'll go to prison,' Kel whined. 'I don't know why you won't help to pay them. After all, you're getting half the diamonds.'

'Yes, yes,' Uncle Ben said impatiently cutting him off.

Madison heard leather creak. One of them had just sat down on the sofa.

'You'd better fill me in. What have you arranged?' Uncle Ben sounded resigned.

More leather creaked. She assumed they were both sitting.

'They've got him working inside the prison. He's not a happy boy. He'll probably jump at the chance to work with the road gang. He's to be transferred to them in a fortnight. He'll escape the first day out.'

'What makes you sure Theron will go for it?'

Alex! What are they planning?

'Wouldn't you? The guards will make it so easy he'll have to try it.'

'He might get away, did you consider that?'

Kel's laugh contained genuine mirth. 'I don't think so, Uncle Ben. They'll be ready for him. Besides, I've told them no recapture, no money.'

'There's more to this than just keeping Theron out of the desert isn't there? Why are you doing it?'

Yes, why, you little shit!

'Five years isn't long enough. He'll be out in three if he behaves. I want him put away for much longer than that.'

There was a long silence as Uncle Ben digested this. Then, 'What if he's shot?'

Another genuine laugh. 'What if he is?'

'It's as good as murder. I want Theron out of our way as well as you but I don't want any part in murder.'

Leather creaked. One of them stood up. 'It's not murder, Uncle Ben. How can it be murder?'

The other one stood. 'It is if you've told the guard to shoot.' Uncle Ben's voice had gone quiet as he made the same connection, at the same time, as Madison. Kel *had* told the guard to shoot. Alex would walk straight into a trap.

'Don't worry,' Kel soothed. 'Nothing will go wrong. Trust me.'

'Oh God!' Madison thought. 'All the evidence I need and I can do nothing.' She realised she could hear a clock ticking and turned her head sideways to find it. It was on the bedside table. It was 10.55.

'You bring that licence to me tomorrow. I'll expect you before ten.'

Don't go, Uncle Ben, please don't go. Kel knows I've heard every word. He's planning to kill me.

She might, just might, have been able to convince him she enjoyed his sexual advances. If she could then maybe he would have let her go. But now?

Footsteps passed the bedroom door. The front door opened. 'One more thing before I leave. I've had word that last shipment reached Amsterdam safely. We should be paid next month. You'll have to warn your men to be careful. Jwaneng is seriously off limits. If they're caught in there and you're implicated there'll be nothing I can do for you.'

'Just remember, Uncle Ben, if I go down, so do you.'

'Why are you like this? I'm your uncle.'

'Insurance, dear Uncle.'

The door banged shut.

Come back, Uncle Ben. God help me!

Footsteps coming back. The door handle turned. The telephone rang again. Kel put his head around the door grinning. 'Don't go away now. This'll be the one I was waiting for.'

Again the minutes ticked away. 11.05. She couldn't make much sense of what he was saying but she heard him say, 'Transfer all the money into my account,' and, a little later, 'Yes of course, but it's got to look as though the transfer came from my uncle. You can do that? Good man.' Then, as he was saying goodbye, 'Talk to you next week, Karl?'

11.10. *Come on, Mummy, where are you?*

At 11.10 Alex stopped running and bent double, winded. *Think. I've got to think.* The South African border was about nine miles east. He could make it well before morning. He decided to head for the Tlokweng Road. It meant a risk of being seen but he could make better time than if he cut through the bush. A donkey brayed close by and he nearly jumped out of his skin. Then, adopting the trotting run of the Bushmen, Alex set off again.

Paul and three of his friends were playing poker at his house. At 11.15, his doorbell rang persistently and urgently. A woman stood there wringing her hands. 'I'm Pamela Carter. Madison's mother.'

'Come in.' He stood back but she shook her head.

'Maddie's in trouble. I know it. Please, can you help?'

'Come in,' he said again. 'Please.' He led her into the lounge. 'What's the problem?'

She wrapped her arms around her body. He could see she was close to breaking down. 'That scheme of yours. Have you any idea what you are asking of my daughter?'

'She told you?'

'There are no secrets between the two of us. She's dreading it.'

He led her to the couch and she sank into it. 'I know,' he said quietly, sitting next to her. 'But what else could we do?'

'She'd have done it you know. She would not have let you down. But the idea was so repulsive to her she had to try something else first. She hasn't come home. I'm worried.'

The game of poker was forgotten by the other three. They crowded around Pamela Carter. 'What's she done?' one of them asked.

She lost the battle with the tears and they slid down her face. 'She went out just after nine. She said she was going to try and find the licence at Kel's house. She said anything was better than letting him come near her. She . . .' Pamela Carter choked on her words, '. . . she said if she wasn't back by eleven I was to come and let you know.'

'Shit!' Paul said. 'Bloody little fool.'

Mrs Carter jumped to her feet. 'No she isn't. She's brave and desperate. You had no right to involve her in your stupid plans.' She flung back her head, set her jaw and grated, 'Are you going to help or not?'

'Let's go,' Paul snapped, furious with Madison and with himself. 'Are you guys in?'

'Try and stop us,' one of them snapped back.

Kel came back into the room. 'Where were we, darling?' He bent down and ripped the tape off her mouth. It hurt like hell but she steeled herself not to cry out.

Stall. I've got to stall.

'Remember that time you were caught up the tree outside my room?' Her lips were stinging. Her voice didn't sound as though it belonged to her. She was almost mindless with fear.

'So what?' he sneered.

'I knew you were there,' she lied.

He was unwinding the tape from her ankles. With the pressure off, her shins pulsated with relief. 'I don't believe you.'

'I knew you were there the first time, too. The time you got Alex into trouble.'

He sniggered. 'Daddy *would* be pleased.'

Her eyes nearly gave her away. Hatred, loathing and fear

clouded her head. With a supreme effort she kept them from showing in her eyes. 'Could I please have a drink of water?'

She could see he was about to refuse. 'Please,' she begged. 'My throat is terribly dry.'

He caught the innuendo. 'Can't have that, darling.'

He was gone two minutes. *11.13. Where are you Mummy?*

He came back with a glass of neat brandy.

'I can't drink that!' she protested. 'Please, all I want is some water.'

But he placed his hand under her head and raised it and tipped the glass towards her mouth. The liquid burned her throat and she choked, spitting it up. 'Drink it down, bitch.' The glass tipped towards her again. He held it there, hard against her mouth, and she had no option but to swallow.

Choking and gasping she shook her head but he held fast until the glass was empty. 'Good girl.' He placed the glass on the floor. 'Now . . .'

'Don't you want to know why I broke in?'

'I know why you broke in. Did you find it?'

'No.'

'I'll just make sure, darling.'

Stall him. He's easily stalled. She looked at the clock. 11.18.

He stormed back into the room. 'Where is it, bitch?'

Her courage and strength were deserting her. She began to cry but he slapped her face hard. 'Where?' Then he laughed. 'Don't worry, I'll find it.'

He found it with his first attempt, screwed it up in a little ball and threw it into a corner of the room. 'Why are you doing this?' she sobbed.

'You're a friend of Theron's aren't you? That's reason enough. Besides,' he sneered, 'the little look I got outside your room was enough to make me want to see more.' He reached out and pinched her on the breast. Although she was wearing a tracksuit it hurt as much as if she were naked. 'You've got the best jugs I've seen.' He pinched again, watching her face carefully.

She tried to hide the pain of it but failed.

He licked his lips. 'You've got guts, Madison, I'll give you that.' His hand moved to her nipple and he squeezed hard.

Madison screamed.

'That's it, darling. That's it.' He squeezed again. 'There's plenty more where that came from.'

Sobbing with pain and outrage, Madison heaved as hard as she could and lashed out with her foot. Kel side-stepped easily.

'Going to fight me, eh?' He was ripping at the buttons on his shirt. 'Good.'

His shirt came off, buttons flying. He stood on one leg and removed a shoe and sock, hopping slightly to keep his balance. 'You're going to like this, darling.' He was glassy-eyed with anticipation and lust. The other shoe and sock came off. He fell on her and kissed her full on the mouth, a wet, slack-lipped kiss that made her moan with revulsion. Then he licked her face like a dog would, lapping at her mouth, the corner of her eyes, her ears, her forehead. He was smiling the whole time.

Suddenly he got off her and stood. 'Back in a minute.'

Frantic, she looked at the clock. 11.22. Her face was wet from his tongue. She was whimpering in fear but when he returned she gave a small scream of pure terror. He was holding a butcher's knife.

'Don't. Please don't,' she begged.

'This?' He looked at the knife as if wondering how it got into his hand. Then he laughed. 'Don't worry about this, darling. Not yet anyway.'

He unbuckled his belt and dropped his trousers, stepping out of them and kicking them away. 'This . . .' he said, holding the knife towards her, '. . . is to remove your clothes.'

What happened next was a blur of movement. She had not heard or seen the bedroom door open. Her eyes were fixed on that insanely cruel face. Kel was walking towards her smiling when suddenly he was flying sideways, the knife leaving his hand and clattering loudly against the wall. Men's voices shouted, a chair overturned, the solid thump of fist on flesh, then someone was unlocking the handcuffs and she was enveloped in the strong safe protection of someone's arms, she had no idea who. It didn't matter who. Then it did matter who and she drew back to see one of Paul's friends and grabbed for him again and he held her tightly while she clung to him shaking and crying.

'I wouldn't have hurt her, I didn't mean her any harm.' Kel's face was bloody and he was blubbering and cringing away against the wall. 'I only wanted to frighten her.'

Paul ran his hand through dark hair which had fallen over one eye. He looked grimly satisfied. Another of his friends handcuffed Kel and pushed him out of the room. Paul came to the bed. 'Can you stand up?'

She nodded.

'Well do it.'

She got shakily to her feet and was wrapped in his arms.

'You bloody little fool.'

She nodded into his chest.

He leaned away and cupped her chin, looking intently into her eyes. 'Did he hurt you?'

'A bit.' Her voice wobbled with emotion.

'You smell like a brewery.' He gently brushed hair back from her face.

Her entire body shook and tears coursed down her cheeks.

'Come here.' He held her again and whispered into her hair. 'I'm sorry, Madison. I had no idea you felt so repulsed by what I asked you to do. I'm so sorry.'

She'd have forgiven him anything just to continue the feeling of safety which was slowly creeping through her body.

The couple of policemen on duty late on Wednesday evening did not know what to do with Kel when he was brought to them, handcuffed and bleeding. They knew who he was. More importantly, they knew who his uncle was. After some lengthy discussions, and after Paul and his three friends steadfastly refused to hand Kel over to anyone other than Alistair McKeith, the Head of Botswana's Criminal Investigation Department, they telephoned McKeith at his home.

McKeith arrived looking sour and dishevelled twenty minutes later. 'This had better be worth it, Theron,' he growled in a broad Scots accent. 'Get that man into the cells,' he roared to the hapless police on duty. 'You . . .' he stabbed a finger at Paul, '. . . you lot get in here.'

The four men followed him into his office, a mess of old furniture and overflowing files, bare window, linoleum floor and two wooden chairs. Looking out of place on the wide windowsill, a large and flourishing rubber plant. 'My wife,' McKeith grouched, following Paul's gaze. He rubbed sleep from his eyes then grinned, 'At least, it's her plant,' he amended.

'Thank Christ!' one of Paul's friends murmured.

McKeith looked sour again. 'What the hell is going on?' He heard Paul out in complete silence, his expression never changing. 'Where's the bloody girl then?' he rasped when Paul had finished.

'Give her a break. She's been through hell.' Paul rummaged in his pocket. 'Here's the licence. We'll testify she was hand-cuffed to the bed and being threatened with a knife. The guy was down to his Y-fronts so he was planning more than a tea party. She'll make a statement tomorrow.'

'I could have her arrested as well you know.'

Paul leaned across McKeith's desk and stared him down. 'But you won't will you, Alistair,' he said quietly. 'Kel's family is corrupt, the whole lot of them. Madison has evidence of diamond theft, tampering with government records, giving false evidence at Alex's trial, bribing prison guards and possibly even attempted murder. My brother has spent months inside that hellhole for nothing. No-one has been allowed near him in all that time. Injustice is the nicest word I can think of for what's happened to him.' He drew back and grated, 'Don't even think about arresting Madison.'

McKeith stared at him, unblinking. 'You threatening me, Theron?'

Paul didn't flinch. 'Yes.'

'Yes,' McKeith said softly, then grinned. 'I rather thought you were.' He rose and went to his office door. 'Shemmen,' he bellowed.

A black policeman came on the run and executed a smart salute. 'Don't bloody do that all the time, it drives me potty.' The policeman smothered a grin.

'Get down to the cells and tell that low-life he's under arrest. We can hold him for forty-eight hours.' He looked back into the room. 'That young lady's story better be good.'

'You've got enough on him as it is.'

'Laddie!' McKeith grated. 'I want the lot of them.' He

snapped off his office light. 'Come on, come on, I'd appreciate *some* sleep tonight.'

'What about my brother?'

'Another night won't hurt him. Besides, how far do you
think we'd get at this hour. The Chief Justice will have to sign
an official release. Your brother will be out by tomorrow
afternoon.'

Too keyed up to go to work the next day, while Madison
gave evidence to a charming and sympathetic McKeith who
had clearly been bowled over by her looks, Paul moped
around his house, expecting Alex to appear at any moment.
When his front doorbell rang at 12.30 he rushed to open it.
'Oh, it's you.'

'Thanks a lot.' Madison pushed past him into the house.

'Come in,' he said drily.

'Is he here?'

'Not yet.'

'McKeith promised to get straight onto it.'

He followed her into the lounge. 'How are you feeling?
Was McKeith . . .'

'McKeith was wonderful and I'm fine. The bruises will
heal.'

'Madison, I meant what I said last night. I had no idea you
felt . . .'

She turned to face him. The strain of last night was still
there but the terror was gone. 'I should never have done it.
You were right, it was a stupid thing to do.'

He shook his head. 'You had such a close call. If anything
had happened to you I'd never have forgiven myself.' He
pulled at his ear. 'Oh come here and give me a hug.'

She went into his arms and he said against her hair, 'Shit, Madison, don't ever do anything like that again.'

The doorbell rang again. McKeith stood there. 'May I come in?'

Paul led him into the lounge. 'Has Kel been arrested?'

McKeith looked happy. 'Arrested, incarcerated and singing loudly.'

'How about Uncle Ben?' Madison asked.

McKeith looked even happier. 'Arrested, incarcerated and contemplating the trouble he's in. He hasn't talked yet but he will. His nephew has implicated him in everything.'

'When is my brother going to be released?'

McKeith looked at Paul sympathetically. 'That's why I'm here,' he said quietly. 'Your brother escaped during the night.'

Alex made good time once he reached the road. There was hardly any traffic at that hour. Any vehicles out and about could be seen in plenty of time for him to hide from their penetrating headlights. A mile from the border post he left the road and made his way through the bush to the border fence. He climbed the fence and was into South Africa before dawn.

On the other side was the isolated Marico bushveld. Terrible sandy, rocky country, densely covered with thorn trees and shrubs, sparsely populated, and hotter than hell between September and April. This was the land of the Voortrekkers' descendants. Hardy Afrikaaners who spoke little, worked hard, lived simply and feared God above all else. Years of drought and overgrazing meant the few farmers still in the area needed vast areas of land just to eke out an existence. Twenty thousand acres sounded grand but, in reality, those who ran these large estates were dirt poor, their beasts thin and undersized and their way of life desired by few. The young left as soon as they decently could. The land was farmed by middle-aged and old folk.

Once he was over the border Alex was virtually undetectable. He had no qualms about surviving in the Marico. Compared to the Kalahari, it was paradise. He needed clothes, food and money, in that order. The first two were easy.

In order to protect their clothing from rotting in the extreme heat, the locals' washing was left on lines overnight to dry. Alex found a pair of jeans, a shirt and some socks at the second farm he came to. Outside the back door, he relieved the farmer of his work boots. He was an hour away into the bush before the farmer discovered his loss. The following night, a farm well inside South Africa provided a chicken, some vegetables, an old metal bucket and a small aluminium dish containing water, presumably for the dog. Alex made himself a stew, lighting the fire the way !Ka had showed him, by rubbing two sticks together. He ate the food by dipping the dish into the bucket and scooping it out.

Money was a problem. Not particularly happy about stealing, he drew the line at breaking into a house and taking money. He had to find work and that was not easy. Offering to do menial tasks would look suspicious; whites in South Africa had Africans for that purpose. Three days later, in the tiny town of Thabazimbi some one hundred miles from the Botswana border, he convinced the man who owned the garage that he was a mechanic. It took the proprietor two weeks to discover that Alex's knowledge of engines was rudimentary. By then, however, Alex had collected two weeks' pay. He hitched a lift to Johannesburg.

He needed a job and he needed a place to stay. He bought

a newspaper and sat in a coffee shop, scanning the classifieds. He nearly missed it. His own name jumped off the page at him from the Personal column.

'ALEX THERON! PLEASE PHONE PAUL. BOLAND HAS CLEARED YOUR NAME.'

Alex couldn't believe it. He found a public telephone booth and, with shaking hands, dialled Paul's number. When Paul answered he shouted, 'It's me. Call me back. Got no money.' He read the number out and then hung up. The shrill ringing of the telephone one minute later was the sweetest sound he had ever heard.

'Why didn't you call me?' Paul asked immediately. 'Jesus, Alex, we all thought you were dead.'

'Why didn't you come to see me?' Alex asked back. 'I was in that prison nearly three months. I didn't get a single letter or visitor.'

'Christ, Alex! Every man and his dog tried to see you. No-one was allowed. We all wrote to you. We thought you would at least get our letters.'

'I got nothing.' Alex felt bitter. All that time he believed they had abandoned him.

'A few heads rolled on your behalf,' Paul said. 'The warden has been fired. Madison reported him for not allowing you visitors.'

'How is Madison?'

'She thinks you're dead. She left Botswana a week ago. I think she's in South Africa somewhere. I can find out for you.'

Alex's spirits lifted. 'Is it true, I'm not wanted?'

'You're a free man. It's over, Alex, you can come home.'

Home! What a great word. 'How about the fact that I escaped from prison?'

'Alistair McKeith of CID was a bit put out. He was

planning to organise your release the day after you escaped. He's prepared to overlook it though since, technically, you were a free man when you did it.'

'How did you locate Tim Boland?'

'Same way I located you. In the Personal column. But it wasn't only Tim who cleared your name. Madison was wonderful.' Paul filled Alex in on the night she broke into Kel's house and found the licence. 'It was a close one, Alex. I think Kel planned to kill her.'

'What's happened to Kel?' Alex found his fingers gripping the receiver hard wishing it was Kel's neck.

'He and his uncle are in prison. His uncle got five years but Kel got fifteen.'

Alex's fingers relaxed. Fifteen years in Gaborone prison was more than enough punishment for anyone.

'De Beers are grateful and embarrassed,' Paul continued. 'You've led them to the biggest diamond mine in the southern hemisphere. You'll get your farm now, Alex. Not only are they prepared to pay you for the find, they plan to compensate you for your time in prison. They feel a bit responsible for that. I think you'll be happy with their offer.'

Free! He was free. It was all he could think about.

'Madison . . .'

'Call me tomorrow. I'll find out from her mother where she is.'

'Tomorrow!'

Paul laughed. 'Okay, hang around the phone box. I'll call you back in half-an-hour.'

Madison had gone to the family beach cottage north of Durban. Conserving the little cash he had, Alex thumbed the

400-mile distance in just under ten hours. Arriving at the small resort of Umhloti Beach he did something he did very rarely. He panicked.

How does she feel about me?

'She risked her life for you,' said his heart.

'She's never said she loves you,' his head told him. 'You were an absolute shit to her in the desert,' it added.

Help me, !Ka.

He located the cottage and stood on the road, uncertain and afraid. A dog barked from the garden of the house next door.

'She put up with you in the desert,' his heart said. 'She must love you.'

His head had no answer. He took it as an omen.

No-one answered his knock. He walked around to the back. The cottage was right on the beach. Wooden steps led down from emerald green lawns to the sand below. From the lawn, he had a good view right around the small cove. He could see one solitary figure standing at the water's edge, staring out to sea. Alex made his way towards her, across the soft sand, down to the hard edge, and along to where she stood. It was the longest walk of his life. 'Madison.' He was three yards from her.

She spun around. 'Alex!' Wind whipped her hair across her face and she brushed it back impatiently. 'Is it really you?'

He grinned at her. He was still uncertain.

'You bastard! You thoughtless, unmitigated bastard! Why the hell couldn't you have let us know you were all right?'

Alex reached her in three strides. 'It's okay,' his heart and head agreed. 'She loves you.'

Much, much later, lying in a tangle of sheets and limbs, she said, 'I have a confession to make.'

'What would that be?' His heart was so full of happiness he felt it would explode.

Her fingers traced a pattern on his chest. 'Finding you in Scotland was not an accident.'

He brushed hair off her face gently. 'How did you find me?'

'I met Marv. I knew he was a friend of yours. I asked if he'd heard from you. He said you were going to Stirling to speak to Chrissy's parents.'

Alex remembered a card he wrote Marv to that effect.

Sheets rustled as she turned into him. 'You know how, in old novels, the heroine is ruined by the scoundrel?'

'I'm no scoundrel,' he protested.

'No,' she agreed. 'But I was certainly ruined. No-one else could measure up.'

'I take it you're speaking in general terms here?' he said drily.

She punched him lightly on the shoulder. 'You know what I mean.' Hesitation. 'I did have one or two relationships, I can't lie about that.'

'Heavens,' he murmured, amused. 'How decadent.'

'You don't mind?'

'Lead me to them, Madame. It's pistols at dawn time.' He was laughing at her gently.

He felt the soft pressure of her lips on his skin. 'You know what I love about you most, Alex?'

'My great personality, good looks and charm?'

He should have known better. 'You think like a woman.' She yelped when he tickled her. 'It's true, it's true,' she giggled, trying to squirm away from his fingers. 'You don't suffer from masculine myopia.'

He stopped tickling and pulled her closer. 'What the hell is masculine myopia?'

'Belief that the only way to be with a woman is to own and dominate them.' She laughed at herself. 'Hell, I don't know. It's a male thing.'

He laughed with her. 'Is that it? That's the end of your confession? Male myopia?'

'No.' She hesitated. 'Alex, I'm not proud of the next bit.'

'Tell me,' he said, sensing her reluctance.

'I was at that horrible finishing school when Mummy wrote and told me that Chrissy had died. My heart just broke for you. I knew you would be devastated.' She raised herself on one elbow and looked down into his face. 'Even so, Alex, all I could think was that now, maybe, you'd have time for me. That's why I went out of my way to get expelled. I wanted to get back to Botswana, be closer to you.' She looked at him unhappily. ' I knew you would be in pain and all I was interested in was me. I'm sorry. I still can't forgive myself for that.'

Her hair had fallen forward and he brushed it back, tucking it behind her ear. 'You should,' he said softly, respecting her honesty.

She shook her head. 'By the time I got back to Botswana you'd gone. I thought, "Fine, he'll be back." But you didn't come back. That's when I met Marv and decided to go to Stirling. I guessed you'd turn up some time. I'd nearly given up on ever finding you when you were literally thrown out of that pub at my feet.'

'Don't remind me.'

She grinned at that. 'It was obvious you weren't ready for another relationship,' she went on. 'A couple of times, when you were staying with me, I nearly blurted out the truth. But you needed more time, I could see that. By the time you returned to Botswana I had come to the conclusion that you had loved Chrissy so much there was no room in your heart for me.'

He pulled her down so she lay on his chest. 'The first time I saw you I fell in love with you,' he admitted. 'Each time we ran into each other after that I always seemed to do or say the wrong thing. Then I met Chrissy. Yes, I fell in love with her. I loved her very much. When she died I couldn't handle the pain but it was more than just that. You put your finger on it in Scotland. You said there was guilt and anger. I was full of guilt. I felt I should have known she was ill. I was terribly angry at myself, I missed her and I felt guilty. I just went off the rails.'

He ran his fingers over her bare shoulders. 'It took a long time,' he said softly. 'I can only guess now that it was because I was so young. But I'm over Chrissy. There is no ghost.'

'Are you sure, Alex? I couldn't live with a ghost.' She looked up and grinned. 'I'm too bloody vain.'

He grinned back. 'I wouldn't do that to you, Madison. You scare me too much.'

They laughed and he kissed her again.

'I must have been blind in Scotland,' he said finally.

'No,' she said quietly. 'You had only just opened your eyes. It was too soon.' She kissed his chest. 'When we bumped into each other in Gabs I thought I could feel something between us.'

'I felt that too.'

'That's why I wanted to go with you.'

'It's why I didn't want you there.' He laughed at himself. 'Bit of latent chivalry if you like.'

'You were so awful to me in the Kalahari . . .' she said, her voice muffled against his chest, '. . . you kept trying to get rid of me.'

'And you wouldn't bloody go,' he said lightly, smiling at the memory of her stubbornness to give in.

'It was my last chance to get you to notice me.'

Alex tightened his arms around her and rolled, so he was leaning over her. 'Oh I noticed you, Madison darling,' he said, kissing her gently.

She wound her arms around his neck. 'I love you,' she whispered.

Looking at her face close to his Alex realised he was seeing the face of his future, the face which would always be there, the faces of their children.

NINETEEN

God, I hate August! The wind, blowing in from the desert, picked up sand and dust and hustled it through the air, stinging his eyes until they grew red and sore. It was so dry he got an electric shock every time he touched metal. The land had turned dusty white and dead looking. His cattle, their backs hunched against the flying sand, searched morosely for fodder, eating the dry, dust-laden grasses which had most of the goodness burned out by frost, their big soft eyes reproachful against nature's unkindness. August made them short-tempered and difficult to work with. He sympathised. August made him short-tempered and difficult to work with too.

Leaning over the railing of his verandah, he grinned. 'Silly old fart, you feel like this every year. At your age, you should know better.' He eyed the rose garden. Everything else had the good sense to wait for September, but not the roses. Gamely, they struggled into flower early. Each year, blasted by flying sand and dirt, they had an air of desperate determination. Next to August he didn't much like roses either.

The rooster was out again, scratching under the roses, pecking the ground hopefully. 'There's nothing there, old fella,' he called. 'Get back to your women.' The rooster glanced at him briefly, his feathers flying out in the wind giving him a fluffy look, then went on pecking.

Normally the garden delighted him. Terraces of green lawn, tumbling splashes of colour from flowering shrubs, the deep shade of deciduous trees, quiet tucked away corners. But in August the lawns were burned brown, the shrubs were scrappy, the trees still bare and the quiet nooks no match for the wind and sand.

God, I hate August! He moved back to his chair against the wall of the house. There, protected by the solid bulk of the kitchen where it jutted out and formed an L-shape, the wind couldn't reach him. The years had been kind to Alex. He walked straight and tall, with an easy fluid stride. Hair, thick and curly still, was peppered with grey. Blue-green eyes, a little faded, held serenity and humour. He picked up Sam's letter. 'All the other boys get twice the allowance I get. Please, Dad, I need more money.' Alex rattled the letter irritably. The boy was incorrigible. Just what did a sixteen-year-old need with so much money? Neither Claire, nor Mickey, had asked for more.

'I used to get by on two shillings a week,' he grumbled to no-one in particular, although the rooster, who had abandoned the roses and was now advancing hopefully up the verandah steps, clucked sympathetically. 'Scram,' he told the bird. The rooster obeyed, dropping his calling card as he went.

Alex sat back and looked across his desperate garden to his equally desperate farm. Despite the dust devils, the lifeless leaves on evergreen trees and bushes, so encrusted with grit not even the gusting wind could shift the layers of dust, despite the Limpopo river lying in sluggish brown pools and his skinny, winter starved cattle with heads drooped in disconsolate misery, he knew he loved this place. Next month, with luck, would come the spring rains, bringing soft green grass into sparkling relief against the white sandy soil. In November or December, the hard summer rains put new life into the river so that it tumbled and flowed and flushed out the green and brown algae which formed in stagnant pools.

He should have gone away, he said that every year. Marv and Pru, and all the other farmers in the area, went away every August. But some stubborn instinct made him stay. Perhaps it was a time to look back, he didn't know. He just knew that each year he stayed on his farm and cursed the weather and remembered.

He remembered it now as clearly as though it was yesterday. All those years ago.

As soon as he had arrived back in Botswana with Madison, two men were clamouring to see him: Tim Boland and Alistair McKeith. Alex had decided to deal with the bad first.

'You're a damned fool,' McKeith snapped irritably. 'You might have been shot.'

'But I wasn't,' Alex said mildly. He had expected an earbashing from Alistair.

'You could have been.'

'Okay.'

McKeith stared at him. 'One more day. That's all. If you'd waited . . .'

'How was I to know?'

'Even half a day would have done it.'

'Okay.'

The policeman breathed heavily. 'You taking the piss, Theron?'

'No sir.'

'I could arrest you.'

'Yes, sir.'

McKeith glared.

Alex gazed innocently back.

'Here.' McKeith passed two pieces of paper over his desk. 'You are now officially pardoned and officially released from prison.'

Alex glanced at them. 'Thank you.'

'And here.' He passed Alex a cheque. 'You're entitled to be paid for the work you did inside.'

Alex looked. The cheque was for an amount of sixty-three rand and forty-six cents. He passed it back. 'Donate it to the police fund.'

McKeith digested this. Then, 'You bitter about this, son?'

'Bitter?' Alex thought a moment. Then he grinned. 'To be perfectly honest, fucking livid doesn't come close.'

McKeith laughed. 'You're all right, Theron. Get out of here. Way I hear it you lead a charmed life. Go and enjoy it.'

Alex rose and put out his hand. 'Thanks,' he said simply.

The policeman took it. 'Try to stay out of trouble, son.'

Alex smiled. 'On second thoughts I will take that cheque.'

'Why?'

'I intend to frame it.'

De Beers had been more than generous. The biggest gemstone diamond pipe in the world had been found exactly where he and Madison had been digging.

Tim Boland had been reinstated when the full extent of

Kel's activities became known. The government had readily agreed to erase all trace of the Prohibited Immigrant order which had ejected him from Botswana. The gardener, who had been paid by Kel to lay false charges against Tim for racist comments and behaviour, was located but Tim Boland refused to lay charges in return. 'It wasn't his fault. Up against Kel and his family, the poor man had no choice.' He rehired the man and in doing so, earned himself the gardener's respect and loyalty which far exceeded that of a close personal friend.

'Basically we're not obliged to pay you anything.' Tim Boland made Alex sweat a bit first. 'The land at Jwaneng belongs to Botswana. You picked up nothing on the surface and you're not entitled to anything found under the ground.' Nails tapped on his desk. He was, Alex observed, in one of his pretentious moods.

'True enough,' Alex agreed. 'But would you have found the pipe without us?'

'Eventually, yes.'

'And how much money would De Beers have spent looking?'

Tim Boland tried to stop it but his professional smile sneaked into real. 'Nice one, Theron.'

'Actually,' Alex went on as though he hadn't spoken, 'at a guess I imagine you'd have blown a good three to five million rand.'

Tim laughed. 'You wouldn't be related to an economist I know by any chance would you?'

Alex leaned forward. 'Tell me, Tim, how big is this?'

Tim's eyes were alive with excitement. 'Bigger than your wildest dreams. You hit the jackpot, you and your Bushmen friends. The geologists are full of the mutters.'

418

'What are you doing for the San? I assume you'll be cordoning off a large area of what used to be their hunting ground. How are they to be compensated?'

Again Tim Boland's real grin emerged. 'Don't you worry about that. De Beers have a reputation to maintain. We're not in the habit of taking without giving something in return. We've joined forces with that Bushman curio scheme you started. We have a team of people working on a package for the Bushmen that will knock your eyes out. No, it's you who is giving us the headache.'

'Why?' Alex shifted uncomfortably in the elegant but inadequate chair.

'Like I said, technically we don't have to give you a thing.' A quick professional smile. 'But while we were not directly responsible for you spending three months in prison, nor was it our idea that you jump the fence and go leaping off to South Africa, and we can't possibly be blamed for the fact that you made no contact with anyone for a whole month who could easily have acquainted you with the status quo . . .' Tim took a deep breath and finished with a rush, 'We feel morally obliged to make amends.'

'How moral is this obligation likely to be?' Alex asked quickly in case another barrage of words was on its way.

Tim made no attempt to conceal his delight. 'How does a million rand sound?'

Alex sat, stunned. He hadn't expected anything like that much. 'You're kidding?' he managed finally.

Tim grinned. 'I'm not kidding. If the land belonged to you it would cost us at least twice that much to buy it back. If you hadn't led us to the pipe, as you pointed out, we'd have spent anything up to five million finding it. It's a fair offer, young man, what do you say?'

419

All Alex could do was nod.

'We're not announcing the find for a couple of years,' Boland said. 'The industry isn't ready for another large mine.' He put a piece of paper in front of Alex. 'Sign this. It's a confidentiality agreement. If word of this find leaks out and we trace it back to you, we'll sue.'

'Word's already out,' Alex protested. 'It's the worst kept secret around.'

Tim Boland just looked at him politely.

'Pass the pen,' Alex said.

Alex and Madison found their land. Nearly 6,000 acres of the best Botswana bushland, near Marv and Pru. They built their house overlooking the Limpopo River.

They were married in November. Paul was best man. He announced his engagement to Ingrid, the stunning blonde daughter of the Swedish Ambassador, during the reception.

Pa, who was staying with Paul in Gaborone for a while, looked happy and proud enough to burst.

Pat came to the wedding with a feisty auburn haired Zambian girl called Jill and the news that he was setting up a construction business in Gaborone. When Alex asked him if he and Jill intended to get married, Pat said, 'Jesus, mother of Mary, boyo, I'm too old for all that sentimental stuff.' But Alex could see the deep affection between them.

Marthe and Jacob were there. Older and more craggy, it didn't stop them demonstrating the Charleston during the reception.

Willie actually wore something other than American cowboy boots.

Artie came down from Rhodesia. He had misread the

invitation and was the only man there in a dinner suit. No trouble to Artie, who whipped off his coat, tied the cummerbund around his head, rolled up his sleeves and danced all night. He was surprisingly light on his feet.

Bob smiled a lot.

Pamela Carter looked almost as stunning as her daughter. 'I always liked you, Alex. Thank God my daughter has had the good sense to marry you.'

Marv and Pru, still very much in love, confessed that Alex's marriage was an event they'd almost given up ever attending.

It hasn't all been plain sailing, Alex mused, sitting on his verandah watching the rooster. *There have been downs as well as ups.*

Their first child, a boy, had not gone full term and had been stillborn. It had taken Madison nearly a year to contemplate another child. She became convinced that there was something wrong with her, that she would never be able to bear Alex children, despite medical opinion to the contrary. Alex watched his lovely young wife suffer and grieve. He offered love and understanding but he knew he could never know the same sense of loss.

Claire was born in 1977, a beautiful replica of Alex, who captured his heart and had Marv saying smugly, 'That girl's got you around her little finger.' Pa visited them three weeks after her birth and fell in love with the baby as much as Alex. He planned to return to Shakawe but stayed four weeks, reluctant to return to his solitary existence. One night he simply died in his sleep. 'A heart attack,' the doctor told them. Alex thought not. Pa was a wily old man—Alex believed he died because he did not believe he could be happier now his sons were settled. He had gone to join his beloved Peta,

421

whom he had never ceased to love. His responsibilities on this earth were over. Alex missed Pa but he was happy for him.

Mickey, or Michael-John as he had been christened, was born the year after Claire. He was the image of Madison.

'A boy and a girl,' Madison said. 'That's perfect. I don't want any more.'

Sam had other ideas and arrived two years later. He had Alex's looks and Madison's personality and was more demanding than the other two put together but they loved him to pieces and wondered how they had not planned to have him.

When Mickey suffered complications from measles at five, and the doctor told them to expect the worst, Alex went into the desert to search for !Ka's old clan. The San danced a curing dance for the boy. Alex returned home to find Mickey wan but recovering. 'By rights, the boy should have died. He obviously has a strong constitution,' the doctor told them. Alex and Madison knew otherwise.

Paul married his beautiful Ingrid a year after Alex and Madison's wedding. She was a gifted commercial artist and photographer. Economists continued to be in demand but Paul, seeing the way the country was heading, set up a marketing consultancy so he and Ingrid could work together. This led to their handling advertising budgets as well as offering marketing advice and Paul, much to his surprise, found himself at the head of Botswana's first, and most successful advertising agency. With his head for figures and practical mind, together with Ingrid's creative flair the two of them were quickly in demand. They lived and worked together happily, Ingrid taking time out to have two daughters.

In 1976 Botswana withdrew from the Rand Monetary Area and issued its own currency, pula and thebe. It took a while to get used to buying things with rain and shields but, in time, the translations lost significance.

In 1980, when Sir Seretse Khama died, Alex and Madison joined the other citizens of Botswana in mourning. The man had given Botswana its headstart. With his wise and calm leadership, the country was well able to look after itself. It was a legacy to be proud of. He took one of the world's poorest nations and led it through a political and financial minefield, to emerge at the other end as a peaceful, fully democratic and economically strong country. The new president, Dr Quett Masire, friend and political partner of Sir Seretse, said, 'We have no option other than to continue on where this great man left off.'

A severe drought in the mid-eighties had Alex selling their cattle at prices so low he wondered if they would ever recover. A freak flood and heavy rain brought good grazing back but the drought wasn't over and the grasses dried up again. With not enough cattle on the property, a fire raged through the tinder dry bush. They lost two sheds, a set of cattle yards and nearly nine miles of fencing.

The world was changing and Botswana changed with it. But no-one was prepared for the year the waters from Angola failed to flow into the Okavango Swamps. The Delta remained dry. Some people believed the earth had tilted on its axis by the merest whisper, upsetting the natural flow of the water. Others blamed interference by the Angolans who, now their war was virtually over, had turned their attention to technology and, as part of this, water conservation. No-one knew for certain but some believed the Angolans had diverted the flow. But when the waters failed to come three years in succession and the birds and animals either died of hunger and thirst or migrated away, Alex knew his Botswana would never be the same again. It was still, however, the only place on earth he ever wanted to be.

Pat and Jill had been regular visitors. They had not married but lived together in a very large house overlooking the Gaborone dam. On a visit to South Africa in 1996 Pat had been pulled up for speeding and, while the policeman was writing out the ticket, the driver of an articulated lorry which was also going too fast had seen the police car, hit the brakes and jack-knifed, killing himself, the policeman and Pat and Jill.

Marv and Pru, who called a halt at seven children, had grown portly with contentment. They were a delightfully noisy family, secure in their numbers, with love in abundance for each other. Madison and Pru became close friends.

The screen door banged. 'What do you think?' she asked, coming to him and picking up Sam's letter.

'I think,' he said slowly, 'that you are more beautiful now than when I first laid eyes on you.'

'About Sam?' Her eyes sparkled.

'I think I love you more now than I did then.'

'Alex!' she protested. 'You get like this every August. What about Sam?'

He looked at her. The curtain of hair had been sensibly cropped but she kept it longish on top which gave her a classic elegance. There was no hint of grey as yet in that black silkiness. Her eyes remained clear grey. No wrinkles, no worry lines. Her body showed no signs of four babies. 'Come,' he said, rising.

'Sam,' she said gently.

'Bugger Sam,' he smiled back.

'Sam,' she repeated.

'Okay, okay, we'll up his allowance.'

'You're a darling.' She kissed his cheek.

'I know that.'

Her hands were on his shoulders. He looked into her eyes. Her face was no longer just his future, it was his past and his present too. He was content. He wrapped her in his arms. 'I want you,' he whispered.

'It's the middle of the afternoon.' Her voice in his ear sent a shiver through him.

'The servants are off duty.'

'I know,' she said dreamily. 'I told them not to hurry back.'